D0182123

By Connie Willis

TERRA INCOGNITA

A LOT LIKE CHRISTMAS

CROSSTALK

THE BEST OF CONNIE WILLIS

ALL ABOUT EMILY

ALL CLEAR

BLACKOUT

ALL SEATED ON THE GROUND

D.A.

INSIDE JOB

PASSAGE

TO SAY NOTHING OF THE DOG

BELLWETHER

UNCHARTED TERRITORY

REMAKE

IMPOSSIBLE THINGS

DOOMSDAY BOOK

LINCOLN'S DREAMS

FIRE WATCH

TERRA INCOGNITA

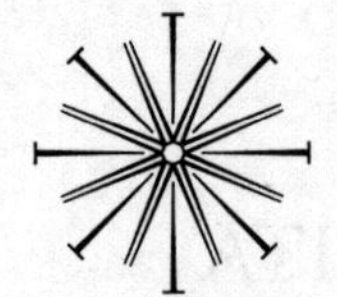

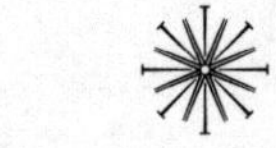

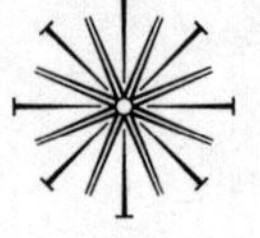

TERRA INCOGNITA

Three Tales

CONNIE WILLIS

Del Rey | New York

Terra Incognita is a work of fiction. Names, characters, places and incidents either are products of the author's imagination or are used fictitiously. Any resemblance to actual persons, living or dead, events, or locales is entirely coincidental.

2018 Del Rey Trade Paperback Edition

Published in the United States by Del Rey, an imprint of Random House, a division of Penguin Random House LLC, New York.

Del Rey and the House colophon are registered trademarks of Penguin Random House LLC.

Most of the stories in this work have been previously published by Del Rey Spectra. *Uncharted Territory* was originally published in paperback form in 1994 by Del Rey Spectra. *Remake* was originally published in paperback form in 1995 by Del Rey Spectra. *D.A.* was originally published in hardcover in 2007 by Subterranean Press.

LIBRARY OF CONGRESS CATALOGING-IN-PUBLICATION DATA

Names: Willis, Connie, author.
Title: Terra incognita : three novellas / Connie Willis.
Description: New York : Del Rey, 2018.
Identifiers: LCCN 2018022918 | ISBN 9781524796860 (paperback)
Subjects: LCSH: Science fiction, American. | BISAC: FICTION / Short Stories (single author). | FICTION / Science Fiction / Adventure. | FICTION / Satire.
Classification: LCC PS3573.I45652 A6 2018 | DDC 813/.54—dc23
LC record available at https://lccn.loc.gov/2018022918

Printed in the United States of America on acid-free paper

randomhousebooks.com

2 4 6 8 9 7 5 3 1

Book design by Virginia Norey
Map design by GDS/Jeffrey L. Ward

To Fred Astaire and Robert A. Heinlein,
who made it look easy

CONTENTS

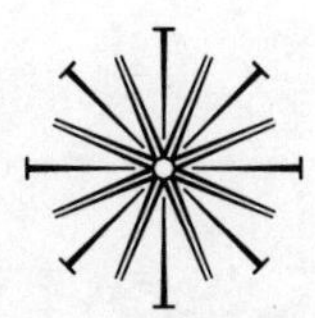

UNCHARTED TERRITORY

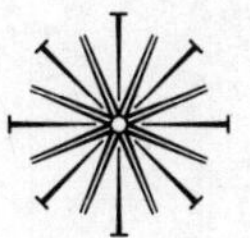

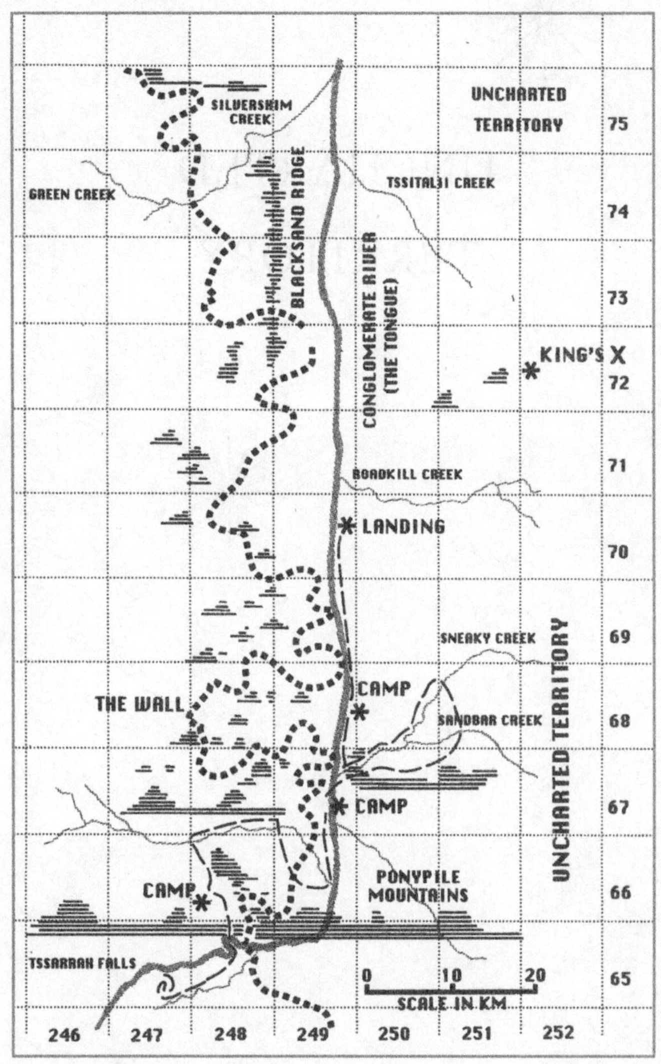

UNCHARTED TERRITORY
SILVERSKIM CREEK
GREEN CREEK
TSSITAL3I CREEK
BLACKSAND RIDGE
CONGLOMERATE RIVER (THE TONGUE)
KING'S X
BOADKILL CREEK
LANDING
SNEAKY CREEK
CAMP
THE WALL
SANDBAR CREEK
CAMP
UNCHARTED TERRITORY
CAMP
PONYPILE MOUNTAINS
TSSARRAH FALLS
0
10
20
SCALE IN KM
75
74
73
72
71
70
69
68
67
66
65
246
247
248
249
250
251
252

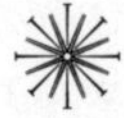

Expedition 183: Day 19

WE WERE STILL THREE KLOMS FROM KING'S X WHEN CARson spotted the dust. "What on hell's that?" he said, leaning forward over his pony's pommelbone and pointing at nothing that I could see.

"Where?" I said.

"Over there. All that dust."

I still couldn't see anything except the pinkish ridge that hid King's X, and a couple of luggage grazing on the scourbrush, and I told him so.

"My shit, Fin, what do you mean you can't—" he said, disgusted. "Hand me the binocs."

"You've got 'em," I said. "I gave 'em to you yesterday. Hey, Bult!" I called up to our scout.

He was hunched over the log on his pony's saddlebone, punching in numbers. *"Bult!"* I shouted. "Do you see any dust up ahead?"

He still didn't look up, which didn't surprise me. He was busy doing his favorite thing, tallying up fines.

"I gave the binocs back to you," Carson said. "This morning when we packed up."

"This morning?" I said. "This morning you were in such an

all-fired hurry to get back to King's X and meet the new loaner you probably went off and left 'em lying in camp. What's her name again? Evangeline?"

"Evelyn Parker," he said. "I was not in a hurry."

"How come you ran up two-fifty in fines breaking camp, then?"

"Because Bult's on some kind of fining *spree* the last few days," he said. "And the only hurry I've been in is to finish up this expedition before every dime of our wages goes for fines, which looks like a lost cause now that you lost the binocs."

"You weren't in a hurry yesterday," I said. "Yesterday you were all ready to ride fifty kloms north on the off-chance of running into Wulfmeier, and then C.J. calls and tells you the new loaner's in and her name's Eleanor, and all of a sudden you can't get home fast enough."

"Evelyn," Carson said, getting red in the face, "and I still say Wulfmeier's surveying that sector. You just don't like loaners."

"You're right about that," I said. "They're more trouble than they're worth." I've never met a loaner yet that was worth taking along, and the females are the worst.

They come in one variety: whiners. They spend every minute of the expedition complaining—about the outdoor plumbing and the dust and Bult and having to ride ponies and everything else they can think of. The last one spent the whole expedition yowling about "terrocentric enslaving imperialists," meaning Carson and me, and how we'd corrupted the "simple, noble indigenous sentients," meaning Bult, which was bad enough. But then she latched onto Bult and told him our presence "defiled the very atmosphere of the planet," and Bult started trying to fine us for breathing.

"I laid the binocs right next to your bedroll, Fin," Carson said, reaching behind him to rummage in his pack.

"Well, I never saw 'em."

"That's because you're half blind," he said. "You can't even see a cloud of dust when it's coming right at you."

Well, as a matter of fact, we'd been arguing long enough that now I could, a kicked-up line of pinkish cloud close to the ridge.

"What do you think it is? A dust tantrum?" I said, even though a tantrum would've been meandering all over the place, not keeping to a line.

"I don't know," he said, putting his hand up to shade his eyes. "A stampede maybe."

The only fauna around here were luggage, and they didn't stampede in dry weather like this, and anyway, the cloud wasn't wide enough for a stampede. It looked like the dust churned up by a rover or a gate opening.

I kicked my terminal on and asked for whereabouts on the gatecrashers. It'd shown Wulfmeier on Dazil yesterday when Carson'd been so set on going after him, and now the whereabouts showed him on Starting Gate, which meant he probably wasn't either place. But he'd have to be crazy to open a gate this close to King's X, even if there was anything underneath here—which there wasn't. I'd already run terrains and subsurfaces—especially knowing we were on our way home.

I squinted at the dust, wondering if I should ask for a verify. I could see now it was moving fast, which meant it wasn't a gate, or a pony, and the dust was too low for the heli. "Looks like the rover," I said. "Maybe the new loaner—what was her name? Ernestine?—is as jumped for you as you are for her, and she's coming out here to meet you. You better comb your mustache."

He wasn't paying any attention. He was still rummaging in his pack, looking for the binocs. "I laid 'em right next to your bedroll when you were loading the ponies."

"Well, I didn't see 'em," I said, watching the dust. It was a good thing it wasn't a stampede, it would have run us over while we stood there arguing about the binocs. "Maybe Bult took 'em."

"Why on hell would Bult take 'em?" Carson bellowed. "His are a hell of a lot fancier than ours."

They were, with selective scans and programmed polarizers, and Bult had hung them around the second joint of his neck and was peering through them at the dust. I rode up next to him. "Can you see what's making the dust?" I asked.

He didn't take the binocs down from his eyes. "Disturbance of land surface," he said severely. "Fine of one hundred."

I should've known it. Bult could've cared less about what was making the dust so long as he could get a fine out of it. "You can't fine us for dust unless we make it," I said. "Give me the binocs."

He bent his neck double, took the binocs off, and handed them to me, and then hunched over his log again. "Forcible confiscation of property," he said into his log. "Twenty-five."

"Confiscation!" I said. "You're not going to fine me with confiscating anything. I *asked* if I could borrow them."

"Inappropriate tone and manner in speaking to an indigenous person," he said into the log. "Fifty."

I gave up and put the binocs up to my eyes. The cloud of dust looked like it was right on top of me, but no clearer. I upped the resolution and took another look. "It's the rover," I called to Carson, who'd gotten off his pony and was taking everything out of his pack.

"Who's driving?" he said. "C.J.?"

I hit the polarizers to screen out the dust and took another look. "What'd you say this loaner's name was, Carson?"

"Evelyn. Did C.J. bring her out with her?"

"It's not C.J. driving," I said.

"Well, who on hell is it? Don't tell me one of the indidges stole the rover again."

"Unfair accusation of indigenous person," Bult said. "Seventy-five."

"You know how you always get mad over the indidges giving things the wrong names?" I said.

"What on hell does that have to do with who's driving the rover?" Carson said.

"Because it looks like the indidges aren't the only ones doing it," I said. "It looks like now Big Brother's doing it, too."

"Give me those binocs," he said, grabbing for 'em.

"Forcible confiscation of property," I said, holding them away from him. "Looks like you could've taken your time this morning and not gone off in such a hurry you forgot ours."

I handed the binocs back to Bult, and just to be contrary, he handed them to Carson, but the rover was close enough now we didn't need them.

It roared up in a cloud of dust, skidded to a halt right on top of a roadkill, and the driver jumped out and strode over to us without even waiting for the dust to clear.

"Carson and Findriddy, I presume," he said, grinning.

Now usually when we meet a loaner, they don't have eyes for anybody but Bult (or C.J., if she's there and the loaner's a male), especially if Bult's unfolding himself off his pony the way he was now, straightening out his back joints one after the other till he looks like a big pink Erector set. Then, while the loaners are still picking their jaws up out of the dirt, one of the ponies keels over or else drops a pile the size of the rover. It's tough to compete with. So we usually get noticed last or else have to say something like "Bult's only dangerous when he senses your fear" to get their attention.

But this loaner didn't so much as glance at Bult. He came straight over to me and shook hands. "How do you do?" he said eagerly, pumping my hand. "I'm Dr. Parker, the new member of your survey team."

"I'm Fin—" I started.

"Oh, I know who *you* are, and I can't *tell* you what an *honor* it is to meet you, Dr. Findriddy!"

He let go of my hand and started in on Carson's. "When C.J. told me you weren't back yet, I couldn't wait till you arrived to meet you," he said, jerking Carson's hand up and down. "Findriddy and Carson! The famous planetary surveyors! I can't believe I'm shaking hands with you, Dr. Carson!"

"It's kind of hard for me to believe, too," Carson said.

"What'd you say your name was, again?" I asked.

"Dr. Parker," he said, grabbing my hand to shake it again. "Dr. Findriddy, I've read all your—"

"Fin," I said, "and this is Carson. There's only four of us on the planet, counting you, so there's not much call for fancy titles. What do you want us to call you?" but he'd already left off pumping my hand and was staring past Carson.

"Is that the Wall?" he said, pointing at a bump on the horizon.

"Nope," I said. "That's Three Moon Mesa. The Wall's twenty kloms the other side of the Tongue."

"Are we going to see it on the expedition?"

"Yeah. We have to cross it to get into uncharted territory," I said.

"Great. I can't wait to see the Wall and the silvershim trees," he said, looking down at Carson's boots, "and the cliff where Carson lost his foot."

"How do you know about all this stuff?" I asked.

He looked back and forth at us in amazement. "Are you kidding? Everybody knows about Carson and Findriddy! You're famous! Dr. Findriddy, you're—"

"Fin," I said. "What do you want us to call you?"

"Evelyn," he said. He looked from one to the other of us. "It's a British name. My mother was from England. Only they pronounce it with a long 'e.' "

"And you're an exozoologist?" I said.

"Socioexozoologist. My speciality's sex."

"C.J.'s the one you want, then," I said. "She's our resident expert."

He blushed a nice pink. "I've already met her."

"She told you her name yet?" I said.

"Her name?" he said blankly.

"What C.J. stands for," I said. "She must be slipping," I said to Carson.

Carson ignored me. "If you're an expert on sex," Carson said, looking over at Bult, who was heading for the rover, "you can help us tell which one Bult is."

"I thought the Boohteri were a simple two-sex species," Evelyn said.

"They are," Carson said, "only we can't tell which one's which."

"All their equipment's on the inside," I said, "not like C.J.'s. It—"

"Speaking of which, did she have supper ready?" Carson said. "Not that it makes any difference to us. At this rate we'll still be out here tomorrow morning."

"Oh. Of course," Evelyn said, looking dismayed, "you're eager to get back to headquarters. I didn't mean to keep you. I was just so excited to actually meet you!" He started off for the rover, where Bult was hunched over the front tire.

He unfolded three leg joints when Evelyn came up. "Damage to indigenous fauna," he said. "Seventy-five."

Evelyn said to me, "Have I done something wrong?"

"Hard not to in these parts," I said. "Bult, you can't fine Evelyn for running over a roadkill."

"Running over—" Evelyn said. He leaped in the rover and roared it back off the roadkill, and then jumped out again. "I didn't see it!" he said, peering at its flattened brown body. "I didn't mean to kill it! Honestly, I—"

"You can't kill a roadkill just by parking a rover on it," I said, poking it with my toe. "You can't even wake it up."

Bult pointed at the tire tracks Evelyn'd just made. "Disruption of land surface. Twenty-five."

"Bult, you can't fine Evelyn," I said. "He's not a member of the expedition."

"Disruption of land surface," Bult said, pointing at the tire tracks.

"Shouldn't I have come out here in the rover?" Evelyn said worriedly.

"Sure you should," I said, clapping him on the shoulder, "'cause now you can give me a ride home. Carson, bring in my pony for me." I opened the door of the rover.

"I'm not getting stuck out here with the ponies while you ride back in style," Carson said. "*I'll* ride in with Evelyn, and *you* bring the ponies."

"Can't we all go back in the rover?" Evelyn said, looking upset. "We could tie the ponies to the back."

"The rover can't go that slow," Carson muttered.

"You've got no reason to get back early, Carson," I said. "I've got to check the purchase orders, and the pursuants, *and* fill out the report on the binocs you lost." I got in the rover and sat down.

"*I* lost?" Carson said, getting red in the face again. "I laid 'em—"

"Expedition member riding in wheeled vehicle," Bult said.

We turned around to look at him. He was standing beside his pony, talking into his log. "Disruption of land surface."

I got out of the rover and stalked over to him. "I told you, you can't fine somebody who's not a member of the expedition."

Bult looked at me. "Inappropriate tone and manner." He straightened some finger joints at me. "You member. Cahsson member. Yahhs?" he said in the maddening pidgin he uses when he's not tallying fines.

But his message was clear enough. If either of us rode back with Evelyn, he could fine us for using a rover, which would take the next six expeditions' wages, not to mention the trouble we'd get into with Big Brother.

"You expedition, yahhs?" Bult said. He held out his pony's reins to me.

"Yeah," I said. I took the reins.

Bult grabbed his log off his pony's saddlebone, jumped in the rover, and folded himself into a sitting position. "We go," he said to Evelyn.

Evelyn looked questioningly at me.

"Bult here'll ride in with you," I said. "We'll bring the ponies in."

"How on hell are we supposed to bring three ponies in when they'll only walk two abreast?" Carson said.

I ignored him. "See you back at King's X." I slapped the side of the rover.

"Go fahhst," Bult said. Ev started the rover up and waved and left us eating a cloud of dust.

"I'm beginning to think you're right about loaners, Fin," Carson said, coughing and smacking his hat against his leg. "They're nothing but trouble. And the males are the worst, especially after C.J. gets to 'em. We'll spend half the expedition listening to him talk about her, and the other half keeping him from labeling every gully in sight Crissa Canyon."

"Maybe," I said, squinting at the rover's dust, which seemed to be veering off to the right. "C.J. said Evelyn got in this morning."

"Which means she's had almost a whole day to give him her pitch," he said, taking hold of Bult's pony's reins. It balked and dug in its paws. "And she'll have at least another two hours to work her wiles before we get these ponies in."

"Maybe," I said, still watching the dust. "But I figure a presentable-looking male like Ev can jump just about any female he wants without having to do anything for it, and you notice he didn't stay at King's X with C.J. He came tearing out here to meet *us*. I think he might be smarter than he looks."

"That's what you said the first time you saw Bult," Carson said, yanking on Bult's pony's reins. The pony yanked back.

"And I was right, wasn't I?" I said, going over to help. "If he wasn't, he'd be here with these ponies, and *we'd* be halfway to King's X." I took over the reins, and he went around behind the pony to push.

"Maybe," he said. "Why wouldn't he want to meet us? After all, we're planetary surveyors. We're famous!"

I pulled and he pushed. The pony stayed put. "Get moving, you rock-headed nag!" Carson said, shoving on its back end. "Don't you know who we are?"

The pony lifted its tail and dumped a pile.

"My *shit*!" Carson said.

"Too bad Evelyn can't see us now," I said, holding the reins over my shoulder and hauling on the pony. "Findriddy and Carson, the famous explorers!"

Off in the distance, to the right of the ridge, the dust disappeared.

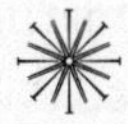

Interim: At King's X

IT TOOK US FOUR HOURS TO MAKE IT INTO KING'S X. BULT'S pony keeled over twice and wouldn't get up, and when we got there, Ev was waiting out at the stable to ask us when we were going to start on the expedition. Carson gave him an inappropriate-in-tone-and-manner answer.

"I know you just got back and have to file your reports and everything," Ev said.

"And eat," Carson muttered, limping around his pony, "and sleep. And kill me a scout."

"It's just that I'm so excited to see Boohte," Ev said. "I still can't believe I'm really *here,* talking to—"

"I know, I know," I said, unloading the computer. "Findriddy and Carson, the famous surveyors."

"Where's Bult?" Carson asked, unstrapping his camera from his pony's saddlebone. "And why isn't he out here to unload his pony?"

Evelyn handed Carson Bult's log. "He said to tell you these are the fines from the trip in."

"He wasn't *on* the trip in," Carson said, glaring at the log. "What on hell are these? 'Destruction of indigenous flora.' 'Damage to sand formations.' 'Pollution of atmosphere.' "

I grabbed the log away from Carson. "Did Bult give you directions back to King's X?"

"Yes," Ev said. "Did I do something wrong?"

"Wrong?!" Carson spluttered. "*Wrong?!*"

"Don't get in a sweat," I said. "Bult can't fine Ev till he's a member of the expedition."

"But I don't understand," Ev said. "What did I do wrong? All I did was drive the rover—"

"Stir up dust, make tire tracks," Carson said, "emit exhaust—"

"Wheeled vehicles aren't allowed off government property," I explained to Ev, who was looking amazed.

"Then how do you get around?" he asked.

"We don't," Carson said, glaring at Bult's pony, which looked like it was getting ready to keel over again. "Explain it to him, Fin."

I was too tired to explain anything, least of all Big Brother's notion of how to survey a planet. "You tell him about the fines while I go get this straightened out with Bult," I said, and went across the compound to the gate area.

In my log, there's nothing worse than working for a government with the guilts. All we were doing on Boohte was surveying the planet, but Big Brother didn't want anybody accusing them of "ruthless imperialist expansion" and riding roughshod over the indidges the way they did when they colonized America.

So they set up all these rules to "preserve planetary ecosystems" (which was supposed to mean we weren't allowed to build dams or kill the local fauna) and "protect indigenous cultures from technological contamination" (which was supposed to mean we couldn't give 'em firewater and guns), and stiff fines for breaking the rules.

Which is where they made their first mistake, because they paid the fines to the indidges, and Bult and his tribe knew a good thing when they saw it, and before you know it we're being fined for making footprints, and Bult's buying technological contamination right and left with the proceeds.

I figured he'd be in the gate area, up to his second knee joint in stuff he'd bought, and I was right. When I opened the door, he was prying open a crate of umbrellas.

"Bult, you can't charge us with fines the rover incurred," I said.

He pulled out an umbrella and examined it. It was the collapsible kind. He held the umbrella out in front of him and pushed a button. Lights came on around the rim. "Destruction of land surface," he said.

I held out his log to him. "You know the regs. 'The expedition is not responsible for violations committed by any person not an official member of the expedition.'"

He was still messing with the buttons. The lights went off. "Bult member," he said, and the umbrella shot out and open, barely missing my stomach.

"Watch it!" I jumped back. "You can't incur fines, Bult."

Bult put down the umbrella and opened a big box of dice, which would make Carson happy. His favorite occupation, next to blaming me, is shooting craps.

"Indidges can't incur fines!" I said.

"Inappropriate tone and manner," he said.

I was too tired for this, too, and I still had the reports and the whereabouts to do. I left him unpacking a box of shower curtains and went across to the mess.

I opened the door. "Honey, I'm home," I called.

"Hello!" C.J. sang out cheerfully from the kitchen, which was a switch. "How was your expedition?"

She appeared in the doorway, smiling and wiping her hands on a towel. She was all done up, clean face and fixed-up hair and a shirt that was open down to thirty degrees north. "Dinner's almost ready," she said brightly, and then stopped and looked around. "Where's Evelyn?"

"Out in the stable," I said, dumping my stuff on a chair, "talking to Carson, the planetary surveyor. Did you know we're famous?"

"You're filthy," she said. "And you're late. What on hell took you so long? Dinner's cold. I had it ready two hours ago." She jabbed a finger at my stuff. "Get that dirty pack off the furniture. It's bad enough putting up with dust tantrums without you two dragging in dirt."

I sat down and propped my legs up on the table. "And how was your day, sweetheart?" I said. "Get a mud puddle named after you? Jump any loaners?"

"Very funny. Evelyn happens to be a very nice young man who understands what it's like to be all alone on a planet for weeks at a time with nobody for hundreds of kloms and who knows what dangers lurking out there—"

"Like losing that shirt," I said.

"You're not exactly in a position to criticize my clothes," she said. "When's the last time you changed *yours*? What have you been doing, rolling in the mud? And get those boots off the furniture. They're disgusting!" She smacked my legs with the dish towel.

This was as much fun as talking to Bult. If I was going to be raked over the coals, it might as well be by the experts. I heaved myself out of the chair. "Any pursuants?"

"If you mean official reprimands, there are sixteen. They're on the computer." She went back to the kitchen, her shirt flapping. "And get cleaned up. You're not coming to the table looking like that."

"Yes, dear," I said, and went over to the console. I fed in the expedition report and took a look at the subsurfaces I'd run in Sector 247-72, and then called up the pursuants.

There were the usual loving messages from Big Brother: We

weren't covering enough sectors, we weren't giving enough f-and-f indigenous names, we were incurring too many fines.

"Pursuant to language used by members of survey expeditions, such members will refrain from using derogatory terms in reference to the government, in particular, abbreviations and slang terms such as 'Big Brother' and 'morons back home.' Such references imply lack of respect, thereby undermining relations with the indigenous sentients and obstructing the government's goals. Members of survey expeditions will henceforth refer to the government by its proper title in full."

Evelyn and Carson came in. "Anything interesting?" Carson asked, leaning over me.

"We're wearing our mikes turned up too high," I said.

He clapped me on the shoulder. "I'm gonna go check the weather and then take a bath," he said.

I nodded, looking at the screen. He left, and I started through the pursuants again and then looked back behind me. Ev was leaning over me, his chin practically on my shoulder.

"Do you mind if I watch?" he said. "It's so exc—"

"I know, I know," I said. "There's nothing more exciting than reading a bunch of memos from Big Brother. Oh. Sorry," I said, pointing at the screen, "we're not supposed to call them that. We're supposed to use appropriate titles. There's nothing more exciting than reading memos from the Third Reich."

Ev grinned, and I thought, *Yep, smarter than he looks.*

"Fin," C.J. called from the door of the mess. She'd unstripped her blouse another ten degrees. "Can I borrow Evelyn for a minute?"

"You bet, Crissa Jane," I said.

She glared at me.

"That's what C.J. stands for, you know," I said to Ev. "Crissa Jane Tull. You'll need to remember that for when we go on expedition."

"Fin!" she snapped. "Ev," she said sweetly, "can you come help me with dinner?"

"Sure," Ev said, and was after her like a shot. All right, not that much smarter.

I went back to the pursuants. We weren't showing "proper respect for indigenous cultural integrity," which meant who knows what, we hadn't filled out Subsection 12-2 of the minerals report for Expedition 158, we had left two gaps of uncharted territory on Expedition 162, one in Sector 248-76 and the other in Sector 246-73.

I knew what the 246-73 gap was but not the other one, and I doubted if it was still a gap. We'd been over a lot of the same territory the next-to-last expedition.

I called up the topographicals and asked for a chart overlay. Big Bro—Hizzoner was right for once. There were two holes in the chart.

Carson came in, carrying a towel and a clean pair of socks. "We fired yet?"

"Just about," I said. "How's the weather look?"

"Rain down in the Ponypiles start of next week. Otherwise, nothing. Not even a dust tantrum. Looks like we can go anywhere we want."

"What about in charted territory? Up along 76?"

"Same thing. Clear and dry. Why?" he said, coming over to look at the screen. "What've you got?"

"I don't know yet," I said. "Probably nothing. Go get cleaned up."

He went off toward the latrine. Sector 248-76. That was over on the other side of the Tongue and, if I remembered right, close to Silvershim Creek. I frowned at the screen a minute, and then asked for Expedition 181's log and started fast-forwarding it.

"Is that the expedition you were just on?" Ev said, and I jerked around to find him hanging over me again.

"I thought you were helping C.J. in the kitchen," I said, cutting the log off.

He grinned. "It's too hot in there. Were you sending the log of the expedition to NASA?"

I shook my head. "The log goes out live. It transmits straight to C.J. and she sends it on through the gate. I was just finishing up the expedition summary."

"Do you send all the reports?"

"Nope. Carson sends the topographicals and the f-and-f; I send the geologicals and the accountings." I asked for the tally of Bult's fines.

Ev looked uneasy. "I wanted to apologize to you for driving the rover. I didn't know it was against regs to use nonindigenous transportation. The last thing I wanted to do on my first day was to get you and Dr. Carson in trouble."

"Don't worry about it. We still had wages left over this expedition, which is better than we've made out the last two. The only things that really get you in trouble are killing fauna and naming something after somebody," I said, staring at him, but he didn't look especially guilty. C.J. must not have gotten around to her sales pitch yet.

"Anyway," I said, "we're used to trouble."

"I know," he said earnestly. "Like the time you got caught in the stampede and nearly got trampled, and Dr. Carson rescued you."

"How'd you know about that?" I asked.

"Are you kidding? You're—"

"Famous. Right," I said. "But how—"

"Evelyn," C.J. called, dripping honey with every syllable, "can you help me set the table?" and he was off again.

I got 181's log again, and then changed my mind and asked for the whereabouts. I checked them for the two times we'd been in Sector 248-76. Wulfmeier'd been on Starting Gate both times, which didn't prove anything. I asked for a verify on him.

"Nahhd khompt," Bult said.

I looked up. He was standing next to the computer, pointing his umbrella at me.

"I need the computer, too," I said, and he reached for his log. "Besides, it's almost dinnertime."

"Nahhd tchopp," he said, moving around behind me so he could see the screen. "Forcible confiscation of property."

"That's what it is, all right," I said, wondering which was worse, being stuck with his bayonet of an umbrella or another fine. Besides, I couldn't find out what I needed to know with all these people hanging over my shoulder. And dinner was ready. Evelyn pushed the kitchen door open with his shoulder and brought out a platter of meat. I asked for the catalog.

"Here you go," I said, standing up. "Nieman Marcus at your disposal. Go at it. Tchopp."

Bult sat down, shot his umbrella open, and started talking to the computer. "One dozen pair digiscan polarized field glasses," he said, "with telemetry and object enhancement functions."

Ev stared.

"One 'High Rollers Special' slot machine," Bult said.

Ev came over with the platter. "Bult can speak English?" he said.

I grabbed a chunk of meat. "Depends. When he's ordering stuff, yeah. When you're talking to him, not much. When you're trying to negotiate satellite surveys or permission to set up a gate, *no hablo inglés*." I grabbed another hunk of meat.

"*Stop* that!" C.J. said, bringing in the vegetables. "Honestly, Fin, you've got the manners of a gatecrasher! You could at least wait till we get to the table!" She set the vegetables down. "Carson! Dinner's ready!" she called, and went back into the kitchen.

He came in, wiping his hands on a towel. He'd washed up and shaved around his mustache. He came over close to me. "Find anything?" he muttered.

"Maybe."

Ev, still holding the meat platter, was looking at me inquiringly.

I said, "I found out those binocs you lost are gonna cost us three hundred."

"*I* lost?" Carson said. "You're the one who lost 'em. I laid 'em right next to your pack. Why on hell's it three hundred?"

"Possible technological contamination," I said. "If they turn up on an indidge, it'll be five hundred you lost us."

"*I* lost us!" he said.

C.J. came in, carrying a bowl of rice. She'd switched her shirt for one with even lower coordinates, and lights around the edges like the ones on Bult's umbrella.

"You were the one in a hurry to get back here and meet *Evelyn,*" I said. I pulled a chair out from the table, stepped over it, and sat down.

He grabbed the platter out of Ev's hands. "Five hundred. My *shit*!" He set the platter on the table. "How much were the rest of the fines?"

"I don't know," I said. "I haven't tallied 'em yet."

"Well, what on hell were you doing all this time?" He sat down. "It's plain to see you weren't taking a bath."

"C.J.'s cleaned up enough for both of us," I said. "What're the lights for?" I asked her.

Carson grinned. "They're like those landing strip beacons, so you can find your way down."

C.J. ignored him. "You sit here by me, Evelyn."

He pulled out her chair, and she sat down, managing to lean over so we could all see the runway.

Ev sat down next to her. "I can't believe I'm actually eating dinner with Carson and Findriddy! Tell me about your expedition. I'll bet you had a lot of adventures."

"Well," Carson said, "Fin lost the binocs."

"Have you decided when we leave on the next expedition yet?" Ev asked.

Carson gave me a look. "Not yet," I said. "A few days, probably."

"Oh, good," C.J. crooned, leaning in Ev's direction. "That'll give us more time to get to know each other." She latched onto his arm.

"Is there anything I can do to help so we can leave sooner?" Ev said. "Loading the ponies or something? I'm just so eager to get started."

C.J. dropped his arm in disgust. "So you can spend three weeks sleeping on the ground and listening to these two?"

"Are you kidding?" he said. "I put in four years ago for the chance to go on an expedition with Carson and Findriddy! What's it like, being on the survey team with them?"

"What's it like?" She glared at us. "They're rude, they're dirty, they break every rule in the book, and don't let all their bickering fool you—they're just like *that.*" She crossed one finger over another. "Nobody has a chance against the two of them."

"I know," Ev said. "On the pop-ups, they—"

"What are these pop-ups?" I said. "Some kind of holo?"

"They're DHVs," Ev said, as if that explained everything. "There's a whole series of them about you and Carson and Bult." He stopped and looked around at Bult, hunched over the computer under his umbrella. "Doesn't Bult eat with you?"

"He's not allowed to," Carson said, helping himself to the meat.

"Regs," I said. "Cultural contamination. Asking him to eat at a table and use silverware is imperialistic. We might corrupt him with Earth foods and table manners."

"Small chance of that," C.J. said, taking the meat platter away from Carson. "You two don't *have* any table manners."

"So while we eat," Carson said, plopping potatoes on his plate, "he sits there ordering demitasse cups and place settings for twelve. Nobody ever said Big Brother was big on logic."

"Not Big Brother," I said, shaking my finger at Carson. "Pursuant to our latest reprimand, members of the expedition will henceforth refer to the government by its appropriate title."

"What, Idiots Incorporated?" Carson said. "What other brilliant orders did they come up with?"

"They want us to cover more territory. And they disallowed one of our names. Green Creek."

Carson looked up from his plate. "What on hell's wrong with Green Creek?"

"There's a senator named Green on the Ways and Means Committee. They couldn't prove any connection, though, so they just fined us the minimum."

"There're people named Hill and River, too," Carson said. "If one of them gets on the committee, what on hell do we do then?"

"I think it's ridiculous that you can't name things after people," C.J. said. "Don't you, Evelyn?"

"Why can't you?" Ev asked.

"Regs," I said. "'Pursuant to the practice of naming geological formations, waterways, etc., after surveyors, government officials, historical personages, etc., said practice is indicative of oppressive colonialist attitudes and lack of respect for indigenous cultural traditions, etc., etc.' Hand the meat over."

C.J.'d picked up the platter, but she didn't pass it. "Oppressive! It is not. Why shouldn't we have something named after us? We're the ones stuck on this horrible planet all alone in uncharted territory for months at a time and with who knows what dangers lurking. We should get something."

Carson and I have heard this pitch a hundred or so times. She used to try it on us before she decided the loaners were more susceptible.

"There are hundreds of mountains and streams on Boohte.

You can't tell me there isn't some way you could name *one* of them after somebody. I mean, the government wouldn't even notice."

Well, she's wrong there. Their Imperial Majesties check every single name, and even if all we tried to sneak past them was a bug named C.J., we could get tossed off Boohte.

"There's a way you can get something named after you, C.J.," Carson said. "Why didn't you say you were interested?"

C.J. narrowed her eyes. "How?"

"Remember Stewart? He was one of the first pair of scouts on Boohte," he explained to Ev. "Got caught in a flash flood and swept smack into a hill. Stewart's Hill, they named it. *In memoriam*. All you've got to do is take the heli out tomorrow and point it at whatever you want named after you, and—"

"Very funny," C.J. said. "I'm serious about this," she said to Ev. "Don't you think it's natural to want to have some sign that you've *been* here, so after you're gone you won't be forgotten, some monument to what you've done?"

"My *shit,*" Carson said, "if you're talking about doing stuff, Fin and I are the ones who should have something named after us! How about it, Fin? You want me to name something after you?"

"What would I do with it? What I *want* is the meat!" I held out my hands for it, but nobody paid any attention.

"Findriddy Lake," Carson said. "Fin Mesa."

"Findriddy Swamp," C.J. said.

It was time to change the subject, or I was never going to get any meat. "So, Ev," I said. "You're a sexozoologist."

"Socioexozoologist," he said. "I study instinctive mating behaviors in extraterrestrial species. Courtship rituals and sexual behaviors."

"Well, you've come to the right place," Carson said. "C.J.—"

C.J. cut in, "Tell me about some of the interesting species you've studied."

"Well, they're all interesting, really. Most animal behaviors are instinctive, they're hardwired in, but reproductive behavior is really complicated. It's part hardwiring, part survival strategies, and the combination produces all these variables. The charlizards on Ottiyal mate inside the crater of an active volcano, and there's a Terran species, the bowerbird, which constructs an elaborate bower fifty times his size and then decorates it with orchids and berries to attract the female."

"Some nest," I said.

"Oh, but it's not the nest," Ev said. "The nest is built in front of the bower, and it's quite ordinary. The bower is just for courtship. Sentients are even more interesting. The Inkicce males cut off their toes to impress the female. And the Opantis' courtship ritual—they're the indigenous sentients on Jevo—takes six months. The Opanti female sets a series of difficult tasks the male must perform before she allows him to mate with her."

"Just like C.J.," I said. "What kind of tasks do these Opantis have to do for the females? Name rivers after them?"

"The tasks vary, but they're usually the giving of tokens of esteem, proofs of valor, feats of strength."

"How come the male's always the one who has to do all the courting?" Carson said. "Giving 'em candy and flowers, proving they're tough, building bowers while the female just sits there making up her mind."

"Because the male is concerned only with mating," Ev said. "The female is concerned with ensuring the optimum survival of her offspring, which means she needs a strong mate or a smart one. The male doesn't do all the courting, though. The females send out response signals to encourage and attract the males."

"Like landing lights?" I said.

C.J. glared at me.

"Without those signals, the courtship ritual breaks down and can't be completed," Ev said.

"I'll keep that in mind," Carson said. He pushed back from the table. "Fin, if we're gonna start in two days, we'd better take a look at the map. I'll go get the new topographicals." He went out.

C.J. cleared off the table, and I threw Bult off the computer and set up the map, filling in the two holes with extrapolated topographics before I went back over to the table.

Ev was bending over the map. "Is that the Wall?" he said, pointing at the Tongue.

"Nope. That's the Tongue. *That's* the Wall," I said, sticking my hand in the middle of the holo to show him its course.

"I hadn't realized it was so long," he said wonderingly, tracing its meandering course along the Tongue and into the Ponypiles. "Which part is uncharted territory?"

"The blank part," I said, looking at the huge western expanse of the map. The charted area looked like a drop in the bucket.

Carson came back in and called Bult and his umbrella over, and we discussed routes.

"We haven't mapped any of the northern tributaries of the Tongue," Carson said, circling an area in light marker. "Where can we cross the Wall, Bult?"

Bult leaned over the table and pointed stiffly at two different places, making sure his finger didn't go into the holo.

"If we cross down here," I said, taking the marker away from Carson, "we can cut across here and follow Blacksand Ridge up." I lit a line up to Sector 248-76 and through the hole. "What do you think?"

Bult pointed at the other break in the Wall, holding his hinged finger well above the table. "Fahtsser wye."

I looked across at Carson. "What do you think?"

He looked steadily back at me.

"Will we get to see the trees that have the silver leaves?" Ev said.

"Maybe," Carson said, still looking at me. "Either way looks good to me," he said to Bult. "I'll have to check on the weather and see which one'll work. It looks like there's a lot of rain down here." He poked his finger at the route Bult'd marked. "And we'll have to run terrains. Fin, you want to do that?"

"You bet," I said.

"I'll check the weather, and see if we can work a route through some silvershims for Evie here."

He went out. "Can I watch you run the terrains?" Ev asked me.

"You bet," I said. I went over to the computer.

Bult was on it again, hunched under his umbrella, buying a roulette wheel.

"I've got to figure the easiest route," I said. "You can come back to the mall when I'm done."

He got out his log. "Discriminatory practices," he said.

That was a new one. "Why all these fines, Bult?" I said. "You saving up to buy a—" I was about to say "casino" but the last thing I wanted to do was give him any ideas. "To buy something big?" I ended up.

He reached for his log again.

"I need the computer if you want me to enter those fines you ran up with the rover today," I said.

He hesitated, wondering whether fining me for "attempt to bribe indigenous scout" would be worth more than the rover's fines, and then unfolded himself joint by joint and let me sit down.

I stared at the screen. There was no point in running terrains when I already knew the route I wanted, and I couldn't look at the log with Bult and Ev there either. I started tallying the fines.

After a few minutes, C.J. came in and dragged Ev off to convince him Big Brother wouldn't catch him if he named one of the hills Mount C.J., but Bult was still hovering behind me, his umbrella aimed at my back.

"Don't you need to go unpack all those umbrellas and shower curtains you bought?" I said, but he didn't budge.

I had to wait till everybody was bedded down, including C.J., who'd flounced into her bunk in a hide-nothing nightie and then leaned out to say good night to Ev and give him one last eyeful, before I could take a look at that log.

I figured Bult would be in the gate area, unpacking his purchases, but he wasn't. Which meant he was still "tchopping," and I'd never get time alone on the computer. But he wasn't in the mess either.

I checked the kitchen and then started over to the stables. Halfway there, I caught sight of a half circle of lights out by the ridge. I didn't have any notion of what he was doing clear out there—probably trying to collect fines from the luggage, but at least he wasn't hogging the computer.

I walked out far enough to make sure it was him and not just his umbrella, and then went back into the mess and asked Starting Gate for a verify on Wulfmeier. I got it, which didn't mean anything either. Bult could make more selling fake verifies than he makes off us.

I asked for a trace, then checked on the rest of the gatecrashers. We had beacons on Miller and Abeyta, and Shoudamire was in the brig on the *Powell,* which left Karadjk and Redfox. They were out on the Arm.

The trace showed Wulfmeier on Dazil until yesterday afternoon. I thought about it, and then asked for the log and frame-by-frame coordinates and leaned back to watch it.

I'd been right. Sector 248-76 was next to the Wall, about twenty kloms down from where we'd crossed, an area of grayish igneous hills covered with knee-high scourbrush, which was probably the reason we'd skirted it.

I asked for an aerial. C.J.'d sideswiped 248-76 on one of her trips home. I put privacies on and asked for visuals. It looked the way I remembered it—hills and scourbrush, a few roadkill. The visual said fine-grained schist with phyllosilicates all the way down. I asked for the earlier log. That expedition, we were south of it. It was hills and scourbrush on that end, too.

The schist we'd found on Boohte wasn't gold-bearing, and there were no signs of salt or drainage anomalies, so it wasn't an anticline. And we'd had good reasons for missing it both times—the first time we'd been following the Wall, looking for a break, and the second time we were trying to avoid 246-73. I couldn't see any indications either time that Bult was avoiding it. Even if he was, it was probably because the ponies would balk at the steepness of the hills.

On the other hand, we'd gone right by it twice, and you could hide almost anything in those hills. Including a gate.

I erased my transactions, took the privacies off, and walked back to the bunkhouse to talk to Carson.

Ev was leaning against the door. He looked so sappy-eyed and relaxed I wondered if C.J.'d broken down and given him a jump. She used to and then tried to get the loaners to name something for her afterward, but half the time they forgot, and she decided it worked better the other way around. But I figured the way she was looking at him at dinner it was just possible.

"What are you doing out here?" I asked him.

"I couldn't sleep," he said, looking out in the direction of the ridge. "I still can't convince myself I'm really here. It's beautiful."

He had that right. All three of Boohte's moons were up, strung out in a row like an expedition and turning the ridge a purplish-blue. I leaned against the other side of the door.

"What's it like, out in uncharted territory?" he said.

"It's like those mating customs of yours," I said. "Part instinct, part survival strategies, way too many variables. Mostly, it's a lot of dust and triangulations," I said, even though I knew he wouldn't believe me. "And ponypiles."

"I can't wait," he said.

"Then you'd better be getting to bed," I said, but he didn't move.

"Did you know a lot of species perform their courtship rituals by moonlight?" he said. "Like the whippoorwill and the Antarrean cowfrog."

"And teenagers," I said, and yawned. "We'd better be getting to bed. We've got a lot to do in the morning."

"I don't think I could sleep," he said, still with that dopey look. I began to wonder if I'd been wrong about him being all that smart.

"I saw the vids, but they don't do it justice," he said, looking at me. "I had no idea everything would be so beautiful."

"You should be using that line on C.J. and her nightie," Carson said, poking his head around the door. He was wearing his liner and his boots. "What on hell's going on out here?"

"I was telling Ev how he'd better get to bed so we can start in the morning," I said, looking at Carson.

"Really?" Ev said. The sappy-eyed look disappeared. *"Tomorrow?"*

"Sunup," I said, "so you'd better get back to your bunk. It's the last chance you'll have at a mattress for two weeks," but he didn't show any signs of leaving, and I couldn't talk to Carson with him hanging over me.

"Where are we going?"

"Uncharted territory," I said. "But you'll be asleep in the saddlebone and miss it if you don't get to bed."

"Oh, I couldn't possibly sleep now!" he said, gazing out at the ridge. "I'm too excited!"

"You'd better pack your gear, then," Carson said.

"I'm all packed."

C.J. came out, pulling a hide-nothing robe on over her nightie.

"We're leaving at sunup," I told her.

"Oh, but you can't go *yet,*" she said, and yanked Ev inside.

Carson motioned me out halfway between the bunkhouse and the stable. "What did you find?"

"A hole in Sector 248-76. We've missed it twice, and Bult was leading both times."

"Fossil strata?"

"No. Metamorphic. It's probably nothing, but Wulfmeier was on Dazil yesterday afternoon, *and* verified on Starting Gate. I don't think he's either place."

"What do you think he's doing? Mining?"

"Maybe. Or using it as headquarters while he looks around."

"Where'd you say it was?"

"Sector 248-76."

"My shit," he said softly. "That's awfully close to 246-73. If it is Wulfmeier, he's bound to find it. You're right. We'd better get out there." He shook his head. "I wish we weren't stuck taking this loaner with us. What was he doing out here? Resting between rounds with C.J.?"

"We were discussing mating customs," I said.

"Sexozoologist!" he said. "Sex can mess up an expedition quicker than anything."

"Ev can handle C.J. Besides, she's not going on the expedition."

"It's not C.J. I'm worried about."

"What *are* you worried about, then? Him trying to name one of the tributaries Crissa Creek? Him building a nest fifty times his size? What?"

"Never mind," he said, and stomped off toward the gate area. "I'll tell Bult," he said. "You load the ponies."

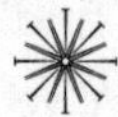

Expedition 184: Day 1

We ended up having C.J. fly us as far as the Tongue. Carson and I tallied up how long it would take to get to uncharted territory and how many fines we'd run up on the way and decided it was cheaper to go by heli, even with the airborne vehicle fines. And C.J. was overjoyed to have a few last chances at Ev. She kept him up front with her the whole way.

"Quit lollygagging with Evie and send him back here," Carson called to C.J. when the Tongue came in sight. "We've got to check his gear."

He came back into the bay immediately, looking as excited as a kid. "Are we in uncharted territory yet?" he asked, squatting down and looking out through the open hatch.

"We charted all this side of the river last time," I said. "The regs are no alcohol, no tobacco, no rec drugs, no caffeine. You carrying any of those?"

"No," he said.

I handed him his mike, and he stuck it on his throat. "No advanced technology except for scientific equipment, no cameras, no lasers or firearms."

"I've got a knife. Can I take that?"

"Only if you don't kill anything indigenous with it," I said.

"If you get the urge to kill something, kill Fin," Carson said. "There's no fine on us."

The heli swooped down to the Tongue and hovered above the near shore. "You're the first out," I said, pushing him over to the door. "It's too big a fine to land," I shouted. "C.J.'s going to hover it. We'll throw down the gear to you."

He nodded and got ready to jump. Bult elbowed him aside, shot his umbrella open, and floated down like Mary Poppins.

"Second out," I shouted. "Don't land on any flora if you can help it."

He nodded again, looking down at Bult, who already had his log out.

"Wait!" C.J. said, and came shooting out of her pilot's seat and past Ev and me. "I couldn't let you go without saying good-bye, Ev," she said, and flung her arms around his neck.

"What on hell are you doing, C.J.?" Carson said. "Do you know how big the fine is for crashing a heli?"

"It's on automatic," she said, and planted a wet one on Ev. "I'll be waiting," she said breathily. "Good luck, I hope you find lots of things to name."

"We're all waiting," I said. "All right, you told her good-bye, Ev. Now, jump."

"Don't forget," C.J. whispered, and leaned forward to kiss him again.

"Now," I said, and gave him a push. He jumped, and C.J. latched onto the edge of the bay and glared at me. I ignored her and started handing the bedrolls and the surveying equipment down to him.

"Don't set the terminal on any flora," I shouted down to him, too late. He'd already laid it in a patch of scourbrush.

I glanced at Bult, but he'd gone down to the river's edge and was looking at the other side with his binocs.

"Sorry," Ev shouted to me. He jerked the terminal back up and looked around for a bare spot.

"Stop gossiping and jump," Carson said behind me, "so I can get the ponies unloaded."

I grabbed the supply packs and handed them down to Ev. "Stand back," I shouted to him, scanning the ground for a clear patch.

"What on hell's keeping you?" Carson shouted. "They're going to unload before I unload them."

I picked a bare spot and jumped, but before I'd so much as hit, Carson yelled, "Lower, C.J.," and I nearly cracked my head on the heli when I straightened up.

"Lower!" Carson bellowed over his shoulder, and C.J. dipped the heli down. "Fin, take the reins, dammit. What on hell are you waiting for? Lead 'em off."

I grabbed for the dangling reins, which did about as much good as it always does, but Carson always thinks the ponies are gonna suddenly turn rational and jump off. They reared and shied and backed Carson against the side of the heli's bay, like always, and Carson said, like always, "You rock-headed morons, get off me!" which Bult entered in his log.

"Verbal abuse of indigenous fauna."

"You're gonna have to push 'em off," I said, like always, and climbed back on.

"Ev," I shouted down, "we're bringing this down as far as it'll go. Signal C.J. when it touches the tops of the scourbrush."

C.J. circled the heli and came in lower. "Up a little," Evelyn said, gesturing with his hand. "Okay."

We were half a meter from the ground. "Let's try it one more time," Carson said, like always. "Take the reins."

I did. This time they squashed him against the back of C.J.'s seat.

"Goddammit, you shit-brained sonsabitches," he shouted, swatting at their hind ends. They backed against him some more.

I maneuvered around to Carson's side and picked up a hind paw of the one that was standing on his bad foot. The pony went over like it'd been doped, and we dragged it to the edge of the bay and pushed it out. It landed with an *oof* and laid there.

Evelyn hurried over. "I think it's hurt," he said.

"Nope," I said. "Just sulking. Stand back."

We upended the other three and dumped them on top of the first one and jumped down.

"Shouldn't we do something?" Evelyn said, looking anxiously at the heap.

"Not till we're ready to go," Carson said, picking up his gear. "They can't shit in that position. Come on, Bult. Let's get packed."

Bult was still over by the Tongue, but he'd dropped his binocs and was squatting on the bank, peering into the centimeter-deep water.

"Bult!" I shouted, walking over to him.

He stood up and got out his log. "Disturbance of water surface," he said, pointing up at the hovering heli. "Generation of waves."

"There's not enough water for a wave," I said, sticking my hand in it. "There's hardly enough to wet your finger."

"Introduction of foreign body into waterway," Bult said.

"Foreign—" I started, and was drowned out by the heli. It flew over the Tongue, rippling the centimeter's worth of water, and came back around, skimming the bushes. C.J. swooped past us, blowing kisses.

"I know, I know," I said to Bult, "disturbance of waterway."

He stalked over to a clump of scourbrush, unfolded an arm under it, and came up with two wiry leaves and a shriveled berry. He held them out to me. "Destruction of crop," he said.

C.J. banked and turned, waving, and headed off northeast. I'd told her to swing over Sector 248-76 on her way home and try to get an aerial. I hoped she wasn't so busy flirting with Ev that she'd forget.

Ev was looking south at the mountains. "Is that the Wall?" he said.

"Nope. The Wall's off that direction," I said, pointing across the Tongue. "Those are the Ponypiles."

"Are we going there?" Ev said, looking sappy-eyed again.

"Not this trip. We'll follow the Tongue south a few kloms and then head northwest."

"Will you two stop sightseeing and get over here and load these ponies?" Carson shouted. He had the ponies up and was strapping the wide-angle to Speedy's pommelbone.

"Yes, ma'am," I said. Ev and I picked our way over to him between grass clumps. "Don't worry about the Wall," I told Ev. "We'll see plenty of it. We have to cross it to get to where we're going, and after we do we'll follow it all the way north to Silvershim Creek."

"Not unless we get these ponies loaded," Carson said. "Here," he said, handing the reins of one of the ponies to Ev. "Get Cyclone loaded."

"Cyclone?" Ev said, looking warily at the pony, which looked to me like it was getting ready to fall over again.

"There's nothing to it," I said. "Ponies—"

"Fin's right," Carson said. "Just don't make any sudden movements. And if he tries to throw you, hang on for dear life, no matter what. Cyclone doesn't get violent except when he senses fear."

"Violent?" Ev said, looking nervous. "I haven't had much experience riding."

"You can ride mine," I said.

"Diablo?" Carson said. "You think that's a good idea after what happened before? No, I think you'd better ride Cyclone."

He held out the stirrup. "You just put your foot in here and take hold of the pommelbone nice and slow," he said.

Ev took hold of the pommel like it was a hand grenade. "There, there, Cyclone," he murmured, bringing his foot up in slow motion to the stirrup. "Nice Cyclone."

Carson looked across at me, the edges of his mustache quaking. "Isn't he doing good, Fin?"

I ignored him and went on attaching the wide-angles to Useless's chest.

"Now swing your other leg up and over, real slow. I'll hold him till you're on," Carson said, holding on tight to the bridle. Evelyn did it and got a death grip on the reins.

"Giddyap!" Carson shouted and smacked the pony on the flank. The pony took a step forward, and Ev dropped the reins and grabbed for the pommelbone. The pony took two more steps toward Carson, lifted its tail, and dumped a pile the size of Everest.

Carson came over to me, laughing fit to kill.

"What are you picking on Ev for?" I said.

He laughed awhile before he answered. "You said he was smarter than he looks. I was just checking it out."

"You should be checking out your scout," I said, pointing at Bult, who had his binocs up to his eyes again, "if you want to depart any time today."

He laughed some more and went over to talk to Bult. I finished attaching the surveying equipment. Bult had his log out, and from the looks of it Carson was yelling at him again.

I swung up onto Useless and rode over to where Ev was sitting on his pony. "Looks like we'll be here awhile," I said. "Sorry about Carson. It's his idea of a joke."

"I figured that out," he said. "Finally. What's his real name?" he said, gesturing at the pony. It took a step forward and stopped.

"Speedy," I said.

"And this is as fast as it goes."

"Sometimes it doesn't go this fast," I said.

Useless lifted its tail and unloaded.

"Tell me they don't do this all the time," Ev said.

"Not like this," I said. "Sometimes after we have 'em in the heli they get the runs."

"Great," he said. "I suppose sudden movements don't spook them?"

"Nothing spooks them," I said, "not even nibblers chewing on their toes. If they're scared or they don't want to do something, they just stand there and won't budge."

"What don't they like?"

"People riding them," I said. "Hills. They won't go up more than a two percent grade. Backtrailing over their own paw-prints. Going more than two abreast. Going more than a klom an hour."

Ev was looking at me warily, like I was putting him on, too.

I held up my hand. "Scout's honor," I said.

"But you can walk faster than that," he said.

"Not when there's a fine for footprints."

He leaned sideways to look at Useless's paws. "But they leave footprints, don't they?"

"They're indigenous," I said.

"But how do you cover any territory?"

"We don't, and Big Bro yells at us," I said, looking over at the Tongue. Carson had given up yelling and was watching Bult talk into his log. "Speaking of which, I'd better fill you in on the rest of the regs. No personal holo or picture-taking, no souvenirs, no picking wildflowers, no killing of fauna."

"What if you're attacked?"

"Depends. If you think you can survive the heart attack you'll have when you see the fine and all the reports you'll have to fill out, go ahead. Letting it kill you might be easier."

He looked suspicious again.

"We probably won't run into anything dangerous where we're going," I said.

"What about nibblers?"

"They're farther north. Hardly any of the f-and-f are dangerous, and the indidges are peaceful. They'll rob you blind, but they won't hurt you. You wear your mike all the time." I reached over and took it off and stuck it back on lower down on his chest. "If you get separated, wait where you are. Don't go trying to find anybody. That's the surest way to get yourself killed."

"I thought you said the f-and-f weren't dangerous?"

"They're not. But we're going to be in uncharted territory. That means landslides, lightning, roadkill holes, flash floods. You can cut your hand on scourbrush and get blood poisoning, or get too far north and freeze to death."

"Or get caught in a luggage stampede."

I wondered how he knew about that. The pop-ups, whatever they were. "Or wander off and never be found again," I said. "Which is what happened to Stewart's partner, Segura. And you won't even get a hill named after you. So you stay where you are, and after twenty-four hours you call C.J. and she'll come and get you."

He nodded. "I know."

I was going to have to find out what these pop-ups are. "You call C.J.," I said, "and you let her worry about finding the rest of us. If you're injured and can't call, she'll know where you are by your mike."

I paused, trying to remember what else I should tell him. Carson was yelling at Bult again. I could hear him clear over by the ponies.

"No giving the indidges gifts," I said, "no teaching them how to make a wheel or build a cotton gin. If you figure out what sex Bult is, no fraternizing. No yelling at the indidges," I said, looking over at Carson.

He was coming this way, his mustache quivering again, but he didn't look like he was laughing this time.

"Bult says we can't cross here," he said. "He says there's no break in the Wall here."

"When we looked at the map, he said there was," I said.

"He says it's been repaired. He says we'll have to ride south to the other one. How far is it?"

"Ten kloms," I said.

"My shit, that'll take us all morning," he said, squinting off in the direction of the Wall. "He didn't say anything about it being repaired when we did the map. Call C.J. Maybe she got an aerial of it on her way home."

"She didn't," I said. Swinging north to Sector 248-76, she wouldn't have gotten any pictures of where we were going.

"Dammit," he said, taking his hat off, looking like he was going to throw it on the ground and then thinking the better of it. He looked at me and then stomped back toward the Tongue.

"You stay here," I said to Ev. I dismounted and caught up to Carson. "You think Bult's got it figured out?" I asked him as soon as we were out of Ev's earshot.

"Maybe," he said. "So what do we do?"

I shrugged. "Go south to the next break. It's no farther from the northern tributaries, and by that time we'll know if we have to check 248-76. I sent C.J. up there to do an aerial." I looked at Bult, who was still talking into his log. "Maybe he doesn't have it figured out. Maybe there are just more fines this way."

"Which is just what we need," he said glumly.

He was right. Our departure fines came to nine hundred, and it took a half hour to tally them up. Then it took Bult another half hour to get his pony loaded, decide he wanted his umbrella, unload everything to find it and load it again, and by that time Carson had used inappropriate manner and tone and thrown his hat on the ground, and we had to wait while Bult added those on.

It was ten o'clock before we finally got started, Bult leading off under his lighted umbrella, which he'd tied to his pony's pommelbone, Ev and I side by side, and Carson in the rear, where he couldn't swear at Bult.

C.J.'d landed us at the top end of a little valley, and we followed it south, keeping close to the Tongue.

"You can't see much from here," I told Ev. "This really only goes another klom or so, and then you should get a better view of the Wall. And five kloms down, it comes right up next to the Tongue."

"Why is it called the Tongue? Is that a translation of the Boohteri name for it?"

"The indidges don't have a name for it. Or half the stuff on this planet." I pointed at the mountains ahead of us. "Take the Ponypiles. Biggest natural formation on the whole continent, and they don't have a name for it, or most of the f-and-f. And when they do give stuff names, they don't make any sense. Their name for the luggage is *tssuhlkahttses*. It means 'dead soup.' And Big Brother won't let us give things sensible names."

"Like the Tongue?" he said, grinning.

"It's long, it's pink, and it's hanging out like it's going 'aah' for a doctor. What else would you call it? That's not its name anyway. The Tongue's just what we call it. The name on the map's Conglomerate River, after the rocks it was flowing between up where we named it."

"An unofficial name," Ev said half to himself.

"Won't work," I said. "We already named Tight-ass Canyon after C.J. She wants something named after her officially. Passed, approved, and on the topographicals."

"Oh," he said, and looked disappointed.

"What about that?" I said. "Any species besides Homo sap have to carve a female's name on a tree to get a jump?"

"No," he said. "There's a species of water bird on Choom where the males build plaster dikes around the females that look a lot like the Wall."

Speaking of which, there it was. The valley had been climbing and opening out as we rode, and all of a sudden we were at the top of a rise and looking out across what looked like one of C.J.'s aerials.

It was flat all the way to the feet of the Ponypiles, with the Tongue slicing through it like a map boundary. Boohte's got as many oxides as Mars, and lots of cinnabar, so the plains are pink. There were mesas here and there off to the west, and a couple of cinder pyramids, and the blue of the distance turned them a nice lavender. And meandering around them and over the mesas, down to the Tongue and then away again, arched white and shining in the sun, was the Wall. At least Bult hadn't been lying about the break. The Wall marched unbrokenly as far as I could see.

"There she is," I said. I turned and looked at Ev.

His mouth was hanging open.

"Hard to believe the Boohteri built it, isn't it?"

Ev nodded without closing his mouth.

"Carson and I have this theory that they didn't," I said. "We think some poor species of indidges who lived here before built it, and then Bult and his pals fined them out of it."

"It's beautiful," Ev, who hadn't heard me, said. "I had no idea it was so long."

"Six hundred kloms," I said. "And getting longer. An average of two new chambers a year, according to C.J.'s aerials, not counting repaired breaks."

Which meant our theory didn't wash at all, but neither did the idea of the indidges doing all the work.

"It's even more beautiful than the pop-ups," Ev said, and I was going to ask him what exactly pop-ups were, but I didn't think he'd hear that either.

I remembered the first time I'd seen the Wall. I'd only been on Boohte a week. We'd spent the whole time struggling up a draw in pouring rain and *I'd* spent the whole time wondering how I'd let Carson talk me into this, and we came out on top of a mesa a lot higher than what we were now, and Carson said, "There she is. All yours."

Which got us a pursuant on incorrect imperialistic attitudes and how "Pursuant to proprietorship, planets are *not* owned."

I looked over at Ev. "You're right. It is presentable-looking."

Bult finished writing up his fines, and we started out across it. He was still keeping close to the Tongue, and after half a klom he got out his binocs, looked through them at the water, and shook his head, and we plodded on.

It was already after noon, and I thought about getting lunch out of my pack, but the ponies were starting to drag and Ev was intent on the Wall, which was close to the Tongue here, so I waited.

The Wall disappeared behind a low step-mesa for a hundred meters and then curved down almost to the Tongue, and Carson's pony apparently decided he'd gone far enough and stopped, swaying.

"Uh-oh," I said.

"What is it?" Ev said, dragging his eyes away from the Wall.

"Rest stop. Remember how I told you they're not dangerous?" I said, watching Carson, who'd gotten down off his pony and was standing clear. "Well, that's if they don't fall over with your legs under 'em. Think you can get down off him faster than you got on?"

"Yes," Ev said, jumping down and away like he expected Speedy to explode.

I tightened the straps on the computer, dismounted, and

stepped back. Up ahead, Carson's pony had stopped swaying, and Carson had gone back up to it and was trying to untie the food packs.

Ev and I walked up and watched him struggle with the line. The pony dumped a pile practically on Carson's foot and started swaying again.

"Tim-berr," I said, and Carson jumped back. The pony took a couple of tottering steps forward and fell over, its legs out stiff at its side.

The pack was half under it, and Carson started yanking it out from under the motionless carcass. Bult unfolded himself and stepped decorously off his pony holding his umbrella, and the rest of the ponies went over like dominoes.

Ev went over to Carson and stood looking down on him. "Don't make any sudden movements," he said.

Carson stomped past me. "What are *you* laughing at?" he said.

We had lunch and incurred a few fines, but I didn't get a chance to talk to Carson alone. Bult stuck like glue to us, talking into his log, and Ev kept asking questions about the Wall.

"So they make the chambers one at a time," he said, looking across at it. We were on the wrong side of the Wall here, so all you could see were the back walls of the chambers, looking like they'd been plastered and painted a whitish-pink. "How do they build them?"

"We don't know. Nobody's ever seen them doing it," Carson said. "Or seen them doing anything worthwhile," he added darkly, watching Bult tallying up, "like finding us a way across it so we can get on with this expedition."

He went over to Bult and started talking to him in an inappropriate manner.

"And what *are* the chambers?" Ev asked. "Dwellings?"

"And storerooms for all the stuff Bult buys, and landfills. Some of them are decorated, with flowers hanging in the opening and nibbler bones laid out in a design in front of the door. Most of them stand empty."

Carson stomped back, his mustache quaking. "He says we can't cross here either."

"The other break's been repaired, too?" I said.

"No. Now he says there's something in the water. *Tssi mitss.*"

I looked over at the Tongue. It was flowing over quartzite sand here and was clear as glass. "What's that?"

"Your guess is as good as mine. It translates as 'not there.' I asked him how much farther we have to go, and all he'll say is 'sahhth.' "

Sahhth apparently meant halfway to the Ponypiles because he didn't even glance at the Tongue again once we had the ponies up and moving, and he didn't even bother to lead. He motioned Ev and me ahead and went back to ride with Carson.

Not that we could get lost. We'd charted all this territory before, and all we had to do was keep close to the Tongue. The Wall dipped away from the water and off toward a line of mesas, and we went up a hill through a herd of luggage, grazing on dirt, and came out at another Scenic Point.

The thing about these long vistas is that you're not going to see anything else for a while, and we'd already catalogued the f-and-f along here. There weren't any, anyway—a lot of luggage, some tinder grass, an occasional roadkill. I ran geological contours and double-checked the topographicals, and then, since Ev was busy gawking at the scenery, ran the whereabouts.

Wulfmeier was on Starting Gate after all. He'd been picked up by Big Brother for removing ore samples. So he wasn't in Sector 248-76, and we could've spent another day at King's X, eating C.J.'s cooking and catching up on reports.

Speaking of which, I figured I might as well finish them up now. I asked for Bult's purchase orders.

He must've worked fast while we were at King's X. He'd spent all his fines and then some. I wondered if that was why we were heading south, because he'd *tchopped* himself into a hole.

I went through the list, weeding out weapons and artificial building materials and trying to figure out what he was going to do with three dozen dictionaries and a chandelier.

"What are you doing?" Ev said, leaning across to look at the log.

"Screening out contraband," I said. "Bult's not allowed to order anything with weapon potential, which in his case should have included umbrellas. It's hard to catch everything."

He leaned farther across. "You're marking them 'out of stock.'"

"Yeah. If we tell him he can't order them, he fines us for discrimination, and he hasn't figured out yet that he doesn't have to pay for out-of-stock items, which keeps him from ordering even more stuff."

He looked like he was going to keep asking questions, so I called up the topographical instead and said, "Tell me some more about these mating customs you're an expert on. Are there any species who give their girlfriends dictionaries?"

He grinned. "Not that I've run across so far. Gift-giving is a major part of a majority of species' courtship rituals, though, including *Homo sapiens*. Engagement rings, and the traditional candy and flowers."

"Mink coats. Condos. Islands in the Tobo Sea."

"There are several theories about its significance," Ev said. "Most zoologists think the bestowing of a gift proves the male's ability to obtain and defend territory. Some socioexozoologists believe gift-giving is a symbolic enactment of the sex act itself."

"Romantic," I said.

"One study found gift-giving triggered pheromones in the female, which in turn produced chemical changes in the male that led to the next phase of the courtship ritual. It's hardwired into the brain. Sexual instincts pretty much override rational thought."

Which is why females'll run off with the first male who smiles at them, I thought, and why C.J. had been acting like an idiot at the landing. Speaking of which, here she was calling on the transmitter. "Home Base to Findriddy. Come in, Fin."

"What is it?" I said, taking off my mike and moving it up so she could hear me.

"You got a reprimand," she said. "'Pursuant to relations between members of the survey expedition and native planet dwellers. All members of the expedition will show respect for the ancient and noble cultures of indigenous sentients and will refrain from making terrocentric value judgments.'"

Which could have waited till we got back from the expedition. "What did you really call for, C.J.?" I asked. As if I didn't know.

"Is Evelyn there? Can I talk to him?"

"In a minute. Did you get a picture of that northwest section?"

There was a long pause before her answer came back. "I forgot."

"What do you mean, you forgot?"

"I had other things on my mind. The heli prop sounded funny."

"On hell it did. The only thing on your mind was jumping Ev."

"I don't know what you're so upset about," she said. "That whole area's charted, isn't it?"

"Here's Ev," I said. I patched her through and showed Ev the transmit button, and then looked back at Carson.

He'd want to know what I'd found out or hadn't found out, but he and Bult were too far back to shout at, and besides, I didn't want Bult figuring out why we'd picked the route we had.

If he hadn't already. We'd long since passed the second break in the Wall, and he didn't show any signs of crossing the Tongue.

"I'll try," Ev said earnestly into his mike. "I promise."

It's about time for a dust storm, I thought, looking at the sky. Carson usually likes to have one on the first day anyway, just in case something comes up where we need one, but he was deep in conversation with Bult, probably trying to talk him into crossing the Tongue.

"I miss you, too, C.J.," Ev said.

Nothing was stopping me from pointing the camera at a likely suspect and doing one myself, but there wasn't so much as a haze on the horizon. The Wall was only half a klom off along this stretch, and sometimes there are little kick-up breezes along it, but not today. The air was as still as a roadkill.

"Look!" Ev said, and I thought he was talking to C.J., but he said, "Fin, what's that?" and pointed at a shuttlewren that was flying toward us.

"Tssillirah," I said. "We call them shuttlewrens."

"Why?" he said, watching the little bird fly over my head and back toward the other two ponies.

I didn't waste breath answering. The shuttlewren circled Carson's head and started back for us, flapping its stubby pinkish wings like it was about to wear out. It made two trips around Ev's hat and started back for Carson again.

"Oh," Ev said, turning around to see it making the circuit again, flapping for dear life. "How long can it keep that up?"

"A long time. We had one follow us for fifty kloms like that one time up by Turquoise Lake. Carson figured up it flew almost seven hundred kloms."

Ev started asking for stuff on his log. "What does the Boohteri name for them mean?" he asked me.

"Wide mud," I said, "and don't ask what that's supposed to mean. Maybe they build their nests out of mud. But there's no mud around here."

Or dust, I thought. I went back to thinking about dust storms.

If Bult and Carson had been up ahead of us, I'd've taken my foot out of the stirrup and dragged it in the dirt to stir up some dust, but the way it was, Bult would catch me, and Ev would stop talking about shuttlewrens and ask what I was doing.

I looked back at Carson and waved, thinking maybe that would signal him to do something, but he was so busy talking to Bult I couldn't get his attention. The shuttlewren, on its tenth lap, skimmed the top of his hat, but that didn't get his attention either.

"Oh, look!" Ev said.

I turned back around. He was half up in the saddle, pointing off toward the Wall. I couldn't see what at, which meant neither could the scans.

"Where?" I said.

"Over there," he said, pointing.

I finally saw what he was looking at—a couch potato lying down behind a roundleaf bush and looking like a ponypile with fur.

I didn't think the scan had enough res to pick it up, but I said, "I don't see anything," to stall while I set the camera on a narrow focus to the far left of it, just in case.

"Over *there,*" Ev said. "Is that—"

I cut him off before he could get more specific. "My shit!" I shouted. "Put the shield on. That's a . . ." and hit the disconnect.

"What is it?" Ev said, reaching for his knife. "Is it dangerous?"

"What?" I said, locking the disconnect in for twelve minutes.

"That!" Ev said, waving his hand in the direction of the couch potato. "That brown thing over there."

"Oh, *that,*" I said. "That's a couch potato. It's not dangerous. Herbivore. Lies down most of the time, except to eat. I didn't notice it lying there." I set my watch alarm for ten minutes.

"Then what were you looking at?" he said, staring worriedly at the horizon.

"The weather," I said. "We get dust tantrums close to the Wall, and they play hob with the transmitter." I punched the transmitter's "send" three or four times and then held it down. "C.J., you there? Calling Home Base. Come in, Home Base." I shook my head. "It's out. I was afraid of that."

"I didn't see any dust," Ev said.

"They're only a meter or so wide," I said, "and nearly invisible unless they're in your line of sight." I hit a few more keys at random. "I better go tell Carson."

I yanked hard on the pony's reins and prodded it in the sides. "Carson," I called. "We got a problem."

Carson was still deep in conversation with Bult. I gave the pony another prod, and it gave me an evil look and started backing. At this rate, the dust storm'd be over before I even made it back there. I should've made it twenty minutes. "C.J., you there?" I said into the transmitter, just to make sure it was off, and got down off the pony.

"Hey, Carson," I yelled, "the transmitter's down." I walked back to his pony. "Wind's picking up," I said. "Looks like we're in for a dust tantrum."

"When?" he said with a glance at Bult, who was busy digging for his log to fine me for being off Useless.

"Now," I said.

"How long do you think it'll last?"

"Awhile," I said, looking speculatively at the sky. "Twelve minutes, maybe twelve and a half."

"Rest stop," Carson called, and Bult leaped off his pony and stalked over to look at my footprints.

Carson walked off in the direction of the couch potato. I looked back at Ev. He was standing with his head up and his mouth open, watching the shuttlewren. I caught up with Carson, and we squatted so we wouldn't attract the attention of the shuttlewren.

"What's wrong?" he said.

"Nothing," I said. "I just thought we should have one dust storm before we crossed into uncharted territory."

"You could have waited, then," Carson said. "We're not crossing anytime soon."

"Why not? Is this break fixed, too?"

He shook his head. *"Tssi mitsse,* which means 'big *tssi mitss,'* which I figure translates as he's going to see to it we don't get anywhere near Sector 248-76. What did you find out from C.J.? Did the aerial show anything?"

"She didn't get it. She was too busy batting her eyes at Ev and forgot."

"Forgot?!" he said. He stood up. "I told you he was going to louse up this expedition. I suppose you were too busy pointing out the sights to run whereabouts either."

I stood up and faced him. "What on hell's that supposed to mean?"

"It means you two've been so busy talking I figured you'd forgotten all about a little detail like what's going on in 248-76. What on hell's interesting enough to talk about all day long, anyway?"

"Mating customs," I said.

"Mating customs," he said disgustedly. "That's why you didn't run whereabouts?"

"I did run them. Whatever's in that sector, it's not Wulfmeier. He's on Starting Gate, and he's under arrest. I got a verify."

Carson stared south at the Ponypiles. "Then what on hell's Bult up to?"

The shuttlewren changed course in midflap and started toward us. "I don't know," I said, taking off my hat and waving with it to keep it away. "Maybe the indidges have got a gold mine up there. Maybe they're secretly building Las Vegas with all the stuff Bult's ordered." The 'wren circled my head and made a pass at Carson. "Maybe Bult's just trying to run up our fines by taking us the long way around. Did he say how much farther we'd have to go before we could cross the Tongue?"

"Sahhth," Carson said, mimicking Bult holding his umbrella and pointing. "If we go much farther south, we'll be in the Pony-piles. Maybe he's going to lead us into the mountains and drown us in a flash flood."

"And then fine us for being foreign bodies in a waterway." My watch beeped. "Looks like it's starting to clear up," I said. I picked up a handful of dirt, and we started back for the ponies.

Bult met us halfway. "Taking of souvenirs," he said, pointing sternly at the dirt in my hand. "Disturbances of land surface. Destruction of indigenous flora."

"Better transmit all those right away," I said, "before you forget."

I went over to Ev's and my ponies, the shuttlewren tailing me. While Ev was watching it circle his head, I blew dirt off my hand onto the camera lens and then swung up and looked at my watch. A minute to go.

I messed with the transmitter a little and called to Carson, "I think I've got it fixed. Come on, Ev."

I messed some more for Ev's benefit, taking off a chip and snapping it back into place, but I didn't need to have bothered. He was still gawking at the shuttlewren.

"Is that shuttlewren a male?" he asked.

"Beats me. You're the expert on sex." I released the disconnect, counted to three, hit it again, and counted to five. "Calling Ki–" I said, and kicked it on again. "–ng's X, come in, C.J."

"C.J. here," she said. "Where on hell did you go?"

"Nothing serious, C.J. Just a dust tantrum. We're too close to the Wall," I said. "Is the camera back on?"

"Yes. I don't see any dust."

"We just caught the edge of it. It lasted about a minute. I've been spending the rest of the time trying to get the transmitter up and running."

"It's funny," she said slowly, "how a minute's worth of dust could do so much damage."

"It's one of the chips. You know how sensitive they are."

"If they're so sensitive, how come all that dust from the rover didn't jam them?"

"The rover?" I said, looking around blankly like one might drive up.

"When Evelyn drove out to meet you yesterday. How come the transmitter didn't cut out then?"

Because I'd been too busy worrying about Wulfmeier and wrestling the binocs away from Bult to even think of it, I thought. I'd stood there coughing and choking in the rover's dust and it hadn't even crossed my mind. My shit, that was all we needed, for C.J. to catch on to our dust storms. "No accounting for technology," I said, knowing she was never going to buy it. "Transmitter's got a mind of its own."

Carson came up. "You talking to C.J.? Ask her if she's got an aerial of the Wall along here. I want to know where the breaks are."

"Sure," I said, and hit disconnect again. "We got a problem. C.J.'s asking questions about the dust storm. She wants to know why the transmitter didn't go out with all that dust from the rover."

"The rover?" he said, and I could see it dawn on him like it had on me. "What did you tell her?"

"That the transmitter's temperamental."

"She'll never buy that," he said, glaring at Ev, who was watching the shuttlewren start another lap. "I told you he'd cause trouble."

"It's not Ev's fault. We're the ones who didn't have sense enough to recognize a dust storm when we saw it. I'm going back on. What do I tell her?"

"That it's dust getting in the chip that does it," he said, stomping back to his pony, "not just dust in the air."

Which maybe would have worked, except two expeditions ago I'd told her it was dust in the air that did it.

"Come on, Ev," I said. He came over and got on his pony, still watching the shuttlewren. I took my finger off the disconnect. "—ase, come in, Home Base."

"Another dust storm?" C.J. said sarcastically.

"There must still be some dust in the chip," I said. "It keeps cutting out."

"How come the sound cuts out at the same time?" she said.

Because we're still wearing our mikes too high, I thought.

"It's funny," she went on. "While you were out, I took a look at the meteorologicals Carson ran before you left. They don't show any wind for that sector."

"No accounting for the weather either, especially this close to the Wall," I said. "Ev's right here. You want to talk to him?"

I patched him in before she could answer, thinking sex wasn't always such a bad thing on an expedition. It would take her mind off the dust anyway.

Bult and Carson rode in a wide circle around us to get in the lead again, and we followed, Ev still talking to C.J., which mostly consisted of listening and saying "yes" every once in a while, and "I promise." The shuttlewren followed us, too, making the circuit back and forth like a sheep dog.

"What kind of nests do the shuttlewrens have?" Ev asked.

"We've never seen them," I said. "What did C.J. have to say?"

"Not much. Their nests are probably in this area," he said, looking across the Tongue. The Wall was almost up next to the bank, and there were a few scourbrush in the narrow space between, but nothing that looked big enough to hide a nest. "The behavior they're exhibiting is either protective, in which case it's a female, or territorial, in which case it's a male. You say they've followed you for long distances. Have you ever been followed by more than one at a time?"

"No," I said. "Sometimes one'll fall away and another one'll take over, like they're working in shifts."

"That sounds like territorial behavior," he said, watching the shuttlewren make the turn past Bult. It was flying so low it brushed Bult's umbrella, and he looked up and then hunched over his fines again. "I don't suppose there's any way to get a specimen?"

"Not unless it has a coronary," I said, ducking as it skimmed my hat. "We've got holos. You can ask the memory."

He did, and spent the next ten minutes poring over them while I worried about C.J. We'd talked her into believing the transmitter could be taken out by a gust of dust that wouldn't even show on the log, and then I'd stood there yesterday and let the transmitter get totally smothered with it and hadn't even had the sense to disconnect.

And now that she was suspicious, she wouldn't let it go. She was probably checking all the logs for dust storms right now and comparing them to the meteorologicals.

Bult and Carson were looking in the water again. Bult shook his head.

"The staking out of territory is a courtship ritual," Ev said.

"Like gangs," I said.

"The male butterfish sweeps an area of ocean bottom clear of pebbles and shells for the female and then circles it constantly."

I looked at the shuttlewren, which was rounding Bult's umbrella again. Bult put down his log and collapsed the umbrella.

"The Mirgasazi on Yoan stake out a block of airspace. They're an interesting species. Some of the females have bright feathers, but they're not the ones the males are interested in."

The shuttlewren flapped past us and up to Bult and Carson again. It rounded the bend, and Bult shot his umbrella open. The shuttlewren fell in midflap, and Bult stabbed it with the tip of the umbrella a couple of times.

"I knew I should have put umbrellas on the weapons list," I said.

"Can I have it?" Ev said. "To see if it's a male?"

Bult unfolded his arm, picked up the shuttlewren, and rode on, plucking the feathers off it. When he had half of them off, he stuck the shuttlewren in his mouth and bit it in half. He offered Carson half. Carson shook his head, and Bult crammed the whole thing in.

"Guess not," I said. I leaned down and got a feather and handed it to him.

He was watching Bult chew. "Shouldn't there be a fine for that?" he said.

"'All members of the expedition shall refrain from making value judgments regarding the indigenous sentients' ancient and noble culture,'" I said.

I picked up the pieces Bult spit out, which didn't amount to much, and gave 'em to Ev. And looked off at the horizon.

The Wall curved back away from the Tongue and out across the plain in a straight line. Beyond it, there was a scattering of scourbrush and trees. There wasn't any wind, the leaves were hanging limp. What we needed was a good dust storm to throw C.J. off, but there wasn't so much as a breeze.

It wasn't C.J.'s figuring the dust storms out that worried me. She'd try to blackmail us into naming something after her, but she'd been doing that for years. But I didn't want her talking about it over the transmitter for Big Brother to hear. If they started looking at the log, they'd be able to see for themselves. There was no way there'd been a dust tantrum in this weather. There wasn't even any air. The feathers Bult was spitting out up ahead fell straight down.

Half a klom later, we ran into a dust tantrum that was more

like a full-blown rage. It got in the transmitter (but not before we'd gotten a full five minutes of it on the log), and up our noses and down our throats, and made it so dark we had to navigate by following the lights on Bult's umbrella.

By the time we got clear of it, it was getting dark for real, and Bult started looking for a good place to camp, which meant someplace knee-deep in flora so he could get the maximum in fines out of us. Carson wanted to get across the Tongue first, but Bult peered solemnly into the water and pronounced *tssi mitsse,* and while Carson was yelling, "Where? I don't see a damn thing!" the ponies started to sway, so we camped where we were.

We set up camp in a hurry, first because we didn't want to have to unload the ponies after they were down, and then because we didn't want to be stumbling around in the dark, but all three of Boohte's moons were up before we got the transmitter unloaded.

Carson went off to tie the ponies up downwind, and Ev helped me spread out the bedrolls.

"Are we in uncharted territory?" he asked.

"Nope," I said, shaking the dust out of my bedroll. "Unless you count what's on us." I spread the bedroll out, making sure it wasn't on any flora. "Speaking of which, I'd better go call C.J. and tell her where we are." I handed Carson's bedroll to him and started over to the transmitter.

"Wait," he said.

I stopped and turned back to look at him.

"When I talked to C.J., she wanted to know why the dust tantrum hadn't shown up on the log."

"And what did you tell her?"

"I said it came in at an angle and blindsided us. I said it blew up so fast I didn't even see it till you shouted, and by that time we were in the middle of it."

I told Carson he was smarter than he looked, I thought.

"How come you did that?" I said. "C.J.'d probably give you a free jump for telling her we blew up that storm ourselves."

"Are you kidding?" he said, looking so surprised I was sorry I'd said it. Of course he wouldn't betray us. We were Findriddy and Carson, the famous explorers who could do no wrong, even if he'd just caught us red-handed.

"Well, thanks," I said, and wondered exactly how smart he was and what explanation I could get away with. "Carson and I had things we needed to discuss, and we didn't want Big Brother listening."

"It's a gatecrasher, isn't it? That's why the expedition left in such a hurry and why you keep running whereabouts when there isn't supposed to be anybody but us on the planet. You think somebody's illegally opened a gate. Is that why Bult's leading us south, to try to keep us from catching him?"

"I don't know what Bult's doing," I said. "He could have kept us away from a gatecrasher by crossing where we were this morning and leading us up along the Wall past Silvershim Creek. He didn't have to drag us clear down here. Besides," I said, looking at Bult, who was down by the Tongue with Carson and the ponies, "he doesn't like Wulfmeier. Why would he try to protect him?"

"Wulfmeier?" Ev said, sounding excited. "Is that who it is?"

"You know Wulfmeier?"

"Of course. From the pop-ups," he said.

Well, I should have known.

"What do you think he's doing?" Ev said. "Trading with the indigenous sentients? Mining?"

"I don't think he's doing anything. I got a verify this morning that he's on Starting Gate."

"Oh," he said, disappointed. In the pop-ups, we must have gone after gatecrashers with lasers blasting. "But you want to go there just to make sure?"

"If Bult ever lets us cross the Tongue," I said.

Carson came stomping up. "I ask Bult if it's safe to water the ponies, and he pretends to look in the water and says, '*tssi mitss* nah,' so I say, 'Well, fine, since there aren't any *tssi mitss,* we can cross first thing in the morning,' and he hands me a pair of dice and says, 'Sahthh. Brik lilla fahr.'" He squatted down and rummaged in his pack. "My shit, 'lilla fahr' is practically in the Ponypiles." He glared at the mountains. "What on hell is he up to? And don't give me that stuff about fines." He pulled out the water-analysis kit and straightened up. "He's got enough already to buy himself a different planet. Fin, did you get that aerial of the Wall from C.J. yet?"

"I was just calling her," I said. He stomped off, and I went over to the transmitter.

"What can I do?" Ev said, tagging after me like a shuttlewren. "Should I gather some wood for a fire?"

I looked at him.

"Don't tell me," he said, catching my expression. "There's a fine for gathering wood."

"And starting a fire with advanced technology, and burning indigenous flora," I said. "We usually try to wait till Bult gets cold and builds one."

Bult didn't show any signs of getting cold, even though the wind over the Ponypiles that had sent that dust tantrum into us had a chill to it, and after supper he gave Carson some more dice, and then went off and sat under his umbrella out by the ponies.

"What on hell's he doing now?" Carson said.

"He probably went to get the battery-powered heater he bought last expedition," I said, rubbing my hands together. "Tell us some more about mating customs, Ev. Maybe a little sex'll warm us up."

"Speaking of which, Evie, have you figured out which brand Bult is yet?" Carson said.

As near as I could tell, Ev hadn't so much as looked at Bult since we started, except when Bult was snacking on the shuttle-wren, but he spoke right up.

"Male," he said.

"How do you figure that?" Carson said, and I was wondering, too. If it was table manners he was going by, that wasn't any sign. Every indidge I'd seen ate like that, and most of them didn't bother about taking the feathers off first.

"His acquisitive behavior," Ev said. "Collecting and hoarding property is a typical male courtship behavior."

"I thought collecting stuff was a female behavior," I said. "What about all those diamonds and monograms?"

"Gifts the male gives to the female are symbols of the male's ability to amass and defend wealth or territory," Ev said. "By collecting fines and purchasing manufactured goods, Bult is demonstrating his ability to gain access to the resources necessary for survival."

"Shower curtains?" I said.

"Utility isn't the issue. The male burin fish collects large quantities of black rock clams, which are of no practical value, since the burin fish only eats flora, and piles them into towers as part of the courtship ritual."

"And that impresses the female?" I said.

"Ability to amass wealth is indicative of the genetic superiority of the male, and therefore the increased chance of survival for her offspring. Of course she's impressed. There are other qualities that impress her, too. Size, strength, the ability to defend territory, like that shuttlewren we saw this afternoon—"

Which the female shuttlewrens probably hadn't been very impressed with, I thought.

"—virility, youth—"

Carson said, "You mean we're here freezing our hind ends off because Bult's trying to impress some *female*?" He stood up. "I told you sex can louse up an expedition faster than anything else." He grabbed up the lantern. "I'm not gonna end up with frostbite just because Bult wants to show his genes to some damn female."

He went stomping off into the dark, and I watched the bobbing lantern, wondering what had gotten into him all of a sudden and why Bult wasn't following him with his log if what Ev said was true. Bult was still sitting out by the ponies—I could see the lights on his umbrella.

"The indigenous sentients on Prii built bonfires as part of their courtship ritual," Ev said, rubbing his hands together to warm them. "They're extinct. They burned down every forest on Prii in less than five hundred years time." He tipped his head back and looked at the sky. "I still can't believe how beautiful everything is."

It was presentable-looking. There were a bunch of stars, and the three moons were jostling for position in the middle of the sky. But my teeth were chattering, and there was a strong whiff of ponypile from downwind.

"What are the names of the moons?" he said.

"Larry, Curly, and Moe," I said.

"No, really. What are the Boohteri names?"

"They don't have names for them. Don't get any idea of naming one after C.J., though. They're Satellite One, Two, and Three until Big Brother surveys them, which it won't anytime soon since the Boohteri won't agree to satellite surveys."

"C.J.?" he said, like he'd forgotten who she was. "They don't look anything like they did on the pop-ups. Nothing on Boohte has, except you. You look exactly like I thought you would."

"These pop-ups you're always talking about? What are they? Holo books?"

"DHVs." He got up, went over to his bedroll, and squatted down to get something out from under it. He came back, holding a flat square the size of a playing card, and sat down beside me.

"See?" he said, and opened the flat card up like a book. "Episode Six," he said.

Pop-ups was a good name for them. The picture seemed to jump out of the middle of the card and into the space between us, like the map back at King's X, only this was full-size and the people were moving and talking.

There was a presentable-looking female standing next to a horse made up to be a pony and a squatty pink thing like a cross between an accordion and a fireplug. They were having an argument.

"He's been gone too long," the female said. She had on tight pants and a low-slung shirt, and her hair was long and shiny. "I'm going to go find him."

"It's been nearly twenty hours," the accordion said. "We must report in to Home Base."

"I'm not leaving here without him," the female said, and swung up on the horse and galloped away.

"Wait!" the accordion shouted. "You can't! It's too dangerous!"

"Who's that supposed to be?" I said, sticking my finger into the accordion.

"Stop," Ev said, and the scene froze. "That's Bult."

"Where's his log?" I said.

"I told you things were different from what I'd expected," he said, sounding embarrassed. "Go back."

There was a flicker, and we were back at the beginning of the scene.

"He's been gone too long!" Tight Pants said.

"If that's Bult, then who's that supposed to be?" I said.

"You," he said, sounding surprised.

"Where's Carson?" I said.

"In the next scene."

There was another flicker, and we were at the foot of a cliff, with big, fake-looking boulders all around. Carson was sitting at the bottom of the cliff, sprawled out against one of the boulders with a big gash in the side of his head and a fancy mustache that curled at the ends. Carson's mustache had never looked that good, not even the first time I saw him, and they had the nibblers all wrong, too—they looked like guinea pigs with false teeth—but what they were doing to Carson's foot was pretty realistic. I hoped they got to the part where I found him pretty soon.

"Next scene," I said, and it flickered to me coming straight down the cliff in those tight pants, blasting at the nibblers with a laser.

Which wasn't the way it happened at all. Unless I'd wanted to go down the same way Carson did, there was no way off the cliff. The nibblers had run off when I yelled, but I'd had to go back along the cliff till I came to a chimney and work my way down and back around, and it took three hours. The nibblers had run off again when they heard me coming, but they hadn't been gone long.

Tight Pants jumped the last ten feet and knelt down beside Carson, and started tearing strips she couldn't afford to lose off her shirt and tying them around Carson's foot, which only looked a little bloody around the toes, sobbing her eyes out.

"I didn't cry," I said. "You got any others?"

"Episode Eleven," Ev said, and the cliff flicked into a silvershim grove. Tight Pants and Fancy Mustache were surveying the grove with an old-fashioned transit and sextant, and the accordion was writing down the measurements.

It looked like somebody'd cut up pieces of aluminum foil and hung them on a dead branch, and Carson was wearing a blue fuzzy vest that I had a feeling was supposed to be luggage fur.

"Findriddy!" the accordion said, looking up sharply. "I hear someone coming!"

"What are you two doing?" Carson said, and walked right into a silvershim. He looked around, his arms full of sticks. "What on *hell* is this?"

"You and me," I said.

"A pop-up," Ev said.

"Turn it off!" Carson said, and the other Carson and Tight Pants and the silvershims compressed into a black nothing. "What on hell's the matter with you, bringing advanced technology on an expedition? Fin, you were supposed to see to it he followed the regs!" He dumped the sticks with a clatter onto where the accordion'd been standing. "Do you know how big a fine Bult could slap us with for that?"

"I . . . I didn't know . . ." Ev was stammering, stooping down to pick up the pop-up before Carson stepped on it. "It never occurred to me . . ."

"It's no more advanced than Bult's binocs," I said, "or half the stuff he's ordered. And even if it was, he doesn't know anything about it. He's over there tallying up his fines." I pointed off toward the lights of his umbrella.

"How do you know he doesn't know? You can see it for kloms!"

"And you can hear you twice as far!" I said. "The only way he's going to find out about it is if he comes over to see what all the hollering's about!"

Carson snatched the pop-up away from Ev. "What else did you bring?" he shouted, but softer. "A nuclear reactor? A gate?"

"Just another disk," Ev said. "For the pop-up." He pulled a black coin out of his pocket and handed it to Carson.

"What on hell's this?" he said, turning it over.

"It's us," I said. "Findriddy and Carson, Planetary Explorers, and Our Faithful Scout, Bult. Thirteen episodes."

"Eighty," Ev said. "There are forty on each disk, but I only brought my favorites."

"You gotta see 'em, Carson," I said. "Especially your mustache. Ev, is there some way you can tone down the production so we can watch without letting the rest of the neighborhood in on it?"

"Yeah," Ev said. "You just—"

"Nobody's watching anything till we get a fire built and I make sure Bult's out there under that umbrella," he said, and stomped off for about the fourth time.

I got the sticks made into a passable fire by the time he got back, looking mad, which meant Bult *was* there.

"All right," he said, handing the pop-up back to Ev. "Let's see these famous explorers. But keep it down."

"Episode Two," Ev said, laying it on the ground in front of us. "Reduce fifty percent and cloak," and the scene came up, smaller and in a little box this time. Fancy Mustache and Tight Pants were clambering over a break in the Wall. Carson was wearing his blue fuzzy vest.

"You're the one with the fancy mustache," I said, pointing.

"Do you have any idea what kind of fine we'd get for killing a suitcase?" he said. He pointed at Tight Pants. "Who's the female?"

"That's Fin," Ev said.

"Fin?!" Carson said, and let out a whoop. "Fin?! Can't be. Look at her. She's way too clean. And she looks too much like a female. Half the time with Fin, you can't even tell!" He whooped again and slapped his leg. "And look at that chest. You sure that's not C.J.?"

I reached out and slapped the pop-up shut.

"What'd you do that for?" Carson said, holding his middle.

"Time to turn in," I said. I turned to Ev. "I'm gonna keep this in my boot tonight so Bult can't get hold of it," I said, and went over to my bedroll.

Bult was standing next to Carson's bedroll. I glanced out toward the Tongue. The umbrella was still there, burning brightly.

Bult picked up my bedroll to look under it. "Damage to flora," he said, pointing at the dirt underneath.

"Oh, shut up," I said, and crawled in.

"Inappropriate tone and manner," he said, and went back out toward his umbrella.

Carson laughed himself sick for another hour, and I lay there after that an hour or so waiting for them to go to sleep and watching the moons jostling for positions in the sky. Then I got the pop-up out of my boot and opened it on the ground beside me.

"Episode Eight. Reduce eighty percent and cloak," I whispered, and lay there and watched Carson and me sitting on horses in a pouring rain and tried to figure out which expedition this was supposed to be. There was a blue buffalo standing up the hill from where we were, and the accordion was pointing at it. "It is called *soolkases* in the Boohteri tongue," he said, and I knew which one this was, only that wasn't the way it happened.

It had taken us four hours to figure out what Bult was saying. *"Tssilkrothes?"* I remembered Carson shouting.

"Tssuhhtkhahckes!" Bult had shouted back.

"Suitcases?!" Carson said, so mad his mustache looked like it'd shake off. "We can't name them suitcases!" and right then a couple thousand suitcases had come roaring up over the hill at us. My pony stood there like an idiot and nearly got both of us trampled.

In the pop-up version, my pony ran off, and I was the one who stood there looking dumb till Carson galloped up and swung me up behind him. I was wearing high-heeled boots and pants so tight it was no wonder I couldn't run, and Carson was right, she was way too clean, but he hadn't had to fall in the fire laughing about it.

Carson swung me up, and we rode off, my tight pants hugging the horse and my hair streaming out behind me.

"Nothing here's what I expected," Ev had said back at King's X, "except you." Tonight he'd said, "You looked exactly the way I pictured you." Which, I thought, trying to figure out how to make the pop-up run it again, was pretty damn good.

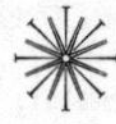

Expedition 184: Day 2

By noon the next day, we were still on this side of the Tongue and still heading south, and Carson was in such a foul mood I steered clear of him.

"Is he always this irritable?" Ev asked me.

"Only when he's worried," I said.

Speaking of which, I was getting a little worried myself.

Carson's water analysis hadn't showed up anything but the usual f-and-f, but Bult had insisted there were *tssi mitss* and led us south to a tributary. There were *tssi mitss* in the tributary, too, and he led us east along it till we came to one of its tributaries. This one didn't have any *tssi mitss,* but it zigzagged down through a draw too steep for the ponies, so Bult led us north along it, looking for a place to cross. At this rate, we'd be back at King's X by suppertime.

But that wasn't what was worrying me. What was worrying me was Bult. He hadn't fined us for anything all morning, not even when we broke camp, and he kept looking off to the south through his binocs. Not only that, but Carson's binocs had turned up. He found them in his bedroll after breakfast.

"Fin!" he'd shouted, dangling them by the strap. "I knew you had 'em. Where'd you find 'em, in your pack?"

"I haven't seen 'em since the morning we left for King's X when you borrowed 'em," I said. "Bult must've had 'em."

"Bult? Why would he've taken 'em?" he said, and gestured at Bult, who was peering through his own binocs at the Ponypiles.

I didn't know, which was what was worrying me. The indidges don't steal, at least that's what Big Brother tells us in the pursuants, and in all the expeditions we'd gone on, Bult hadn't ever taken anything away from us but our hard-earned wages. I wondered what else he might start doing—like take us deep into uncharted territory and then steal our packs and the ponies. Or lead us into an ambush.

I wanted to talk about it with Carson, but I couldn't get close to him, and I didn't want to risk another dust storm. I tried riding up alongside him, but Bult kept his pony dead-even with Carson's and glared at me when I tried to move up.

Ev stuck almost as close to me, asking questions about the shuttlewren and telling me about appetizing mating customs, like the male hanging fly, which spins a big balloon of spit and slobber for the female to mess with while he jumps her.

We finally found a place to cross the creek as it zagged sideways across a momentarily flat space, and headed southwest through a series of low hills, and I did a triangulation and then started running terrains.

"Well, we're in uncharted territory now," I told Ev. "You can start looking around for stuff to name after C.J. so you can get your jump."

"If I wanted a jump, I could get it without that," he said, and I thought, *I bet you could.*

"I know how C.J. feels, though," he said, looking out across the plain. "Wanting to leave some mark. You go through that gate, and you realize how big a planet is, and how insignificant you are. You could be here your whole life and never even leave a footprint."

"Try telling that to Bult," I said.

He grinned. "Okay, maybe footprints. But nothing lasting. That's why I wanted to come on this expedition. I wanted to do something that would make me famous, like you and Carson. I wanted to discover something that would get me on the pop-ups."

"Speaking of which," I said, leaning down to pick up a rock, "how did we get on them?" I stuck the rock in my pack. "How'd they find out about the suitcases? And Carson's foot?"

"I don't know," Ev said slowly, as if the question hadn't ever occurred to him. "Your logs, I guess."

It hadn't been in the logs about my finding Carson right when the twenty-four hours were up, though. We'd told some of the stories to loaners, and one of the female ones had kept a diary. But Carson wouldn't have told her about my crying over him.

The hills through here were covered with scraggly plants. I took a holo of them and then halted Useless, which didn't take much, and dismounted.

"What are you doing?" Ev asked.

"Collecting pieces of the planet for you to leave C.J.'s mark on," I said, digging around the roots of a couple of the plants and sticking them in a plastic bag.

I picked up two more rocks and handed them to him. "Either of these look like a C.J. to you?"

I got back on, watching Bult. He hadn't even noticed I was off my pony, let alone reached for his log. He was peering through his binocs at the hills beyond the tributary.

"Don't you ever wish you could have something named after you, Fin?" Ev was asking.

"Me? Why on hell would I want that? Who the hell remembers who Bryce Canyon or Harper's Ferry are named after even when they've got their names on them? Besides, you can't name a thing just by putting it on a topographical map. That's not the way it works." I gestured at the Ponypiles. "When people get here, they won't call those the Findriddy Mountains. They'll call 'em the Ponypiles. People name things after what they look like, or what happened there, or what the indidge name sounds like, not according to regs."

"People?" Ev said. "You mean gatecrashers?"

"Gatecrashers," I said, "and miners and settlers and shopping-mall owners."

"But what about the regs?" Ev said, looking shocked. "They're supposed to protect the natural ecology and the sovereignty of the indigenous culture."

I nodded my head at Bult. "And you think the indigenous culture wouldn't sell them the whole place for some pop-ups and a couple of dozen shower curtains? You think Big Brother's paying us to survey all this for his health? You think as soon as we find something they want, they won't be down here, regs or no regs?"

Ev looked unhappy. "Like tourists," he said. "Everybody's seen the silvershims and the Wall on the pop-ups, and they all want to come see them."

"And take holos of themselves being fined," I said, even though I hadn't really thought of Boohte as a tourist attraction. "And Bult can sell them dried ponypiles for souvenirs."

"I'm glad I came before the rush," he said, looking at the water ahead. The hills parted on either side of the tributary, and it wouldn't matter whether there were *tssi mitss* or not. A wide sandbar stretched almost the full width of the water.

The ponies picked their way across it like it was quicksand, and Ev just about fell off, trying to lean down to look at it. "The female willowback needs to lay her eggs in still water, so the courtship ritual involves the male doing a swimming dance that dams up sand across the stream."

"And that's what this is?" I said.

"I don't think so. It looks like it's just a sandbar." He sat up in the saddlebone. "The female shale-dwelling lizard scratches a design in the dirt, and then the male scratches the same design on the shale."

I wasn't paying any attention. Bult was peering through the binocs at the hills between us and the Tongue, and Carson's pony was starting to sway. "Here's your big chance, Ev," I said. "Rest stop!"

After Carson and I did the topographicals and we had lunch, I hauled out my rocks and plastic bags and Carson emptied his bug-catcher, and we settled down to naming.

Carson started with the bugs. "Do you have a name for it?" he asked Bult, holding it away from Bult so he couldn't stuff it in his mouth, but Bult didn't even look interested.

He looked at Carson for a minute like he was thinking of something else, and then said what sounded to me like steam hissing and then metal being dragged over granite.

"Tssimrrah?" Carson said.

"Thssahggih," Bult said.

"This'll take a while," I said to Ev.

Figuring out the indidge name for a thing isn't so much about understanding what Bult says as trying to keep it from all sounding the same. F-and-f all sounds like steam escaping in a blizzard, lakes and rivers sound like a gate opening, and rocks all begin with a belching "B," which makes you wonder about the indidges' opinion of Bult. All of them sound more or less the same, and none of them sound like English letters, which is a good thing, or everything would have the same name.

"Thssahggah?" Carson said.

"Shhoomrrrah," Bult said.

I glanced at Ev, who was looking at the rocks and the bagged plants. It was fairly slim pickings—the only rock that didn't look like mud warmed over was horneblende, and the only flower had five ragged-looking petals, but I didn't think Ev would try what the loaners usually did, anyway, which was try to name the first flower we found a chrysanthemum, no matter what it looked like. Chrysa, for short.

Carson and Bult finally agreed on *tssahggah* for the bug, and I took holos of it and of the piece of horneblende and transmitted them and their names.

Bult had the flower and was shaking his head.

"The indidges don't have a name for it," Carson said, looking at Ev. "How about it, Evie? What do you want to call it?"

Ev looked at it. "I don't know. What kind of things can you name them after?"

Carson looked irritated. It was obvious he'd expected "chrysanthemum." "No proper names, no technological references, no Earth landmarks with 'new' in front of them, no value judgments."

"What's left?" Ev said.

"Adjectives," I said, "shapes, colors—except for green—natural references."

Ev was still examining the plant. "It was growing out by the sandbar. How about sandpink?"

Carson looked like he was trying to figure out if there was any way to make sandpink into Crissa. "A pink's an Earth genus, isn't it, Fin?" he growled at me.

"Yeah," I said. "It'll have to be sandblossom. Next?"

Bult had names for the rocks, which took forever, and even he started to look impatient, picking his binocs up and then putting them down without looking through them, and nodding at whatever Carson said.

"Biln," Carson said, and I entered it. "Is that everything?"

"We need to name the tributary," I said, pointing at it. "Bult, do the Boohteri have a name for this river?"

He already had his pony up and was climbing on it. I had to ask him again.

He shook his head, and got down off the pony and picked up his binocs.

Carson came up beside me. "There's something wrong," I said.

"I know," he said, frowning. "He's been jittery all morning."

Bult was looking through his binocs. He took them down from his eyes and then held them up to his ear.

"Let's go," I said, and went to gather up the specimens. "Wagons ho, Ev!"

"What about the tributary?" Ev said.

"Sandbar Creek," I said. "Come on."

Bult was already going. Carson and I grabbed up the specimens and Carson's binocs, but Bult was already up the bank and heading west between the hills.

"What about the other one?" Ev said.

"Other what?" I said, jamming the specimens in my pack. I slung Carson's binocs around the pommelbone.

"The other tributary. Do the Boohteri have a name for it?"

"I doubt it," I said, swinging up onto Useless. Carson was having trouble with his pony. If we waited for him, we were going to lose Bult. "Come on," I said to Ev and started after Bult.

"Accordion Creek," Ev said.

"What?" I said, trying to decide which way Bult had gone. I caught a flash of light from his binocs off to the left and urged the pony that way.

"As a name for the other tributary," Ev said. "Accordion Creek, because of the way it folds back and forth."

"No technological references," I said, looking back at Carson. His pony had stopped and was unloading a pile.

"Oh, right," Ev said. "Then how about Zigzag Creek?"

I caught sight of Bult again. He was on top of the next rise, off his pony, looking through his binocs.

"We've already got a Zigzag Creek," I said, waving to Carson to come ahead. "Up north in Sector 250-81."

"Oh," he said, sounding disappointed. "What else means 'back and forth'? Crooked? Tortuous?"

We caught up to Bult, and I unhooked Carson's binocs from the pommelbone and put them up to my eyes, but I couldn't see anything through them but hills and sandblossoms. I upped the resolution.

"Ladder," Ev was muttering beside me. "No, that's technological . . . crisscross . . . how about Crisscross Creek?"

Well, it was a good try. It wasn't "chrysanthemum," and he'd waited till Carson wasn't there and I was worrying about something else. He was definitely smarter than he looked. But not smart enough.

"Nice try," I said, still scanning the hills with the binocs. "How about Sneaky Creek?" I said as Carson caught up to us. "For the way it tries to slip past you when you're not looking?"

Either Bult had seen what he was looking for through his binocs or he'd given up. He didn't try to ride ahead for the rest of the afternoon, and after our second rest stop, he put his binocs in his pack and got out his umbrella again. When I asked him the name of a bush during the rest stop, he wouldn't answer me.

Ev wasn't talking either, which was fine because I had a lot to think about. Bult might have calmed down, but he still wasn't levying fines, even though the rest stop had been on a hillside covered with sandblossoms, and two or three times I caught him glaring at me from under his umbrella. When his pony wouldn't get up, he kicked it.

I wondered if irritability was a sign of mating behavior, too, or if he was just nervous. Maybe he wasn't just trying to impress some female. Maybe he was taking us home to meet her.

I called C.J. "I need a whereabout on the indidges," I told her.

"And I need a whereabout on you. What are you doing down in 249-68?"

"Trying to cross the Tongue," I said. "Are there any indidges in our sector?"

"Not a one. They're all up by the Wall in 248-85."

Well, at least they weren't in 248-76.

"Any unusual movements?"

"No. Let me talk to Ev."

"Sure thing. Ask him about the creek we named this morning," I said.

I patched him through and thought about Bult some more, and then asked for another whereabout on the gatecrashers. Wulfmeier still showed on Starting Gate, probably trying to come up with the money to pay his fines.

We got back to the Tongue by late afternoon, but it was still hilly, and the Tongue was too narrow and deep for us to cross. We were close to the Wall—it wound up and down over the hills on the other side—and apparently in a shuttlewren's territory again. Ev alternated between watching it make its rounds and trying to shoo it away so Bult couldn't harpoon it.

Bult headed south, winding up over the tops of hills about like the Wall. I shouted ahead to Carson that it was too steep for the ponies, and he nodded and said something to Bult. Bult plodded on, and ten minutes later his pony keeled over in a dead faint.

Ours followed suit, and we sat down and waited for them to recover. Bult took his umbrella halfway up the hill and sat down under it. Carson lay back and put his hat over his eyes, and I got out Bult's purchase orders and went over them again, looking for clues.

"Do you always see shuttlewrens close to the Wall like this?" Ev asked. He had apparently recovered from the tongue-lashing C.J.'d given him.

"I don't know," I said, trying to remember. "Carson, do we always see shuttlewrens when we're close to the Wall?"

"Mmph," Carson said from under his hat.

"These species that give gifts to their mates," I said to Ev, "what other kinds of courting do they do?"

"Fighting," he said, "mating dances, displays of sexual characteristics."

"Migration?" I said, looking up the hill at Bult. The umbrella was sitting propped against the hill, its lights on. Bult wasn't under it. "Where's Bult?"

Carson sat up, putting his hat on. "Which way?"

I stood up. "Over there. Ev, tie up the ponies."

"They're still out cold," he said. "What's going on?"

Carson was already halfway up the hill. I scrambled after him.

"Up this gully," he said, and we clambered up it. It led up between two hills, a trickle of water at the bottom, and then opened out. Carson signaled me to wait and went up a hundred meters.

"What is it?" Ev said, coming up behind me, panting. "Has something happened to Bult?"

"Yeah," I said. "Only he doesn't know it yet."

Carson was back. "Just like we thought," he said. "Dead end. What say you go up there"—he pointed—"and I go around that way?"

"And we meet in the middle," I said, nodding. I headed up the side of the gully with Ev behind me. I ran along the crest of the hill in a half crouch, and then dropped to all fours and crawled the rest of the way.

"What is it?" Ev whispered. "A nibbler?" He looked excited.

"Yeah," I whispered back. "A nibbler."

He pulled his knife out.

"Put that away," I hissed at him. "You're liable to fall on it and kill yourself." He put it away. "Don't worry. It's not dangerous unless it's doing something it shouldn't."

He looked confused.

"Down," I said, and we crawled out onto a ledge looking down on the space where the gully widened out. Below us, I could see the flattened area of a gate and a lean-to made of a tarp on sticks. In front of it was Bult.

A man was standing half under the tarp, holding out a handful of rocks to Bult. "Quartz," the man said. "It's found in igneous outcroppings, like this." He reached forward to show Bult a holo, and Bult stepped back.

"You ever seen anything like this around here?" the man said, holding up the holo.

Bult took another step backward.

"It's only a holo, you moron," the man said, holding it out to Bult. "Did you ever see anything like this around here?" and Carson came strolling into the clearing, carrying his pack.

He stopped short. "Wulfmeier!" he said, sounding surprised and amused. "What on hell are you doing on Boohte?"

"Wulfmeier," Ev breathed beside me. I put my finger to my lips to shush him.

"What's that?" Carson said, pointing at the holo. "A postcard?" He walked up next to Bult. "My pony wandered off, and I came looking for him. Same as Bult. How about you, Wulfmeier?"

I wished I could see Wulfmeier's face from where we were. "Something went wrong with my gate," he said, taking a step back under the tarp and looking behind him. "Where's Fin?" he said, and lowered his hand to his side.

"Right here," I said, and jumped down. "Wulfmeier," I said, holding out my hand. "Fancy meeting you here. Ev," I called up, "come on down here and meet Wulfmeier."

Wulfmeier didn't look up. He looked at Carson, who'd moved off to the side. Ev landed on all fours and stood up quickly.

"Ev," I said, "this is Wulfmeier. We go way back. What are you doing on Boohte? It's restricted."

"I told Carson," he said, looking warily from one to the other of us, "something must have gone wrong with my gate. I was trying to get to Menniwot."

"Really?" I said. "We had a verify that you were on Starting Gate." I walked over to Bult. "What you got there, Bult?"

"I was emptying out my boot, and Bult wanted to see it," Wulfmeier said, still watching Carson.

Bult handed me the chunks of quartz. I examined them. "Tch, tch, taking of souvenirs. Bult, looks like you're going to have to fine him for that."

"I told you, I got them in my shoe. I was walking around, trying to figure out where I was."

"Tch, tch, tch, leaving footprints. Disturbance of land surface." I went over to the gate and peered underneath it. "Destruction of flora." I leaned inside the gate. "What's wrong with it?"

"I got it fixed," Wulfmeier said.

I stepped inside, and came back out again. "Looks like dust, Carson," I said. "We have a lot of trouble with dust. Does it get in the chips? He better check it while we're here, just in case."

Wulfmeier glanced back at the lean-to and over at Ev, and then back at Carson. He moved his hand away from his side.

"Good idea," he said. "I'll get my stuff."

"Better not," I said. "You wouldn't want to overload the gate. We'll send it along afterward." I went up to the gate controls. "Where'd you say you were trying to go? Menniwot?"

He opened his mouth to say something and then closed it. I asked for coordinates and fed the data into the gate. "That should do it," I said. "You shouldn't end up here again."

Carson walked him over to the gate, and he stepped inside. His hand dropped to his side again, and I hit activate and got out of the way.

Carson was already back at the lean-to, rummaging through Wulfmeier's stuff.

"What'd he have?" I said.

"Ore samples. Gold-bearing quartz, argentite, platinum ore." He leafed through the holos. "Where'd you send him?"

"Starting Gate," I said. "Speaking of which, I better go tell them he's coming. And that somebody's been messing with Big Brother's arrest records. Bult, figure up the fines on this stuff, and we'll send 'em special delivery. Come on," I said to Ev, who was standing there looking at the place where the gate had been like he wished there'd been a fight. "We've gotta call C.J."

We started down the gully. "You were great!" Ev said, scrambling over rocks. "I couldn't believe you faced him down like that! It was just like in the pop-ups!"

We came out of the gully and down the hill to where he'd tied the ponies. They were still lying down. "What'll happen to Wulfmeier on Starting Gate?" he asked while I wrestled the transmitter off Useless.

"He'll get fined for faking his location and disturbing land surface."

"But he was gatecrashing!"

"He says he wasn't. You heard him. There was something wrong with his gate. He'd have to have been drilling, trading, prospecting, or shooting luggage for Big Brother to confiscate his gate."

"What about those rocks he was giving Bult? That's trading, isn't it?"

I shook my head. "He wasn't giving them to Bult. He was asking if he'd ever seen anything like them. At least he wasn't pouring oil on the ground and lighting it like the last time we caught him with Bult."

"But that's prospecting!"

"We can't prove that either."

"So he gets fined, and then what?" Ev said.

"He'll scrounge up the money to pay the fines, probably from some other gatecrasher who wants to know where to look, and then he'll try again. Up north, probably, now that he knows where we are." *Up in Sector 248-76,* I thought.

"And you can't stop him?"

"There are four people on this whole planet, and we're supposed to be surveying it, not chasing after gatecrashers."

"But—"

"Yeah. Sooner or later, there'll be one we won't catch. I'm not worried about Wulfmeier—the indidges don't like him, and anything he gets he'll have to find himself. But not all of the gatecrashers are scum. Most of them are people looking for a better place to starve, and sooner or later they'll figure out where a silver mine is from our terrains, or they'll talk the indidges into showing them an oil field. And it'll be all over."

"But the government—what about the regs? What about—"

"Preserving the indigenous culture and the natural ecology? Depends. Big Brother can't stop a mining or drilling operation without sending forces, which means gates and buildings and people taking excursion trips to see the Wall, and forces to protect *them,* and pretty soon you've got Los Angeles."

"You said it depends," Ev said. "On what?"

"On what they find. If it's big enough, Big Brother'll come to get it himself."

"What'll happen to the Boohteri?"

"The same thing that always happens. Bult's a smart operator, but not as smart as Big Brother. Which is why we're putting the money from those out-of-stocks in the bank for him. So he'll have a fighting chance."

I punched "send." "Expedition calling King's X. Come in, King's X." I grinned at Ev. "You know, there *was* something wrong with Wulfmeier's gate."

C.J. came on, and I told her to send a message through the gate to Starting Gate and handed her over to Ev so he could fill her in on the details. "Fin was great!" he said. "You should have seen her!"

Bult and Carson were back. Bult had his log out and was talking into it.

"You find anything?" I said.

"Holos of anticlines and diamond pipes. Couple cans of oil. A laser."

"What about the ore samples? Were they indigenous?"

He shook his head. "Standard Earth samples." He looked at Bult, who'd stopped tallying fines and was going up the hill to get his umbrella. "At least now we know why Bult was leading us down here."

"Maybe." I frowned. "I got the idea he was just as surprised to see Wulfmeier as we were. And Wulfmeier was definitely surprised to see us."

"He'd probably told Bult to sneak off and meet him after dark," he said. "Speaking of which, we'd better get going. I don't want Wulfmeier to come back and find us still here."

"He's not coming back for a while," I said. "He's got a loose T-cable. It'll fall off by the time he gets to Starting Gate."

He smiled. "I still want to make it to the other side of the Wall by tonight."

"If Bult'll let us cross the Tongue," I said.

"Why wouldn't he? He's already had his conference with Wulfmeier."

"Maybe," I said, but Bult didn't go half a klom before he led the ponies across, and not a word about *tssi mitsse,* or otherwise, which shot my theory to pieces.

"You know the best part about that scene back there with Wulfmeier?" Ev said as we splashed across and headed south again. "The way you and Carson worked together. It's even better than on the pop-ups."

I'd watched that pop-up last night. We'd caught Wulfmeier

threatening the accordion and come out punching and kicking, lasers blazing.

"You don't even have to say anything. You both know what the other one's thinking." Ev gestured expansively. "On the pop-ups, they show you working together, but this was like you were reading each other's minds. You do what the other one wants you to do without even being told. It must be great to have a partner like that."

"Fin, where on hell do you think you're going?" Carson said. He was off his pony and untying the cameras. "Stop jabbering about mating customs and come help me. We're camping here."

It wasn't a bad place to camp, and Bult was back to fining us, or at least me, for every step I took, but I was still worried. Carson's binocs disappeared again, and Bult paced back and forth between the three of us while we were setting up camp and eating supper, giving me murderous looks. After supper, he disappeared.

"Where's Bult?" I asked Carson, looking out into the darkness for Bult's umbrella.

"Probably looking for diamond pipes," Carson said, huddling next to the lantern. It was chilly again, and there were big clouds over the Ponypiles.

I was still thinking about Bult. "Ev," I asked, "do any of these species of yours get violent as part of their courtship rituals?"

"Violent?" Ev said. "You mean, toward their mate? Bull zoes sometimes accidentally kill their mates during the mating dance, and spiders and praying mantis females eat the male alive."

"Like C.J.," Carson said.

"I was thinking more of violence against something else, to impress the female," I said.

"Predators sometimes kill prey to present to the female as a gift," Ev said, "if you'd call that violence."

I would, especially if it meant Bult was leading us into a nibbler's nest or over a cliff so he could dump our carcasses at his girlfriend's feet.

"Fahrrr," Bult said, looming out of the darkness. He dumped a big pile of sticks in front of us. "Fahrrr," he said to Carson, and squatted to light it with a chemical igniter. As soon as it was going, he disappeared again.

"Rivalry among males is common in almost all mammals," Ev said, "elephant seals, primates—"

"Homo sap," Carson said.

"Homo sapiens," Ev said, unruffled, "elk, woodcats. In a few cases, they actually fight to the death, but in most it's symbolic combat, designed to show the female who's stronger, more virile, younger—"

Carson stood up.

"Where are you going?"

"To run meteorologicals. I don't like the looks of those clouds over the Ponypiles." You couldn't see the clouds over the Ponypiles, it was so dark, and he'd already run meteorologicals. I'd watched him while we were setting up camp. I wondered if he was worried about Bult and had gone to check on him, but Bult was right here, with another armful of sticks.

"Thanks, Bult," I said. He glared at Ev and then at me again and walked off, still carrying the sticks.

I stood up.

"Where are you going?" Ev said.

"To run a whereabout on Wulfmeier. I want to make sure he made it to Starting Gate." I pulled his pop-up out of my boot and tossed it to him. "Here. Tight Pants and Fancy Mustache'll keep you company."

I went over to the equipment. Carson was nowhere to be seen. I got the log and called up Bult's fines. "Breakdown by day," I said. "Secondary breakdown by person," and watched it for a while, thinking about Bult and the binocs and Ev's mating customs.

When I got back to the fire, Ev was sitting in front of an officeful of terminals, which didn't look much like a Findriddy and Carson adventure.

"What's that?" I said, sitting down beside him.

"Episode One. That's you," he said, pointing at one of the females.

I wasn't wearing tight pants in this one. I was wearing a skimpy little skirt and one of C.J.'s shirts, landing lights and all, and talking into a screen with a geological on it.

Carson strolled into the office in his luggage vest, fringed pants, and a pair of boots the nibblers wouldn't have even had to bite through. His mustache was slicked down and curled up, and all the females simpered at him like he was a buck with big horns.

"I'm looking for someone to go with me to a new planet," he said, his eyes sweeping the room and coming to rest on Skimpy Skirt. Music from somewhere under the terminals started to play, and everything went pinkish. Carson walked over to her desk and stood over her, looking down her blouse.

After a while, he said, "I'm looking for someone who longs for adventure, who's not afraid of danger." He held out his hand, and the music got louder. "Come with me," he said.

"Is that how it was?" Ev said.

Well, my shit, of course it wasn't like that. He'd swaggered in, sat down at my desk, and propped his muddy boots up on it.

"What are you doing here?" I'd said. "You run up too many fines again?"

"Nope," he said, grabbing for my hand. "I wouldn't mind running up a few more fraternizing with the sentients, though. How about it?"

I yanked my hand free. "What are you really doing here?"

"I'm looking for a partner. New planet. Surface survey and naming. Any takers?" He grinned at me. "Lots of perks."

"I'll bet," I said. "Dust, snakes, dehyde food, and no bathrooms."

"And me," he said with that smug grin. "Garden of Eden. Wanta come?"

"Yeah," I said, watching the pop-up go pinker. "That's how it was."

"Come with me," Carson said again to Skimpy Skirt, and she stood up and gave him her hand. A draft from somewhere started blowing her hair and her skimpy skirt.

"It'll be uncharted territory," he said, looking in her eyes.

"I'm not afraid," she said, "as long as I'm with you."

"What on hell's *that* supposed to be?" Carson said, limping up.

"The way you and Fin met," Ev said.

"And I suppose those landing lights are supposed to be Fin's?"

"You finish your meteorologicals?" I cut in before he could say anything about not being able to tell I was a female half the time.

"Yeah," he said, warming his hands over the fire. "Supposed to rain in the Ponypiles. I'm glad we're heading north tomorrow." He looked back at Carson and Skimpy Skirt, who were still holding hands and looking sappy-eyed at each other. "Evie, which adventure did you say this was supposed to be?"

"It's when you first met," Ev said. "When you asked Fin to be your partner."

"*Asked* her?" Carson said. "My shit, I didn't ask her. Big Brother said my partner had to be a female, for gender balance, whatever on hell that is, and she was the only female in the department who knew how to run terrains and geologicals."

"Fahrrr," Bult said, and dumped his load of sticks on Carson's bad foot.

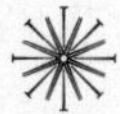

Expedition 184: Day 3

I HAULED MY BEDROLL OUT BY THE PONIES SO I DIDN'T HAVE to listen to Carson, and in the morning I said, "Come on, Ev, you're riding with me. I want to hear all about mating customs from you."

"Chilly around here this morning," Carson said.

I strapped the camera on Useless and cinched it tight.

"I don't like the look of those clouds," Carson said, looking at the Ponypiles. They were covered with low clouds that were spreading out. Half the sky was overcast. "It's a good thing we're heading north."

"Sahhth," Bult said, pointing south. "Brik."

"I thought you said there was a break north of here," Carson said.

"Sahtth," Bult said, glaring at me.

I glared back.

"I don't like the way he's acting," Carson said. "He was gone half the night, and this morning he left a bunch of dice in my bedroll. And Evie says his pop-up's missing."

"Good," I said, climbing up on Useless. "Ev, tell me again about what males do to impress their females."

Bult led us south most of the morning, keeping close to the Tongue, even though the Wall was at least two kloms to the west and there was nothing between us and it but one sandblossom and a lot of pink dirt.

Bult kept sending murderous glances back at me and kicking his pony to make it go faster. Not only did it, our ponies keeping up with it, but they didn't keel over once all morning. I wondered if Bult had been faking rest stops the way we did dust storms. And what else he'd been faking.

Around noon, I gave up waiting for a rest stop and hauled dehydes out of my pack for lunch, and, right after we ate, we came to a creek, which Bult crossed without even looking in, and a handful of silvershims. The whole sky was gray by then, so they didn't look like much.

"Sorry the sun's not out," I told Ev. I looked at their grayish leaves, hanging limp and dusty. "They don't look much like the pop-ups, do they?"

"I'm sorry I lost the pop-up," Ev said. "I put it under my bedroll instead of in my boot." He hesitated. "You didn't know that was how you got chosen to be Carson's partner, did you?"

"Are you kidding?" I said. "That's how Big Brother always does things. C.J. got picked because she was one-sixteenth Navajo." I looked ahead at Carson.

"Why did you come to Boohte?" Ev said.

"You heard the man," I said. "I wanted adventure, I wasn't afraid of danger, I wanted to be famous."

We rode on a ways. "Is that really why?" Ev said.

"Let's change the subject," I said. "Tell me about mating customs. Did you know there's a fish on Starsi that's so dumb it thinks it's being courted when it's not?"

A half a klom after the silvershims, Bult turned west toward the Wall. It bulged out to meet us, and where it did, a whole section was down, a heap of shiny white rubble with high-water marks on it. A flood must've taken it out, even though it was an awfully long way from the Tongue.

Bult led us over the break and, finally, north, keeping next to the Wall all the way back up to the creek we'd crossed. Ev was excited about seeing the front side of the Wall, even though only a few of the chambers looked like they'd been lived in lately, and even more excited about a shuttlewren that tried to dive-bomb us riding through the break.

"Their territory obviously involves the Wall in some way," he said, leaning sideways to get a look inside. "Have you ever seen one of their nests in the chambers?"

If he leaned over any farther, he was going to fall off his pony. "Rest stop!" I called up to Carson and Bult, and pulled back on the reins. "Come on, Ev," I said, and dismounted. "It's against regs to go inside the chambers, but you can peek in."

He looked up ahead at Bult, who had his log out and was glaring back at us. "What about the fine for leaving footprints?"

"Carson can pay it," I said. "Bult hasn't fined him in two days." I went over to a chamber and looked inside the door.

They're not real doors, more like a hole poked in the middle of the side, and there's no floor either. The sides curve up like an egg. There was a bunch of sandblossoms laid out on the bottom of this one, and in the middle of it one of the American flags Bult had bought two expeditions ago.

"Courtship ritual," I said, but Ev was looking up at the curved ceiling, trying to see if there was a nest. "There are several species of birds that nest in the homes of other species. The panakeet on Yotata, the cuckoo."

We started back to the ponies. It was starting to sprinkle. Up ahead, Bult was getting his umbrella out of his pack and putting it up. Carson was off his pony stomping back to us. "Fin, what on hell do you think you're doing?" he said when he got up to us.

"Taking a rest stop," I said. "We haven't had one all day."

"And we're not going to. We're finally heading north." He took hold of Useless's reins and yanked him forward. "Ev, you stay back here and bring up the rear. Fin's coming up to ride with me."

"I like it back here," I said.

"Too bad," he said, and dragged my pony forward. "You're riding with me. Bult, you lead. Fin and I are riding together."

Bult gave me a murderous glance and lit up his umbrella. He crossed the creek and then rode up along it, going west.

"Now get on," Carson said and mounted his pony. "I want to be away from the mountains by nightfall."

"And that's why I have to ride with you," I said, swinging my leg up, "so I can tell you which way's north? It's that way."

I pointed north. There was a high bluff in that direction and, between it and the Ponypiles, a strip of flat grayish-pink plain, splotched here and there with whitish and dark patches. Bult was heading catty-corner across the flat, still following the stream, his pony leaving deep pawprints in the soft ground.

"Thanks," Carson said. "The way you been acting, I didn't figure you knew which end was up, let alone north."

"What on hell's that supposed to mean?"

"It means you haven't been paying attention to anything since Evelyn showed up and started talking about mating customs. I'd've thought you'd've run out of species by now."

"Well, we haven't," I snapped.

"You're supposed to be surveying, not listening to the loaners. In case you haven't noticed, we're in uncharted territory, we don't have any aerials, Bult's half a klom ahead of us—" He pointed up ahead.

Bult's pony was drinking out of the stream. It was still sprinkling, but Bult turned off his umbrella and collapsed it.

"—and who knows where he's going. He could be leading us into a trap. Or around in circles till the food runs out."

I looked ahead at Bult. He'd crossed the creek and ridden a little way up the other side. His pony was taking another drink.

"Maybe Wulfmeier's back and Bult's leading us straight to him. And you haven't looked at a screen all morning. You're supposed to be running subsurfaces, not listening to Evie Darling talk about sex."

"Listening to him is one hell of a lot more fun than listening to you tell me how to do my job!" I kicked the log on and asked for a subsurface. Up ahead, Bult's pony was stopped and drinking again. I looked down at the stream. Where it cut the low banks, the rock looked like mudstone. "Cancel subsurface," I said.

"You haven't been paying attention to anything," Carson said. "You lose the binocs, you lose the pop-up—"

"Shut up," I said, looking at the bluff, backing the full length of the plain. The plain tilted slightly to its base. "Terrain," I said. "No. Terrain cancel." I looked out at the closest whitish patch. Where the drops of rain were sticking to it, it was pocked with pink.

"You were supposed to keep the pop-up in your boot. If Bult gets hold of it—"

"Shut up," I said. Where Bult's pony had walked there were fifteen-centimeter-deep pawprints in the grayish-brown dirt. The ones up ahead were dark on the bottom.

"If you'd have been paying attention, you'd have realized Wulfmeier—" Carson was saying.

"My shit!" I said, "Dust storm!" and jammed the disconnect. "Shit."

Carson jerked around in the saddlebone as if he expected to see a dust tantrum roaring down on him, and then jerked back and stared at me.

"Subsurface," I said to the terminal. I pointed at the pony's pawprints. "Offline, and no trace."

Carson stared at the pawprints. "Is everything off?" he said.

"Yes," I said, checking the cameras to make sure.

"Are you running a subsurface?"

"I don't have to," I said, waving at the plain. "It's right there on top. Shit, shit, shit."

Evelyn rode up. "What is it?" he asked.

"I knew he was up to something," Carson said, looking ahead at Bult. He was off his pony and squatting down at the edge of a dark patch. "I *told* you I thought he was leading us into a trap."

"What *is* it?" Ev said, pulling his knife out. "Nibblers?"

"No, it's a couple of royal saps," Carson said. "Was the log on?"

"Of course it was on," I snapped. "This is uncharted. Terrain, offline and no trace," I said, but I already knew what it was going to show. A bluff backing a tilted plain. Mudstone. Salt. Seepage. A classic anticline, just like in Wulfmeier's holos. Shit, shit, shit.

"What *is* it?" Evelyn said.

The terrain came up on the screen. "Subsurface overlay," I said.

"Nahtth," Bult called.

I looked up. He had his umbrella up and was pointing with it at the bluff.

"The sneak," Carson said. "Where's he leading us now?"

"We've got to get out of here," I said, scanning the subsurface. It was worse than I thought. The field was fifteen kloms square, and we were right in the middle of it.

"He wants us to follow him," Carson said. "He probably wants to show us a gusher. We've got to get out of here."

"I know," I said, scanning the subsurface. The salt dome went the whole length of the bluff and all the way to the foot of the Ponypiles.

"What do we do?" Carson said. "Go back to the Wall?"

I shook my head. The only sure way out of this was the way we'd come, but the ponies wouldn't backtrail, and the subsurface showed a secondary fault south of the creek. If we went off at an angle, we were liable to run into seep, and we obviously couldn't go north.

"Distance overlay," I said. "Offline and no trace."

"We can't stay offline all day," Carson said. "C.J.'s already suspicious."

"I *know,*" I said, looking desperately at the map. We couldn't go west. It was too far, and the subsurface showed seepage that way. "We've got to go south," I said, pointing at the foothills of the Ponypiles. "We need to get up on that spur so we'll be up above the natural table."

"Are you sure?" Carson said, coming around to look at the screen.

"I'm sure. The rocks are gypsum." Which is frequently associated with an anticline. Shit, shit, shit.

"And then what? Go up into the Ponypiles in that weather?" He pointed at the low clouds.

"We've got to go somewhere. We can't stay here. And any other way's liable to lead us straight into Oklahoma."

"All right," he said, getting up on his pony. "Come on, Ev. We're going."

"Shouldn't we wait for Bult?" Ev said.

"My shit, no. He's already gotten us in enough trouble. Let him find his own way out. That goddamn Wulfmeier. You lead," he said to me, "and we'll follow."

"You stay right behind me," I said, "and holler if you see something I don't."

Like an anticline. Like an oil field.

I looked at the screen, wishing it would show a path for us to follow, and started slowly across the plain, watching for seep and hoping the ponies wouldn't suddenly go in knee-deep. Or decide to keel over.

It started to drizzle, and then rain, and I had to wipe the screen off with my hand. "Bult's following us," Carson said when we were halfway to the spur.

I looked back. He had his umbrella down and was kicking his pony to catch up.

"What are we going to tell him?" I said.

"I don't know," he said. "Damn Wulfmeier. This is all his fault."

And mine, I thought. *I should have recognized the signs in the terrain. I should have recognized the signs in Bult.*

The ground turned paler, and I ran a geological and got a mix of gypsum and sulfur in with the mudstone. I wondered if I could risk turning the transmitter back on, and about that time Useless stepped in seep over his paw. It started to drizzle again.

It took us an hour and a half to get out of the oil field and the rain and up into the first hills of the spur. They were gypsum, too, eroded by the wind into flattened and whorled mounds that looked exactly like ponyshit. It apparently hadn't rained as much up here. The gypsum was dry and powdery, and before we'd climbed fifty meters we were coated in pinkish dust and spitting plaster.

I found a stream, and we waded the ponies up it to get the oil off their paws. They balked at the cold water and the incline, and I finally got off and walked Useless, yanking on its reins and cursing it every step of the way up.

Bult had caught up. He was right behind Ev, dragging on his pony's reins and watching Carson thoughtfully. Ev was looking thoughtful, too, and I hoped that didn't mean he'd figured things out, but it didn't look like it. He craned his neck to look at a shuttlewren flying reconnaissance above us.

I needed to get the transmitter back on, but I wanted to make sure we were out of camera range of the anticline first. I dragged Useless up above a clear pool and into a little hollow with rocks on all sides, and unloaded the transmitter.

Ev came up. "I've got to ask you something," he said urgently, and I thought, *Shit, I knew he was smarter than he looked,* but all he said was "Is the Wall close to here?"

I said I didn't know, and he climbed up the rocks to look for himself. Well, I thought, at least he hadn't said anything about how well Carson and I worked together in a crisis.

I erased the subsurfaces and geologicals and reran the log to see how bad the damage was and then reconnected the transmitter.

"Now what happened?" C.J. said. "And don't tell me it was another dust storm. Not when it was raining."

"It wasn't a dust storm," I said. "I thought it was, but it was a wall of rain. It hit us before I could get the equipment covered."

"Oh," she said as if I'd stolen her thunder. "I didn't think you could have a dust storm in that mud you were going through."

"We didn't," I said. I told her where we were.

"What are you doing up there?"

"We got worried about a flash flood," I said. "Did you get the subsurface and terrain?" I asked. "I was working on them when the rain hit."

There was a pause while she checked and I wiped my hand across my mouth. It tasted like gypsum. "No," she said. "There's an order for a subsurface and then a cancel."

"A cancel?" I said. "I didn't cancel anything. That must have happened when the transmitter went down. What about aerials? Have you got anything on the Ponypiles?" I gave her our coordinates.

There was another pause. "I've got one east of the Tongue, but nothing close to where you are." She put it on the screen. "Can I talk to Evelyn?"

"He's drying off the ponies. And, no, he hasn't named anything for you yet. But he's been trying."

"He has?" she said, sounding pleased, and signed off without asking anything else.

Ev came back. "The Wall is just the other side of those rocks," he said, wiping dust off his pants. "It goes over the top of the ridge up there."

I told him to go dry off the ponies and reran the log again. The footprints did look like mud, especially with the rain pocking the gray-brown dirt, and it was cloudy, so there wasn't any iridescence. And there wasn't a subsurface. Or an aerial.

But there was me, saying to cancel the subsurface. And the terrain was right there on the log for them to see—the sandstone bluff and the grayish-brown dirt and the patches of evaporated salt.

I looked at the ponies' pawprints. They looked a little like mud, maybe, but they wouldn't when they did the enhances. Which there was no way they wouldn't. Not with C.J. talking about phony dust storms, not when we'd had the transmitter down for over two hours.

I should go tell Carson. I looked down toward the pool, but I didn't see him, and I didn't feel like going to look for him. I knew what he was going to say—that I should have realized it was an anticline, that I wasn't paying attention, that it was my fault and I was a crummy partner. Well, what did he expect? He'd only picked me because of my gender.

Carson came clambering up the rocks. "I got a look at Bult's log," he said. "He didn't write up any fines down there."

"I know," I said. "I already checked. What'd he say?"

"Nothing. He's sitting up in one of those Wall chambers with his back to the door."

I thought about that.

"His feelings are probably hurt that we didn't pay him for

leading us there. Wulfmeier obviously offered him money to show him where there was an oil field." He took off his hat. There was a line of gypsum dust where the brim had been. "I told him we got worried about the rain, that we thought that plain might flood, so we decided to come up here."

"That won't keep him from leading us straight back down there now that it's stopped," I said.

"I told him you wanted to run geologicals on the Ponypiles." He put his hat back on. "I'm gonna go look for a way past the field." He squatted down beside me. "How bad is it?"

"Bad," I said. "You can see the tilt and the mudstone on the log, and I'm on, canceling the subsurface."

"Can you fix any of it?"

I shook my head. "We had the transmitter off too long. It's already through the gate."

"What about C.J.?"

"I told her we ran into rain. She thinks the pawprints are mud. But Big Brother won't."

He came around to look at the screen. "It's that bad?"

"It's that bad," I said bitterly. "Any fool can see it's an anticline."

"Meaning I should've noticed it," he said, bristling. "I wasn't the one dawdling behind talking about sex." He threw his hat down on the ground. "I told you he was going to louse up this expedition."

"Don't you dare blame this on Ev!" I said. "He wasn't the one yelling at me for half an hour while the scans got the whole damned anticline on film!"

"No, he was the one busy noticing birds! And watching pop-ups! Oh, he's been a lot of use! The only thing he's done this whole expedition is try to get a jump out of you!"

I slammed the erase button, and the screen went black. "How do you know he hasn't already gotten one?" I stomped past him. "At least Ev can tell I'm a female!"

I stormed down the rocks, so mad I could have killed him, fine or no fine, and ended up sitting on a gypsum ponypile next to the pool, waiting for him to go off and look for a way down.

After a few minutes, he did, clambering up beside the stream without a glance in my direction. I saw Ev come down from the Wall and say something to him. Carson barged past him and went out along the spur, and Ev stood there staring after him, looking bewildered, and then looked down at me.

He was right about one thing, in all his talk about mating customs. When the hardwiring kicks in, it overrides rational thought, all right. And common sense. I was mad at myself for not seeing the anticline and madder at Carson, and half sick about what was going to happen when Big Brother saw that log. And I was covered with dried-on gypsum dust and oil and reeking of ponypiles. And, on the pop-ups, my face was always washed.

But that was no reason to do what I did, which was to strip off my pants and shirt and wade into that pool. If Bult saw me, I'd be fined for polluting a waterway and Carson would have killed me for not running an f-and-f check first, but Bult was sulking up in the Wall, and the water was so clear you could see every rock on the bottom. It spilled down over rounded boulders into the pool and poured out through a carved-out spout below.

I waded out to the middle, where it was chest-deep, and ducked under.

I stood up, scrubbed gypsum plaster off my arms, and ducked under again. When I came up, Ev was leaning against my gypsum ponypat.

"I thought you were up at the Wall watching shuttlewrens," I said, smoothing back my hair with both hands.

"I was," he said. "I thought you were with Carson."

"I was," I said, looking at him. I sank into the water, my arms out. "Have you figured out the shuttlewrens' courtship ritual?"

"Not yet," he said. He sat down on the rock and took his boots off. "Did you know the mer-apes on Chichch mate in the water?"

"You sure know a hell of a lot of species," I said, treading water. "Or do you just make them up?"

"Sometimes," he said, unbuttoning his shirt. "When I'm trying to impress a female."

I paddled out to where the water came up to my shoulders and stood up. The current was faster here. It rippled past my legs. "It won't work on C.J. The only thing that'll impress her is Mount Crissa Jane."

He peeled off his shirt. "It's not C.J. I'm trying to impress." He pulled off his socks.

"It's not a good idea to take your boots off in uncharted territory," I said, swimming toward him through the deep water. The current rippled past my legs again.

"The female mer-ape invites the male into the water by swimming toward him," he said. He stripped off his pants and stepped into the water.

I stood up. "Don't come in," I said.

"The male enters the water," he said, wading in, "and the female retreats."

I stood still, peering into the water. I felt the zag, wider this time, and looked where it should be. All I could see was a ripple over the rocks, like air above hot ground.

"Step back," I said, putting my hand up. I walked carefully toward him, trying not to disturb the water.

"Look, I didn't mean to—"

"Slowly," I said, bending down to get the knife out of my boot. "One step at a time."

He looked wildly down at the water. "What is it?" he said.

"Don't make any sudden movements," I said.

"What is it?" he said. "Is there something in the water?" and splashed wildly out of the water and up onto the ponypile.

What looked like a blurring of the current zagged toward me, and I plunged the knife down with a huge splash, hoping I was aiming at the right place.

"What is it?" Ev said.

Now that its blood was spreading in the water, I could see it, and it was definitely *e.* Its body was longer than Bult's umbrella, and it had a wide mouth. "It's a *tssi mitsse,*" I said.

It was also indigenous fauna, and I'd killed it, which meant I was in big trouble. But blood in the water and a fish you couldn't see weren't exactly small trouble. I got away from the blood and out of the water.

Ev was still crouching bare-beamed on the rock. "Is it dead?" he said.

"Yeah," I said, drying off my hair with my shirt and then putting it on. "And so am I." I started pulling the rest of my clothes on.

He got down off the gypsum, looking anxious. "You're not hurt, are you?"

"No," I said, looking in the water and wishing I had been. At least then I could have claimed "self-defense" on the reports.

The blood had spread over the lower half of the pool and was spilling over the spout into the stream. The *tssi mitsse* was drifting toward the spout, too, and I didn't see any activity around it, but I wasn't going back in the water to get it.

I left Ev getting his clothes on and went up to the ponies, which were all lying squeezed in among the rocks. Their paws were still wet, and I thought about us walking them up the stream, and Bult not saying a word. Nobody on this expedition was doing their job.

I took a grappling hook and Bult's umbrella and went down to get the *tssi mitsse* out of the water. Ev was buttoning his shirt and looking embarrassedly at Bult, who was over by the spout, hunched over and looking at the bloody water. I sent Ev to get the holo camera. Bult unfolded himself. He had his log, and he looked pointedly at the umbrella in my hand.

"I know, I know. Forcible confiscation of property," I said. It didn't much matter. Bult's fines were nothing compared to the penalty for killing an indigenous life-form.

The *tssi mitsse* had floated in close to the bank. I hooked it with the umbrella handle and pulled it to the edge and onto the bank, stepping away from it in a hurry, in case it wasn't dead, but Bult went right over to it, unfolded an arm, and started poking his hand into its side.

"Tssi mitss," he said.

"You're kidding," I said. "How big are the big ones?"

It was over a meter long and was perfectly visible now that it was out of the water, with transparent jellylike flesh that must have the same refraction index as water.

"Tith," Bult said, pulling the mouth back. "Keel bait."

They looked like they could kill bite, all right, or at least take off a foot. There were two long, sharp teeth on either side of its mouth and little serrated ones in between, and that was good. At least it hadn't been a harmless algae-eater.

Ev came back with the camera. He handed it to me, looking at the *tssi mitss*. "It's huge," he said.

"That's what you think," I said. "You'd better go find Carson."

"Yeah," he said, and stood there, hesitating. "I'm sorry I jumped out of the water like that."

"No harm done," I said.

I took holos and measurements and brought down the scale to weigh it. When I started to pick it up by the head, Bult said, "Keel bait," and I dropped it with a thud and then took a closer look at its teeth.

Definitely not an algae-eater. The long teeth on either side weren't teeth. They were fangs, and when I ran an analysis of the venom, it ate right through the vial.

I hauled the *tssi mitss* by the tail up the rocks to camp and started in on the reports. "Accidental killing of indigenous fauna," I told the log. "Circumstances—" and then sat and stared at the screen.

Carson came back, scrambling up the rocks from the direction of the pool and stopping short when he saw the *tssi mitss*. "Are you all right?"

"Yeah," I said, looking at the screen. "Don't touch the teeth. They're full of acid."

"My shit," he said softly. "Is this what was in the Tongue when Bult wouldn't let us cross?"

"Nope. This is the small version," I said, wishing he'd get on with it.

"It didn't bite you? You're sure you're all right?"

"I'm sure," I said, even though I wasn't.

He squatted down and looked at it. "My shit," he said again. He looked up at me. "Evie says you were in the pool when you killed it. What on hell were you doing in there?"

"I was taking a bath," I said, looking at the screen.

"Since when do you take baths in uncharted territory?"

"Since I ride all afternoon through gypsum dust," I said. "Since I get covered with oil, trying to wash it off the ponies. Since I find out you can't even tell half the time whether I'm female or not."

He stood up. "So you take off all your clothes and go in swimming with Evie?"

"I didn't take off all my clothes. I had my boots on." I glared at him. "And I don't have to have my clothes off for Ev to be able to tell I'm a female."

"Oh, right, I forgot, he's the expert on sex. Is that what that was down at the pool, some kind of mating dance?" He kicked at the carcass with his bad foot.

"Don't do that," I said. "I've got enough to worry about without having to fill out a form for desecrating remains."

"Worry about!" he said, his mustache quivering. "*You've* got enough to worry about? You know what *I've* got to worry about? What on hell you're going to do next." He kicked the *tssi mitss* again. "You let Wulfmeier open a gate right under our noses, you lead us into an oil field, you take a bath and nearly get yourself killed."

I slammed the terminal off and stood up. "And I lost the binocs! Don't forget that! You want a new partner, is that what you're saying?"

"A new–?"

"A new partner," I said. "I'm sure there are plenty of females to choose from who'd traipse off with you to Boohte the way I did."

"That's what all this is about, isn't it?" Carson said, frowning at me. "It's not about Evie at all. It's about what I said the other night about picking you as a partner."

"You *didn't* pick me, remember?" I said furiously. "*Big Brother* picked me. For gender balance. Only it obviously didn't work because half the time you can't tell which gender I am."

"Well, I sure can right now. You're acting worse than C.J. We been partners for a hundred and eighty expeditions–"

"Eighty-four," I said.

"We've been eating dehydes and putting up with C.J. and getting fined by Bult for eight years. What on hell difference does it make how I picked you?"

"You *didn't* pick me. You sat there with your feet up on my desk and said, 'Wanta come?' and I came, just like that. And now I find out all you cared about is that I could do topographicals."

"All I cared about–?" He kicked the *tssi mitss* again, and a big piece of clear jelly flew off. "I rode into that luggage stampede and got you. I never even looked at any of those female loaners.

What do you want me to do? Send you flowers? Bring you a dead fish? No, wait, I forgot, you got one of those for yourself. Lock horns with Evie so that you can tell which one of us is younger and's got both feet? What?"

"I want you to leave me alone. I have to finish these reports," I said, and looked at the screen. "I want you to go away."

Nobody said a word during supper, except Bult, who fined me for dusting off a lump of gypsum before I sat down. It started to rain and all evening Carson kept going out to the edge of the overhang and looking at the sky.

Ev sat in a corner, looking miserable, and I worked on the reports. Bult didn't show any inclination to build any more fires. He sat in the opposite corner watching pop-ups until Carson took it away from him and snapped it shut, and then he opened his umbrella, nearly poking me in the eye with it, and went off up to the Wall.

I wrapped up in my bedroll and worked on the reports some more, but it was too cold. I went to bed. Ev was still sitting in the corner, and Carson was still watching the rain.

I woke up in the middle of the night with water dripping on my neck. Ev was still asleep in his bedroll, snoring, and Carson was sitting in the corner, with the pop-up spread out in front of him. He was watching the scene in Big Brother's offices, the scene where he asked me to go with him.

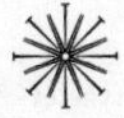

Expedition 184: Day 4

In the morning, he was gone. It was raining really hard, and the wind had started to blow. There was a stream running through the middle of the overhang and pooling at the back. The foot of Ev's bedroll was already wet.

It was a lot colder, and I figured Carson had gone after firewood, but when I went outside his pony was gone.

I climbed up to the Wall to look for Bult. He wasn't in any of the chambers. I went back down to the pool.

He wasn't there, and the pool wasn't either. Water was pouring everywhere over the rocks, white with gypsum. The ponypile Ev had crouched on was completely covered.

I climbed back up to the Wall and followed it over the ridge. Bult was at the top, looking south toward what you could see of the Ponypiles, which wasn't much, the clouds were so low.

"Where's Carson?" I shouted over the rain.

He looked west and then down at the oil field we'd crossed yesterday. "Dan nah," he said.

"He took one of the ponies," I shouted. "Which way did he go?"

"Nah see liv," he said. "Nah goot-bye."

"He didn't say good-bye to anybody," I said. "We've got to find him. You go up along the ridge, and I'll check the way we came up."

But the way we came up was flowing with water, too, and too slick for a pony to have gotten down, and when I went up to the overhang to get Ev, the whole back half was underwater and Ev was piling everything on a damp ledge.

"We've got to move the equipment," he said when he saw me. "Where's Carson?"

"I don't know," I said. I found another overhang higher up, not as deep and tilted up toward the back, and we carried the transmitter and the cameras up. When I went down for the rest of the equipment, I found Carson's log. And his mike.

Bult came back, sopping wet. "Nah fine," he said.

And apparently he doesn't want to be found, I thought, turning the mike over in my hands.

"That overhang isn't going to work," Ev said. "There's water spilling down the side."

We moved the equipment again, into a carved-out hollow away from the stream. It was deep, and the bottom was dry, but by afternoon there was a river running past it, spilling down catty-corner from the ridge, and by morning we'd be cut off from the ponies. And any way out if the water rose.

I went looking again. Water was pouring from both overhangs we'd been in, and there was no way we could get to the other side of the stream, even without *tssi mitss* in it. I climbed up onto the ridge. It was high enough, but we'd never last out here in the open. I tried not to think about Carson, out in this somewhere with nothing but his bedroll. And no mike.

A shuttlewren dived at my head and around to the Wall again. "Better get in out of this," I said.

I went back down to the hollow and got Ev and Bult. "Come

on," I said, picking up the transmitter. "We're moving." I led them up to the ridge and over to the Wall. "In here," I said.

"I thought this was against the regs," Ev said, stepping over the rounded bottom of the door.

"So's everything else," I said. "Including drowning and polluting the waterways with our bodies."

Bult stepped over the door and set his equipment down, and got out his log. "Trespassing on Boohteri property," he said into it.

It took us four trips to get everything up, and then we still had the ponies, which were all lying in a waterlogged pile and wouldn't get up. We had to push them up through the rocks, protesting all the way. It was dark before we got them to the Wall.

"We aren't going to put them in the same chamber with us, are we?" Ev said hopefully, but Bult was already lifting them over the door, paw by paw.

"Maybe we could knock out a door between this passage and the next one," Ev said.

"Destruction of Boohteri property," Bult said, and got out his log.

"At least with the ponies we'll have something to eat," I said.

"Destruction of alien life-form," Bult said into his log.

Destruction of alien life-form. I should get busy on those reports.

"Where was Carson going?" Ev said as if he'd just remembered he was missing.

"I don't know," I said, looking out at the rain.

"Carson would've waded right in when he saw that thing and killed it," Ev said.

Yeah, I thought, *he would have. And then yelled at me for not running an f-and-f check.*

"They would have done a pop-up about it," he said, and I

thought, *Yeah, and I know what that would have looked like. Old Tight Pants without her pants yelling, "Help, help!" and a fish with false teeth lunging up out of the water, and Carson splashing in with a laser and blasting it to hell.*

"I told you to get out of the water, and you did," I said. "I would've jumped out myself if I hadn't been so far out."

"Carson wouldn't have," he said. "He would have come to get you."

I looked out at the darkness and the rain. "Yeah," I said. He would have. If he'd known where I was.

Expedition 184: Day 5

It took me all the next day to fill out the reports on the *tssi mitss,* which was probably a good thing. It kept me from standing in the door of the Wall like Ev, staring out at the rain and the rising water.

And it kept me from thinking about Stewart, and how he'd drowned in a flash flood, and about his partner Annie Segura, who'd gone off looking for him and never been found. It kept me from thinking about Carson, washed up somewhere along the Tongue. Or sitting at the bottom of a cliff.

The chamber wasn't much of an improvement on the overhang. The ponies got the runs, and the shuttlewren flew frantically back and forth around our heads. With the rounded floor, there was no place to sit, and the wind kept blowing rain in. Ev and I could've used one of Bult's shower curtains.

Bult didn't need one. He sat under his umbrella watching pop-ups all day. Carson had left them behind, too. I tried to take it away from him, which got me a fine, and then made Ev show him how to make it not take up the whole chamber, but as soon as Ev went back to watching out the door, Bult put it back to full size.

"He's been gone too long," Tight Pants said, swinging up onto her horse, which was in the middle of the ponies. "I'm going to find him."

"It's been nearly twenty hours," the accordion said. "We must report in to Home Base."

"It's been more than twenty-four hours," Ev said, coming back in from the door. "Aren't we supposed to call C.J.?"

"Yeah," I said, and started filling in Form R-28-X, Proper Disposal of Indigenous Fauna Remains. In all those trips up the ridge in the pouring rain, I hadn't thought to bring the *tssi mitss,* which meant I was going to get slapped with another fine.

"Are you going to call her?" Ev said.

I kept filling out the report.

Toward evening C.J. called. "The scans have been showing the same thing all day," she said.

"It's raining. We're waiting it out in a cave."

"But you're all all right?"

"We're fine," I said.

"Do you want me to come pull you out?"

"No."

"Can I talk to Ev?"

"No," I said, looking at him. "He's out with Carson seeing how bad the flooding is." I signed off.

"I wouldn't have told her," Ev said.

"I know," I said, looking at Bult.

Carson and Fin were standing in front of him. "It'll be uncharted territory," Carson said, holding out his hand.

"I'm not afraid," Fin said, "as long as I'm with you."

"What are you going to do?" Ev said.

"Wait," I said.

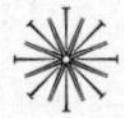

Expedition 184: Day 6

The next morning the rain let up a little and then started again. The roof of the chamber developed a leak, right over where we had the equipment piled, and we had to move it over next to the ponies.

It was getting a little crowded. During the night four roadkill had dragged themselves over the door, and the shuttlewren went crazy, wheeling and circling at the top of the chamber, making passes at Ev and me, and at Tight Pants climbing down the cliff.

Bult wasn't watching. He'd gotten up for the hundredth time and gone outside to stand on the ridge.

"What's he doing?" Ev said, watching the shuttlewrens.

"Looking for Carson," I said. "Or a way out of here."

There wasn't any way out. Water was flowing off of every mound, carrying what looked like half the Ponypiles with it, and a raging stream cut across the end of the ridge.

"Where do you think Carson is?" Ev said.

"I don't know," I said. During the night, it had occurred to me that Wulfmeier might have gotten his gate fixed and come back to get even. And Carson was alone, no mike, nothing.

I couldn't tell Ev that, and while I was trying to think of something I could, Ev said, "Fin, come look at this."

He was peering up at the leak in the ceiling. The shuttlewren was making little dives at it.

"It's trying to repair it," Ev said thoughtfully. "Fin, do you still have those parts of the one Bult ate?"

"There wasn't much left," I said, but I dug in my pack and got them out.

"Oh, good," he said, examining the fragments. "I was afraid he'd eaten the beak." He settled down against the wall with them.

The pop-up was still on. Fin was binding up the stub of Carson's foot and bawling. "It's all right," Carson was saying. "Don't cry."

The pop-up went dark and words appeared in the middle of the chamber. The credits. "Written by Captain Jake Trailblazer."

"Look at this," Ev said, bringing over one of the shuttlewren pieces. "See how the beak is flat, like a trowel? Can I run an analysis?"

"Sure." I went over to the door and looked out. Bult was standing on the ridge, where the stream cut across, in the rain.

"I should have figured it out before," Ev said, looking at the screen. "Look at how high the door is. And why would the Boohteri make a curved floor like that?" He stood up and looked at the leak again. "You said you've never seen the Boohteri building one of the chambers?" he said. "Is that right?"

"Yeah."

"Do you remember me telling you about the bowerbird?" he said.

"The one that builds a nest fifty times its size?"

"It's not a nest. It's a courtship chamber."

I couldn't see where this was going. We already knew the indidges used the Wall for courting.

"The male Adelie penguin gives a round stone to the female as a courting gift. But the stone doesn't belong to him. He stole it from another nest." He looked expectantly at me. "Who does that sound like?"

Well, Carson and I'd always said we thought somebody else built the Wall. I looked up at the shuttlewren. "But it's too small to build something like this, isn't it?" I said.

"The bowerbird's bower is fifty times its size. And you said the Wall was only growing by two new chambers a year. Some species only mate every three years, or five. Maybe they work on it several years."

I looked at the curved walls. Three to five years work, and then the imperialistic indidges move in and take it over, knock the door out to make it bigger, put up flags. I wondered what Big Brother was going to say when he heard about this.

"It's just a theory," Ev said. "I need to run probabilities on size and strength and take samples of the Wall's composition."

"It sounds like a pretty good theory," I said. "I've never seen Bult use a tool. Or order one either." The Boohteri word for the wall was "ours," but so was the word for most of Carson's and my wages. And that was Ev's pop-up he'd been watching.

"I'll need a specimen," Ev said, looking speculatively at the shuttlewren making frantic circles around us.

"Go ahead," I said, ducking. "Wring its neck. I'll write up the reports."

"First, I want to get this on holo," he said, and spent the next hour filming the shuttlewren poking at the leak. It didn't do anything to it that I could see, but by midmorning the ceiling had stopped leaking, and there was a tiny patch of new-looking white shiny stuff on the ceiling.

Bult came in, with his umbrella and two dead shuttlewrens.

"Give that to me," I said, and snatched one away from him.

He glared at me. "Forcible confiscation of property."

"Exactly." I handed it to Ev. "'Ours.' You'd better stick it in your boot."

Ev did, and Bult watched him, glaring, and then stuffed the other one in his mouth and went outside. Ev got out his knife and started chipping flakes off of the Wall.

The rain was letting up, and I went out and took a look around. Bult was standing where the stream cut across the ridge, staring up into the Ponypiles. While I watched, he splashed across and went on along the ridge.

The stream must be down, and the pool definitely was. Milky water was still spilling off every surface, but you could see Ev's ponypat rock and the spout at the bottom of the pool. Off to the west the clouds were starting to thin.

I went back up to the ridge. Bult had disappeared. I went into the chamber and started stuffing things in my pack.

"Where are you going?" Ev said. He'd looked around to make sure it wasn't Bult and then started scraping again.

"To find Carson," I said, fixing the straps so I could put the pack on my back.

"You can't," he said, holding the knife. "It's against the regs. You're supposed to stay where you are."

"That's right." I took off my mike and handed it and Carson's to him. "You wait here till afternoon and then call C.J. to come get you. We're only sixty kloms from King's X. She'll be here in a flash." I stepped over the door.

"But you don't know where he is," Ev said.

"I'll find him," I said, but I didn't have to. He and Bult were coming across the stream talking, their heads bent together. Carson was limping.

I ducked back in the chamber, dumped my pack on the floor, and asked for R-28-X, Proper Disposal of Indigenous Fauna Remains.

"What are you doing?" Ev said. "I want you to take me with you. It's uncharted territory. I don't think you should go look for

Carson by yourself," and Carson appeared in the door. "Oh," Ev said, surprised.

Carson stepped over the door and into the middle of the pop-up Bult had been watching. It was raining, and Fin was standing watching two thousand luggage bear down on her. Carson swung into the saddle and galloped toward her.

Carson snapped the pop-up shut. "How wide do you think the field is?" he said to me.

"Eight kloms. Maybe ten. That's how long the bluff is," I said. I handed him his mike. "You lost this."

He put it on. "Are you sure eight is as far as it goes?"

"No, but after that there's caprock, so there won't be any seepage. If we don't run a subsurface, we'll be okay," I said. "Is that where you were, finding a way past it?"

"I want to leave by noon," he said, and walked over to Bult. "Come on, we've got work to do."

They squatted in a corner, and Carson emptied out his pockets. Wherever he'd been, he'd collected lots of f-and-f. He had three plants in plastic bags, a holo of some kind of ungulate, and a whole pocketful of rocks.

He ignored us, which didn't bother Ev, who was busy dissecting his specimen. I packed up everything and got the wide-angles on the ponies.

Carson picked up one of the rocks and handed it to Bult. It was a crystal of some kind, transparent with triangular faces. By rights, I should be running a mineralogical to see if it already had a name, but I wasn't about to say anything to Carson, not when he was so pointedly not looking at me.

"Do the Boohteri have a name for this?" Carson asked Bult.

Bult hesitated, as if looking for some cue from Carson, and then said, *"Thitsserrrah."*

"Tchahtssillah?" Carson said.

Books are supposed to begin with a belching "b," but Bult nodded. *"Tchatssarrah."*

"Tssirrroh?" Carson said.

They went on like that for fifteen minutes while I strapped the terminal on my pony and rolled up the bedrolls.

"Tssarrrah?" Carson said, sounding irritated.

"Yahss," Bult said. *"Tssarrrah."*

"Tssarrrah," Carson said. He stood up, went over to my pony, and entered the name. Then he went back to where Bult was squatting and started picking up the plastic bags. "We'll do the rest of these later. I don't want to spend another night in the Ponypiles."

And what was that all about? I thought, watching him put the plants in his pack.

Ev was still working on his specimen. "Come on," I said. "We're leaving."

"Just a couple more holos," he said, grabbing up the camera.

"What's he doing?" Carson said.

"Gathering data," I said.

Ev had to take holos of the outside, too, and scrape a sample of the outside surface.

It was another half hour before he was finished, and Carson acted fidgety the whole time, swearing at the ponies and looking at the clouds. "It looks like it's going to rain," he kept saying, which it didn't. The rain was obviously over. The clouds were breaking up, and the puddles were already drying.

We finally set off a little past midday, Bult and Carson in the lead and Ev bringing up the rear, taking holos of the Wall and the shuttlewren who was supervising our departure.

The stream that had cut across the ridge was already down to a trickle. We followed it down to where it connected with the Tongue, and began following it east.

It made a wide canyon here with room on the far side for ponies. Bult knelt down on the bank and inspected it, though I didn't see how he'd be able to see a *tssi mitss* in the muddy pink water. But they must all have been washed downriver in the flood because he gave the go-ahead and we waded the ponies across and started up the canyon.

After the first klom or so, the bank got too rocky to be muddy and the clouds started to drift off. The sun even came out for a few minutes. Ev messed with his specimen, Carson and Bult talked and gestured, deciding which way to go, and I fumed. I was so mad I could've killed Carson. I'd been picturing him washed up in some gulch, half eaten by a nibbler, for the last three days. And not so much as a word when he came back about how on hell he'd made it through the flood or where on hell he'd been.

We began to climb, and I could hear a faint roar up ahead.

"Do you hear that?" I asked Ev.

He had his head in his screen, working on his shuttlewren theory, and I had to ask him again.

"Yeah," he said, looking up blankly. "It sounds like a waterfall," and a couple of minutes later there was one. It was just a cascade, and not very high, but right above it the river twisted out of sight, so it was a real waterfall and not just a rough section of river, and we'd gotten above where the rain started, so the water ran a nice, clear brownish color.

The gypsum piles made a whole series of bubbling zigzag rushes, and it was presentable-looking enough I figured Ev would at least make a try at naming it after C.J., but he didn't even look up from his screen and Carson rode right past it.

"Aren't we gonna name it?" I hollered ahead to him.

"Name what?" he said, as blank as Ev when I'd asked him about the roar.

"The waterfall."

"The water—?" he said, turning fast to look not at the waterfall, which was right in front of him, but up ahead.

"The *water*fall," I said, pointing at it with my thumb. "You know. Water. Falling. Don't we need to name it?"

"Of course," he said. "I just wanted to see what was up ahead first," which I didn't believe for a minute. Naming it hadn't so much as crossed his mind till I said it, and when I'd pointed at it he'd had an expression on his face I couldn't make out. Mad? Relieved?

I frowned. "Carson—" I started, but he'd already twisted around to look at Bult.

"Bult, do the indidges have a name for this?" he said.

Bult looked, not at the waterfall, but at Carson, with a questioning expression, which was peculiar, and Carson said, "He hasn't been this far up the Tongue. Ev, you got any ideas?"

Ev looked up from his screen. "According to my calculations, a shuttlebird could construct a Wall chamber in six years," he said happily, "which matches the mating period of the blackgull."

"What about Crisscross Falls?" I said.

Carson didn't even look annoyed, which was even more peculiar. "What about Gypsum Falls? We haven't used that yet, have we?"

"They'd have to begin building before maturation," Ev said, "which means the mating instinct would have to be activated at birth."

I checked the log. "No Gypsum Falls."

"Good," Carson said and set off again before I even had it entered.

We'd never named a weed that fast, let alone a waterfall, and Ev had apparently forgotten all about C.J. and sex, unless he thought there'd be plenty of other waterfalls to pick from. He might be right. I could still hear the roar of water, even when we went around the curve in the canyon, and around the next curve it got even louder.

Bult and Carson had stopped up above the waterfall and were

consulting. "Bult says this isn't the Tongue," Carson said when we came up. "He says it's a tributary, and the Tongue's farther south."

He hadn't said that. Carson had just told me the Boohteri hadn't been up this far, and besides, Bult hadn't opened his mouth. And Carson looked preoccupied, the way Bult had right before the oil field episode.

But Carson was already splashing us back across the river and up the side of the canyon, not even looking at Bult to see which way he was going. He stopped at the top. "This way?" he asked Bult, and Bult gave him that same questioning look and then pointed off up a hill. And what was he leading us into now? *If* he was the one leading us.

We were above the gypsum now, the soapy slopes giving way to a brownish-rose igneous. Bult led us up a break in another, steeper hill, and toward a clump of silvershim trees. They were old ones, as tall as pines and in full leaf. They would have been blinding if the sun had been out, which it looked like it might be again in a minute.

"Here're the silvershims you were so anxious to see," I said to Ev, and after talking to his screen he raised his head and looked at them.

"They'd look a lot better if we were out in the sun," I said, and right then it put in an appearance and lit them up.

"I told you," I said, putting up my hand to shade my eyes.

Ev looked dazed, and no wonder. They glittered like one of C.J.'s shirts, the leaves shimmering and reflecting in the breeze.

"Not much like the pop-ups, is it?" I said.

"*That's* what gives the Wall its shiny texture!" he said, and slapped his forehead with the flat of his hand. "That was the only part I couldn't figure out, what gave it that shine." He started taking holos. "The shuttlewrens must chew the leaves up."

Well, so much for the silvershims he'd come all the way to

Boohte to see. Was C.J. going to be mad when she found out Ev had forgotten her and taken up with some leaf-chewing, plaster-spitting bird!

The ponies had slowed to a crawl, and I would have been happy to take a rest stop and sit and look at the trees for a few minutes, but Bult and Carson rode on through the middle of them. When Bult wasn't looking, I picked a handful of the leaves and handed them to Ev, but I doubted if Bult would have fined me if he'd seen me. He was too busy looking ahead at a stream we were coming to.

It wasn't much bigger than the trickle up on top of the ridge, and it was coming from the wrong direction, but Bult claimed it was the Tongue. We started up it, winding in and out between the trees till the igneous on either side began to shut them out. It stacked up in squarish piles like old red bricks, and I grabbed a loose piece and ran an analysis. Basalt with cinnabar and gypsum crystals mixed in. I hoped Carson knew where he was going, because there was no room to backtrail here.

The canyon was getting steeper, too, and the ponies started to complain. The stream climbed up in a little series of cascades that chortled instead of roaring, and the banks turned into reddish-brown blocks, as steep as stairs.

The ponies'll never make it, I thought, and wondered if that was what Carson was up to—leading us into some defile so steep we'd have to carry the ponies through it on our shoulders just for spite. Carson'd have to carry his, too, though, and the way he was kicking his and swearing at it I didn't think he was playacting.

Carson's pony stopped and leaned back so far on his rear legs I thought he was going to pitch back onto me. Carson got off and pulled on the reins. "Come on, you beam-headed, rock-brained hind end," he shouted, leaning right in his pony's face, which must have scared him because he dumped a huge pile and started to topple over, but the rock wall stopped him.

"Don't you *dare* try that," Carson bellowed, "or I'll dump you in this stream for the *tssi mitss* to eat. Now come on!" He gave a mighty yank on the reins, and the pony stepped back, dislodged a rock, which went clattering down into the stream, and took off up the steps like he was being chased.

I hoped my pony would get the hint, and he did. He lifted his tail and plopped a big pile. I got off and took hold of his reins. Bult took out his log and looked at Ev expectantly.

"Come on, Ev," I said.

Ev looked up from his screens, blinking in surprise. "Where are we going?" he said, like he hadn't so much as noticed we weren't still meandering through the silvershims.

"Up a cliff," I said. "It's a mating custom."

"Oh," he said, and dismounted. "The shuttlewren's flight range puts the silvershims well within range. I need to run tests on the plaster's composition to make sure, but I can't do that till I get back to King's X."

I knotted the reins tight under Useless's mouth, and whispered, "You lazy, broken-down copy of a horse, I'm going to do everything Carson's ever threatened you with and some he hasn't even thought of, and if you shit one more time before we're out of this canyon, I'll pull that pommelbone right out of your neck."

"What on hell's keeping you?" Carson said, coming back down the steps. He didn't have his pony.

"I'm not carrying this pony," I said.

He sidestepped the piles and got behind Useless and pushed for a while.

"Turn her around," he said.

"It's too narrow," I said. "You know ponies won't backtrail."

"Yeah," he said, and took the reins and yanked her around till she was nose to nose with Ev's pony. "Come on, you poor imitation of a cow, let alone a horse," he said, and pulled, and she backed right up the canyon.

"You're smarter than you look," I called after him as he went back for Ev's.

"You ain't seen nothin' yet," he said.

We didn't have any more trouble with the ponies—they hung their heads like they'd been outsmarted and plodded steadily upward, but it still took us the better part of an hour to climb half a klom, and we were going nowhere. The stream shrank to a trickle and half disappeared between the rocks. It obviously wasn't the Tongue, and Carson must have had the same idea, because the next side canyon we came to he led us into it back the direction we'd come.

It was just as steep and twice as narrow. I didn't have to stop and take mineral samples, I just scraped them off with my legs as we rode past. The basalt blocks got smaller and began to look like a brick wall, and between them there were zigzag veins of the triangle-faceted crystals Carson had brought home. They acted like prisms, flashing pieces of the spectrum across the narrow canyon when the sun hit them.

Just about when I'd decided the canyon was going to run into a bricked-up dead end, we climbed up and onto the flat and back into silvershims.

We were on a wide overhang with trees growing right up to the edge, and I could see, off to the right, the Tongue far below and hear the roar of its waterfalls. Carson ignored it and rode off through the middle of the trees, heading straight for the far edge, not even bothering now to pretend Bult was leading.

I was right, I thought, *he is leading us over a cliff,* and came out of the trees. He'd tied his pony to a trunk and was standing close to the edge, looking out across the canyon. Ev rode up, and then Bult, and we just sat there on our ponies, gawking.

"Well, what do you know?" Carson said, trying to sound astonished. "Will you look at that? It's a waterfall."

That cascade with the gypsum piles was a waterfall. There was no word for what this was, except that it was obviously the Tongue, meandering through the silvershim forests on the far side and then plunging a good thousand meters into the canyon below us.

"My shit!" Ev said, and dropped his shuttlewren. "My *shit*!"

My sentiments exactly. I'd seen holos of Niagara and Yosemite Falls when I was a kid, and they were pretty impressive, but they were only water. This—

"My *shit*!" Ev said again.

We were standing a good five hundred meters above the canyon floor and opposite a rose brick cliff that rose up another two hundred meters. The Tongue leaped out of a narrow V in the top of it and flung itself like a suicide down into the canyon with a roar I should never have mistaken for a cascade, throwing up a billow of mist and spray I could almost feel, and crashing into the swirling green-white water below.

The sun ducked under a cloud and then came out again, and the waterfall exploded like fireworks. There was a double rainbow across the top of the spray, and that one was probably from the water's refracting the sunlight, but the rest of them were from the cliff. It was crisscrossed with veins of the prismatic crystal, and they sparkled and glittered like diamonds, flashing chunks of rainbow onto the cliff, onto the falls, into the air, across the whole canyon.

"My *shit*!" Ev said again, hanging on to his pony's reins like they could hold him up. "That's the most beautiful thing I've ever seen!"

"Lucky us stumbling onto it this way," Carson said, and I turned to look at him. He had his thumbs in his belt loops and was looking smug. "If we'd kept on up that canyon," he said, "we'd have missed it altogether."

Lucky, my boots, I thought. *All that dragging us through silvershims and up steps and consulting with Bult like you didn't know where you were going. This is what you were doing while I was waiting for you in the Wall, worried sick. Off chasing rainbows.*

He must have found it by following the Tongue, looking for a way around the anticline, and then gone off wandering up cliffs and in and out of side canyons, searching for the best vantage point to show it to us from. If we'd stayed on the Tongue, the way he probably had when he found it, we'd have caught a half glimpse of it around some bend, or heard the roar get louder and guessed what was coming, instead of having it burst on us all at once like some view of rainbow heaven.

"Really lucky!" Carson said, his mustache quivering. "So what do you want to name it?"

"Name it?" Ev's head jerked around to look at Carson, and I thought, *Well, so much for birds and scenery, we're back to sex.*

"Yeah," Carson said. "It's a natural landmark. It's gotta have a name. How about Rainbow Falls?"

"*Rainbow* Falls?" I snorted. "It's gotta have a better name than that," I said. "Something big, something that'll give some idea of what it looks like. Aladdin's Cave."

"Can't name it after a person."

"Prism Falls. Diamond Falls."

"Crystal Falls," Ev said, still staring at it.

He'd never get it past them. Chances were Big Brother, ever vigilant, would spot it and send us a pursuant that said Crissa Jane Tull worked on the survey team and the name was ineligible, and this time they'd be able to prove a connection, and we'd get fined to within an inch of our lives.

It was too bad, because Crystal Falls was the perfect name for it. And until Big Brother caught it, Ev would get a lot of jumps out of C.J.

"Crystal Falls," I said. "You're right. It's perfect."

I looked at Carson, wondering if he was thinking the same

thing, but he wasn't even listening. He was looking at Bult, who had his head bent over his log.

"What's the Boohteri name for the waterfall, Bult?" Carson asked, and Bult glanced up, said something I couldn't hear, and looked down at his log again.

I left Ev drooling into the canyon and went over by them, thinking, *Great, it's going to end up being called Dead Soup Falls or, worse, Ours.*

"What'd he say?" I shouted to Carson.

"Damage to rock surface," Bult said. He was catching up his fines. "Damage to indigenous flora."

I figured he was going to have to add, "Inappropriate tone and manner," but Carson didn't look so much as annoyed. "Bult," he shouted, but only because of the roar, "what do you call it?"

He looked up again and stared vaguely off to the left of the waterfall. I took the opportunity to snatch the log out of his hands.

"The waterfall, you pony-brained nonsentient!" I said, pointing, and he shifted his gaze in the right direction, though who on hell knows what he was really looking at—a cloud, maybe, or some rock slung halfway down the cliff.

"Do the Boohteri have a name for the waterfall?" Carson said patiently.

"Vwarrr," Bult said.

"That's the word for water," Carson said. "Do you have a name for this waterfall?" and Bult looked at Carson with that peculiar questioning look, and I thought, amazed, *He's trying to figure out what Carson wants him to say.*

"You said your people had never been in the mountains," Carson said, prompting him, and Bult looked like he'd just remembered his line.

"Nah nahm."

"You can't call it Nah Nahm," Ev said from behind us. "You've got to name it something beautiful. Something grand!"

"Grand Canyon!" I said.

"Something like Heart's Desire," Ev said. "Or Rainbow's End."

"Heart's Desire," Carson said thoughtfully. "That's not bad. Bult, what about the canyon? Do the Boohteri have a name for that?"

Bult knew his line this time. "Nah nahm."

"Crown Jewels Canyon," Ev said. "Starshine Falls."

"It should really be an indidge name," Carson said piously. "Remember what Big Brother said. 'Every effort should be made to discover the indigenous name of all flora, fauna, and natural landmarks.'"

"Bult just told you," I said. "They don't have a name for it."

"What about the cliff, Bult?" Carson said, looking hard at Bult. "Or the rocks? Do the indidges have a name for those?"

Bult looked like he needed a prompter, but Carson didn't seem mad. "What about the crystals?" he said, digging in his pocket. "What did you name that crystal?"

The roaring of the falls seemed to get louder.

"Thitsserrrah," Bult said.

"Yeah," Carson said. *"Tssarrrah*. You said Crystal Falls, Ev. We'll name it *Tssarrrah* after the crystals."

The roar got so loud it made me go dizzy, and I grabbed on to the pony.

"Tssarrrah Falls," Carson said. "What do you think, Bult?"

"Tssarrrah," Bult said. "Nahm."

"How about you?" Carson said, looking at me.

Ev said, "I think it's a beautiful name."

I walked over to the edge of the overhang, still feeling dizzy, and sat down.

"That settles it," Carson said. "Fin, you can send it in. Tssarrrah Falls."

I sat there listening to the roar and watching the glittering spray. The sun went in behind a cloud and burst out again, and rainbows darted across and above the cliff like shuttlewrens, sparkling like glass.

Carson sat down beside me. "Tssarrah Falls," he said. "It was lucky the indidges had a word for those crystals. Big Brother's been wanting us to give more stuff indigenous names."

"Yeah," I said. "Lucky. What does *tssarrah* mean, did Bult say?"

"'Crazy female,' probably," he said. "Or maybe 'heart's desire.'"

"How much did you have to bribe him with? Next year's wages?"

"That was what was funny," he said, frowning. "I was going to give him the pop-up since he likes it so much. I figured I might have to give him a lot more than that after the oil field, but I asked him if he'd help, and he said yes, just like that. No fines, nothing."

I wasn't surprised.

"Did you get the name sent?" he said.

I looked at the falls for a long minute. The water roared down, dancing with rainbows. "I'll do it on the way down. Hadn't we better get going?" I said, and stood up.

"Yeah," he said, looking south at where the clouds were accumulating again. "Looks like it's going to rain again."

He held out his hand, and I yanked him to his feet. "You didn't have any business going off like that," I said.

He still had hold of my hand. "You didn't have any business nearly getting yourself killed." He let go of my hand. "Bult, come on, you've got to lead us back down."

"How on hell are we supposed to do that when the ponies won't backtrail?" I said, but Bult's pony walked right through the silvershims and down into the narrow canyon, and ours followed single file without so much as a balk.

"Dust storms aren't the only things being faked around here," I muttered.

Nobody heard me. Carson was up behind Bult, still doing the leading, down the side canyon, back through the one where the ponies had given us so much trouble, and then into another side canyon. I let them get ahead and looked back at Ev. He was bent over his terminal, probably looking at shuttlewren stats. I called C.J.

After I talked to her, I looked ahead and caught a glimpse of the side of the falls. The rainbows were lighting up the sky. Ev caught up to me. "They'll never get it on the pop-ups like it really was," he said.

"No," I said. "They won't."

The canyon widened, and we could see the falls from an angle, the water leaping sideways off the crystal-studded cliff and straight down.

"Speaking of which," Ev said, "what's Carson's first name?"

I'd told Carson he was smart. "What?"

"His first name. I got to thinking that I don't know it. On the pop-ups, you never call each other anything but Findriddy and Carson."

"It's Aloysius," I said. "Aloysius Byron. His initials are A.B.C. Don't tell him I told you."

"*His* first name's Aloysius," he said thoughtfully. "And yours is Sarah."

As smart as they come.

"Did you know that in some species the males all compete for the most desirable female?" he said, smiling wryly. "Most of them don't stand a chance, though. She always picks the one who's the bravest. Or the smartest."

"Speaking of which, you were pretty smart to figure out the shuttlewrens built the Wall."

He brightened. "I still have to prove it," he said. "I'm going to have to run content analyses and work/size probabilities when I get back to King's X. And write it up."

"It'll be on the pop-ups, too," I said. "You'll be famous. Ev Parker, socioexozoologist."

"You think so?" he said, as if it hadn't occurred to him before.

"I know so. A whole episode."

He looked hard at me. "It's you, isn't it? You're the one writing the episodes. You're Captain Jake Trailblazer."

"Nope," I said, "but I know who is." *And her initials are C.J.T.,* I thought. "My shit, you may get a whole series."

The canyon opened out, and we were on another overlook, as big as a field this time, and lower down. Off to one side, there was a way down, a slope leading back along the canyon to its floor. Beyond the canyon you could see the plains, pink and lavender. I could see the bluff that backed the anticline off to the east, too far off the scans to notice anything.

"Rest stop," Bult said, and got off his pony. He sat down under a silvershim and opened out the pop-up.

"Do you hear that?" Carson said, looking up in the sky.

"It's C.J.," I said. "I told her to come get Ev so he can work on his theory. He's gotta run some tests."

"Is she doing aerials?" he said, looking anxiously back in the direction of the bluff.

"I told her to go south and come in over the Ponypiles, that we needed an aerial of them," I said.

"What about on the way back?"

"Are you kidding? She's going to have Ev with her. She won't be running any aerials with him in the heli. My shit, she probably forgot to do the aerials on the way down, she was so excited."

Carson looked at me questioningly. The heli swooped in and hovered above the field. C.J. jumped down from the bay, ran across to Ev, and practically knocked him down, kissing him.

"What's all that about?" Carson said, watching them.

"Courtship ritual," I said. "I told her Ev named the falls after her. I told her he named it Crystal Falls." I looked at Carson. "It was the only way he was ever going to get a jump. On this planet, anyway."

They were still in a clinch.

"When she finds out what we really named it," Carson said, grinning, "she's gonna be really mad. When are you gonna tell her?"

"I'm not," I said. "That's the name I sent."

He quit grinning. "What on hell did you do that for?"

"The other day Ev almost got a name past me. Crisscross Creek. You were worrying about what Bult was up to, and I was busy trying to load everything on the ponies, and when he asked me what we were going to name that little stream we crossed, I wasn't paying any attention. It wouldn't have gotten past Big Brother, but it got past me. Because I was busy worrying about something else."

Ev and C.J. had come out of their clinch and were looking at the waterfall. C.J. was making squealing noises that practically drowned out the falls.

"Crystal Falls won't get past Big Brother either," Carson said. "And *Tssarrrah* Falls would have."

"I know," I said, "but maybe they'll be so busy yelling at us over naming it that and killing the *tssi mitss* that they'll forget about the oil field."

He stared at Ev. C.J. was kissing him again. "What about Evie?"

"He won't tell," I said.

"What about Bult? How do we know he won't lead us out of these mountains and straight into another anticline? Or a diamond deposit?"

"That's not a problem either. All you've got to do is tell him."

He turned and looked at me. "Tell him what?"

"Can't you tell when somebody's got a crush on you? Making

you fires, watching your scenes on the pop-ups over and over, giving you presents—"

"What presents?"

"All those dice. The binocs."

"They were *our* binocs."

"Yeah, well, the indidges seem to have a little trouble with that word. He gave you half a shuttlewren, too. And an oil field."

"*That's* why he said he'd help me with the waterfall." He stopped. "I thought Ev said he was a male."

"He is," I said, grinning. "And apparently he's got as much trouble telling what sex we are as we did with him."

"He thinks I'm a *female*?"

"It's an easy enough mistake," I said, grinning. I started to walk away.

He grabbed my arm and swung me around to face him. "You're sure you want to do this? We could get fired."

"No, we won't. We're Findriddy and Carson. We're too famous to get fired." I smiled at him. "Besides, they can't. After this expedition, we're going to owe them our wages for the next twenty."

We went over to C.J. and Ev, who were glued together again. "Ev, you and your pony go back with C.J. to King's X," I said. "You've gotta get that theory on the Wall written up."

"Evelyn told me about his theory," C.J. said. I wondered when he'd had the time. "And how he saved you from the *tssi mitss*."

"We're gonna go ahead and finish out the expedition," Carson said, dragging Ev's pony over. "I thought we'd survey the Ponypiles as long as we're here."

We heaved the pony into the bay, and told C.J. to swing west over the Ponypiles and then north on the way home and try to get an aerial.

She wasn't paying any attention. "Take all the time you need surveying," she said, climbing on. "And don't worry about us. We'll be fine." She went forward.

Carson handed Ev his pack. "If you could take holos of the Wall at different places, I'd appreciate it," Ev said. "And samples of the plaster."

Carson nodded. "Anything else we can do?"

Ev looked up at the heli. "You've already done quite a bit." He shook his head, grinning. "Crystal Falls," he said, looking at me. "I still think we should've named it Heart's Desire."

He climbed up into the bay, and C.J. took off, dipping so close to the ground we both ducked.

"Maybe we did too much," Carson said. "I hope C.J. isn't so grateful she kills him."

"I wouldn't worry about it," I said. The heli circled the canyon like a shuttlewren and swooped down in front of the falls for a last look. They flew off, straight north across the plains, which meant we weren't going to get any aerials.

"We're just postponing the inevitable, you know," he said, looking after the heli. "Sooner or later Big Brother's going to figure out we've been having way too many dust storms, or Wulfmeier'll stumble onto that vein of silver in 246-73. If Bult doesn't figure out what he could get for this place and tell them first."

"I've been thinking about that," I said. "Maybe it wouldn't be as bad as we think. They didn't build the Wall, did you know that? They just moved in afterward, clunked the natives on the head, and took over. Bult'd probably own Starting Gate and half of Earth inside a year."

"And build a dam over the falls," he said.

"Not if it was a national park," I said. "You heard what Ev said about how he'd wanted to see the silvershims and the Wall, especially when they find out who built it. I figure people would come a long way to see something like this." I gestured at the falls. "Bult could charge admission."

"And fine them for leaving footprints," he said. "Speaking of which, what's to stop Bult from getting a crush on you once I tell him I'm not a female?"

"He thinks I'm a male. You said yourself, half the time you can't tell what sex I am."

"And you're never going to let me forget it, are you?"

"Nope," I said.

I went over to where Bult was sitting, watching the pop-up of Carson holding Skimpy Skirt's hand. "Come with me," Carson said.

"Come on, Bult," I said. "Let's get going."

Bult shut the pop-up and handed it to Carson.

"Congratulations," I said. "You're engaged."

Bult got out his log. "Disturbance of land surface," he said to me. "One-fifty."

I climbed up on Useless. "Let's go."

Carson was looking at the falls again. "I still think we should've named it Tssarrrah Falls," he said. He went over to his pony and started rummaging in his pack.

"What on hell are you doing now?" I said. "Let's go!"

"Inappropriate tone and manner," Bult said into his log.

"I wasn't talking to you," I said. "What are you looking for?" I said to Carson.

"The binocs," Carson said. "Have you got 'em?"

"I gave 'em to you," I said. "Now, come on."

He got on his pony and we started off down the slope after Bult. Out beyond the cliff, the plain was turning purple in the late afternoon. The Wall curved down out of the Ponypiles and meandered across it, and beyond it you could see the mesas and rivers and cinder cones of uncharted territory, spread out before me like a present, like a bowerbird's treasures.

"You did not give the binocs back to me," Carson said. "If you lost 'em again—"

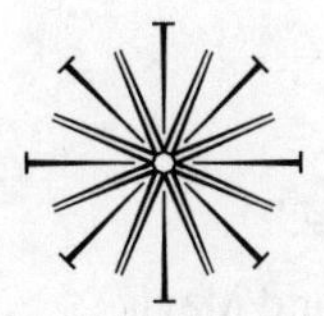

REMAKE

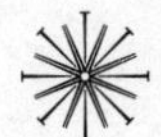

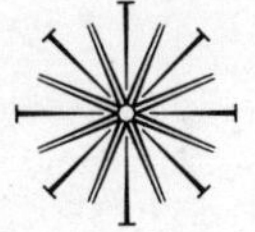

"Not much is impossible."

—Steve Williams, Industrial Light and Magic

"The girl seems to have talent,
but the boy can do nothing."

—Vaudeville booking report on Fred Astaire

HOUSE LIGHTS DOWN

Before Titles

I SAW HER AGAIN TONIGHT. I WASN'T LOOKING FOR HER. IT WAS an early Spielberg liveaction, *Indiana Jones and the Temple of Doom,* a cross between a shoot-'em-up and a VR ride and the last place you'd expect tap shoes, and it was too late. The musical had kicked off, as Michael Caine so eloquently put it, in 1965.

This liveaction was made in '84, at the very beginning of the computer graphics revolution, and it had a few CG sections: digitized Thugees being thrown off a cliff and a pathetically clunky morph of a heart being torn out. It also had a Ford Tri-Motor plane, which was what I was looking for when I found her.

I needed the Tri-Motor for the big good-bye scene at the airport, so I'd accessed Heada, who knows everything, and she'd said she thought there was one in one of the liveaction Spielbergs, the second Indy maybe. "It's close to the end."

"How close?"

"Fifty frames. Or maybe it's in the third one. No, that's a dirigible. The second one. How's the remake coming, Tom?"

Almost done, I thought. *Three years off the AS's and still sober.*

"The remake's stuck on the big farewell scene," I said, "which is why I need the plane. So what do you know, Heada? What's the latest gossip? Who's ILMGM being taken over by this month?"

"Fox-Mitsubishi," she said promptly. "Mayer's frantic. And the word is, Universal's head exec is on the way out. Too many addictive substances."

"How about you?" I said. "Are you still off the AS's? Still assistant producer?"

"Still playing Melanie Griffith in *Working Girl,*" she said. "Does the plane have to be color?"

"No. I've got a colorization program. Why?"

"I think there's one in *Casablanca.*"

"No, there's not," I said. "That's a two-engine Lockheed."

She said, "Tom, I talked to a set director last week who was on his way to China to do stock shots."

I knew where this was leading. I said, "I'll check the Spielberg. Thanks," and signed off before she could say anything else.

The Ford Tri-Motor wasn't at the end, or in the middle, which had one of the worst mattes I'd ever seen. I worked my way back through it at 48 per, thinking it would have been easier to do a scratch construct, and finally found the plane almost at the beginning. It was pretty good—there were close-ups of the door and the cockpit, and a nice medium shot of it taking off. I went back a few frames, trying to see if there was a close-up of the propellers, and then said, "Frame 1-001," in case there was something at the very beginning.

Trademark Spielberg morph of the old Paramount Studios mountain into opening shot, this time of a man-sized silver gong. Cue music. Red smoke. Credits. And there she was, in a chorus line, wearing silver tap shoes and a silver-sequined leotard with tuxedo lapels. Her face was made up thirties style—red lips, Harlow eyebrows—and her hair was platinum blond.

It caught me off guard. I'd already searched the eighties, looking in everything from *Chorus Line* to *Footloose,* and not found any sign of her.

I said, "Freeze!" and then, "Enhance right half," and leaned forward to look at the enlarged image to make sure, as if I hadn't already been sure the instant I saw her.

"Full screen," I said, "forward realtime," and watched the rest of the number. It wasn't much—four lines of blondes in sequined top hats and ribboned tap shoes doing a simple chorus routine that could have been lifted from *42nd Street*, and was about as good. There must not have been any dancing teachers around in the eighties either.

The steps were simple, mostly trenches and traveling steps, and I thought it had probably been one of the very first ones Alis did. She had been this good when I saw her practicing in the film hist classroom. And it was too Berkeley-esque. Near the end of the number, it went to angles and a pan shot of red scarves being pulled out of tuxedo pockets, and Alis disappeared. The Digimatte couldn't have matched that many switching shots, and I doubted if Alis had even tried. She had never had any patience with Busby Berkeley.

"It isn't dancing," she'd said, watching the kaleidoscope scene in *Dames* that first night in my room.

"I thought he was famous for his choreography," I'd said.

"He is, but he shouldn't be. It's all camera angles and stage sets. Fred Astaire always insisted his dances be shot full-length and in one continuous take."

"Frame ten," I said so I wouldn't have to put up with the mountain morph again, and started through the routine again. "Freeze."

The screen froze her in midkick, her foot in the silver tap shoe extended the way Madame Dilyovska of Meadowville had taught her, her arms outstretched. She was supposed to be smiling, but she wasn't. She had a look of intentness, of careful concentration under the scarlet lipstick, the penciled brows, the look she had worn that first night, watching Ginger Rogers and Fred Astaire on the freescreen.

"Freeze," I said again, even though the image hadn't moved, and sat there for a long time, thinking about Fred Astaire and looking at her face, that face I had seen under endless wigs, in endless makeups, that face I would have known anywhere.

TITLE UP

Opening Credits and Dissolve to Pan Shot of Party Scene

MOVIE CLICHE #14: The Party.
Disjointed snatches of bizarre conversation, excessive AS consumption, assorted outrageous behavior.

SEE: ***Notorious; Greed; The Graduate; Risky Business; Breakfast at Tiffany's; Dance, Fools, Dance; The Party.***

SHE WAS BORN THE YEAR FRED ASTAIRE DIED. HEDDA TOLD ME that the first time I met Alis. It was at one of the dorm parties the studios sponsor. There's one every week, ostensibly to show off their latest CG innovations and try to tempt hackate film-school seniors into a life of digitizing and indentured servitude, really so their execs can score some chooch (of which there is never enough) and some popsy (of which there is plenty, all of it in white halter dresses and platinum hair). Hollywood at its finest, which is why I stay away, but this one was being sponsored by ILMGM, and Mayer had promised me he'd be there.

I'd been doing a paste-up for him, digitizing his studio exec boss's popsy into a River Phoenix movie. I wanted to give Mayer the opdisk and get paid before the boss found a new face. I'd already done the paste-up twice and fed in the feedback bypasses three times because he'd switched girlfriends, and this last time the new face had insisted on a scene *with* River Phoenix, which meant I'd had to watch every River Phoenix movie ever made, of which there are a lot—he was one of the first actors copyrighted. I wanted to get the money before Mayer's boss changed partners again. The money and some AS's.

The party was crammed into the dorm lounge, like always—freshies and faces and hackates and hangers-on. The usual suspects. There was a big fibe-op freescreen in the middle of the room. I glanced up at it, hoping to God it wasn't the new River Phoenix movie, and was surprised to see Fred Astaire and Ginger Rogers, dancing up a flight of stairs. Fred was wearing tails, and Ginger was in a white dress that flared into black at the hem. I couldn't hear the music over the party din, but it looked like the Continental.

I couldn't see Mayer. There was a guy in an ILMGM baseball cap and a beard—the hackates' uniform—standing under the freescreen with a remote, holding forth to a couple of CG majors. I scanned the crowd, looking for suits and/or somebody I knew who'd give me some chooch.

"Hi," one of the faces said breathily. She had platinum hair, a white halter dress, and a beauty mark, and she was very splatted. Her eyes weren't focusing at all.

"Hi," I said, still scanning the crowd. "And who are you supposed to be? Jean Harlow?"

"Who?" she said, and I wanted to believe that that was because of whatever AS she was doing, but it probably wasn't. Ah, Hollywood, where everybody wants to be in the movies and nobody's ever bothered to watch one.

"Jeanne Eagels?" I said. "Carole Lombard? Kim Basinger?"

"No," she said, trying to focus. "Marilyn Monroe. Are you a studio exec?"

"Depends. Do you have any chooch?"

"No," she said sadly. "All gone."

"Then I'm not a studio exec," I said. I could see an exec, though, over by the stairs, talking to another Marilyn. The Marilyn was wearing a white halter dress just like the one I was talking to had on.

I've never understood why the faces, who have nothing to sell but an original personality, an original face, all try to look like somebody else. But I guess it makes sense. Why should they be different from everybody else in Hollywood, which has always been in love with sequels and imitations and remakes?

"Are you in the movies?" my Marilyn persisted.

"Nobody's in the movies," I said, and started toward the studio exec through the crush.

It was harder work than hauling the *African Queen* through the reeds. I edged my way between a group of faces talking about a rumor that Columbia Tri-Star was hiring warmbodies, and then a couple of geekates in data helmets who were at some other party altogether, and over to the stairs.

I couldn't tell it wasn't Mayer till I got close enough to hear the exec's voice—studio execs are as bad as Marilyns. They all look alike. And have the same line.

". . . looking for a face for my new project," he was saying. The new project was a remake of *Back to the Future* starring, natch, River Phoenix. "It's a perfect time to rerelease," he said, leaning down the Marilyn's halter top. "They say we're *this* close"—he held his thumb and forefinger together, almost touching—"to getting the real thing."

"The real thing?" the Marilyn said in a fair imitation of Marilyn Monroe's breathy voice. She looked more like her than mine had, though she was a little thick in the waist. But the faces don't worry about that as much as they used to. A few extra pounds can be didged out. Or in. "You mean time travel?"

"I mean time travel. Only it won't be in a DeLorean. It'll be in a time machine that looks like the skids. We've already come up with the graphics. The only thing we don't have is an actress to play opposite River. The director wanted to go with Michelle Pfeiffer or Lana Turner, but I told him I think we should go with an unknown. Somebody with a new face, somebody special. You interested in being in the movies?"

I'd heard this line before. In *Stage Door*. 1937.

I waded back into the party and over to the freescreen, where the baseball-cap-and-beard was holding forth to some freshies. ". . . programmed for any shots you want. Dolly shots, split screens, pans. Say you want a close-up of this guy." He pointed up at the screen with the remote.

"Fred Astaire," I said. "That guy is Fred Astaire."

"You punch in 'close-up'—"

Fred Astaire's face filled the screen, smiling.

"This is ILMGM's new edit program," the baseball cap said to me. "It picks angles, combines shots, makes cuts. All you need is a full-length base shot to work from, like this one." He hit a button on the remote, and a full-length shot of Fred and Ginger replaced Fred's face. "Full-length shots are hard to come by. I had to go all the way back to the b-and-w's to find anything long enough, but we're working on that."

He hit another button, and we were treated to a view of Fred's mouth, and then his hand. "You can do any edit program you want," Baseball Cap said, watching the screen. Fred's mouth again, the white carnation in his lapel, his hand. "This one takes the base shot and edits it using the shot sequence of the opening scene from *Citizen Kane*."

A medium shot of Ginger, and then of the carnation. I wondered which one was supposed to be Rosebud.

"It's all preprogrammed," Baseball Cap said. "You don't have to do a thing. It does everything."

"Does it know where Mayer is?" I asked.

"He *was* here," he said, looking vaguely around and then back at the screen, where Fred was going through his paces. "It can extrapolate long shots, aerials, two-shots."

"Have it extrapolate somebody who knows where Mayer is," I said, and went back over the side and into the water. The party was getting steadily more crowded. The only ones with any room at all to move were Fred and Ginger, swirling up and down the staircase.

The exec I'd seen before was in the middle of the room, pitching to the same Marilyn, or a different one. Maybe he knew where Mayer was. I started toward him and then spotted Hedda in a pink strapless sheath and diamond bracelets. *Gentlemen Prefer Blondes.*

Hedda knows everything, all the news, all the gossip. If anybody knew where Mayer was, it'd be Hedda. I waded my way over to her, past the exec, who was explaining time travel to the Marilyn. "It's the same principle as the skids," he said. "The Casimir effect. The randomized electrons in the walls create a negative-matter region that produces an overlap interval."

He must have been a hackate before he morphed into an exec.

"The Casimir effect lets you overlap space to get from one skids station to another, and the same thing's theoretically possible for getting from one parallel timefeed to another. I've got an opdisk that explains it all," he said, running his hand down her haltered neck. "How about if we go up to your room and take a look at it?"

I squeezed past him, hoping I wouldn't come up covered with leeches, and hauled myself out next to Hedda. "Mayer here?" I asked.

"Nope," she said, her platinum head bent over an assortment of cubes and capsules in her pink-gloved hand. "He was here for a few minutes, but he left with one of the freshies. And when the party started, there was a guy from Disney nosing around. The word is, Disney's scouting a takeover of ILMGM."

Another reason to get paid now. "Did Mayer say if he was coming back?"

She shook her head, still deep in her study of the pharmacy.

"Any chooch in there?" I said.

"I think these are," she said, handing me two purple-and-white capsules. "A face gave me this stuff, and he told me which was which, but I can't remember. I'm pretty sure those are the chooch. I took some. I can let you know in a minute."

"Great," I said, wishing I could take them now. Mayer's leaving with a freshie might mean he was pimping again, which meant another paste-up. "What's the word on Mayer's boss? His new girlfriend dump him yet?"

She looked instantly interested. "Not that I know of. Why? Did you hear something?"

"No." And if Hedda hadn't either, it hadn't happened. So Mayer'd just taken the freshie up to her dorm room for a quick pop or a quicker line or two of flake, and he'd be back in a few minutes, and I might actually get paid.

I grabbed a paper cup from a Marilyn swaying past and downed the capsules.

"So, Hedda," I said, since talking to her was better than to the baseball cap or the time-travel exec, "what other gossip you putting in your column this week?"

"Column?" she said, looking blank. "You always call me Hedda. Why? Is she a movie star?"

"Gossip columnist," I said. "Knew everything that was going on in Hollywood. Like you. So what is? Going on?"

"Viamount's got a new automatic foley program," she said promptly. "ILMGM's getting ready to file copyrights on Fred

Astaire *and* Sean Connery, who finally died. And the word is, Pinewood's hiring warmbodies for the new *Batman* sequel. And Warner's—" She stopped in midword and frowned down at her hand.

"What's the matter?"

"I don't think it's chooch. I'm getting a funny . . ." She peered at her hand. "Maybe the yellow ones were the chooch." She fished through her hand. "This feels more like ice."

"Who gave them to you?" I said. "The Disney guy?"

"No. This guy I know. A face."

"What does he look like?" I asked. Stupid question. There are only two varieties: James Dean and River Phoenix. "Is he here?"

She shook her head. "He gave them to me because he was leaving. He said he wouldn't need them anymore, and besides, he'd get arrested in China for having them."

"China?"

"He said they've got a liveaction studio there, and they're hiring stunt doubles and warmbodies for their propaganda films."

And I'd thought doing paste-ups for Mayer was the worst job in the world.

"Maybe it's redline," she said, poking at the capsules. "I hope not. Redline always makes me look like shit the next day."

"Instead of like Marilyn Monroe," I said, looking around the room for Mayer. He still wasn't back. The time-travel exec was edging toward the door with a Marilyn. The data-helmet geekates were laughing and snatching at air, obviously at a much better party than this one. Fred and Ginge were demonstrating another editing program. Rapid-fire cuts of Ginger, the ballroom curtains, Ginger's mouth, the curtains. It must be the shower scene from *Psycho*.

The program ended and Fred reached for Ginger's outstretched hand, her black-edged skirt flaring with momentum, and spun her into his arms. The edges of the freescreen started going to soft-focus. I looked over at the stairs. They were blurring, too.

"Shit, this isn't redline," I said. "It's klieg."

"It is?" she said, sniffing at it.

It is, I thought disgustedly, and what was I supposed to do now? Flashing on klieg wasn't any way to do a meeting with a sleaze like Mayer, and the damned stuff isn't good for anything else. No rush, no halluces, not even a buzz. Just blurred vision and then a flash of indelible reality. "Shit," I said again.

"If it is klieg," Hedda said, stirring it around with her gloved finger, "we can at least have some great sex."

"I don't need klieg for that," I said, but I started looking around the room for somebody to pop. Hedda was right. Flashing during sex made for an unforgettable orgasm. Literally. I scanned the Marilyns. I could do the exec's casting couch number on one of the freshies, but there was no way to tell how long that would take, and it felt like I only had a few minutes. The Marilyn I'd talked to before was over by the freescreen listening to the studio exec's time-travel spiel.

I looked over at the door. A girl was standing in the doorway, gazing tentatively around at the party as if she were looking for somebody. She had curly light brown hair, pulled back at the sides. The doorway behind her was dark, but there had to be light coming from somewhere because her hair shone like it was backlit.

"Of all the gin joints in all the world . . ." I said.

"Joint?" Hedda said, deep in her pill assortment. "I thought you said it was klieg." She sniffed it.

The girl had to be a face, she was too pretty not to be, but the hair was wrong, and so was the costume, which wasn't a halter dress and wasn't white. It was black, with a green fitted weskit, and she was wearing short green gloves. Deanna Durbin? No, the hair was the wrong color. And it was tied back with a green hair ribbon. Shirley Temple?

"Who's that?" I muttered.

"Who?" Hedda licked her gloved finger and rubbed it in the powder the pills had left on her glove.

"The face over there," I said, pointing. She had moved out of the doorway, over against the wall, but her hair was still catching the light, making a halo of her light brown hair.

Hedda sucked the powder off her glove. "Alice," she said.

Alice who? Alice Faye? No, Alice Faye'd been a platinum blonde, like everybody else in Hollywood. And she wasn't given to hair ribbons. Charlotte Henry in *Alice in Wonderland*?

Whoever the girl had been looking for—the White Rabbit, probably—she'd given up on finding him and was watching the freescreen. On it, Fred and Ginger were dancing around each other without touching, their eyes locked.

"Alice who?" I said.

Hedda was frowning at her finger. "Huh?"

"Who's she supposed to be?" I said. "Alice Faye? Alice Adams? *Alice Doesn't Live Here Anymore*?"

The girl had moved away from the wall, her eyes still on the screen, and was heading toward the baseball cap. He leaped forward, thrilled to have a new audience, and started into his spiel, but she wasn't listening to him. She was watching Fred and Ginge, her head tilted up toward the screen, her hair catching the light from the fibe-op feed.

"I don't think any of this stuff is what that face told me," Hedda said, licking her finger again. "It's her name."

"What?"

"Alice," she said. "A-l-i-s. It's her name. She's a freshie. Film hist major. From Illinois."

Well, that explained the hair ribbon, though not the rest of the getup. It wasn't Alice Adams. The gloves were 1950s, not '30s, and her face wasn't angular enough to be trying for Katharine Hepburn. "Who's she supposed to be?"

"I wonder which one of these is ice," Hedda said, poking around in her hand again. "It's supposed to make the flash go away faster. She wants to dance in the movies."

"I think you've had enough pill potluck," I said, reaching for her hand.

She squeezed it shut, protecting the pills. "No, really. She's a dancer."

I looked at her, wondering how many unmarked pills she'd taken before I got here.

"She was born the year Fred Astaire died," she said, gesturing with her closed fist. "She saw him on the fibe-op feed and decided to come to Hollywood to dance in the movies."

"*What* movies?" I said.

She shrugged, focusing on her hand again.

I looked over at the girl. She was still watching the screen, her face intent. "Ruby Keeler," I said.

"Huh?" Hedda said.

"The plucky little dancer in *42nd Street* who wants to be a star." Only she was about twenty years too late. But just in time for a little popsy, and if she was wide-eyed enough to believe she could make it in the movies, it ought to be a piece of cake getting her up to my room.

I shouldn't have to explain time travel to her, like the exec. He was talking earnestly to a Marilyn wearing black fringe and holding a ukelele. *Some Like It Hot.*

"See, you're turning me down in this timefeed," he was saying, "but in a parallel timefeed we're already popping." He leaned closer. "There are hundreds of thousands of parallel timefeeds. Who *knows* what we're doing in some of them?"

"What if I'm turning you down in all of them?" the Marilyn said.

I squeezed past her fringe, thinking she might work out if Ruby didn't, and started through the crowd toward the screen.

"Don't!" Hedda said loudly.

At least half the room turned to look at her.

"Don't what?" I said, coming back to her. She was looking past me at Alis, and her face had the bleak, slightly dazed look klieg produces.

"You just flashed, didn't you?" I said. "I told you it was klieg. And that means I'll be doing the same thing shortly, so if you'll excuse me—"

She took hold of my arm. "I don't think you should—" she said, still looking at Alis. "She won't . . ." She was looking worriedly at me. Mildred Natwick in *She Wore a Yellow Ribbon,* telling John Wayne to be careful.

"Won't what? Give me a pop? You wanna bet?"

"No," she said, shaking her head like she was trying to clear it. "You . . . she knows what she wants."

"So do I. And thanks to your Russian-roulette approach to pharmaceuticals, it promises to be an unforgettable experience. If I can get Ruby up to my room in the next ten minutes. Now, if there are no further objections . . ." I said, and started past her.

She started to put out her hand, like she was going to grab my sleeve, and then let it drop.

The exec was talking about negative-matter regions. I went around him and over to the screen, where Alis was looking up at Fred's face, the staircase, Ginger's black-edged skirt, Fred's hand.

She was as pretty in close-up as she had been in the establishing shot. Her caught-back hair was picking up the flickering light from the screen and her face had an intent, focused look.

"They shouldn't do that," she said.

"What? Show a movie?" I said. "'You have to show a movie at a party. It's a Hollywood law.'"

She turned and smiled delightedly at me. "I know that line.

It's from *Singin' in the Rain*," she said, pleased. "I didn't mean the movie. It's them editing it like that." She looked back up at the screen. Or down. It was doing an aerial now, and all you could see were the tops of Fred and Ginger's heads.

"I take it you don't like Vincent's edit program?" I said.

"Vincent?"

I nodded toward the baseball cap, who was off in a corner doing a line of illy. "Doesn't he remind you of Vincent Price in *House of Wax*?"

The edit program was back to quick cuts—the steps, Fred's face, close-up of a step. The baby carriage scene from *Potemkin*.

"In more ways than one," I said.

"Fred Astaire always insisted they shoot his dances in a full-length shot and in one continuous take," she said without taking her eyes off the screen. "He said it's the only way to film dancing."

"He did, huh? No wonder I like the original better." I looked at her. "I've got it up in my room."

And that made her turn away from Ginger's flashingly cut feet, shoulder, hair, and look at me. It was the same intent, focused look she had had watching the screen, and I felt the edges start to blur.

"No cuts, no camera angles," I said rapidly. "Nothing preprogrammed. Full-length and in one continuous take. Want to come up and take a look?"

She looked back at the freescreen. Fred's chest, his face, his knees. "Yes," she said. "You've got the real movie? Not colorized or anything?"

"The real thing," I said, and led her up the stairs.

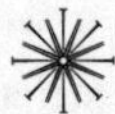

RUBY KEELER: ***[Nervously]*** **I've never been in a man's apartment before.**

ADOLPHE MENJOU: ***[Pouring champagne]*** **You've never been in Hollywood before.** ***[Handing her glass]*** **Here, my dear, this will relax you.**

RUBY KEELER: ***[Hovering near door]*** **You said you had a screen test application up here. Shouldn't I fill it out?**

ADOLPHE MENJOU: ***[Turning down lights]*** **Later, my dear, after we've had a chance to get to know each other.**

"I'VE GOT ANYTHING YOU COULD WANT," I TOLD ALIS ON the way up. "All the ILMGMs and the Warner and Fox-Mitsubishi libraries, at least everything that's been digitized, which should be everything you'd want." I led her down the hall. "The Fred Astaire–Ginger Rogers movies were Warner, weren't they?"

"RKO," she said.

"Same thing." I keyed the door. "Here we are," I said, and opened it into my room.

She took a trusting step inside and then stopped at the sight of the arrays covering three walls with their mirrored screens. "I thought you said you were a student," she said.

Now was not the time to tell her I hadn't been to class in over a semester. "I am," I said, leaning past her so she'd step forward into the room and picking up a shirt. "Clothes all over the floor, bed's not made." I lobbed the shirt into the corner. "*Andy Hardy Goes to College.*"

She was looking at the digitizer and the fibe-op-feed hookup. "I thought only the studios had Crays."

"I do work for them to help pay for tuition," I said. And keep me in chooch.

"What kind of work?" she said, looking up at her own face's reflection in the silvered screens, and now was not the time to tell her I specialized in procuring popsy for studio execs either.

"Remakes," I said. I smoothed out the blankets. "Sit down."

She perched on the edge of the bed, knees together.

"Okay," I said, sitting down at the comp. I asked for the Warner library menu. "The Continental's in *Top Hat,* isn't it?"

"*The Gay Divorcée,*" she said. "Near the end."

"Main screen, end frame, and back at 96," I said. Fred and Ginge leaped onto the screen and up over a table. "Rew at 96 frames per sec," and they jumped down off the table and back through breakfast to the ballroom.

I rew'd to the beginning of the number and let it go. "Do you want sound?" I said.

She shook her head, her face already intent on the screen, and maybe this hadn't been such a great idea. She leaned forward, and the same concentrated look she'd had downstairs came into her face, as if she were trying to memorize the steps. I might as well not have been in the room, which hadn't exactly been the idea in bringing her up here.

"Menu," I said. "Fred Astaire and Ginger Rogers movies." The menu came up. "Aux screen one, *Swing Time,*" I said. There was usually a big dance finale in these things, wasn't there? "End frame and back at 96."

There was. On the top left-hand screen, Fred in tails spun Ginge in a silver dress. "Frame 102-044," I said, reading the code at the bottom. "Forward realtime to end and repeat. Continuous loop. Screen two, *Follow the Fleet,* screen three, *Top Hat,* screen four, *Carefree*. End frame and back at 96."

I started continuous loops on them and went through the rest of the Fred and Ginger list, filling most of the left-hand array with their dancing: turning, tapping, twirling, Fred in tails, sailor's uniform, riding tweeds, Ginger in long, slinky dresses that flared out below the knee in a froth of feathers and fur and glitter. Waltzing, tapping, gliding through the Carioca, the Yam, the Piccolino. And all of them full-length. All of them without cuts.

Alis was staring at the screens. The careful, intent look was gone, and she was smiling delightedly.

"Anything else?"

"*Shall We Dance,*" she said. "The title number. Frame 87-1309."

I set it running on the bottom row. Fred in meticulous tails, dancing with a chorus of blondes in black satin and veils. They all held up masks of Ginger Rogers's face, and they put them up in front of their faces and flirted away from Fred, their masks as stiff as faces.

"Any other movies?" I said, calling up the menu again. "Plenty of screens left. How about *An American in Paris*?"

"I don't like Gene Kelly," she said.

"Okay," I said, surprised. "How about *Meet Me in St. Louis*?"

"There isn't any dancing in it except the 'Under the Bamboo Tree' number with Margaret O'Brien. It's because of Judy Garland. She was a terrible dancer."

"Okay," I said, even more surprised. "*Singin' in the Rain*? No, wait, you don't like Gene Kelly."

"The 'Good Morning' number's okay."

I found it, Gene Kelly with Debbie Reynolds and Donald

O'Connor, tapping up steps and over furniture in wild exuberance. Okay.

I scanned the menu for movies that didn't have Gene Kelly or Judy Garland in them. "*Good News*?"

" 'The Varsity Drag,' " she said, nodding. "It's right at the end. Do you have *Seven Brides for Seven Brothers*?"

"Sure. Which number?"

"The barnraising," she said. "Frame 27-986."

I called it up. I looked for something with Ruby Keeler in it. "*42nd Street*?"

She shook her head. "It's a Busby Berkeley. There's no dancing in it except for one background shot of a rehearsal and about sixteen bars in the 'Pettin' in the Park' number. There's never any dancing in Busby Berkeleys. Do you have *On the Town*?"

"I thought you didn't like Gene Kelly."

"Ann Miller," she said. "The 'Prehistoric Man' number. Frame 28-650. She's technically pretty good when she sticks to tap."

I don't know why I was so surprised or what I'd expected. Starstruck adoration, I guess. Ruby Keeler gushing, "Gosh, Mr. Ziegfeld, a part in your show! That'd be wonderful!" Or maybe Judy Garland, gazing longingly at the photo of Clark Gable in *Broadway Melody of 1938*. But she didn't like Judy, and she'd dismissed Gene Kelly as airily as if he was an auditioning chorus girl in a Busby Berkeley. Who she didn't like either.

I filled out the array with Fred Astaire, who she *did* like, though none of his color movies were as good as the b-and-w's, and neither were his partners. Most of them just hung on while he swung them around, or struck a pose and let him dance circles, literally, around them.

Alis wasn't watching them. She'd gone back to the center screen and was watching Fred, full-length, swirling Ginger weightlessly across the floor.

"So that's what you want to do," I said, pointing. "Dance the Continental?"

She shook her head. "I'm not good enough yet. I only know a few routines. I could do that," she said, pointing at the Varsity Drag, and then at the cowboy number from *Girl Crazy*. "And maybe that. Chorus, not lead."

And that wasn't what I expected either. The one thing the faces have in common under their Marilyn beauty marks is the unshakable belief they've got what it takes to be a star. Most of them don't—they can't act or show emotion, can't even do a reasonable imitation of Norma Jean's breathy voice and sexy vulnerability—but they all think the only thing standing between them and stardom is bad luck, not talent. I'd never heard any of them say, "I'm not good enough."

"I'm going to need to find a dancing teacher," Alis was saying. "You don't know of one, do you?"

In Hollywood? She was as likely to find one as she was to run into Fred Astaire. Less likely.

And what if she *was* smart enough to know how good she was? What if she'd studied the movies and criticized them? None of it was going to bring back musicals. None of it was going to make ILMGM start shooting liveactions again.

I looked up at the arrays. On the bottom row, Fred was trying to find the real Ginger in among the masks. On the third screen, top row, he was trying to talk her into a pop—she twirled away from him, he advanced, she returned, he bent toward her, she leaned languorously away.

All of which I'd better get on with or I was going to flash with Alis still sitting there on the edge of the bed, clothes on and knees together.

I asked for sound on screen three and sat down next to Alis on the bed. "I think you're good enough," I said.

She glanced at me, confused, and then realized I was picking up on her "I'm not good enough" line. "You haven't seen me dance," she said.

"I wasn't talking about dancing," I said, and bent forward to kiss her.

The center screen flashed white. "Message," it said. "From Heada Hopper." She'd spelled Hedda with an "a." I wondered if Hedda'd had another revelatory flash and was interrupting to tell it to me.

"Message override," I said, and stood up to clear the screen, but it was too late. The message was already on the screen.

"Mayer's here," it read. "Shall I send him up? Heada."

The last thing I wanted was Mayer up here. I'd have to make a copy of the paste-up and take it down to him. "River Phoenix file," I said to the computer, and shoved in a blank opdisk. "*Where the Boys Are*. Record remake."

The dancing screens went blank, and Alis stood up. "Should I go?" she said.

"No!" I said, rummaging for a remote. The comp spit out the disk, and I snatched it up. "Stay here. I'll be right back. I've just got to give this to a guy."

I handed her the remote. "Here. Hit 'M' for menu, and ask for whatever you want. If the movie you want isn't on ILMGM, you can call up the other libraries by hitting 'file.' I'll be back before the Continental's over. Promise."

I started out the door. I wanted to shut the door to keep her there, but it looked more like I'd be right back if I left it open. "Don't leave," I said, and tore downstairs.

"Heada" was waiting for me at the foot of the stairs. "Sorry," she said. "Were you popping her?"

"Thanks to you, no," I said, scanning the room for Mayer. The room had gotten even more crowded since Alis and I left. So had the screen—a dozen Fred and Gingers were running split-screen circles around each other.

"I wouldn't have interrupted you," Heada said, "but you asked before if Mayer was here."

"It's okay," I said. "Where is he?"

"Over there." She pointed in the direction of the Freds and Gingers. Mayer was under them, listening to Vincent explain his edit program and twitching from too much chooch. "He said he wanted to talk to you about a job."

"Great," I said. "That means his boss has got a new girlfriend, and I've got to paste in a new face."

She shook her head. "Viamount's taking over ILMGM and Arthurton's going to head Project Development, which means Mayer's boss is out, and Mayer's scrambling. He's got to distance himself from his boss *and* convince Arthurton he should keep him instead of bringing in his own team. So this job is probably a bid to impress Arthurton, which could mean a remake, or even a new project. In which case . . ."

I'd stopped listening. Mayer's boss was out, which meant the disk in my hand was worth exactly nothing, and the job he wanted to see me about was pasting Arthurton's girlfriend into something. Or maybe the girlfriends of the whole Viamount board of directors. Either way, I wasn't going to get paid.

". . . in *which* case," Heada was saying, "his coming to you is a good sign."

"Golly," I said, clasping my hands together. "This could be my big break."

"Well, it could," she said defensively. "Even a remake would be better than these pimping jobs you've been doing."

"They're all pimping jobs." I started through the crush toward Mayer.

Heada squeezed through after me. "If it *is* an official project," she said, "tell him you want a credit."

Mayer had moved to the other side of the freescreen, probably trying to get away from Vincent, who was right behind him, still talking. Above them, the crowd on the screen was still revolving, but slower and slower, and the edges of the room were starting to soft-focus. Mayer turned and saw me, and waved, all in slow motion.

I stopped, and Heada crashed into me. "Do you have any slalom?" I said, and she started fumbling in her hand again. "Or ice? Anything to hold off a klieg flash?"

She held out the same assortment of capsules and cubes as before, only not as many. "I don't think so," she said, peering at them.

"Find me something, okay?" I said, and squeezed my eyes shut, hard, and then opened them again. The soft-focus receded.

"I'll see if I can find you some lude," she said. "Remember, if it's the real thing, you want a credit." She slipped off toward a pair of James Deans, and I went up to Mayer.

"Here you go," I said to Mayer, and tried to hand him the disk. I wasn't going to get paid, but it was at least worth a try.

"Tom!" Mayer said. He didn't take the disk.

Heada was right. His boss was out.

"Just the guy I've been looking for," he said. "What have you been up to?"

"Working for you," I said, and tried again to hand him the disk. "It's all done. Just what you ordered. River Phoenix, close-up, kiss. She's even got four lines."

"Great," he said, and pocketed the disk. He pulled out a palmtop and punched in numbers. "You want this in your online account, right?"

"Right," I said, wondering if this was some kind of bizarre preflashing symptom: actually getting what you wanted. I looked around for Heada. She wasn't talking to the James Deans anymore.

"I can always count on you for the tough jobs," Mayer said. "I've got a new project you might be interested in." He put a friendly arm around my shoulder and led me away from Vincent. "Nobody knows this," he said, "but there's a possibility of a merger between ILMGM and Viamount, and if it goes through, my boss and his girlfriends'll be a dead issue."

How does Heada do it? I thought wonderingly.

"It's still just in the talking stages, of course, but we're all very excited about the prospect of working with a great company like Viamount."

Translation: It's a done deal, and "scrambling" isn't even the word. I looked down at Mayer's hands, half expecting to see blood under his fingernails.

"Viamount's as committed as ILMGM is to the making of quality movies, but you know how the American public is about mergers. So our first job, *if* this thing goes through, is to send them the message: 'We care.' Do you know Austin Arthurton?"

Sorry, Heada, I thought, *it's another pimping job.*

"What's the job?" I said. "Didging in Arthurton's girlfriend? Boyfriend? German shepherd?"

"Jesus, no!" he said, and looked around to make sure nobody'd heard that. "Arthurton's totally straight, vegetarian, clean, a real Gary Cooper type. He's completely committed to convincing the public the studio's in responsible hands. Which is where you come in. We'll supply you with a memory upgrade and automatic print-and-send, and I'll have you paid on receipt through the feed." He waved the disk of his old boss's girlfriend at me. "No more having to track me down at parties." He smiled.

"What's the job?"

He didn't answer. He looked around the room, twitching. "I see a lot of new faces," he said, smiling at a Marilyn in yellow feathers. *There's No Business Like Show Business*. "Anything interesting?"

Yes, up in my room, and I want to flash on her, not you, Mayer, so get to the point.

"ILMGM's taken some flak lately. You know the rap: violence, AS's, negative influence. Nothing serious, but Arthurton wants to project a positive image—"

And he's a real Gary Cooper type. I was wrong about its being a pimping job, Heada. It's a slash-and-burn.

"What does he want out?" I said.

He started to twitch again. "It's not a censorship job, just a few adjustments here and there. The average revision won't be more than ten frames. Each one'll take you maybe fifteen minutes, and most of them are simple deletes. The comp can do those automatically."

"And I take out what? Sex? Chooch?"

"AS's. Twenty-five a movie, and you get paid whether you have to change anything or not. It'll keep you in chooch for a year."

"How many movies?"

"Not that many. I don't know exactly."

He reached in his suit pocket and handed me an opdisk like the one I'd given him. "The menu's on here."

"Everything? Cigarettes? Alcohol?"

"All addictive substances," he said, "visuals, audios, and references. But the Anti-Smoking League's already taken the nicotine out, and most of the movies on the list have only got a couple of scenes that need to be reworked. A lot of them are already clean. All you'll have to do is watch them, do a print-and-send, and collect your money."

Right. And then feed in access codes for two hours. A wipe was easy, five minutes tops, and a superimpose ten, even working from a vid. It was the accesses that were murder. Even my River Phoenix–watching marathon was nothing compared to the hours I'd spend reading in accesses, working my way past authorization guards and ID-locks so the fibe-op source wouldn't automatically spit out the changes I'd made.

"No, thanks," I said, and tried to hand him back the disk. "Not without full access."

Mayer looked patient. "You know why the authorization codes are necessary."

Sure. So nobody can change a pixel of all those copyrighted movies, or harm a hair on the head of all those bought-and-paid-for stars. Except the studios.

"Sorry, Mayer. Not interested," I said, and started to walk away.

"Okay, okay," he said, twitching. "Fifty per and full exec access. I can't do anything about the fibe-op-feed ID-locks and the Film Preservation Society registration. But you can have complete freedom on the changes. No preapproval. You can be creative."

"Yeah," I said. "Creative."

"Is it a deal?" he said.

Heada was sidling past the screen, looking up at Fred and Ginger. They were in close-up, gazing into each other's eyes.

At least the job would pay enough for my tuition and my own AS's, instead of having to have Heada mooch for me, instead of taking klieg by mistake and having to worry about flashing on Mayer and carrying an indelible image of him around in my head forever. And they're all pimping jobs, in or out. Or official.

"Why not?" I said, and Heada came up. She took my hand and slipped a lude into it.

"Great," Mayer said. "I'll give you a list. You can do them in any order. A minimum of twelve a week."

I nodded. "I'll get right on it," I said, and started for the stairs, popping the lude as I went.

Heada pursued me to the foot of the stairs. "Did you get the job?"

"Yeah."

"Was it a remake?"

I didn't have time to listen to what she'd say when she found out it was a slash-and-burn. "Yeah," I said, and sprinted back up the stairs.

There really wasn't any hurry. The lude would give me half an hour at least and Alis was already on the bed. If she was still there. If she hadn't gotten her fill of Fred and Ginge and left.

The door was half open the way I'd left it, which was either a good or a bad sign. I looked in. I could see the near bank. The array was blank. *Thanks, Mayer. She's gone, and all I've got to show for it is a Hays Office list. If I'm lucky, I'll get to flash on Walter Brennan taking a swig of rotgut whiskey.*

I started to push the door open, and stopped. She was there after all. I could see her reflection in the silvered screens. She was sitting on the bed, leaning forward, watching something. I pushed the door farther open so I could see what. The door scraped a little against the carpet, but she didn't move. She was watching the center screen. It was the only one on. She must not have been able to figure out the other screens from my hurried instructions, or maybe one screen was all she was used to back in Bedford Falls.

She was watching with that focused look she had had downstairs, but it wasn't the Continental. It wasn't even Ginger dancing side by side with Fred. It was Eleanor Powell. She and Fred were tap-dancing on a dark polished floor. There were lights in the background, meant to look like stars, and the floor reflected them in long, shimmering trails of light.

Fred and Eleanor were in white—him in a suit, no tails, no top hat this time, her in a white dress with a knee-length skirt that swirled out when she swung into the turns. Her light brown hair was the same length as Alis's and was pulled back with a white headband that glittered, catching the light from the reflections.

Fred and Eleanor were dancing side by side, casually, their arms only a little out to the sides for balance, their hands not even close to touching, matching each other step for step.

Alis had the sound off, but I didn't need to hear the taps, or the music, to know what this was. *Broadway Melody of 1940,* the second half of the "Begin the Beguine" number. The first half was a tango, formal jacket and long white dress, the kind of stuff Fred did with all his partners, except that he didn't have to cover for Eleanor Powell or maneuver fancy steps around her. She could dance as well as he did.

And the second half was this—no fancy dress, no fuss, the two of them dancing side by side, full-length shot and one long, unbroken take. He tapped a combination, she echoed it, snapping the steps out in precision time, he did another, she answered, neither of them looking at the other, each of them intent on the music.

Not "intent." Wrong word. There was no concentration in them at all, no effort; they might have made up the whole routine just now as they stepped onto the polished floor, improvising as they went.

I stood there in the door, watching Alis watch them as she sat there on the edge of the bed, looking like sex was the furthest thing from her mind. Heada was right—this had been a bad idea. I should go back down to the party and find some face who wasn't locked at the knees, whose big ambition was to work as a warmbody for Columbia Tri-Star. The lude I'd just taken would hold off any flash long enough for me to talk one of the Marilyns into coming on cue.

And Ruby Keeler'd never miss me—she was oblivious to everything but Fred Astaire and Eleanor Powell doing a series of rapid-fire tap breaks. She probably wouldn't even notice if I brought the Marilyn back up to the bed to pop. Which is what I should do, while I still had time.

But I didn't. I leaned against the door, watching Fred and Eleanor and Alis, watching Alis's reflection in the blank screens of the right-hand array. Fred and Eleanor were reflected in the screens, too, their images superimposed on Alis's intent face on the silver screens.

And "intent" wasn't the right word for her either. She had lost that alert, focused look she'd had watching the Continental, counting the steps, trying to memorize the combinations. She had gone beyond that, watching Fred and Eleanor dance side by side, their hands not touching, and they weren't counting either, they were lost in the effortless steps, in the easy turns, lost in the dancing, and so was Alis. Her face was absolutely still watching them, like a freeze frame, and Fred Astaire and Eleanor Powell were somehow still, too, even as they danced.

They tapped, turning, and Eleanor danced Fred back across the floor, facing him now but still not looking at him, her steps reflections of his, and then they were side by side again, swinging into a tap cadenza, their feet and the swirling skirt and the fake stars reflected in the polished floor, in the screens, in Alis's still face.

Eleanor swung into a turn, not looking at Fred, not having to, the turn perfectly matched to his, and they were side by side again, tapping in counterpoint, their hands almost touching, Eleanor's face as still as Alis's, intent, oblivious. Fred tapped out a ripple, and Eleanor repeated it, and glanced sideways over her shoulder and smiled at him, a smile of awareness and complicity and utter joy.

I flashed.

The klieg usually gives you at least a few seconds warning, enough time to do something to hold it off or at least close your eyes, but not this time. No warning, no telltale soft-focus, nothing.

One minute I was leaning against the door, watching Alis

watch Fred and Eleanor tippity-tapping away, and the next: freeze frame, cut! print, and send, like a flashbulb going off in your face, only the afterimage is as clear as the picture, and it doesn't fade, it doesn't go away.

I put my hand up in front of my eyes, like somebody trying to shield themselves from a nuclear blast, but it was too late. The image was already burned into my neocortex.

I must've staggered back against the door, too, and maybe even cried out, because when I opened my eyes, she was looking at me, alarmed, concerned.

"Is something wrong?" she said, scrambling off the bed and taking my arm. "Are you okay?"

"I'm fine," I said. Fine. She was holding the remote. I took it away from her and clicked the comp off. The screen went silver, blank except for the reflection of the two of us standing there in the door. And superimposed on the reflection another reflection—Alis's face, rapt, absorbed, watching Fred and Eleanor in white, dancing on the starry floor.

"Come on," I said, and grabbed Alis's hand.

"Where are we going?"

Someplace. Anyplace. A theater where some other movie is showing. "Hollywood," I said, pulling her out into the hall. "To dance in the movies."

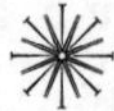

Camera whip-pans to medium shot: LAIT station sign. Diamond screen, "Los Angeles Instransit" in hot pink caps, "Westwood Station" in bright green.

WE TOOK THE SKIDS. MISTAKE. THE BACK SECTION WAS closed off, but they were still practically empty—a few knots of tourates on their way home from Universal Studios clumped together in the middle of the room, a couple of druggates asleep against the back wall, three others over by the far side wall, laying out three-card monte hands on the yellow warning strip, one lone Marilyn.

The tourates were watching the station sign anxiously, like they were afraid they'd miss their stop. Fat chance. The time between Instransit stations may be inst, but it takes the skids a good ten minutes to generate the negative-matter region that produces the transit, and another five afterward before they turn on the exit arrows, during which time nobody was going anywhere.

The tourates might as well relax and enjoy the show. What there was of it. Only one of the side walls was working, and half of it was running a continuous loop of ads for ILMGM, which apparently didn't know it'd been taken over yet. In the center of the wall, a digitized lion roared under the studio trademark in glowing gold: "Anything's Possible!" The screen blurred and went to swirling mist while a voiceover said, "ILMGM! More Stars Than There Are in Heaven," and then announced names while said stars appeared out of the fog. Vivien Leigh tripping toward us in a huge hoop skirt; Arnold Schwarzenegger roaring in on a motorcycle; Charlie Chaplin twirling his cane.

"Constantly working to bring you the brightest stars in the firmament," the voiceover said, which meant the stars currently in copyright litigation. Marlene Dietrich, Macaulay Culkin at age ten, Fred Astaire in top hat and tails, strolling effortlessly, casually toward us.

I'd dragged Alis out of the dorm to get away from mirrors and the Beguine and Fred, tippity-tapping away on my frontal lobe, to find something different to look at if I flashed again, but all I'd done was exchange my screen for a bigger one.

The other wall was even worse. It was apparently later than I'd thought. They'd shut the ads off for the night, and it was nothing but a long expanse of mirror. Like the polished floor Fred Astaire and Eleanor Powell had danced on, side by side, their hands nearly–

I focused on the reflections. The druggates looked dead. They'd probably taken capsules Heada told them were chooch. The Marilyn was practicing her pout in the mirror, flinching forward with a look of openmouthed surprise, and splaying her hand against her white pleated skirt to keep it from billowing up. The steam grating scene from *The Seven Year Itch*.

The tourates were still watching the station sign, which read La Brea Tar Pits. Alis was watching it, too, her face intent, and even in the fluorescents and the flickering light of ILMGM upcoming remakes, her hair had that curious backlit look. Her feet were apart, and she held her hands out, braced for sudden movement.

"No skids in Riverwood, huh?" I said.

She grinned. "Riverwood. That's Mickey Rooney's hometown in *Strike Up the Band,*" she said. "We only had a little one in Galesburg. And it had seats."

"You can squeeze more people in during rush hour without seats. You don't have to stand like that, you know."

"I know," she said, moving her feet together. "I just keep expecting us to move."

"We already did," I said, glancing at the station sign. It had changed to Pasadena. "For about a nanosecond. Station to station and no in-between. It's all done with mirrors."

I stood on the yellow warning strip and put my hand out toward the side wall. "Only they're not mirrors. They're a curtain of negative matter you could put your hand right through. You need to get a studio exec on the make to explain it to you."

"Isn't it dangerous?" she said, looking down at the yellow warning strip.

"Not unless you try to walk through them, which ravers sometimes try to do. There used to be barriers, but the studios made them take them out. They got in the way of their promos."

She turned and looked at the far wall. "It's so big!"

"You should see it during the day. They shut off the back part at night. So the druggates don't piss on the floor. There's another room back there"—I pointed at the rear wall—"that's twice as big as this."

"It's like a rehearsal hall," Alis said. "Like the dance studio in *Swing Time*. You could almost dance in here."

"'I won't dance,'" I said. "'Don't ask me.'"

"Wrong movie," she said, smiling. "That's from *Roberta.*"

She turned back to the mirrored side wall, her skirt flaring out, and her reflection called up the image of Eleanor Powell next to Fred Astaire on the dark, polished floor, her hand—

I forced it back, staring determinedly at the other wall, where a trailer for the new *Star Trek* movie was flashing, till it receded, and then turned back to Alis.

She was looking at the station sign. Pasadena was flashing. A line of green arrows led to the front, and the tourates were following it through the left-hand exit door and off to Disneyland.

"Where are we going?" Alis said.

"Sightseeing," I said. "The homes of the stars. Which should be Forest Lawn, only they aren't there anymore, They're back up on the silver screen working for free."

I waved my hand at the near wall, where a trailer for the remake of *Pretty Woman,* starring, natch, Marilyn Monroe, was showing.

Marilyn made an entrance in a red dress, and the Marilyn stopped practicing her pout and came over to watch. Marilyn flipped an escargot at a waiter, went shopping on Rodeo Drive for a white halter dress, faded out on a lingering kiss with Clark Gable.

"Appearing soon as Lina Lamont in *Singin' in the Rain,*" I said. "So tell me why you hate Gene Kelly."

"I don't hate him exactly," she said, considering. "*American in Paris* is awful, and that fantasy thing in *Singin' in the Rain,* but when he dances with Donald O'Connor and Frank Sinatra, he's actually a good dancer. It's just that he makes it look so *hard.*"

"And it isn't?"

"No, it *is.* That's the point." She frowned. "When he does jumps or complicated steps, he flails his arms and puffs and pants. It's like he wants you to know how hard it is. Fred Astaire doesn't do that. His routines are lots harder than Gene Kelly's, the steps are *terrible,* but you don't see any of that on the screen. When he dances, it doesn't look like he's working at all. It looks easy, like he just that minute made it up—"

The image of Fred and Eleanor pushed forward again, the two of them in white, tapping casually, effortlessly, across the starry floor—

"And he made it look so easy you thought you'd come to Hollywood and do it, too," I said.

"I know it won't be easy," she said quietly. "I know there aren't a lot of liveactions—"

"Any," I said. "There aren't *any* liveactions being made. Unless you're in Bogota. Or Beijing. It's all CGs. 'No actors need apply.'"

Dancers either, I thought, but didn't say it. I was still hoping to get a pop out of this, if I could hang on to her till the next flash. If there was a next flash. I was getting a killing headache, which wasn't supposed to be a side effect.

"But if it's all computer graphics," Alis was saying earnestly, "then they can do whatever they want. Including musicals."

"And what makes you think they want to? There hasn't been a musical since 1996."

"They're copyrighting Fred Astaire," she said, gesturing at the screen. "They must want him for something."

Something is right, I thought. *The sequel to* The Towering Inferno. *Or snuffporn movies.*

"I said I knew it wouldn't be easy," she said defensively. "You know what they said about Fred Astaire when he first came to Hollywood? Everybody said he was washed up, that his sister was the one with all the talent, that he was a no-talent vaudeville hoofer who'd never make it in movies. On his screen test, somebody wrote, 'Thirty, balding, can dance a little.' They didn't think he could do it either, and look what happened."

There were movies for him to dance in, I didn't say, but she must have seen it in my face because she said, "He was willing to work really hard, and so am I. Did you know he used to rehearse his routines for weeks before the movie even started shooting? He wore out six pairs of tap shoes rehearsing for *Carefree.* I'm willing to practice just as hard as he did," she said. "I know I'm not good enough. I need to take ballet, too. All I've had is jazz and tap. And I don't know very many routines yet. Plus, I'm going to have to find somebody to teach me ballroom."

Where? I thought. *There hasn't been a dancing teacher in Hollywood in twenty years. Or a choreographer. Or a musical.* CGs might have killed the liveaction, but they hadn't killed the musical. It had died all by itself back in the sixties.

"I'll need a job to pay for the dancing lessons, too," she was saying. "The girl you were talking to at the party—the one who looks like Marilyn Monroe—she said maybe I could get a job as a face. What do they do?"

Go to parties, stand around trying to get noticed by somebody who'll trade a pop for a paste-up, do chooch, I thought, wishing I had some.

"They smile and talk and look sad while some hackate does a scan of them," I said.

"Like a screen test?" Alis said.

"Like a screen test. Then the hackate digitizes the scan of your face and puts it into a remake of *A Star Is Born* and you get to be the next Judy Garland. Only why do that when the studio's already got Judy Garland? And Barbra Streisand. And Janet Gaynor. And they're all copyrighted, they're already stars, so why would the studios take a chance on a new face? And why take a chance on a new movie when they can do a sequel or a copy or a remake of something they already own? And while we're at it, why not *star* remakes in the remake? Hollywood, the ultimate recycler!"

I waved my hand at the screen where ILMGM was touting coming attractions. "*The Phantom of the Opera,*" the voiceover said. "Starring Anthony Hopkins and Meg Ryan."

"Look at that," I said. "Hollywood's latest effort—a remake of a remake of a silent!"

The trailer ended, and the loop started again. The digitized lion did its digitized roar, and above it a digitized laser burned in gold: "Anything's Possible!"

"Anything's possible," I said, "if you have the digitizers and the Crays and the memory and the fibe-op feed to send it out over. And the copyrights."

The golden words faded into fog, and Scarlett simpered her way out of it toward us, holding up her hoop skirt daintily.

"Anything's possible, but only for the studios. They own everything, they control everything, they—"

I broke off, thinking, *There's no way she'll give me a pop after that little outburst. Why didn't you just tell her straight out her little dream's impossible?*

But she wasn't listening. She was looking at the screen, where the copyright cases were being trotted out for inspection. Waiting for Fred Astaire to appear.

"The first time I ever saw him, I knew what I wanted," she said, her eyes on the wall. "Only 'wanted' isn't the right word. I mean, not like you want a new dress—"

"Or some chooch," I said.

"It's not even that kind of wanting. It's . . . there's a scene in *Top Hat* where Fred Astaire's dancing in his hotel room and Ginger Rogers has the room below him, and she comes up to complain about the noise, and he tells her that sometimes he just finds himself dancing, and *she* says—"

" 'I suppose it's some kind of an affliction,' " I said.

I'd expected her to smile at that, the way she had at my other movie quotes, but she didn't.

"An affliction," she said seriously. "Only that isn't it either, exactly. It's . . . when he dances, it isn't just that he makes it look easy. It's like all the steps and rehearsing and the music are just practice, and what he does is the real thing. It's like he's gone beyond the rhythm and the time steps and the turns to this other place. . . . If I could get there, do that . . ."

She stopped. Fred Astaire was sauntering toward us out of the mist in his top hat and tails, tipping his top hat jauntily forward with the end of his cane. I looked at Alis.

She was looking at him with that lost, breathless look she had had in my room, watching Fred and Eleanor, side by side, dressed in white, turning and yet still, silent, beyond motion, beyond—

"Come on," I said, and yanked on her hand. "This is our stop," and followed the green arrows out.

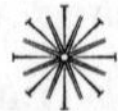

SCENE: Hollywood première night at Grauman's Chinese Theatre. Searchlights crisscrossing the night sky, palm trees, screaming fans, limousines, tuxedos, furs, flashbulbs popping.

WE CAME OUT ON HOLLYWOOD BOULEVARD, ON THE CORNER of Chaos and Sensory Overload, the worst possible place to flash.

It was a DeMille scene, as usual. Faces and tourates and freelancers and ravers and thousands of extras milling among the vid places and VR caves. And among the screens: drops and freescreens and diamonds and holos, all showing trailers edited à la *Psycho* by Vincent.

Trump's Chinese Theater had two huge dropscreens in front of it, running promos of the latest remake of *Ben-Hur*. On one of them, Sylvester Stallone in a bronze skirt and digitized sweat was leaning over his chariot, whipping the horses.

You couldn't see the other. There was a vid-neon sign in front of it that said Happy Endings, and a holoscreen showing Scarlett O'Hara in the fog, saying, "But, Rhett, I love you."

"Frankly, my dear—I love you, too," Clark Gable said, and crushed her in his arms. "I've always loved you!"

"The cement has stars in it," I said to Alis, pointing down. It was too crowded to see the sidewalk, let alone the stars. I led her out into the street, which was just as crowded, but at least it was moving, and down toward the vid places.

Hawkers from the VR caves crushed flyers into our hands, two dollars off reality, and River Phoenix pushed up. "Drag? Flake? A pop?"

I bought some chooch and popped it right there, hoping it would stave off a flash till we got back to the dorm.

The crowd thinned out a little, and I led Alis back onto the sidewalk and past a VR cave advertising, "A hundred percent body hookup! A hundred percent realistic!"

A hundred percent realistic, all right. According to Heada, who knows everything, simsex takes more memory than most of the VR caves can afford, and half of them slap a data helmet on the customer, add some noise to make it look like a VR image, and bring in a freelancer.

I towed Alis around the VR cave and straight into a herd of tourates standing in front of a booth called A Star Is Born and gawking at a vid-pitch. "Make your dreams come true! Be a movie star! $89.95, including disk. Studio-licensed! Studio-quality digitizing!"

"I don't know, which one do you think I should do?" a fat female tourate was saying, flipping through the menu.

A bored-looking hackate in a white lab coat and James Dean pompadour glanced at the movie she was pointing at, handed her a plastic bundle, and motioned her into a curtained cubicle.

She stopped halfway in. "I'll be able to watch this on the fibe-op feed, won't I?"

"Sure," James Dean said, and yanked the curtain across.

"Do you have any musicals?" I asked, wondering if he'd lie to me like he had to the tourate. She wasn't going to be on the fibe-op feed. Nothing gets on except studio-authorized changes.

Paste-ups and slash-and-burns. She'd get a tape of the scene and orders not to make any copies.

He looked blank. "Musicals?"

"You know. Singing? Dancing?" I said, but the tourate was back wearing a too-short white robe and a brown wig with braids looped over her ears.

"Stand up here," James Dean said, pointing at a plastic crate. He fastened a data harness around her large middle and went over to an old Digimatte compositor and switched it on.

"Look at the screen," he said, and the tourates all moved so they could see it. Storm troopers blasted away, and Luke Skywalker appeared, standing in a doorway over a dropoff, his arm around a blank blue space in the screen.

I left Alis watching and pushed through the crowd to the menu. *Stagecoach, The Godfather, Rebel Without a Cause.*

"Okay, now," James Dean said, typing onto a keyboard. The female tourate appeared on the screen next to Luke. "Kiss him on the cheek and step off the box. You don't have to jump. The data harness'll do everything."

"Won't it show in the movie?"

"The machine cuts it out."

They didn't have any musicals. Not even Ruby Keeler. I worked my way back to Alis.

"Okay, roll 'em," James Dean said. The fat tourate smooched empty air, giggled, and jumped off the box. On the screen, she kissed Luke's cheek, and they swung out across a high-tech abyss.

"Come on," I said to Alis, and steered her across the street to Screen Test City.

It had a multiscreen filled with stars' faces, and an old guy with the pinpoint eyes of a redliner. "Be a star! Get your face up on the silver screen! Who do you want to be, popsy?" he said, leering at Alis. "Marilyn Monroe?"

Ginger Rogers and Fred Astaire were side by side on the bottom row of the screen. "That one," I said, and the screen zoomed till they filled it.

"You're lucky you came tonight," the old guy said. "He's going into litigation. What do you want? Still or scene?"

"Scene," I said. "Just her. Not both of us."

"Stand in front of the scanner," he said, pointing, "and let me get a still of your smile."

"No, thank you," Alis said, looking at me.

"Come on," I said. "You said you wanted to dance in the movies. Here's your chance."

"You don't have to do anything," the old guy said. "All I need's an image to digitize from. The scanner does the rest. You don't even have to smile."

He took hold of her arm, and I expected her to wrench away from him, but she didn't move.

"I want to dance in the movies," she said, looking at me, "not get my face digitized onto Ginger Rogers's body. I want to dance."

"You'll be dancing," the old guy said. "Up there on the screen for everybody to see." He waved his free hand at the milling cast of thousands, none of whom were looking at his screen. "And on opdisk."

"You don't understand," she said to me, tears welling up in her eyes. "The CG revolution—"

"Is right there in front of you," I said, suddenly fed up. "Simsex, paste-ups, snuffshows, make-your-own remakes. Look around, Ruby. You want to dance in the movies? This is as close as you're going to get!"

"I thought you understood," she said bleakly, and whirled before either of us could stop her, and plunged into the crowd.

"Alis, wait!" I shouted, and started after her, but she was already far ahead. She disappeared into the entrance to the skids.

"Lose the girl?" a voice said, and I turned and glared. I was opposite the Happy Endings booth. "Get dumped? Change the ending. Make Rhett come back to Scarlett. Make Lassie come home."

I crossed the street. It was all simsex parlors on this side, promising a pop with Mel Gibson, Sharon Stone, the Marx Brothers. A hundred percent realistic. I wondered if I should do a sim. I stuck my head in the promo data helmet, but there wasn't any blurring. The chooch must be working.

"You shouldn't do that," a female voice said.

I pulled my head out of the helmet. A freelancer was standing there, blond, in a torn net leotard and a beauty mark. *Bus Stop*. "Why go for a virtual imitation when you can have the real thing?" she breathed.

"Which is what?" I said.

The smile didn't fade, but she looked instantly on guard. Mary Astor in *The Maltese Falcon*. "What?"

"This real thing. What is it? Sex? Love? Chooch?"

She half put up her hands, like she was being arrested. "Are you a narc? 'Cause I don't know what you're talking about. I was just making a comment, okay? I just don't think people should settle for VRs, is all, when they could talk to somebody real."

"Like Marilyn Monroe?" I said, and wandered on down the sidewalk past three more freelancers. Marilyn in a white halter dress, Madonna in brass cones, Marilyn in pink satin. The real thing.

I scored some more chooch and a line of tinseltown from a James Dean too splatted to remember he was supposed to be selling the stuff, and ate it, walking on past the snuffshows, but somewhere I must have gotten turned around because I was back at Happy Endings, watching the holoscreen. Scarlett ran into the fog after Rhett, Butch and Sundance leaped forward into a hail of gunfire, Humphrey Bogart and Ingrid Bergman stood in front of an airplane looking at each other.

"Back again, huh?" the hawker said. "Best thing for a broken heart. Kill the bastards. Get the girl. What'll it be? *Lost Horizon*? *Terminator 9*?"

Ingrid was telling Bogie she wanted to stay, and Bogie was telling her it was impossible.

"What happy endings do people come up with for this?" I asked him.

"*Casablanca*?" He shrugged. "The Nazis show up and kill the husband, Ingrid and Bogart get married."

"And honeymoon in Auschwitz," I said.

"I didn't say the endings were any good."

On the screen, Bogie and Ingrid were looking at each other. Tears welled up in her eyes, and the edges of the screen went to soft-focus.

"How about *Shadowlands*?" the guy said, but I was already shoving through the crowd, trying to reach the skids before I flashed.

I almost made it. I was past the chariot race when a Marilyn crashed into me and I went down, and I thought, *Natch, I'm going to flash on cement,* but I didn't.

The sidewalk blurred and then went blinding, and there were stars in it, and Fred and Eleanor, all in white, danced easily, elegantly through the milling crowd, and superimposed across them was Alis, watching them, her face lost and sorrowful. Like Ingrid's.

FADE TO BLACK

MONTAGE: No sound, HERO, seated at comp, punches keys and deletes AS's as scene onscreen changes. Western saloon, elegant nightclub, fraternity house, waterfront bar.

WHATEVER EFFECT MY JUDGE HARDY LECTURE HAD HAD ON Alis, it didn't make her give up on her dream and head back to Meadowville. She was at the party again the next week.

I wasn't. I'd gotten Mayer's list and a notice that my scholarship had been canceled due to "nonperformance," and I was working on Mayer's list just to stay in the dorm. And in chooch.

I didn't miss anything, though. Heada came up to my room halfway through the party to fill me in. "The takeover's definitely on," she said. "Mayer's boss's been moved to Development, which means he's on the way out. Warner's filing a countersuit on Fred Astaire. It goes to court tomorrow."

Alis should have had her face pasted onto Ginger's while she had the chance. She'd never get a chance to dance with him now.

"Vincent's at the party," she said. "He's got a new decay morph."

"What a pity I've got to miss that," I said.

"What are you doing up here anyway?" she said, fishing.

"You've never missed a party before. Everybody's down there. Mayer, Alis—" She paused, watching my face.

"Mayer, huh?" I said. "I've got to talk to him about a raise. Do you know who drinks in the movies? Everybody." I took a swig of scotch to illustrate. "Even Gary Cooper."

"Should you be doing that stuff?" Heada said.

"Are you kidding? It's cheap, it's legal, *and* I know what it is." And it was pretty good at keeping me from flashing.

"Is it safe?" Heada, who thought nothing of snorting white stuff she found on the floor, was reading the bottle warily.

"Of course it's safe. *And* endorsed by W. C. Fields, John Barrymore, Bette Davis, and E.T. And the major studios. It's in every movie on Mayer's list. *Camille, The Maltese Falcon, Gunga Din*. Even *Singin' in the Rain*. Champagne at the party after the première." The one where Donald O'Connor said, "You have to show a movie at a party. It's a Hollywood law." I finished off the bottle. "Also *Oklahoma.* Poor Judd is dead. Dead drunk."

"Mayer was hitting on Alis at the party," she said, still looking at me.

Yeah, well, that was inevitable.

"Alis was telling him how she wanted to dance in the movies."

That was inevitable, too.

"I hope they'll be very happy," I said. "Or is he saving her to give to Gary Cooper?"

"She can't find a dancing teacher."

"Well, I'd love to stay and chat," I said, "but I've got to get back to the Hays Office." I called up *Casablanca* again and started deleting liquor bottles.

"I think you should help her," Heada said.

"Sorry," I said. " 'I stick my neck out for nobody.' "

"That's a quote from a movie, isn't it?"

"Bingo," I said. I deleted the crystal decanter Humphrey Bogart was pouring himself a drink out of.

"I think you should find her a dancing teacher. You know a lot of people in the business."

"There *aren't* any people in the business. It's all CGs, it's all ones and zeros and didge-actors and edit programs. The studios aren't even hiring warmbodies anymore. The only *people* in the business are dead, along with the liveaction. Along with the musical. Kaput. Over. 'The end of Rico.'"

"That's a quote from the movies, too, isn't it?"

"Yes," I said, "which are also dead, in case you couldn't tell from Vincent's decay morph."

"You could get her a job as a face."

"Like the one you've got?"

"Well, then, a job as a hackate, as a foley, or a location assistant or something. She knows a lot about movies."

"She doesn't want to hack," I said, "and even if she did, the only movies she knows about are musicals. A location assistant's got to know everything, stock shots, props, frame numbers. Be a perfect job for you, Heada. Now I really have to get back to playing Lee Remick."

Heada looked like she wanted to ask if that was a movie, too.

"*The Hallelujah Trail,*" I said. "Temperance leader, battling demon rum." I tipped the bottle up, trying to get the last drops out. "You have any chooch?"

She looked uncomfortable. "No."

"Well, what have you got? Besides klieg. I don't need any more doses of reality."

"I don't have anything," she said, and blushed. "I'm trying to taper off a little."

"You?!" I said. "What happened? Vincent's decay morph get to you?"

"No," she said defensively. "The other night, when I was on the klieg, I was listening to Alis talk about wanting to be a dancer, and I suddenly realized there was nothing I wanted, except chooch and getting popped."

"So you decided to go straight, and now you and Alis are going to tap-dance your way to stardom. I can see it now, your names up in lights—Ruby Keeler and Una Merkel in *Gold Diggers of 2018*!"

"No," she said, "but I decided I'd like to be like her, that I'd like to want something."

"Even if that something is impossible?"

I couldn't make out her expression. "Yeah."

"Well, giving up chooch isn't the way to do it. If you want to figure out what it is you want, the way to do it is to watch a lot of movies."

She looked defensive again.

"How do you think Alis came up with this dancing thing? From the movies. She doesn't just want to dance in the movies, she wants to be Ruby Keeler in *42nd Street*—the plucky little chorus girl with a heart of gold. The odds are stacked against her, and all she's got is determination and a pair of tap shoes, but don't worry. All she has to do is keep hoofing and hoping, and she'll not only make it big, she'll save the show *and* get Dick Powell. It's all right there in the script. You didn't think Alis came up with it on her own, did you?"

"Came up with what?"

"Her *part*," I said. "That's what the movies do. They don't entertain us, they don't send the message: 'We care.' They give us lines to say, they assign us parts: John Wayne, Theda Bara, Shirley Temple, take your pick."

I waved at the screen, where the Nazi commandant was ordering a bottle of Veuve Clicquot '26 he wasn't going to get to drink. "How about Claude Rains sucking up to the Nazis? No, sorry, Mayer's already playing that part. But don't worry, there are enough parts to go around, and everybody's got a featured role, whether they know it or not, even the faces. They think they're playing Marilyn, but they're not. They're doing Greta Garbo as Sadie Thompson. Why do you think the execs keep doing all these remakes? Why do they keep hiring Humphrey Bogart and Bette Davis? It's because all the good parts have already been cast, and all we're doing is auditioning for the remake."

She looked at me so intently I wondered if she'd lied about giving up AS's and was doing klieg. "Alis was right," she said. "You do love the movies."

"What?"

"I never noticed, the whole time I've known you, but she's right. You know all the lines and all the actors, and you're always quoting from them. Alis says you act like you don't care, but underneath you really love them, or you wouldn't know them all by heart."

I said, in my best Claude Rains, " 'My dear Ricky, I suspect that underneath that cynical shell you are at heart a sentimentalist.' Ruby Keeler does Ingrid Bergman in *Spellbound*. Did Dr. Bergman have any other psychiatric observations?"

"She said that's why you do so many AS's, because you love movies and you can't stand seeing them being butchered."

"Wrong," I said. "You don't know everything, Heada. It's because I pushed Gregory Peck onto a spiked fence when we were kids."

"See?" she said wonderingly. "Even when you're denying it, you do it."

"Well, this has been fun, but I have to get back to work butchering," I said, "and you have to get back to deciding whether you want to play Sadie Thompson or Una Merkel." I turned back to the screen. Peter Lorre was clutching Humphrey Bogart's lapels, begging him to save him.

"You said everybody's playing a part, whether they know it or not," Heada said. "What part am I playing?"

"Right now? Thelma Ritter in *Rear Window*. The meddling friend who doesn't know when to keep her nose out of other people's business," I said. "Shut the door when you leave."

She did, and then opened it again and stood there watching me. "Tom?"

"Yeah?" I said.

"If I'm Thelma Ritter and Alis is Ruby Keeler, what part are you playing?"

"King Kong."

Heada left, and I sat there for a while, watching Humphrey Bogart stand by and let Peter Lorre get arrested, and then got up to see if there were any AS's on the premises. There was klieg in the medicine cabinet, just what I needed, and a bottle of champagne from one time when Mayer brought a face up to watch me paste her into *East of Eden*. I took a swig. It was flat, but better than nothing. I poured some in a glass and ff'd to the "Play it again, Sam" scene.

Bogart slugged down a drink, the screen went to soft-focus, and he was pouring Ingrid Bergman champagne in front of a matte that was supposed to be Paris.

The door opened.

"Forget to give me some gossip, Heada?" I said, taking another swallow.

It was Alis. She was wearing a pinafore and puffed sleeves. Her hair was darker, and had a big bow in it, but it had that same backlit look to it, framing her face with radiance.

Fred Astaire tapped a ripple on the polished floor, and Eleanor Powell repeated it and turned to smile at him—

I downed the rest of the champagne in one gulp and poured some more. "Well, if it isn't Ruby Keeler," I said. "What do you want?"

She stayed in the doorway. "The musicals you showed me the other night, Heada said you might be willing to loan me the opdisks."

I took a drink of champagne. "They aren't on disk. It's a direct fibe-op feed," I said, and sat down at the comp.

"Is that what you do?" she said from behind me. She was standing looking over my shoulder at the screen. "You ruin movies?"

"That's what I do," I said. "I protect the moviegoing public from the evils of demon rum and chooch. Mostly demon rum. There aren't all that many movies with drugs in them. *Valley of the Dolls, Postcards from the Edge,* a couple of Cheech and Chongs, *The Thief of Bagdad.* I also remove nicotine if the Anti-Smoking League didn't get there first." I deleted the champagne glass Ingrid Bergman was raising to her lips. "What do you think? Tea or cocoa?"

She didn't say anything.

"It's a big job. Maybe you could do the musicals. Want me to access Mayer and see if he'll hire you?"

She looked stubborn. "Heada said you could make opdisks for me off the feed," she said stiffly. "I just need them to practice with. Till I can find a dancing teacher."

I turned around in the chair to look at her. "And then what?"

"If you don't want to lend them to me, I could watch them here and copy down the steps. When you're not using the comp."

"And then what?" I said. "You copy down the steps and practice the routines and then what? Gene Kelly pulls you out of the chorus—no, wait, I forgot, you don't like Gene Kelly—Gene Nelson pulls you out of the chorus and gives you the lead? Mickey Rooney decides to put on a show? What?"

"I don't know. When I find a dancing teacher—"

"There *aren't* any dancing teachers. They all went home to Meadowville fifteen years ago, when the studios switched to computer animation. There aren't any soundstages or rehearsal halls or studio orchestras. There aren't any *studios,* for God's sake! All there is is a bunch of geekates hacking away on Crays and a bunch of corporation execs telling 'em what to do. Let me show you something." I twisted back around in the chair. "Menu," I said. "*Top Hat.* Frame 97-265."

Fred and Ginge came up on the screen, spinning around in the Piccolino. "You want to bring musicals back. We'll do it right here. Forward at 5." The screen slowed to a sequence of frames. Kick and. Turn and. Lift.

"How long did you say Fred had to practice his routines?"

"Six weeks," she said tonelessly.

"Too long. Think of all that rehearsal-hall rent. And all those tap shoes. Frame 97-288 to 97-631, repeat four times, then 99-006 to 99-115, and continuous loop. At 24." The screen slid into realtime, and Fred lifted Ginge, lifted her again, and again, effortlessly, lightly. Lift, and lift, and kick and turn.

"Does that kick look high enough to you?" I said, pointing at the screen. "Frame 99-108 and freeze." I fiddled with the image, raising Fred's leg till it touched his nose. "Too high?" I eased it back down a little, smoothed out the shadows. "Forward at 24."

Fred kicked, his leg sailing into the air. And lift. And lift. And lift. And lift.

"All right," Alis said. "I get the point."

"Bored already? You're right. This should be a production number." I hit multiply. "Eleven, side by side," I said, and a dozen Fred Astaires kicked in perfect synch, lift, and lift, and lift, and lift. "Multiply rows," I said, and the screen filled with Fred, lifting, kicking, tipping his top hat.

I turned around to look at Alis. "Why would they want you when they can have Fred Astaire? A hundred Fred Astaires? A thousand? And none of them have trouble learning a step, none of them get blisters on their feet or throw temper tantrums or have to be paid or grow old or—"

"Get drunk," she said.

"You want Fred drunk?" I said. "I can do that, too. Frame 97-412 and freeze." Fred Astaire stopped in midturn, smiling. "Frame 97—" I said, and the screen went silver and then to legalese. "The character of Fred Astaire is currently unavailable for fibe-op transmission. Copyright ownership suit *ILMGM* v. *RKO-Warner* . . ."

"Oops. Fred's in litigation. Too bad. You should have taken that paste-up while you had the chance."

She wasn't looking at the screen. She was looking at me, her gaze alert, focused, the way it had been on the Piccolino. "If you're so sure what I want is impossible, why are you trying so hard to talk me out of it?"

Because I don't want to see you down on Hollywood Boulevard in a torn net leotard. I don't want to have to stick your face in a River Phoenix movie so Mayer's boss can pop you.

"You're right," I said. "Why the hell am I?" I turned to the comp and said, "Print accesses, all files." I ripped the hardcopy out of the printer. "Here. Take my fibe-op accesses and make all the disks you want. Practice till your little feet bleed." I thrust it at her.

She didn't take it.

"Go on," I said, and pressed it into her unresponsive hand. "Who am I to stand in your way? In the immortal words of Leo the Lion, anything's possible. Who cares if the studios have got all the copyrights and the fibe-op sources and the digitizers and the accesses? We'll sew our own costumes. We'll build our own sets. And then, right before we open, Bebe Daniels'll break her leg and you'll have to go on for her!"

She crumpled up the hardcopy, looking like she'd like to throw it at me. "How would you know what's possible and impossible? You don't even *try*. Fred Astaire—"

"Is tied up in court, but don't let that stop you. There's still

Ann Miller. And *Seven Brides for Seven Brothers*. And Gene Kelly. Oh, wait, I forgot, you're too good for Gene Kelly. Tommy Tune. And don't forget Ruby Keeler."

She threw it.

I picked the hardcopy up and uncrumpled it. " 'Temper, temper, Scarlett,' " I drawled, smoothing it out. I tucked it in the pocket of her pinafore and patted it. "Now get out there on that stage. It's showtime! The whole cast's counting on you. Remember, you're going out there a youngster, but you've got to come back a star."

Her hand clenched, but she didn't throw the hardcopy again. She wheeled, skirt flaring like Eleanor's white one. I had to close my eyes against the sudden image of Fred and Eleanor dancing on the polished floor, the phony stars shimmering in endless ripples, and missed Alis's exit.

She slammed the door behind her, and the image receded. I opened it and leaned out. "Be so good you'll make me hate you," I called after her, but she was already gone.

SCENE: Busby Berkeley production number. Giant revolving fountain with chorus girls in gold lamé on each level, filling champagne glasses in the flowing fountain. Move in to close-up of champagne glass, then to close-up of bubbles, inside each bubble a chorus girl in gold-sequined tap pants and halter top, tap-dancing.

ALIS DIDN'T COME BACK AGAIN AFTER THAT. HEADA WENT out of her way to keep me posted—she hadn't found a dancing teacher, the Viamount takeover was a done deal, Columbia Tri-Star was doing a remake of *Somewhere in Time*.

"There was this Columbia exec at the party," Heada told me, perched on my bed. "He said they've been doing experiments with images projected into negative-matter regions, and there's a measurable lag. He says they're *this* close"—she did the thumb-and-forefinger bit—"to inventing time travel."

"Great," I said. "Alis can go back to the thirties and take dancing lessons from Busby Berkeley himself."

Only she didn't like Busby Berkeley, and after taking all the AS's out of *Footlight Parade* and *Gold Diggers of 1933,* neither did I.

She was right about there not being any dancing in his movies. There was a glimpse of tapping feet in *42nd Street,* a rehearsal going on in the background of a plot exposition scene, a few bars in "Pettin' in the Park" for Ruby, who danced about as well as

Judy Garland. Otherwise, it was all neon violins and revolving wedding cakes and fountains and posed platinum-haired chorus girls, every one of whom had probably been a studio exec's popsy. Overhead kaleidoscope shots and pans and low-angle shots from underneath chorus girls' spread-apart legs that would have given the Hays Office fits. But no dancing.

Lots of drinking, though—speakeasies and backstage parties and silver flasks stuck in chorus girls' garters. Even a production number in a bar, with Ruby Keeler as Shanghai Lil, a popsy who'd done a lot of hooch and a lot of sailors. A hymn to alcohol's finer qualities.

Of which there were many. It was cheap, it didn't do as much damage as redline, and if it didn't give you the blessed forgetfulness of chooch, it stopped the flashing and put a nice soft-focus on things in general. Which made it easier to work on Mayer's list.

It also came in assorted flavors—pink ladies for *Topper,* elderberry wine for *Arsenic and Old Lace,* a nice Chianti for *Silence of the Lambs.* In between, I drank champagne, which had apparently been in every movie ever made, and cursed Mayer, and deleted beakers and laboratory flasks from the cantina scene in *Star Wars.*

I went to the next party, and the one after that, but Alis wasn't there. Vincent was, demonstrating another program, and the studio exec, still pitching time travel to the Marilyns, and Heada.

"That stuff wasn't klieg after all," she told me. "It was some designer chooch from Brazil."

"Which explains why I keep hearing the Beguine."

"Huh?"

"Nothing," I said, looking around the room. Vincent's program must be a weeper simulator. Jackie Cooper was up on the screen, in a battered top hat and a polka-dot tie, blubbering over his dead dog.

"She's not here," Heada said.

"I was looking for Mayer," I said. "He's going to have to pay me double for *The Philadelphia Story*. The thing's full of alcohol. Sherry before lunch, martinis out by the pool, champagne, cocktails, hangovers, ice packs. Cary Grant, Katharine Hepburn, Jimmy Stewart. The whole cast's stinking."

I took a swig from the crème de menthe I had left over from *Days of Wine and Roses*. "The visuals will take at least three weeks, and that doesn't include the lines. 'I have the hiccups,' and 'Oh, I wonder if I might borrow a drink.' "

"She was here earlier," Heada said. "One of the execs was hitting on her."

"No, no, *I* say, 'I wonder if I might borrow a drink,' and *you* say, 'Certainly. Coals to Newcastle.' " I took another drink.

"Should you be doing so much alcohol?" Heada, the chooch queen, said.

"I have to," I said. "It's the bad effect of watching all these movies. Thank goodness ILMGM's remaking them so no one else will be corrupted." I drank some more crème de menthe.

Heada looked at me sharply, like she'd been doing klieg again. "ILMGM's doing a remake of *Time After Time*. The exec told Alis he thought he could get her a part in it."

"Great," I said, and went over to look at Vincent's program.

Audrey Hepburn was up on the screen now, standing in the rain and sobbing over her cat.

"This is our new tears program," Vincent said. "It's still in the experimental stage."

He said something to his remote, and the screen split. A computerized didge-actor sobbed alongside Audrey, clutching what looked like a yellow rug. Tears weren't the only thing in the experimental stage.

"Tears are the most difficult form of water simulation to do," Vincent said. The Tin Woodman was up there now, rusting his joints. "It's because tears aren't really water. They've got mucoproteins and lysozymes and a high salt content. It affects the index of refraction and makes them hard to reproduce," he said, sounding defensive.

He should. The didge-woodman's tears looked like Vaseline, oozing out of digitized eyes. "You ever program VRs?" I said. "Of, say, a movie scene like the one you used for the edit program a couple of weeks ago? The Fred Astaire and Ginger Rogers scene?"

"A virtual? Sure. I can do helmet and full-body data. Is this something you're working on for Mayer?"

"Yeah," I said. "Could you have the person take, say, Ginger Rogers's place, so she's dancing with Fred Astaire?"

"Sure. Foot and knee hookups, nerve stimulators. It'll feel like she's really dancing."

"Not feel like," I said. "Can you make it so she actually dances?"

He thought about it awhile, frowning at the screen. The Tin Woodman had disappeared. Ingrid Bergman and Humphrey Bogart were at the airport saying good-bye.

"Maybe," Vincent said. "I guess. We could put on some sole-sensors and rig a feedback enhance to exaggerate her body movements so she could shuffle her feet back and forth."

I looked at the screen. There were tears welling up in Ingrid's eyes, glimmering like the real thing. They probably weren't. It was probably the eighth take, or the eighteenth, and a makeup girl had come out with glycerine drops or onion juice to get the right effect. It wasn't the tears that did it anyway. It was the face, that sweet, sad face that knew it could never have what it wanted.

"We could do sweat enhancers," Vincent said. "Armpits, neck."

"Never mind," I said, still watching Ingrid. The screen split, and a didge-actress stood in front of a didge-airplane, oozing baby oil.

"How about a directional sound hookup for the taps and endorphins?" Vincent said. "She'll swear she was really dancing with Gene Kelly."

I drank the rest of the crème de menthe and handed him the empty bottle and then went back up to my room and hacked away at *The Philadelphia Story* for two more days, trying to think of a good reason for Jimmy Stewart to carry Katharine Hepburn and sing "Somewhere Over the Rainbow" without being sloshed, and pretending I needed one.

Mayer would hardly care, and neither would his tight-assed boss. And nobody else watched liveactions. If the plot didn't make sense, the hackates who did the remake could worry about it. They'd probably remake the remake anyway. Which was also on the list.

I called it up. *High Society*. Bing Crosby and Grace Kelly. Frank Sinatra playing Jimmy Stewart. I ff'd through the last half of it, searching for inspiration, but it was even more awash with AS's. *And* it was a musical. I went back to *Story* and tried again.

It was no use. Jimmy Stewart had to be drunk in the swimming pool scene to tell Katharine Hepburn he loved her. Katharine had to be drunk for her fiancé to dump her and for her to realize she still loved Cary Grant.

I gave up on the scene and went back to the one before it. It was just as bad. There was too much exposition to cut it, and most of it was in Jimmy Stewart's badly slurred voice. I rewound to the beginning of the scene and turned the sound up, getting a match so I could overdub his dialogue.

"Are you still in love with her?" Jimmy Stewart said, leaning belligerently toward Cary Grant.

"Mute," I said, and watched Cary Grant say something imperturbable, his face revealing nothing.

"Insufficient," the comp said. "Additional match data needed."

"Yeah." I turned the sound up again.

"Liz thinks you are," Jimmy Stewart said.

I rew'd to the beginning of the scene and froze it for the frame number, and then went through the scene again.

"Are you still in love with her?" Jimmy Stewart said. "Liz thinks you are."

I blanked the screen and accessed Heada. "I need to find out where Alis is," I said.

"Why?" she said suspiciously.

"I think I've found her a dancing teacher," I said. "I need her class schedule."

"Sorry," she said. "I don't know it."

"Come on, you know everything," I said. "What happened to 'I think you should help her'?"

"What happened to 'I stick my neck out for nobody'?"

"I told you, I found her somebody to teach her to dance. An old woman out in Palo Alto. Ex-chorus girl. She was in *Finian's Rainbow* and *Funny Girl* back in the seventies."

She was still suspicious, but she gave her schedule to me. Alis was taking Moviemaking 101, basic comp graphics stuff, and a film hist class, The Musical 1939–80. It was clear out in Burbank.

I took the skids and a bottle of *Public Enemy* gin and went out to find her. The class was in an old studio building UCLA had bought when the skids were first built, on the second floor.

I opened the door a crack and looked in. The prof, who looked like Michael Caine in *Educating Rita,* a movie with way too many AS's in it, was standing in front of a blank, old-fashioned comp monitor with a remote, holding forth to a scattering of students, mostly hackates taking it for their movie content elective, some Marilyns, Alis.

"Contrary to popular belief, the computer graphics revolution didn't kill the musical," the prof said. "The musical kicked off," he paused to let the class titter, "in 1965."

He turned to the monitor, which was no bigger than my array screens, and clicked the remote. Behind him, cowboys appeared, leaping around a train station. *Oklahoma.*

"The musicals, with their contrived story lines, unrealistic song-and-dance sequences, and simplistic happy endings, no longer reflected the audience's world."

I glanced at Alis, wondering how she was taking this. She wasn't. She was watching the cowboys, with that intent, focused look, and her lips were moving, counting the beats, memorizing the steps.

". . . which explains why the musical, unlike film noir and the horror movie, has not been revived in spite of the availability of such stars as Judy Garland and Gene Kelly. The musical is irrelevant. It has nothing to say to modern audiences. For example, *Broadway Melody of 1940 . . .*"

I retreated up the uneven steps and sat there, working on the gin and waiting for him to finish. He did, finally, and the class trickled out. A trio of faces, talking about a rumor that Disney was going to use warmbodies in *Grand Hotel,* a couple of hackates, the prof, snorting flake on his way down the steps, another hackate.

I finished off the gin. Nobody else came out, and I wondered if I'd somehow missed Alis. I went to see. The steps had gotten steeper and more uneven while I sat there. I slipped once and grabbed on to the banister, and then stood there a minute, listening. There was a clatter and then a thunk from inside the room, and the faint sound of music. The janitor?

I opened the door and leaned against it.

Alis, in a sky-blue dress with a bustle, and a flowered hat, was dancing in the middle of the room, a blue parasol perched on her shoulder. A song was coming from the comp monitor, and Alis was high-stepping in time with a line of bustled, parasoled girls on the monitor behind her.

I didn't recognize the movie. *Carousel,* maybe? *The Harvey Girls*? The girls were replaced by high-stepping boys in derbies and straw hats, and Alis stopped, breathing hard, and pulled the remote out of her high-buttoned shoe. She rewound, stuck the remote back in her shoe, and propped the parasol against her shoulder. The girls appeared again, and Alis pointed her toe and did a turn.

She had piled the desks in stacks on either side of the room, but there still wasn't enough room. When she swung into the second turn, her outstretched hand crashed into them, nearly knocking them over. She reached for the remote again, rew'd, and saw me. She clicked the screen off and took a step backward. "What do you want?"

I waggled my finger at her. "Give you a little advice. 'Don't want what you can't have.' Michael J. Fox, *For Love or Money*. Bar scene, party, nightclub, three bottles of champagne. Only not anymore. Yours truly has done his job. Right down the sink."

I swung my arm to demonstrate, like James Mason in *A Star Is Born,* and the chairs went over.

"You're splatted," she said.

"'Nope.'" I grinned. "Gary Cooper in *The Plainsman.*" I walked toward her. "Not splatted. Boiled, pickled, soused, sozzled. In a word, drunk as a skunk. It's a Hollywood tradition. Do you know how many movies have drinking in them? All. Except the ones I've taken it out of. *Dark Victory, Citizen Kane, Little Miss Marker*. Westerns, gangster movies, weepers. It's in all of them. Every one. Even *Broadway Melody of 1940*. Do you know why Fred got to dance the Beguine with Eleanor? Because George Murphy was too tanked up to go on. Forget dancing," I said, making another sweeping gesture that nearly hit her. "What you need to do is have a drink."

I tried to hand her the bottle.

She took another protective step toward the monitor. "You're drunk."

"Bingo," I said. "'Very drunk indeed,' as Audrey Hepburn would say. *Breakfast at Tiffany's*. A movie with a happy ending."

"Why'd you come here?" she said. "What is it you want?"

I took a swig out of the bottle, remembered it was empty, and looked at it sadly. "Came to tell you the movies aren't real life. Just because you want something doesn't mean you can have it. Came to tell you to go home before they remake you. Audrey should've gone home to Tulip, Texas. Came to tell you to go home to Carval." I waited, swaying, for her to get the reference.

"*Andy Hardy Has Too Much to Drink,*" she said. "He's the one who needs to go home."

The screen faded to black for a few frames, and then I was sitting halfway down the steps, with Alis leaning over me. "Are you all right?" she said, and tears were glimmering in her eyes like stars.

"I'm fine," I said. "'Champagne is a great level-el-ler,' as Jimmy Stewart would say. Need to pour some on these steps."

"I don't think you should take the skids in your condition," she said.

"We're all on the skids," I said. "Only place left."

"Tom," she said, and there was another fade to black, and Fred and Ginger were on both walls, sipping martinis by the pool.

"That'll have to go," I said. "Have to send the message 'We care.' Gotta sober Jimmy Stewart up. So what if it's the only way he can get up the courage to tell her what he really thinks? See, he knows she's too good for him. He knows he can't have her. He has to get drunk. Only way he can ever tell her he's in love with her."

I put out my hand to her hair. "How do you do that?" I said. "That backlighting thing?"

"Tom," she said.

I let my hand drop. "Doesn't matter. They'll ruin it in the remake. Not real anyway."

I waved my hand grandly at the screen like Gloria Swanson in *Sunset Boulevard*. "All a 'lusion. Makeup and wigs and fake sets. Even Tara. Just a false front. FX and foleys."

"I think you'd better sit down," Alis said, taking hold of my arm.

I shook it off. "Even Fred. Not the real thing at all. All those taps were dubbed in afterward, and they aren't really stars. In the floor. It's all done with mirrors."

I lurched toward the wall. "Only it's not even a mirror. You can put your hand right through it."

After which things went to montage. I remember trying to get out at Forest Lawn to see where Holly Golightly was buried and Alis yanking on my arm and crying big jellied tears like the ones in Vincent's program. And something about the station sign beeping Beguine, and then we were back in my room, which looked funny, the arrays were on the wrong side of the room, and they all showed Fred carrying Eleanor over to the pool, and I said, "You know why the musical kicked off? Not enough drinking. Except Judy Garland," and Alis said, "Is he splatted?" and then answered herself, "No, he's drunk." And I said, "'I don't want you to think I'm a drinker. I can stop anytime I want to—only I don't want to,'" and waited, grinning foolishly, for the two of them to get the reference, but they didn't. "*Some Like It Hot,* Marilyn Monroe," I said, and began to cry thick, oily tears. "Poor Marilyn."

And then I had Alis on the bed and was popping her and watching her face so I'd see it when I flashed, but the flash didn't come, and the room went to soft-focus around the edges, and I pounded harder, faster, nailing her against the bed so she couldn't get away, but she was already gone and I tried to go after her and ran into the arrays, Fred and Eleanor saying good-bye at the airport, and put my hand up and it went right through and I lost my balance. But when I fell, it wasn't into Alis's arms or into the arrays. It was into the negative-matter regions of the skids.

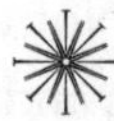

LEWIS STONE: *[Sternly]* I hope you've learned your lesson, Andrew. Drinking doesn't solve your problems. It only makes them worse.

MICKEY ROONEY: *[Hangdog]* I know that now, Dad. And I've learned something else, too. I've learned I should mind my own business and not meddle in other people's affairs.

LEWIS STONE: *[Doubtfully]* I hope so, Andrew. I certainly hope so.

IN *THE PHILADELPHIA STORY*, KATHARINE HEPBURN'S GETTING drunk solved everything: Her stuffed-shirt fiancé broke off the engagement, Jimmy Stewart quit tabloid journalism and started the serious novel his faithful girlfriend had always known he had in him, Mom and Dad reconciled, and Katharine Hepburn finally admitted she'd been in love with Cary Grant all along. Happy endings all around.

But the movies, as I had tried so soddenly to tell Alis, are not Real Life. And all I had done by getting drunk was to wake up in Heada's dorm room with a two-day hangover and a six-week suspension from the skids.

Not that I was going anywhere. Andy Hardy learns his lesson, forgets about girls, and settles down to the serious task of Minding His Own Business, a job made easier by the fact that Heada wouldn't tell me where Alis was because she wasn't speaking to me.

And by Heada's (or Alis's) pouring all my liquor down the drain like Katharine Hepburn in *The African Queen* and Mayer's putting a hold on my account till I turned in last week's dozen. Last week's dozen consisted of *The Philadelphia Story,* which I was only halfway through. So it was heigh-ho, heigh-ho, off to work we go to find twelve squeaky-cleans I could claim I'd already edited, and what better place to look than Disney?

Only *Snow White* had a cottage full of beer tankards and a dungeon full of wine goblets and deadly potions. *Sleeping Beauty* was no better—it had a splatted royal steward who'd drunk himself literally under the table—and *Pinocchio* not only drank beer but smoked cigars the Anti-Smoking League had somehow missed. Even *Dumbo* got drunk.

But animation wipes are comparatively easy, and all *Alice in Wonderland* had was a few smoke rings, so I was able to finish off the dozen and replenish *my* stock of deadly potions so at least I didn't have to watch *Fantasia* cold sober. And a good thing, too. The *Pastoral Symphony* sequence in *Fantasia* was so full of wine it took me five days to clean it up, after which I went back to *The Philadelphia Story* and stared at Jimmy Stewart, trying to think of some way to salvage him, and then gave up and waited for my skids suspension to be over.

As soon as it was, I went out to Burbank to apologize to Alis, but more time must have gone by than I realized because there was a CG class cramming the unstacked chairs, and when I asked one of the hackates where Michael Caine and the film hist class had gone, he said, "That was last semester."

I stocked up on chooch and went to the next party and asked Heada for Alis's class schedule.

"I don't do chooch anymore," Heada said. She was wearing a tight sweater and skirt and black-framed glasses. Marilyn Monroe in *How to Marry a Millionaire*. "Why can't you leave her alone? She's not hurting anybody."

"I want—" I said, but I didn't know what I wanted. No, that wasn't true. What I wanted was to find a movie that didn't have a single AS in it. Only there weren't any.

"The Ten Commandments," I said, back in my room again.

There was drinking in the golden-calf scene and assorted references to "the wine of violence," but it was better than *The Philadelphia Story*. I laid in a supply of grappa and asked for a list of biblical epics, and went to work playing Charlton Heston—deleting vineyards and calling a halt to Roman orgies. Vengeance is mine, saith the Lord.

SCENE: Exterior of the Hardy house in summer. Picket fence, maple tree, flowers by front door. Slow dissolve to autumn. Leaves falling. Tight focus on a leaf and follow it down.

LA-LA-LAND IS A LOT LIKE THE SKIDS. YOU STAND STILL AND stare at a screen, or, worse, your own reflection, and after a while you're somewhere else.

The parties continued, packed with Marilyns and studio execs. Fred Astaire stayed in litigation, Heada avoided me, I drank. In excellent company. Gangsters drank, Navy lieutenants, little old ladies, sweet young things, doctors, lawyers, Indian chiefs. Fredric March, Jean Arthur, Spencer Tracy, Susan Hayward, Jimmy Stewart. And not just in *The Philadelphia Story*. The all-American, "shucks, wah-ah-all," do-the-honorable-thing boy next door got regularly splatted. Aquavit in *The Man Who Shot Liberty Valance,* brandy in *Bell, Book and Candle,* "likker" straight from the jug in *How the West Was Won*. In *It's a Wonderful Life,* he got drunk enough to get thrown out of a bar and ran his car into a tree. In *Harvey,* he spent the entire film pleasantly tipsy, and what in hell was I supposed to do when I got to that movie? What in hell was I supposed to do in general?

Somewhere in there, Heada came to see me. "I've got a question," she said, standing in the door.

"Does this mean you're over being mad at me?" I said.

"Because you practically broke my arms? Because you thought the whole time you were popping me I was somebody else? What's to be mad about?"

"Heada . . ." I said.

"It's okay. Happens to me all the time. I should open a simsex parlor." She came in and sat down on the bunk. "I've got a question."

"I'll answer yours if you answer mine," I said.

"I don't know where she is."

"You know everything."

"She dropped out. The word is, she's working down on Hollywood Boulevard."

"Doing what?"

"I don't know. Probably not dancing in the movies, which should make you happy. You were always trying to talk her out of–"

I cut in with, "What's your question?"

"I watched that movie you told me I was playing a part in. *Rear Window* with Thelma Ritter? And all the meddling you said she did, telling him to mind his own business, telling him not to get involved. It was good advice. She was just trying to help."

"What's your question?"

"I watched this other movie. *Casablanca.* It's about this guy who has a bar in Africa someplace during World War II, and his old girlfriend shows up, only she's married to this other guy–"

"I know the plot," I said. "What part don't you understand?"

"All of it," she said. "Why the bar guy–"

"Humphrey Bogart," I said.

"Why Humphrey Bogart drinks all the time, why he says he won't help her and then he does, why he tells her she can't stay. If the two of them are so splatted about each other, why can't she stay?"

"There was a war on," I said. "They both had work to do."

"And this work was more important than the two of them?"

"Yeah," I said, but I didn't believe it, in spite of Rick's whole "hill of beans" speech. Ilsa's lending moral support to her husband, Rick's fighting in the Resistance weren't more important. They were a substitute. They were what you did when you couldn't have what you wanted. "The Nazis would get them," I said.

"Okay," she said doubtfully. "So they can't stay together. But why can't he still pop her before she leaves?"

"Standing there at the airport?"

"No," she said, very serious. "Before. Back at the bar."

Because he can't have her, I thought. *And he knows it.*

"Because of the Hays Office," I said.

"In real life, she would have given him a pop."

"That's a comforting thought," I said. "But the movies aren't real life. And they can't tell you how people feel. They've got to show you. Valentino rolling his eyes, Rhett sweeping Scarlett off her feet, Lillian Gish clutching her heart. Bogie loves Ingrid and can't have her." I could see her looking blank again. "The bar owner loves his old girlfriend, so they have to *show* you by not letting him touch her or even give her a good-bye kiss. He has to just stand there and look at her."

"Like you drinking all the time and falling off the skids," she said.

Now it was my turn to look blank.

"The night Alis brought you back to my room, the night you were so splatted."

I still didn't get it.

"Showing the feelings," Heada said. "You trying to walk through the skids screen and nearly getting killed and Alis pulling you out."

SCENE: Exterior. The Hardy house. Wind whirls the dead leaves. Slow dissolve to a bare-branched tree. Snow. Winter.

I'd apparently had quite a night that night. I had tried to walk through the skids wall like a druggate on too much rave and then popped the wrong person. A wonderful performance, Andrew.

And Alis had saved me. I took the skids down to Hollywood Boulevard to look for her, checking at Screen Test City and at A Star Is Born, which had a River Phoenix look-alike working there. The Happy Endings booth had changed its name to Happily Ever After and was featuring *Doctor Zhivago,* Omar Sharif and Julie Christie in the field of flowers, smiling and holding a baby. A knot of half-interested tourates were watching it.

"I'm looking for a face," I said.

"Take your pick," the guy said. "Lara, Scarlett, Marilyn—"

"We were down here a few months ago," I said, trying to jog his memory. "We talked about *Casablanca*. . . ."

"I got *Casablanca,*" he said. "I got *Wuthering Heights, Love Story*—"

"This face," I interrupted. "She's about so high, light brown hair—"

"Freelancer?" he said.

"No," I said. "Never mind."

I walked on. There was nothing else on this side except VR caves. I stood there and thought about them, and about the sim-sex parlors farther down and the freelancers hustling out in front of them in torn net leotards, and then went back to Happily Ever After.

"Casablanca," I said, pushing in front of the tourates, who'd decided to get in line. I slapped down my card.

The guy led me inside. "You got a happy ending for it?" he asked.

"You bet."

He sat me down in front of the comp, an ancient-looking Wang. "Now what you do is push this button, and your choices'll come up on the screen. Push the one you want. Good luck."

I rotated the airplane forty degrees, flattened it to two-dimensional, and made it look like the cardboard it had been. I'd never seen a fog machine. I settled for a steam engine, spewing out great belching puffs of cloud, and ff'd to the three-quarter shot of Bogie telling Ingrid, "We'll always have Paris."

"Expand frame perimeter," I said, and started filling in their feet, Ingrid in flats and Bogie in lifts, big, chunky blocks of wood strapped to his shoes with pieces of—

"What in hell do you think you're doing?" the guy said, bursting in.

"Just trying to inject a little reality into the proceedings," I said.

He shoved me out of the chair and started pushing keys. "Get out of here."

The tourates who'd been ahead of me were standing in front of the screen, and a little crowd had formed around them.

"The plane was cardboard and the airplane mechanics were midgets," I said. "Bogie was only five four. Fred Astaire was the son of an immigrant brewery worker. He only had a sixth-grade education."

The guy emerged from the booth steaming like my fog machine.

"'Here's looking at you, kid' took seventeen takes," I said, heading toward the skids. "None of it's real. It's all done with mirrors."

SCENE: Exterior. The Hardy house in winter. Dirty snow on roof, lawn, piled on either side of front walk. Slow dissolve to spring.

I don't remember whether I went back down to Hollywood Boulevard again. I know I went to the parties, hoping Alis would show up in the doorway again, but not even Heada was there.

In between, I raped and pillaged and looked for something easy to fix. There wasn't anything. Sobering up the doctor in *Stagecoach* ruined the giving birth scene. *D.O.A.* went dead on arrival without Edmond O'Brien slugging back shots of bourbon, and *The Thin Man* disappeared altogether.

I called up the menu again, looking for something AS-free, something clean-cut and all-American. Like Alis's musicals.

"Musicals," I said, and the menu chopped itself into categories and put up a list. I scrolled through it.

Not *Carousel*. Billy Bigelow was a lush. So were Ava Gardner in *Show Boat* and Van Johnson in *Brigadoon*. *Guys and Dolls*? No dice. Marlon Brando'd gotten a missionary splatted on rum. *Gigi*? It was full of liquor and cigars, not to mention "The Night They Invented Champagne."

Seven Brides for Seven Brothers? Maybe. It didn't have any saloon scenes or "Belly Up to the Bar, Boys" numbers. Maybe some applejack at the barnraising or in the cabin, nothing that couldn't be taken out with a simple wipe.

"Seven Brides for Seven Brothers," I said to the comp, and poured myself some of the bourbon I'd bought for *Giant*. Howard Keel rode into town, married Jane Powell, and they started up into the mountains in his wagon. I could ff over this whole section—Howard was hardly likely to pull out a jug and offer Jane a swig, but I let it run at regular speed while she twittered on to Howard about her hopes and plans. Which were going to be smashed as soon as she found out she was supposed to cook and clean for his six mangy brothers. Howard giddyapped the make-believe horses and looked uncomfortable.

"That's right, Howard. Don't tell her," I said. "She won't listen to you anyway. She's got to find out for herself."

They arrived at the cabin. I'd expected at least one of the brothers to have a corncob pipe, but they didn't. There was some roughhousing, another song, and then a long stretch of pure wholesomeness till the barnraising.

I poured myself another bourbon and leaned forward, watching for homespun dissipation. Jane Powell handed pies and cakes out of the wagon, and a straw-covered jug I'd have to turn into a pot of beans or something, and they went into the barnraising number Alis had asked for the night I met her. "Ff to end of music," I said, and then, "Wait," which wasn't a command, and they continued galloping through the dance, finished, and started in on raising the barn in record time.

"Stop," I said. "Back at 96," I said, and rew'd to the beginning of the dance. "Forward realtime," I said, and there she was. Alis. In a pink gingham dress and white stockings, with her backlit hair pulled back into a bun.

"Freeze," I said.

It's the booze, I thought. Ray Milland in *Lost Weekend,* seeing pink elephants. Or some effect of the klieg, a delayed flash or something, superimposing Alis's face over the dancers like it had been over the figures of Fred Astaire and Eleanor Powell dancing on the polished floor.

And how often was this going to happen? Every time somebody went into a dance routine? Every time a face or a hair ribbon or a flaring skirt reminded me of that first flash? Deboozing Mayer's movies was bad enough. I didn't think I could take it if I had to look at Alis, too.

I turned the screen off and then on again, like I was trying to debug a program, but she was still there.

I watched the dance again, looking at her face carefully, and then triple-timed to the scene where the brides get kidnapped. The dancer, her light brown hair covered by a bonnet, looked like Alis but not *like* her. I triple-timed to the next dance number, the girls doing ballet steps in their pantaloons and white stockings this time, no bonnets, but whatever it was, her hair or the music or the flare of her skirt, had passed, and she was just a girl who looked like Alis. A girl, who, unlike Alis, had gotten to dance in the movies.

I ff'd through the rest of the movie, but there weren't any more dance numbers and no sign of Alis, and this was all Another Lesson, Andrew, in not mixing bourbon with *Rio Bravo* tequila.

"Beginning credits," I said, and went back and wiped the bottle in the boardinghouse scene and then triple-timed to the barn-raising again to turn the jug into a pan of cornbread, and then thought I'd better watch the rest of the scene to make sure the jug wasn't visible in any of the other shots.

"Print and send," I said, "and forward realtime."

And there she was again. Dancing in the movies.

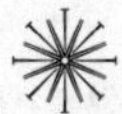

MOVIE CLICHE #15: The Hangover.
(Usually follows #14: The Party.)
Headache, jumping at loud noises, flinching at daylight.

SEE: *The Thin Man, The Tender Trap, After the Thin Man, McLintock!, Another Thin Man, The Philadelphia Story, Song of the Thin Man.*

I ACCESSED HEADA, NO VISUAL. "DO YOU KNOW OF ANYTHING that can sober me up?"

"Fast or painless?"

"Fast."

"Ridigaine," she said promptly. "What's up?"

"Nothing's up," I said. "Mayer's bugging me to work harder on his movies, and I decided the AS's are slowing me down. Do you have any?"

"I'll have to ask around," she said. "I'll get some and bring it over."

That's not necessary, I wanted to say, which would only make her more suspicious. "Thanks," I said.

While I was waiting for her, I called up the credits. They weren't much help. There were seven brides, after all, and the only ones I knew were Jane Powell and Ruta Lee, who'd been in every B picture made in the seventies. Dorcas was Julie Newmeyer, who'd later changed her name to Julie Newmar. When I went back and looked at the barnraising scene again, it was obvious which one she was.

I watched it, listening for the other characters' names. The little blonde Russ Tamblyn was in love with was named Alice, and Dorcas was the tall brunette. I ff'd to the kidnapping scene and matched the other girls to their characters' names. The one in the pink dress was Virginia Gibson.

Virginia Gibson. "Screen Actors Guild directory," I said, and gave it the name.

Virginia Gibson had been in an assortment of movies, including *Athena* and something called *I Killed Wild Bill Hickok*.

"Musicals," I said, and the list shrank to five. No, four. *Funny Face* had Fred Astaire in it, which meant it was in litigation.

There was a knock on the door. I blanked the screen, then decided that would be a dead giveaway. "*Notorious,*" I said, and then chickened out. What if Ingrid Bergman had Alis's face, too? "Cancel," I said, and tried to think of another movie, any movie. Except *Athena*.

"Tom, are you okay?" Heada called through the door.

"Coming," I said, staring at the blank screen. *Saratoga Trunk*? No, that had Ingrid in it, too, and anyway, if this was going to happen all the time, I'd better know it before I took anything else.

"*Notorious,*" I said softly. "Frame 54-119," and waited for Ingrid's face to come up.

"Tom!" Heada shouted. "Is something wrong?"

Cary Grant went out of the ballroom, and Ingrid gazed after him, looking anxious and like she was about to cry. And looking like Ingrid, which was a relief.

"Tom!" Heada said, and I opened the door.

Heada came in and handed me some blue capsules. "Take two. With water. Why didn't you answer the door?"

"I was getting rid of the evidence," I said, pointing at the screen. "Thirty-four champagne bottles."

"I watched that movie," she said, going over to the screen. "It's set in Brazil. It's got stock shots of Rio de Janeiro and Sugarloaf."

"Right as always," I said, and then, casually, "Speaking of which, you know everything, Heada. Do you know if Fred Astaire's been copyrighted yet?"

"No," she said. "ILMGM's appealing."

"How long before these ridigaine take effect?" I said before she could ask why I wanted to know about Fred Astaire.

"Depends on how much you've got in your system," she said. "The way you've been popping it, six weeks."

"Six *weeks*?"

"I'm kidding," she said. "Four hours, maybe less. Are you sure you want to do this? What if you start flashing again?"

I didn't ask her how she knew I'd been flashing. This was, after all, Heada.

She handed me the glass. "Drink lots of water. And pee as much as you can," she said. "What's really up?"

"Slashing and burning," I said, turning back to the frozen screen. I cut out another champagne bottle.

She leaned over my shoulder. "Is this the scene where they run out of champagne, and Claude Rains goes down to the wine cellar and catches Cary Grant?"

"Not when I get through with it," I said. "The champagne's going to be ice cream. What do you think, should the uranium be hidden in the ice-cream freezer or the bag of rock salt?"

She looked at me seriously. "I *think* there's something wrong. What is it?"

"I'm four weeks behind on Mayer's list, and he's twitching down my neck, that's what's wrong. Are you sure these are ridigaine?" I said, peering at the capsules. "They aren't marked."

"I'm sure," she said, still looking suspiciously at me.

I popped the capsules in my mouth and reached for the bourbon.

Heada snatched it out of my hand. "You take them with *water.*" She went into the bathroom, and I could hear the gurgle of the bourbon being poured down the drain.

She came out of the bathroom and handed me a glass of water. "Drink as much as you can. It'll help flush your system faster. No alcohol." She opened the closet, felt around inside, pulled out a bottle of vodka.

"*No* alcohol," she said, unscrewing the cap, and went back into the bathroom to pour it out. "Any other bottles?"

"Why?" I said, sitting down on the bed. "You decide to switch over from chooch?"

"I told you, I quit," she said. "Stand up."

I did, and she knelt down and started fishing under the bed.

"Which is how I know how the ridigaine's going to make you feel," she said, pulling out a bottle of champagne. "You'll want a drink, but don't. You'll just toss it. And I mean toss it." She fumbled with the cork on the bottle. "So don't drink. And don't try to do anything. Lie down as soon as you start feeling anything, headache, shakes. And stay there. You might have halluces. Snakes, monsters . . ."

"Six-foot-tall rabbits named Harvey," I said.

"I'm not kidding," she said. "I felt like I was going to die when I took it. And chooch is a lot easier to quit than alcohol."

"So why'd you quit?" I said.

She gave me a wry look and went back to messing with the cork. "I thought it would make somebody notice me."

"And did they?"

"No," she said, and went back to messing with the cork. "Why did you call and ask me to bring you some ridigaine?"

"I told you," I said. "Mayer—"

She popped the cork. "Mayer's in New York, pimping support for his new boss, who, the word has it, is on the way out. The rumor is, the ILMGM execs don't like his high-handed moralizing. At least when it applies to them." She poured out the champagne and came back in the room. "Any other champagne?"

"Lots," I said, and went over to the comp. "Next frame," I said, and a tubful of champagne bottles came up on the screen. "You want to pour these out, too?" I turned, grinning.

She was looking at me seriously. "What's really up?"

"Next frame," I said. The screen shifted to Ingrid, looking anxious, her hair like a halo. I took the champagne glass out of her hand.

"You saw her again, didn't you?" she said.

Everything.

"Who?" I said, even though it was hopeless. "Yeah," I said. "I saw her." I shut off *Notorious*. "Come here," I said, "I want you to look at something."

"*Seven Brides for Seven Brothers,*" I said to the comp. "Frame 25-118."

The screen lit Jane Powell, sitting in the wagon, holding a basket.

"Forward realtime," I said, and Jane Powell handed the basket to Julie Newmar.

"I thought this was going into litigation," Heada said over my shoulder.

"Over who?" I said. "Jane Powell or Howard Keel?"

"Russ Tamblyn," she said, pointing at him. He'd climbed on the wagon and was gazing soulfully at the little blonde, Alice. "Virtusonic's been using him in snuffporn movies, and ILMGM doesn't like it. They're claiming copyright abuse."

Russ Tamblyn, looking young and innocent, which was probably the point, went off with Alice, and Howard Keel lifted Jane Powell down off the buckboard.

"Stop," I said to the computer. "I want you to look at this next scene," I said to Heada. "At the faces. Forward realtime," I said, and the dancers formed two lines and bowed and curtsied to each other.

I don't know what I'd expected Heada to do—gasp and clutch her heart like Lillian Gish maybe. Or turn to me halfway through and ask, "What exactly is it I'm supposed to be looking for?"

She didn't do either. She watched the entire scene, still and silent, her face almost as focused on the screen as Alis's had been, and then said quietly, "I didn't think she'd do it."

For a moment, I couldn't register what she said for the roaring in my head, the roaring that was saying, "It *is* her. It's not a flash. It *is* her."

"All that talk about finding a dance teacher," Heada was saying. "All that stuff about Fred Astaire. I never thought she'd—"

"Never thought she'd do what?" I said blankly.

"This," she said, waving her hand vaguely at the screen, where the sides of the barn were going up. "That she'd end up as somebody's popsy," she said. "That she'd sign on. Give up. Sell out." She gestured at the screen again. "Did Mayer say which of the studio execs you were doing it for?"

"I didn't do it," I said.

"Well, *somebody* did it," she said. "Mayer must've asked Vincent or somebody. I thought you said she didn't want her face pasted on somebody else's."

"She didn't. She doesn't," I said. "This isn't a paste-up. It's her, dancing."

She looked at the screen. A cowboy brought his hammer down hard on Russ Tamblyn's thumb.

"She wouldn't sell out," I said.

"To quote a friend of mine," she said, "everybody sells out."

"No," I said. "People sell out to get what they want. Getting her face pasted onto somebody else's body isn't what she wanted. She wanted to dance in the movies."

"Maybe she needed the money," Heada said, looking at the screen. Someone whacked Howard Keel with a board, and Russ Tamblyn took a poke at him.

"Maybe she figured out she couldn't have what she wanted."

"No," I said, thinking about her standing there on Hollywood Boulevard, her face set. "You don't understand. No."

"Okay," she said placatingly. "She didn't sell out. It isn't a paste-up." She waved at the screen. "So what is it? How'd she get on there if somebody didn't paste her in?"

Howard Keel shoved a pair of brawlers into the corner, and the barn fell apart, collapsing into a clatter of boards and chagrin. "I don't know," I said.

We both stood there a minute, looking at the wreckage.

"Can I see the scene again?" Heada said.

"Frame 25-200, forward realtime," I said, and Howard Keel reached up again to lift Jane Powell down. The dancers formed their lines. And there was Alis, dancing in the movies.

"Maybe it isn't her," Heada said. "That's why you asked me to bring over the ridigaine, wasn't it, because you thought it might be the alcohol?"

"You see her, too."

"I know," she said, frowning, "but I'm not really sure I know what she looks like. I mean, the times I saw her I was pretty splatted, and so were you. And it wasn't all that many times, was it?"

That party, and the time Heada sent her to ask me for the access, and the episode of the skids. Memorable occasions, all.

"No," I said.

"So it could be it's just somebody else who looks like her. Her hair's darker than that, isn't it?"

"A wig," I said. "Wigs and makeup can make you look really different."

"Yeah," Heada said, as if that proved something. "Or really alike. Maybe this person's wearing a wig and makeup that makes her look like Alis. Who is it, anyway? In the movie?"

"Virginia Gibson," I said.

"Maybe this Virginia Gibson and Alis just look alike. Was she in any other movies? Virginia Gibson, I mean? If she was, we could look at them and see what she looks like, and if this is her or not." She looked concernedly at me. "You'd better let the ridigaine work first, though. Are you having any symptoms yet? Headache?"

"No," I said, looking at the screen.

"Well, you will in a few minutes." She pulled the blankets off the bed. "Lie down, and I'll get you some water. Ridigaine's fast, but it's rough. The best thing is if you can—"

"Sleep it off," I said.

She brought a glass of water in and set it by the bed. "Access me if you get the shakes and start seeing things."

"According to you, I already am."

"I didn't *say* that. I just said you should check out this Virginia Gibson before you jump to any conclusions. *After* the ridigaine does its stuff."

"Meaning that when I'm sober, it won't look like her."

"Meaning that when you're sober, you'll at least be able to see her." She looked steadily at me. "Do you want it to be her?"

"I think I will lie down," I said to get her to leave. "My head aches." I sat down on the bed.

"It's starting to work," she said triumphantly. "Access me if you need anything."

"I will," I said, and lay back.

She looked around the room. "You don't have any more liquor in here, do you?"

"Gallons," I said, gesturing toward the screen. "Bottles, flasks, kegs, decanters. You name it, it's in there."

"It'll just make it worse if you drink anything."

"I know," I said, putting my hand over my eyes. "Shakes, pink elephants, six-foot-tall rabbits, 'and how are you, Mr. Wilson?' "

"*Access* me," she said, and left, finally.

I waited five minutes for her to come back and tell me to be sure and piss, and then another five for the snakes and rabbits to show up, or, worse, Fred and Eleanor, dressed in white and dancing side by side. And thinking about what Heada'd said. If it wasn't a paste-up, what was it? And it couldn't be a paste-up. Heada hadn't heard Alis talking about wanting to dance in the movies. She hadn't seen her, that night down on Hollywood Boulevard, when I offered her a chance at one. She could have been digitized that night, been Ginger Rogers, Ann Miller, anybody she wanted. Even Eleanor Powell. Why would she have suddenly changed her mind and decided she wanted to be a dancer nobody'd ever heard of? An actress who'd only appeared in a handful of movies. One of which starred Fred Astaire.

"We're *this* close to having time travel," the exec had said, his thumb and finger almost touching.

And what if Alis, who was willing to do anything to dance in the movies, who was willing to practice in a cramped classroom with a tiny monitor and work nights in a tourate trap, had talked one of the time-travel hackates into letting her be a guinea pig? What if Alis had talked him into sending her back to 1954, dressed in a green weskit and short gloves, and then, instead of coming back like she was supposed to, had changed her name to Virginia Gibson and gone over to MGM to audition for a part in *Seven Brides for Seven Brothers*? And then gone on to be in six other movies. One of which was *Funny Face*. With Fred Astaire.

I sat up, slowly, so I wouldn't turn my headache into anything worse, and went over to the terminal and called up *Funny Face*.

Heada had said Fred Astaire was still in litigation, and he was. I put a watch-and-warn on both the movie and Fred in case the case got settled. If Heada was right—and when wasn't she?—Warner would turn around and file immediately, but if there was a glitch or Warner's lawyers were busy with Russ Tamblyn, there might be a window. I set the watch-and-warn to beep me and called up the list of Virginia Gibson's musicals again.

Starlift was a World War II b-and-w, which wouldn't give me as clear an image as color, and *She's Back on Broadway* was in litigation, too, for someone I'd never heard of. That left *Athena, Painting the Clouds with Sunshine,* and *Tea for Two,* none of which I could remember ever seeing.

When I called up *Athena,* I could see why. It was a cross between *One Touch of Venus* and *You Can't Take It with You,* with lots of floating chiffon and health-food eccentrics and almost no dancing. Virginia Gibson, in green chiffon, was supposed to be Niobe, the goddess of jazz and tap or something. Whatever she was, it wasn't Alis. It looked like her, especially with her hair pulled back in a Greek ponytail. "And with a fifth of bourbon in you," Heada would have said. And a double dose of ridigaine. Even then, it didn't look as much like her as the dancer in the barnraising scene. I called up *Seven Brides,* and the screen stayed silver for a long moment and then started scrolling legalese. "This movie is currently in litigation and unavailable for viewing."

Well, that settled that. By the time the courts had decided to let Russ Tamblyn be sliced and diced, I'd be chooch-free and able to see it was just somebody who looked like her, or not even that. A trick of lights and makeup.

And there was no point in slogging through any more musicals to drive the point home. Any resemblance was purely alcoholic, and I should do what Doc Heada said, lie down and wait for it to pass. And then go back to slicing and dicing myself. I should call up *Notorious* and get it over with.

"*Tea for Two,*" I said.

Tea was a Doris Day pic, and I wondered if she was on Alis's bad-dancer list. She deserved to be. She smirked her way toothily through a tap routine with Gene Nelson, set in a rehearsal hall Alis would have killed for, all floor space and mirrors and no stacks of desks. There was a terrible Latin version of "Crazy Rhythm," Gordon MacRae singing "I Only Have Eyes for You," and then Virginia Gibson's big number.

And there was no question of her being Alis. With her hair down, she didn't even look that much like her. Or else the ridigaine was kicking in.

The routine was Hollywood's idea of ballet, more chiffon and a lot of twirling around, not the kind of routine Alis would have bothered with. *If* she'd had ballet back in Meadowville, and not just jazz and tap, but she hadn't, and Virginia obviously had, so Alis wasn't Virginia, and I was sober, and it was back to the bottles.

"Forward 64," I said, and watched Doris smirk her way through the title number and an unnecessary reprise. The next number was a big production number. Virginia wasn't in it, and I started to ff again and then stopped.

"Rew to music cue," I said, and watched the production number, counting the frame numbers. A blond couple stepped forward, did a series of toe slides, and stepped back again, and a dark-haired guy and a redhead in a white pleated skirt kicked forward and went into a side-by-side Charleston. She had curly hair and a tied-in-front blouse, and the two of them put their hands on their knees and did a series of cross kicks. "Frame 75-004, forward 12," I said, and watched the routine in slow motion.

"Enhance quadrant 2," and watched the red hair fill the screen, even though there wasn't any need for an enhancement, or for the slowmo, either. No question at all of who it was.

I had known the instant I saw her, the same way I had in the barnraising scene, and it wasn't the booze (of which there was at least fifteen minutes' worth less in my system) or klieg, or a passing resemblance enhanced with rouge and eyebrow pencil. It was Alis. Which was impossible.

"Last frame," I said, but this was the Good Old Days when the chorus line didn't get into the credits, and the copyright date had to be deciphered. MCML. 1950.

I went back through the movie, going to freeze frame and enhance every time I spotted red hair, but I didn't see her again. I ff'd to the Charleston number and watched it again, trying to come up with a theory.

Okay. The hackate had sent her to 1950 (scratch that—the copyright was for the release date—had sent her to 1949) and she had waited around for four years, dancing chorus parts and palling around with Virginia Gibson, waiting for her chance to clunk Virginia on the head, stuff her behind a set, and take her place in *Brides*. So she could impress the producer of *Funny Face* with her dancing so that he'd offer her a part, and she'd finally get to dance with Fred, if only in the same production number.

Even splatted on chooch, I couldn't have bought that one. But it was her, so there had to be an explanation. Maybe, in between chorus jobs, Alis had gotten a job as a warmbody. They'd had them back then. They were called stand-ins, and maybe she got to be Virginia Gibson's because they looked alike, and Alis had bribed her to let her take her place, just for one number, or had connived to have Virginia miss a shooting session. Anne Baxter in *All About Eve*. Or maybe Virginia had an AS problem, and when she'd showed up drunk, Alis had had to take her place.

That theory wasn't much better. I called up the menu again. If Alis had gotten one chorus job, she might have gotten others. I scanned through the musicals, trying to remember which ones had chorus numbers. *Singin' in the Rain* did. That party scene I'd taken all that champagne out of.

I called up the record of changes to find the frame number and ff'd through the nonchampagne, to Donald O'Connor's saying, "You have to show a movie at a party. It's a Hollywood law," through said movie, to the start of the chorus number.

Girls in skimpy pink skirts and flapper hats ran onstage to the tune of "You Are My Lucky Star" and a bad camera angle. I was going to have to do an enhance to see their faces clearly. But there wasn't any need to. I'd found Alis.

And she might have managed to bribe Virginia Gibson. She might even have managed to stuff her and the *Tea for Two* redhead behind their respective sets. But Debbie Reynolds hadn't had an AS problem, and if Alis had crammed her behind a set, *somebody* would have noticed.

It wasn't time travel. It was something else, a comp-generated illusion of some kind in which she'd somehow managed to dance and get it on film. In which case, she hadn't disappeared forever into the past. She was still in Hollywood. And I was going to find her.

"Off," I said to the comp, grabbed my jacket, and flung myself out the door.

MOVIE CLICHE #419: The Blocked Escape. HERO/HEROINE on the run, near escape with bad guys, eludes them, nearly home-free, villain looms up suddenly, asks, "Going somewhere?"

SEE: *The Great Escape, The Empire Strikes Back, North by Northwest, The 39 Steps.*

HEADA WAS STANDING OUTSIDE THE DOOR, ARMS FOLDED, TAPping her foot. Rosalind Russell as the Mother Superior in *The Trouble with Angels.*

"You're supposed to be lying down," she said.

"I feel fine."

"That's because the alcohol isn't out of your system yet," she said. "Sometimes it takes longer than others. Have you peed?"

"Yes," I said. "Buckets. Now if you'll excuse me, Nurse Ratched . . ."

"Wherever you're going, it can wait till you're clean," she said, blocking my way. "I mean it. Ridigaine's not anything to fool with." She steered me back into the room. "You need to stay here and rest. Where were you going anyway? To see Alis? Because if you were, she's not there. She's dropped all her classes and moved out of her dorm."

And in with Mayer's boss, she meant. "I wasn't going to see Alis."

"Where *were* you going?"

It was useless to lie to Heada, but I tried it anyway. "Virginia Gibson was in *Funny Face*. I was going out to try to find a copy of it."

"Why can't you get it off the fibe-op?"

"Fred Astaire's in it. That's why I asked you if he was out of litigation." I let that sink in for a couple of frames. "You said it might just be a likeness. I wanted to see if it's Alis or just somebody who looks like her."

"So you were going out to look for a pirated copy?" Heada said as if she almost believed me. "I thought you said she was in six musicals. They aren't all in litigation, are they?"

"There weren't any close-ups in *Athena,*" I said, and hoped she wouldn't ask why I couldn't enhance. "And you know how she is about Fred Astaire. If she's going to be in anything, it'd be *Funny Face.*"

None of this made any sense, since the idea was supposedly to find something Virginia Gibson was in, not Alis, but Heada nodded when I mentioned Fred Astaire. "I can get you one," she said.

"Thanks," I said. "It doesn't even have to be digitized. Tape'll work." I led her to the door. "I'll stay here and lie down and let the ridigaine do its stuff."

She crossed her arms again.

"I swear," I said. "I'll give you my key. You can lock me in."

"You'll lie down?"

"Promise," I lied.

"You won't," she said, "and you'll wish you had." She sighed. "At least you won't be on the skids. Give me the key."

I handed her the card.

"Both of them," she said.

I handed her the other card.

"Lie *down,*" she said, and shut the door and locked me in.

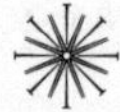

MOVIE CLICHE #86: Locked In.

SEE: *Broken Blossoms, Wuthering Heights, The Phantom Foe, The Palm Beach Story, The Man with the Golden Arm, The Collector.*

WELL, I NEEDED MORE PROOF ANYWAY BEFORE I CONFRONTED Alis, and I was starting to feel the headache I'd lied to Heada about having. I went into the bathroom and followed orders and then laid down on the bed and called up *Singin' in the Rain*.

There weren't any telltale matte lines or pixel shadows, and when I did a noise check, there weren't any signs of uneven degradation. Which didn't prove anything. I could do undetectable paste-ups with a fifth of William Powell's *Thin Man* rye in me.

I needed more data. Preferably something full-length and in one continuous take, but Fred was still in litigation. I called up the list of musicals again. Alis had been wearing a bustle the day I went out to see her, which meant a period piece. Not *Meet Me in St. Louis*. She had said there wasn't any dancing in it. *Show Boat*, maybe. Or *Gigi*.

I went through both of them, looking for parasols and backlit hair, but it took forever, and ff'ing made me dizzy.

"Global search," I said, pressing my hand to my eyes. "Dance routines," and spent the next ten minutes explaining to the comp what a dance routine was. "Forward at 40," I said, and took it through *Carousel.*

The program worked okay, though this was still going to take forever. I debated eliminating ballet, decided the comp wouldn't have any more idea than Hollywood did of what it was, and added an override instead.

"Instant to next routine, cue," I said. "Next, please," and called up *On Moonlight Bay*.

Bay was another Doris Day toothfest, so even with the override it took far too long to get through it, but at least I could "next, please" when I saw there weren't any bustles.

"*Vernon and Irene Castle,*" I said. No, that was a Fred Astaire. *The Harvey Girls*?

I got more legalese. Was everybody in litigation? I called up the menu, scanning it for period pieces.

"*In the Good Old Summertime,*" I said, and then was sorry. It was a Judy Garland, and Alis had been right, there wasn't any dancing in Judy Garland movies. I tried to remember what else she'd said that night in my room and what movies she'd asked for. *On the Town*.

It wasn't in litigation. But her nemesis, Gene Kelly, was in it, leaping around in a white sailor suit and making it look hard. "Next, please," I said, and Ann Miller appeared in a low-cut dress, apple cheeks, and Marilyn figure, tapping her way between dinosaur skeletons. Even with makeup and digital padding, Alis couldn't have been mistaken for her, and I had the feeling that was important, but the clatter of Ann's taps was making my head pound. I "next, please"d to the Meadowville number Alis had said she liked, Vera-Ellen and the overenergetic Gene Kelly in a soft-shoe. Vera-Ellen was a lot more Alis's size, she even had a hair ribbon, but she wasn't Alis either. "Next, please."

Gene Kelly did one of his overblown ballets, Frank Sinatra and Betty Garrett danced a tango with an Empire State Building telescope, and Ann Miller, in an even more low-cut dress, showed up, and then Vera-Ellen. Wearing the green weskit and black skirt Alis had worn to the party that first night. I sat up.

Vera-Ellen took Gene Kelly's hand and spun away from the camera. "Freeze," I said. "Enhance," and there was no mistaking that backlit hair, and sure enough, when she spun back out of the turn, it was Alis, reaching her hand out, smiling delightedly at Gene.

I asked for a menu of Vera-Ellen movies. "*Belle of New York,*" I said.

Legalese. Fred Astaire. Ditto *Three Little Words*. I finally got *The Kid from Brooklyn,* and went through it number by number, but Alis wasn't in it, and there must be some other logic at work here. What? Gene Kelly? He'd been in both *Singin' in the Rain* and *On the Town*.

"*Anchors Aweigh,*" I said.

Gene's costars were Kathryn Grayson and Jose Iturbi, neither of whom were noted for their dancing ability, so I didn't expect there to be any production numbers. There weren't. Gene Kelly danced with Frank Sinatra, with a chorus line of sailors, with a cartoon mouse.

It was another of his overblown fantasy numbers, this time with an animated background and Tom and Jerry and a lot of pre-CG special effects, but he and Tom the Mouse danced a soft-shoe side by side, hand and paw nearly touching, and it almost looked like the real thing.

I accessed Vincent, decided I didn't want this on the feed, and punched in a key override, wishing there was a way I could find out whether Heada was standing guard without opening the door.

There wasn't, but it was okay. She wasn't there. I locked the door in case she came back, and went down to the party. Vincent was demonstrating a new program to a trio of breathless Marilyns.

"Give it a command," Vincent said, pointing at the screen, where Clint Eastwood, dressed in a striped poncho and a concho-banded hat, was sitting in a chair, his hands at his sides like a puppet's. "Go ahead."

The Marilyns giggled. "Stand," one of them said daringly. Clint got woodenly to his feet.

"Take two steps backward," another Marilyn said.

"Mother, may I?" I said. "Vincent, I need to talk to you." I got between him and the Marilyns. "I need to bluescreen some liveaction into a scene. How do I do that?"

"It's easier to do a scratch construct," he said, looking at the screen where Clint was standing, waiting for orders. "Or a paste-up. What kind of liveaction? Human?"

"Yeah, human," I said, "but a paste-up won't work. So how do I bluescreen it in?"

He shrugged. "Set up a pixar and compositor. Maybe an old Digimatte, if you can find one. The tourate traps use them sometimes. The hard part's the patching–lights, perspective, camera angles, edges."

I'd stopped listening. The A Star Is Born place down on Hollywood Boulevard had had a Digimatte. And Heada'd said Alis had gotten a job down there.

"It still won't be as good as a graphic," he was saying. "But if you've got an expert melder, it's possible."

And a pixar, *and* the comp know-how, *and* the accesses. None of which Alis had. "What if you didn't have accesses? Say you wanted to do it without anyone knowing about it?"

"I thought you had full studio access," he said, suddenly interested. "Did Mayer fire you?"

"This is *for* Mayer. I'm taking the AS's out of a hackate movie,"

I said glibly. "*Rising Sun*. There are too many visual references to do a wipe. I've got to do a whole new scene, and I want it to be authentic."

I was counting on his not having seen the movie, or knowing it was made before accesses, a good bet with somebody who'd turn Clint Eastwood into a marionette. "The hero superimposes a fake image over a real one. To catch a criminal."

He was frowning vaguely. "Somebody breaks into the fibe-op feed in this movie?"

"Yeah," I said. "So how do I make it look like the real thing?"

"Source piracy? You don't," he said. "You have to have studio access."

Nowhere fast. "I don't have to show anything illegal," I said, "just talk about how he finds a bypass around the encryptions or breaks into the authorization guards," but he was already shaking his head.

"It doesn't work like that," he said. "The studios have paid too much for their properties and actors to let source piracy happen, and encryptions, authorization guards, navajos, all those can be gotten around. That's why they went to the fibe-op loop. What goes out comes back in."

Up on the screen, Clint had started moving. I glanced up. He was walking in a figure-eight pattern, hands down, head down. Looping.

"The fibe-op feed sends the signal out and back again in a continuous loop. It's got an ID-lock built in. The lock matches the signal coming in against the one that went out, and if they don't match, it rejects the incoming and substitutes the old one."

"Every frame?" I said, thinking maybe the lock only checked every five minutes, enough time to squeeze in a dance routine.

"Every frame."

"Doesn't that take a ton of memory? A pixel-by-pixel match?"

"Brownian check," he said, but that wasn't much better. The

lock would check random pixels and see if they matched, and there'd be no way to know in advance which ones. The only thing you'd be able to change the image to was another one exactly like it.

"What about when you have accesses?" I said, watching Clint make the circuit, around and around. Boris Karloff in *Frankenstein*.

"In that case, the lock checks the altered image for authorization and then allows it past."

"And there's no way to get a fake access?" I said.

He was looking at the screen irritatedly, as if I was the one who'd set Frankenstein in motion. "Sit," he said. Clint sat.

"Stay," I said.

Vincent glared at me. "What movie did you say this was for?"

"A remake," I said, looking over at the door. Heada was coming in. "Maybe I'll just stay with the wipe," I said, and ducked off toward the stairs.

"I still don't see why you insist on doing it by hand," he called after me. "There's no point. I've got a search-and-destroy program—"

I skidded upstairs and punched in the override, cursing myself for locking the door in the first place, opened it, got in bed, remembered the door was supposed to be locked, locked it, and flung myself back on the bed.

Hurrying had not been a good idea. My head had started to pound like the drums in the Latin number in *Tea for Two*.

I closed my eyes and waited for Heada, but it must not have been her in the doorway, or else she had gotten waylaid by Vincent and his dancing dolls. I called up *Three Sailors and a Girl,* but all the "next, please"s made me faintly seasick. I closed my eyes, waiting for the queasiness to pass, and then opened them again and tried to come up with a theory that didn't belong in a movie.

Alis couldn't have bluescreened herself in like Gene Kelly's mouse. She didn't know anything about comps—she'd been taking Basic CG 101 last fall when I got her class schedule out of Heada. And even if she had somehow mastered melds and shading and rotoscoping, she still didn't have the accesses.

Maybe she'd gotten somebody to help her. But who? The undergrad hackates didn't have accesses either, and Vincent wouldn't have understood why she insisted on doing it by hand.

So it had to be a paste-up. And why not? Maybe Alis had finally realized dancing in the movies was impossible, or maybe Mayer'd promised to find her a dancing teacher if she'd pop his boss. She wouldn't be the first face to come to Hollywood and end up on a casting couch.

But if that were the case, she wouldn't have looked like she did. I called up *On the Town* again and peered at it through my headache. Alis leaped lightly around the Empire State Building, animated and happy. I turned it off and tried to sleep.

If it was a paste-up, she wouldn't have had that focused, intent look. Vincent, programs or no programs, could never have captured that smile.

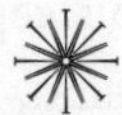

Slow pan from comp screen to clock, showing 11:05, and back to screen. Shot of sailors dancing. Slow pan to clock, showing 3:45.

SOMEWHERE IN THE MIDDLE OF THE NIGHT, IT OCCURRED TO me that there was another reason Mayer couldn't have done a paste-up of Alis. The best reason of all: Heada didn't know about it.

She knew everything, every bit and piece of popsy, every studio move, every takeover rumor. There wasn't anything that got by her. If Alis had given in to Mayer, Heada would have known about it before it happened. And reported it to me, as if it was what I wanted to hear.

And wasn't it? I had told Alis she couldn't have what she wanted, that dancing in the movies was impossible, and it was a paste-up or nothing, and everybody likes to be proven right, don't they?

Especially if they are right. You can't just walk through a movie screen like Mia Farrow in *The Purple Rose of Cairo* and take Virginia Gibson's place. You can't just walk through a looking glass like Charlotte Henry and find yourself dancing with Fred Astaire.

Even if that's what it looks like you're doing. It's a trick of lighting, that's all, and makeup, and too much liquor, too much klieg; and the only cure for that was to follow Heada's orders, piss, drink lots of water, try to sleep.

"*Three Sailors and a Girl,*" I said, and waited for the trick to be revealed.

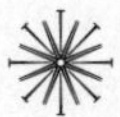

Slow pan from comp screen to clock, showing 4:58, and back to screen. Shot of sailors dancing. Slow pan to clock, showing 7:22.

FEELING BETTER?" HEADA SAID. SHE WAS SITTING ON THE BED, holding a glass of water. "I told you ridigaine was rough."

"Yeah," I said, closing my eyes against the glare from the glass.

"Drink this," she said, and stuck a straw in my mouth. "How's the craving? Bad?"

I didn't want to drink anything, including water. "No."

"You sure?" she said suspiciously.

"I'm sure," I said. I opened my eyes again, and when that went okay, I tried to sit up. "What took you so long?"

"After I found *Funny Face,* I went and talked to one of the ILMGM execs. You were right about its not being Mayer. He's sworn off popsy. He's trying to convince Arthurton he's straight and narrow."

She stuck the straw under my nose again. "I talked to one of the hackates, too. He says there's no way to get liveaction stuff onto the fibe-op source without studio access. He says there are all kinds of securities and privacies and encryptions. He says there are so many, nobody, not even the best hackates, can get past them."

"I know," I said, leaning my head back against the wall. "It's impossible."

"Do you feel good enough to look at the disk?"

I didn't, and there was no point, but Heada put it in and we watched Fred dance circles around Audrey Hepburn and Paris.

The ridigaine was good for something, anyway. Fred was doing a series of swing turns, his feet tapping easily, carelessly, his arms extended, but there wasn't a quiver of a flash or even a soft-focus. My head still ached, but the drumming was gone, replaced by a bleak silence that felt like the aftermath of a flash and had its sharp clarity, its certainty.

I was certain Alis wouldn't have danced in this movie, with its modern dance and its duets, carefully choreographed by Fred to make Audrey Hepburn look like a better dancer than she was. Certain that when Virginia Gibson appeared, she'd be Virginia Gibson, who looked a lot like Alis.

And certain that when I called up *On the Town* and *Tea for Two* and *Singin' in the Rain,* it would still be Alis, no matter how secure the fibe-op loops, no matter how impossible.

Virginia Gibson came on in a gaggle of Hollywood's idea of fashion designers. "You don't see her, do you?" Heada said anxiously.

"No," I said, watching Fred.

"This Virginia Gibson person really does look a lot like Alis," Heada said. "Do you want to try *Seven Brides for Seven Brothers* again, just to make sure?"

"I'm sure," I said.

"Good," she said, standing up briskly. "So, the main thing now that you're clean is to keep busy so you won't think about the craving, and anyway, you need to catch up on Mayer's list before he gets back, and I was thinking maybe I could help you. I've been watching a lot of movies, and I could tell you which ones have AS's in them and where they are. *The Color Purple* has a roadhouse scene where—"

"Heada," I said.

"And *after* you finish the list, maybe you and I could get Mayer to assign us a real remake. I mean, now that we're both clean. You said one time I'd make a great location assistant, and I've been watching a lot of movies. We'd make a great team. You could do the CGs—"

"I need you to do something for me," I said. "There was an ILMGM exec who used to come to the parties who was always using time travel as a line. I need you to find out his name."

"Time travel?" Heada said blankly.

"He said they were *this* close to discovering time travel," I said. "He kept talking about parallel timefeeds."

"You said it wasn't her in *Funny Face,*" she said slowly.

"He kept talking about doing a remake of *Time After Time.*"

She said, still blankly, "You think Alis went back in time?"

"I don't *know,*" I said, and the last word was a shout. "Maybe she found a pair of ruby slippers, maybe she walked up onto the screen like Buster Keaton in *Sherlock Jr.* I don't *know*!"

Heada was looking at me, her eyes full of tears. "But you're going to keep looking for her, aren't you? Even though it's impossible," she said bitterly. "Just like John Wayne in *The Searchers.*"

"And he found Natalie Wood, didn't he?" I said. "Didn't he?" but she was already gone.

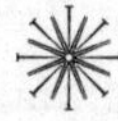

MONTAGE: No sound. HERO, seated at comp, chin on hand, saying, "Next, please," as routine on screen changes. Hula, Latin number, clambake, Hollywood's idea of ballet, hobo number, water ballet, doll dance.

I DIDN'T HAVE ALL THE ALCOHOL OUT OF MY SYSTEM YET. HALF an hour after Heada left, my headache came back with a vengeance. I called up *Two Sailors and a Girl* (or was it *Two Girls and a Sailor*?) and slept for two days straight.

When I got up, I pissed several gallons and then checked to see if Heada had accessed me. She hadn't. I tried to access her, and then Vincent, and started through the movies again.

Alis was in *I Love Melvin,* playing, natch, a chorus girl trying to break into the movies, and in *Let's Dance* and *Two Weeks with Love*. I found her in two Vera-Ellen movies, which I watched twice, convinced that I was somehow missing an important clue, and in *Painting the Clouds with Sunshine,* taking Virginia Gibson's place again in a side-by-side tap routine with Gene Nelson and Virginia Mayo.

I accessed Vincent and asked him about parallel timefeeds. "Is this for *Rising Sun*?" he asked suspiciously.

"*The Time Machine,*" I said. "Paul Newman and Julia Roberts. What *is* a parallel timefeed?" and got an earful of probability and causality and side-by-side universes.

"Every event has a dozen, a hundred, a thousand possible outcomes," he said. "The theory is there's a universe in which every single outcome actually exists."

A universe in which Alis gets to dance in the movies, I thought. *A universe in which Fred Astaire's still alive and the CG revolution never happened.*

I had been looking exclusively through musicals made during the fifties. But if there were parallel timefeeds, and Alis had somehow found a way to get in and out of those other universes, there was no reason she couldn't be in movies made later. Or earlier.

I started through the Busby Berkeleys, short as they were on dancing, and found her tapping without music in *Gold Diggers of 1935* and in the big finale of *42nd Street,* but that was it. I did better (and apparently so had she) in non-Busbys. *Hats Off,* wearing a hat, natch, and *The Show of Shows* and *Too Much Harmony,* "Buckin' the Wind" in a number made for Marilyn, in garters and a white skirt that blew up around her stockinged legs. She was in *Born to Dance,* too, but in the chorus, and I couldn't find her in any other Eleanor Powell movies.

It took me a week to finish the b-and-w's, during which time I couldn't get through to Heada, and she didn't access me. When my comp finally did beep, I didn't wait for her to come on. "Did you find out anything?" I said.

"I found out all right!" Mayer said, twitching. "You haven't sent in a movie in three weeks! I was planning to give the whole package to my boss at next week's meeting, and you're wasting time with *Rising Sun,* which isn't even on the list!"

Which meant Vincent was costarring in the role of Joe Spinell as snitch in *The Godfather II.*

"I needed to replace a couple of scenes," I said. "There were too many visuals to do wipes. One of them's a dance number. You don't know anybody who can dance, do you?" I watched him, looking for some sign, some indication that he remembered

Alis, knew her, had wanted to pop her badly enough that he'd pasted her face in over a dozen dancers'. Nothing. Not even a pause in the twitches.

"There was a face at a couple of the parties a while back," I said. "Pretty, light brown hair, she wanted to dance in the movies."

Nothing. It wasn't Mayer.

"Forget dancers," he said. "Forget *The Time Machine*. Just take the damned alcohol *out*! I want the rest of that list done by Monday, or you'll never work for ILMGM again!"

"You can count on me, Mr. Potter," I said, and let him tell me he was shutting down my credit.

"I want you sober!" he said.

Which, oddly enough, I was.

I took "Moonshine Lullaby" out of *Annie Get Your Gun* and the hookahs out of *Kismet* to show him I'd been listening, and started through the forties, looking for alcohol and Alis, two birds with one ff. She was in *Yankee Doodle Dandy,* and in the hoedown number in *Babes on Broadway,* wearing the pinafore she'd had on the night she'd come to ask me for the disk.

Heada came in while I was watching *Three Little Girls in Blue,* which had an assortment of bustles and Vera-Ellen, but no Alis.

"I found the exec," she said. "He's working for Warner now. He says they're looking at ILMGM as a possible takeover."

"What's his name?" I said.

"He wouldn't tell me anything. He said the reason they haven't rereleased *Somewhere in Time* is because they couldn't decide whether to cast Vivien Leigh or Marilyn Monroe."

"I'll talk to him. What's his name?"

She hesitated. "I talked to the hackates, too. They said last year they were transmitting images through a negative-matter region and got some interference that they thought was a time discrepancy, but they haven't been able to duplicate the results, and now they think it was a transmission from another source."

"How big of a time discrepancy?" I said.

She looked unhappy. "I asked them if they could duplicate the results, could they send a person back into the past, and they said even if it worked, they were only talking about electrons, not atoms, and there was no way anything living could survive a negative-matter region."

Which eliminated parallel timefeeds, and there must be worse to come because Heada was still hovering by the door like Clara Bow in *Wings,* unwilling to tell me the bad news.

"Have you found her in any more movies?" she said.

"Six," I said. "And if it's not time travel, she must have walked up onto the screen like Mia Farrow. Because it's not a paste-up. And it's not Mayer."

"There's another explanation," she said unhappily. "You were pretty splatted there for a while. One of the movies I watched was about a guy who was an alcoholic."

"*The Lost Weekend,*" I said. "Ray Milland," and could already see where this was going.

"He had blackouts when he drank," she said. "He did things and couldn't remember them." She looked at me. "You knew what she looked like. And you had the accesses."

DANA ANDREWS: *[Standing over police sergeant's desk]* She didn't do it, I tell you.

BRODERICK CRAWFORD: Is that so? Then who did?

DANA ANDREWS: I don't know, but I know she couldn't have. She's not that kind of girl.

BRODERICK CRAWFORD: Well, somebody did it. *[Eyes narrowing suspiciously]* Maybe you did it. Where were you when Carson was killed?

DANA ANDREWS: I was out taking a walk.

IT WAS THE LIKELIEST EXPLANATION. I WAS AN EXPERT AT PASTE-ups. And I'd had her face stuck in my head ever since the moment I flashed. And I had full studio access. Motive and opportunity.

I had wanted her, and she had wanted to dance in the movies, and in the wonderful world of CGs, anything is possible. But if I had done it, I wouldn't have given her a two-minute bit in a production number. I'd have deleted Doris Day and her teeth and let Alis dance with Gene Nelson in front of those rehearsal-hall mirrors. If I'd known about the routine, which I hadn't. I'd never even seen *Tea for Two*.

Or I didn't *remember* seeing it. Right after the episode on the skids, Mayer had credited my account for half a dozen Westerns, none of which I remembered doing. But if I had done it, I wouldn't have dressed her in a bustle. I wouldn't have made her dance with Gene Kelly.

I'd put a watch-and-warn on Fred Astaire and *Funny Face*. I changed it to *Broadway Melody of 1940* and asked for a status report on the case. It was close to being settled, but a secondary suit was expected to be filed, and the FPS was considering proceedings.

The Film Preservation Society. Every change was automatically recorded with them, and the studios didn't have any control over them. Mayer hadn't been able to get me out of putting in those codes because they were part and parcel of the fibe-op feed. If it was a paste-up, it would have to be listed in their records.

I called up the FPS's files and asked for the record for *Seven Brides*.

Legalese. I'd forgotten it was in litigation. "*Singin' in the Rain*," I said.

The champagne wipes I'd done in the party scene were listed, along with one I hadn't. "Frame 9-106," it read, and listed the coordinates and the data. Jean Hagen's cigarette holder. It had been done by the Anti-Smoking League.

"*Tea for Two*," I said, and tried to remember the frame numbers for the Charleston scene, but it didn't matter. The screen was empty.

Which left time travel. I went back to doing the musicals, saying, "Next, please!" to conga lines and male choruses and a horrible blackface number I was surprised nobody'd wiped before this. She was in *Can-Can* and *Bells Are Ringing*, both made in 1960, after which I didn't expect to find much. Musicals had gone big-budget around then, which meant buying up Broadway shows and casting box-office properties like Audrey Hepburn and Richard Harris in them who couldn't sing or dance, and then cutting out all the musical numbers to conceal the fact.

And then musicals'd turned socially relevant. As if the coffin had needed any more nails pounded into it.

There was plenty of alcohol in the musicals of the sixties and seventies, though, even if there wasn't much dancing. A gin-soaked father in *My Fair Lady,* a gin-soaked popsy in *Oliver!,* an entire gin-soaked mining camp in *Paint Your Wagon*. Also, saloons, beer, whiskey, red-eye, and a falling-down-drunk Lee Marvin (who couldn't sing or dance, but then neither could Clint Eastwood or Jean Seberg, and who cares? There's always dubbing). The gin-soaked twenties in Lucille Ball's (who couldn't act either, a triple threat) *Mame*.

And Alis, dancing in the chorus in *Goodbye, Mr. Chips* and *The Boy Friend*. Doing the Tapioca in *Thoroughly Modern Millie,* high-stepping to "Put on Your Sunday Clothes" in *Hello, Dolly!* in a sky-blue bustled dress and parasol.

I went out to Burbank. And maybe time travel was possible. At least two semesters had gone by, but the class was still there. And Michael Caine was still giving the same lecture.

"Any number of reasons have been advanced for the demise of the musical," he was intoning, "escalating production costs, widescreen technological complications, unimaginative staging. But the real reason lies deeper."

I stood against the door and listened to him give the eulogy while the class took respectful notes on their palmtops.

"The death of the musical was due not to directorial and casting catastrophes, but to natural causes. The world the musical depicted simply no longer existed."

The monitor Alis had used to practice with was still there, and so were the stacked-up chairs, only now there were a lot more of them. Michael Caine and the class were crammed into a space too narrow for a soft-shoe, and the chairs had been there awhile. They were covered with dust.

"The musical of the fifties depicted a world of innocent hopes and harmless desires." He muttered something to the comp, and Julie Andrews appeared, sitting on an Alpine hillside with a guitar and assorted children. An odd choice for his argument of "simpler times," since the movie'd been made in 1965, the year of the Vietnam buildup. Not to mention its being set in 1939, the year of the Nazis.

"It was a sunnier, less complicated time," he said, "a time when happy endings were still believable."

The screen skipped to Vanessa Redgrave and Franco Nero, surrounded by soldiers with torches and swords. *Camelot.* "That idyllic world died, and with it died the Hollywood musical, never to be resurrected."

I waited till the class was gone and he'd had his snort of flake and asked him if he knew where Alis was, even though I knew it was no use, he wouldn't have helped her, and the last thing Alis would have needed was somebody else to tell her the musical was dead.

He didn't remember her, even after I'd plied him with chooch, and he refused to give me the student list for her class. I could get it from Heada, but I didn't want her looking sympathetic and thinking I'd lost my mind. Charles Boyer in *Gaslight*.

I went back to my room and took Billy Bigelow's drinking and half the plot out of *Carousel,* and went to bed.

An hour later, the comp woke me out of a sound sleep, making a racket like the reactor in *The China Syndrome,* and I staggered over and blinked at it for a good five minutes before I realized it was the watch-and-warn, and *Brides* must be out of litigation, and another minute to think what command to give.

It wasn't *Brides*. It was Fred Astaire, and the court decision was scrolling down the screen: "Intellectual property claim denied, irreproducible art form claim denied, collaborative property claim denied." Which meant Fred's estate and RKO-Warner must have lost, and ILMGM, where Fred had spent all those years covering for partners who couldn't dance, had won.

"*Broadway Melody of 1940,*" I said, and watched the Beguine come up just like I remembered it, stars and polished floor and Eleanor in white, side by side with Fred.

I had never watched it sober. I had thought the silence, the raptness, the quality of still, centered beauty was the effect of the klieg, but it wasn't. They tapped easily, carelessly, across a dark, polished floor, their hands not quite touching, and were as still, as silent as they were that night I watched Alis watching them. The real thing.

And it had never existed, that harmless, innocent world. In 1940, Hitler was bombing the hell out of London and already hauling Jews off in cattle cars. The studio execs were lobbying against war and making deals, the real Mayer was running the studio, and starlets were going pop on a casting couch for a five-second walk-on. Fred and Eleanor were doing fifty takes, a hundred, in a hot airless studio and going home to soak their bleeding feet.

It had never existed, this world of starry floors and backlit hair and easy, careless kick-turns, and the 1940 audience watching it knew it didn't. And that was its appeal, not that it reflected "sunnier, simpler times," but that it was impossible. That it was what they wanted and could never have.

The screen cut to legalese again, RKO-Warner's appeal already under way, and I hadn't seen the end of the routine, hadn't gotten it on tape or even backed it up.

It didn't matter. It was Eleanor, not Alis, and no matter what Heada thought, no matter how logical it was, I wasn't the one doing it. Because if I had been, litigation or no litigation, that was where I would have put her, dancing side by side with Fred, half turning to give him that delighted smile.

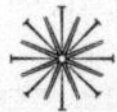

MONTAGE: Tight close-up of comp screen.
Title credits dissolve into one another:
South Pacific, Stand Up and Cheer!, State Fair,
Strike Up the Band, Summer Stock.

EVENTUALLY, I RAN OUT OF PLACES TO LOOK. I WENT DOWN TO Hollywood Boulevard again, but nobody remembered her, and none of the places had Digimattes except A Star Is Born, and it was closed for the night, an iron gate pulled across the front. Alis's other classes had been fibe-op-feed lectures, and her roommate, very splatted, was under the impression Alis had gone back home.

"She packed up all her stuff," she said. "She had all this stuff, costumes and wigs and stuff, and left."

"How long ago?"

"I don't know. Last week, I think. Before Christmas."

I talked to the roommate five weeks after I'd seen Alis in *Seven Brides*. At the end of six weeks, I ran out of musicals. There weren't that many, and I'd watched them all, except for the ones in litigation because of Fred. And Ray Bolger, who Viamount filed copyright on the day after I went out to Burbank.

The Russ Tamblyn suit got settled, beeping me awake in the middle of the night to tell me somebody'd won the right to rape and pillage him on the big screen, and I backed up the barnraising scene and then watched *West Side Story,* just in case. Alis wasn't there.

I watched the "On the Town" routine again and looked up *Painting the Clouds with Sunshine,* convinced there was something important there that I was missing. It was a remake of *Gold Diggers of 1933,* but that wasn't what was bothering me. I put all the routines up on the array in order, easiest to most difficult, as if that might give me some clue to what she'd do next, but it wasn't any help. *Seven Brides for Seven Brothers* was the hardest thing she'd done, and she'd done that six weeks ago.

I listed the movies by date, studio, and dancers, and ran a cross-tabulation on the data. And then I sat and stared at the nonresults for a while. And at the array.

There was a knock on the door. Mayer. I blanked the screen and tried to think of a nonmusical to call up, but my mind had gone blank. "*Philadelphia Story,*" I said finally. "Frame 115-010," and yelled, "Come on in."

It was Heada. "I came to tell you Mayer's going nuclear about your not sending any movies," she said, looking at the screen. It was the wedding scene. Everybody, Jimmy Stewart, Cary Grant, were gathered around Katharine Hepburn, who had a huge hat and a hangover.

"The word is, Arthurton's bringing in a new guy, supposedly to head up Editing," Heada said, "but really to be his assistant, in which case Mayer's out."

Good, I thought, *at least that'll put a stop to the carnage.* But if Mayer got fired, I'd lose my access, and I'd never find Alis.

"I'm working on them right now," I said, and launched into an elaborate explanation of why I was still on *Philadelphia Story*.

"Mayer offered me a job," Heada said.

"So now that he's hired you as a warmbody, you've got a stake in his not getting fired, and you've come to tell me to get busy?"

"No," she said. "Not warmbody. Location assistant. I leave for New York this afternoon."

It was the last thing I expected. I looked over at her and saw she was wearing a blazer and skirt. Heada as studio exec.

"You're leaving?" I said blankly.

"This afternoon," she said. "I came to give you my access number." She took out a hardcopy. "It's asterisk nine two period eight three three," she said, and handed me the piece of paper.

I looked at it, expecting the number, but it was a list of movie titles.

"None of them have any drinking in them," she said. "There are about three weeks' worth. They should stall Mayer for a while."

"Thank you," I said wonderingly.

"Betsy Booth strikes again," she said.

I must have looked blank.

"Judy Garland. *Love Finds Andy Hardy,*" she said. "I told you I've been watching a lot of movies. That's why I got the job. Location assistant has to know all the sets and stock shots and props and be able to find them for the hackate so he doesn't have to digitize new ones. It saves memory."

She pointed at the screen. "*The Philadelphia Story*'s got a public library, a newspaper office, a swimming pool, and a 1936 Packard." She smiled. "Remember when you said the movies taught us how to act and gave us lines to say? You were right. But you were wrong about which part I was playing. You said it was Thelma Ritter, but it wasn't." She waved her hand at the screen, where the wedding party was assembled. "It was Liz."

I frowned at the screen, unable for a moment to remember who Liz was. Katharine Hepburn's precocious little sister? No, wait. The other reporter, Jimmy Stewart's long-suffering girlfriend.

"I've been playing Joan Blondell," Heada said. "Mary Stuart Masterson, Ann Sothern. The girl next door, the secretary who's in love with her boss, only he never notices her, he thinks she's just a kid. He's in love with Tracy Lord, but Joan Blondell helps him anyway. She'd do anything for him, even watch movies."

She stuck her hands in her blazer pockets, and I wondered when she had stopped wearing the halter dress and the pink satin gloves.

"The secretary stands by him," Heada said. "She picks up after him and gives him advice. She even helps him out with his romances, because she knows at the end of the movie he'll finally notice her, he'll realize he can't get along without her, he'll figure out Katharine Hepburn's all wrong for him and the secretary's the one he's been in love with all along." She looked up at me. "But this isn't the movies, is it?" she said bleakly.

Her hair wasn't platinum blond anymore. It was light brown with highlights in it. "Heada," I said.

"It's okay," she said. "I already figured that out. It's what comes of taking too much klieg." She smiled. "In real life, Liz would have to get over Jimmy Stewart, settle for being friends. Audition for a new part. Joan Crawford, maybe?"

I shook my head. "Rosalind Russell."

"Well, Melanie Griffith anyway," she said. "So, anyway, I leave this afternoon, and I just wanted to say good-bye and have you wish me luck."

"You'll be great," I said. "You'll own ILMGM in six months." I kissed her on the cheek. "You know everything."

"Yeah."

She started out the door. "'Here's lookin' at you, kid,'" she said.

I watched her down the hall, and then went back in the room, looking at the list Heada'd given me. There were more than thirty movies here. Closer to fifty. The ones near the bottom had notes after them: "Frame 14-1968, bottle on table," and "Frame 102-166, reference to ale."

I should feed the first twelve in, send them to Mayer to calm him down, but I didn't. I sat on the bed, staring at the list. Next to *Casablanca,* she had written, "Hopeless."

"Hi," Heada said from the door. "It's Tess Trueheart again," and then stood there, looking uncomfortable.

"What is it?" I said, standing up. "Is Mayer back?"

"She's not in 1950," she said, not meeting my eyes. "She's down on Sunset Boulevard. I saw her."

"On Sunset Boulevard?"

"No. On the skids."

Not in a parallel timefeed. Or some never-never land where people walked through the screen into the movies. Here. On the skids. "Did you talk to her?"

She shook her head. "It was morning rush hour. I was coming back from Mayer's, and I just caught a glimpse of her. You know how rush hour is. I tried to get through the crowd to her, but by the time I made it, she'd gotten off."

"Why would she get off at Sunset Boulevard? Did you see her get off?"

"I told you, I just got a glimpse of her through the crowd. She was lugging all this equipment. But she had to have gotten off at Sunset Boulevard. It was the only station we passed."

"You said she was carrying equipment. What kind of equipment?"

"I don't know. Equipment. I *told* you, I—"

"Just got a glimpse of her. And you're sure it was her?"

She nodded. "I wasn't going to tell you, but Betsy Booth's a tough role to shake. And it's hard to hate Alis, after everything she's done." She gestured at her reflections in the array. "Look at me. Chooch-free, klieg-free." She turned and looked at me. "I always wanted to be in the movies and now I am."

She started down the hall again.

"Heada, wait," I said, and then was sorry, afraid her face would be full of hope when she turned around, that there would be tears in her eyes.

But this was Heada, who knows everything.

"What's your name?" I said. "All I have is your access, and I've never called you anything but Heada."

She smiled at me knowingly, ruefully. Emma Thompson in *Remains of the Day*. "I like Heada," she said.

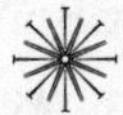

Camera whip-pans to medium shot: LAIT station sign. Diamond screen, "Los Angeles Instransit" in hot pink caps, "Sunset Boulevard" in yellow.

I TOOK THE OPDISK OF ALIS'S ROUTINES AND WENT DOWN TO THE skids. There was nobody on them except a huddle of tourates in mouse ears, a very splatted Marilyn, and Elizabeth Taylor, Sidney Poitier, Mary Pickford, and Harrison Ford, emerging one by one from ILMGM's golden fog. I watched the signs, waiting for Sunset Boulevard and wondering what Alis was doing there. There was nothing down there but the old freeway.

The Marilyn wove unsteadily over to me. Her white halter dress was stained and splotched, and there was a red smear of lipstick by her ear.

"Want a pop?" she said, looking not at me but at Harrison Ford behind me on the screen.

"No, thanks," I said.

"Okay," she said docilely. "How about you?" She didn't wait for me, or Harrison, to answer. She wandered off and then came back. "Are you a studio exec?" she asked.

"No, sorry," I said.

"I want to be in the movies," she said, and wandered off again.

I kept my eyes fixed on the screen. It went silver for a second between promos, and I caught sight of myself looking clean and responsible and sober. Jimmy Stewart in *Mr. Smith Goes to Washington*. No wonder she'd thought I was a studio exec.

The station sign for Sunset Boulevard came up and I got off. The area hadn't changed. There was still nothing down here, not even lights. The abandoned freeway loomed darkly in the starlight, and I could see a fire a long way off under one of the cloverleafs.

There was no way Alis was here. She must have spotted Heada and gotten off here to keep her from finding out where she was really going. Which was where?

There was another light now, a thin white beam wobbling this way. Ravers, probably, looking for victims. I got back on the skids.

The Marilyn was still there, sitting in the middle of the floor, her legs splayed out, fishing through an open palm full of pills for chooch, illy, klieg. *The only equipment a freelancer needs,* I thought, *which at least means whatever Alis is doing it's not freelancing,* and realized I'd been relieved ever since Heada told me about seeing Alis with all that equipment, even though I didn't know where she was. At least she hadn't turned into a freelancer.

It was half past two. Heada had seen Alis at rush hour, which was still four hours away. If Alis went the same place every day. If she hadn't been moving someplace, carrying her luggage. But Heada hadn't said luggage, she'd said equipment. And it couldn't be a comp and monitor, because Heada would have recognized those, and anyway, they were light. Heada had said "lugging." What then? A time machine?

The Marilyn had stood up, spilling capsules everywhere, and was heading over the yellow warning strip for the far wall, which was still extolling ILMGM's cavalcade of stars.

"Don't!" I said, and grabbed for her, a foot from the wall.

She looked up at me, her eyes completely dilated. "This is my stop. I have to get off."

"Wrong way, Corrigan," I said, turning her around to face the front. The sign read Beverly Hills, which didn't seem very likely. "Where did you want to get off?"

She shrugged off my arm and turned back to the screen.

"The way out's that way," I said, pointing to the front.

She shook her head and pointed at Fred Astaire emerging out of the fog. "Through there," she said, and sank down to sitting, her white skirt in a circle. The screen went silver, reflecting her sitting there, fishing through her empty palm, and then to golden fog. The lead-in to the ILMGM promo.

I stared at the wall, which didn't look like a wall, or a mirror. It looked like what it was, a fog of electrons, a veil over emptiness, and for a minute it all seemed possible. For a minute, I thought, *Alis didn't get off at Sunset Boulevard. She didn't get off the skids at all. She stepped through the screen, like Mia Farrow, like Buster Keaton, and into the past.*

I could almost see her in her black skirt and green weskit and gloves, disappearing into the golden fog and emerging on a Hollywood Boulevard full of cars and palm trees and lined with rehearsal halls full of mirrors.

"Anything's possible," the voiceover roared.

The Marilyn was on her feet again and weaving toward the back wall.

"Not that way," I said, and sprinted after her.

It was a good thing she hadn't been headed for the screens this time—I'd never have made it. By the time I got to her, she was banging on the wall with both fists.

"Let me off!" she shouted. "This is my stop!"

"The way off's this way," I said, trying to turn her, but she must have been doing rave. Her arm was like iron.

"I have to get off here," she said, pounding with the flat of her hands. "Where's the door?"

"The door's that way," I said, wondering if this was how I had been the night Alis brought me home from Burbank. "You can't get off this way."

"She did," she said.

I looked at the back wall and then back at her. "Who did?"

"She did," she said. "She went right through the door. I saw her," and puked all over my feet.

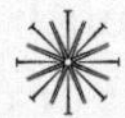

MOVIE CLICHE #12: The Moral.
A character states the obvious, and everybody gets the point.

SEE: *The Wizard of Oz, Field of Dreams, Love Story, What's New Pussycat?*

I GOT THE MARILYN OFF AT WILSHIRE AND TOOK HER TO REHAB, by which time she'd pretty much pumped her own stomach, and waited to make sure she checked in.

"Are you sure you've got time to do this?" she said, looking less like Marilyn and more like Jodie Foster in *Taxi Driver*.

"I'm sure." There was plenty of time, now that I knew where Alis was.

While she was filling out paperwork, I accessed Vincent. "I have a question," I said without preamble. "What if you took a frame and substituted an identical frame? Could that get past the fibe-op ID-locks?"

"An identical frame? What would be the point of that?"

"Could it?"

"I guess," he said. "Is this for Mayer?"

"Yeah," I said. "What if you substituted a new image that matched the original? Could the ID-locks tell the difference?"

"Matched?"

"A different image that's the same."

"You're splatted," he said, and signed off.

It didn't matter. I already knew the ID-locks couldn't tell the difference. It would take too much memory. And, as Vincent had said, what would be the point of changing an image to one exactly like it?

I waited till the Marilyn was in a bed and getting a ridigaine IV and then got back on the skids. After La Brea, there was nobody on them, but it took me till three-thirty to find the service door to the shut-off section and past five to get it open.

I was worried for a while that Alis had braced it shut, which she had, but not intentionally. One of the fibe-op-feed cables was up against it, and when I finally got the door open a crack, all I had to do was push.

She was facing the far wall, looking at the screen that should have been blank in this shut-off section. It wasn't. In the middle of it, Peter Lawford and June Allyson were demonstrating the Varsity Drag to a gymnasium full of college students in party dresses and tuxes. June was wearing a pink dress and pink heels with pompoms, and so was Alis, and their hair was curled under in identical blond pageboys.

Alis had set the Digimatte on top of its case, with the compositor and pixar beside it on the floor, and snaked the fibe-op cable along the yellow warning strip and around in front of the door to the skids feed. I pushed the cable out from the door, gently, so it wouldn't break the connection, and opened the door far enough so I could see, and then stood, half hidden by it, and watched her.

"Down on your heels," Peter Lawford instructed, "up on your toes," and went into a triple step. Alis, holding a remote, ff'd past the song and stopped where the dance started, and watched it, her face intent, counting the steps. She rew'd to the end of the song. She punched a button and everyone froze in midstep.

She walked rapidly in the silly high-heeled shoes to the rear of the skids, out of reach of the frame, and pressed a button. Peter Lawford sang, "—that's how it goes."

Alis set the remote down on the floor, her full-skirted dress rustling as she knelt, and then hurried back to her mark and stood, obscuring June Allyson except for one hand and a tail of the pink skirt, waiting for her cue.

It came, Alis went down on her heels, up on her toes, and into a Charleston, with June behind her from this angle like a twin, a shadow. I moved over to where I could see her from the same angle as the Digimatte's processor. June Allyson disappeared, and there was only Alis.

I had expected June Allyson to be wiped from the screen the way Princess Leia had been for the tourates' scene at A Star Is Born, but Alis wasn't making vids for the folks back home or even trying to project her image on the screen. She was simply rehearsing, and she had only hooked the Digimatte up to feed the fibe-op loop through the processor because that was the way she'd been taught to use it at work. I could see, even from here, that the "record" light wasn't on.

I retreated to the half-open door. She was taller than June Allyson, and her dress was a brighter pink than June's, but the image the Digimatte was feeding back into the fibe-op loop was the corrected version, adjusted for color and focus and lighting. And on some of these routines, practiced for hours and hours in these shut-off sections of the skids, done and redone and done again, that corrected image had been so close to the original that the ID-locks didn't catch it, so close Alis's image had gotten past the guards and onto the fibe-op source. And Alis had managed the impossible.

She flubbed a turn, stopped, clattered over to the remote in her pompomed heels, rew'd to the middle section just before the flub, and froze it. She glanced at the Digimatte's clock, and then punched a button and hurried back to her mark.

She only had another half hour, if that, and then she would have to dismantle this equipment and take it back to Hollywood Boulevard, set it up, open up shop. I should let her. I could show her the opdisk another time, and I had found out what I wanted to know. I should shut the door and leave her to rehearse. But I didn't. I leaned against the door, and stood there, watching her dance.

She went through the middle section three more times, working the clumsiness out of the turn, and then rew'd to the end of the song and went through the whole thing. Her face was intent, alert, the way it had been that night watching the Continental, but it lacked the delight, the rapt, abandoned quality of the Beguine.

I wondered if it was because she was still learning the routine, or if she would ever have it. The smile June Allyson turned on Peter Lawford was pleased, not joyful, and the "Varsity Drag" number itself was only so-so. Hardly Cole Porter.

It came to me then, watching her patiently go over the same steps again and again, as Fred must have done, all alone in a rehearsal hall before the movie had even begun filming, that I had been wrong about her.

I had thought that she believed, like Ruby Keeler and ILMGM, that anything was possible. I had tried to tell her it wasn't, that just because you want something doesn't mean you can have it. But she had already known that, long before I met her, long before she came to Hollywood. Fred Astaire had died the year she was born, and she could never, never, never, in spite of VR and computer graphics and copyrights, dance the Beguine with him.

And all this, the costumes and the classes and the rehearsing, was simply a substitute, something to do instead. Like fighting in the Resistance. Compared to the impossibility of what Alis was unfortunate enough to want, breaking into a Hollywood populated by puppets and pimps must have seemed a snap.

Peter Lawford took June Allyson's hand, and Alis misjudged the turn and crashed into empty air. She picked up the remote to rew, glanced toward the station sign, and saw me. She stood looking at me for a long moment, and then walked over and shut off the Digimatte.

"Don't–" I said.

"Don't what?" she said, unhooking connections. She shrugged a white lab coat on over the pink dress. "Don't waste your time trying to find a dancing teacher because there aren't any?" She buttoned up the coat, and went over to the input and disconnected the feed. "As you can see, I've already figured that out. Nobody in Hollywood knows how to dance. Or if they do, they're splatted on chooch, trying to forget." She began looping the feed into a coil. "Are you?"

She glanced up at the station sign, and then laid the coiled feed on top of the Digimatte and knelt next to the compositor, skirt rustling. "Because if you are, I don't have time to take you home and keep you from falling off the skids and fend off your advances. I have to get this stuff back." She slid the pixar into its case and snapped it shut.

"I'm not splatted," I said. "And I'm not drunk. I've been looking for you for six weeks."

She lifted the Digimatte down and into its case and began stowing wires. "Why? So you can convince me I'm not Ruby Keeler? That the musical's dead and anything I can do, comps can do better? Fine. I'm convinced."

She sat down on the case and unbuckled the pompomed heels. "You win," she said. "I can't dance in the movies." She looked over at the mirrored wall, shoe in hand. "It's impossible."

"No," I said. "I didn't come to tell you that."

She stuck the heels in one of the pockets of the lab coat. "Then what did you come to tell me? That you want your list of accesses back? Fine." She slid her feet into a pair of slip-ons and stood up. "I've learned just about all the chorus numbers and solos anyway, and this isn't going to work for partnered dancing. I'm going to have to find something else."

"I don't want the accesses back," I said.

She pulled off the blond pageboy and shook out her beautiful backlit hair. "Then what do you want?"

You, I thought. *I want you*.

She stood up abruptly and jammed the wig in her other pocket. "Whatever it is, it'll have to wait." She slung the coil of feed over her shoulder. "I've got a job to go to." She bent to pick up the cases.

"Let me help you," I said, starting toward her.

"No, thanks," she said, shouldering the pixar and hoisting the Digimatte. "I can do it myself."

"Then I'll hold the door for you," I said, and opened it.

She pushed through.

Rush hour. Packed mirror to mirror with Ray Milland and Rosalind Russell on their way to work, none of whom turned to look at Alis. They were all looking at the walls, which were going full blast: ILMGM, More Copyrights Than There Are in Heaven. A promo for *Beverly Hills Cop 15,* a promo for a remake of *The Three Musketeers.*

I pulled the door shut behind me, and a River Phoenix, squatting on the yellow warning strip, looked up from a razor blade and a palmful of powder, but he was too splatted to register what he was seeing. His eyes didn't even focus.

Alis was already halfway to the front of the skids, her eyes on the station sign. It blinked Hollywood Boulevard, and she pushed her way toward the exit, with me following in her wake, and out onto the boulevard.

It was still as dark as it gets, but everything was open. And there were still (or maybe already) tourates around. Two old guys in Bermuda shorts and vidcams were at the Happily Ever After booth, watching Ryan O'Neal save Ali MacGraw's life.

Alis stopped at the gated grille of A Star Is Born and fumbled with her key, trying to insert the card without putting any of her stuff down. The two tourates wandered over.

"Here," I said, taking the key. I opened the gate and took the Digimatte from her.

"Do you have Charles Bronson?" one of the oldates said.

"We're not open yet," I said. "I have something I have to show you," I said to Alis.

"What? The latest puppet show? An automatic rehearsal program?" She started setting up the Digimatte, plugging in the cables and fibe-op feed, shoving the Digimatte into position.

"I always wanted to be in *Death Wish,*" the oldate said. "Do you have that?"

"We're not *open,*" I said.

"Here's the menu," Alis said, switching it on for the oldate. "We don't have Charles Bronson, but we have got a scene from *The Magnificent Seven.*" She pointed to it.

"You have to see this, Alis," I said, and shoved in the opdisk, glad I'd preset it and didn't have to call anything up. *On the Town* came up on the screen.

"I have customers to—" Alis said, and stopped.

I had set the disk to "Next, please" after fifteen seconds. *On the Town* disappeared, and *Singin' in the Rain* came up.

Alis turned angrily to me. "Why did you—"

"I didn't," I said. "You did." I pointed at the screen. *Tea for Two* came up, and Alis, in red curls, Charlestoned her way toward the front of the screen.

"It's not a paste-up," I said. "Look at them. They're the movies you've been rehearsing, aren't they? Aren't they?"

On the screen, Alis was high-stepping with her blue parasol.

"You talked about *Singin' in the Rain* that night I met you. And I could have guessed some of the others. They're all full-length shot and in one continuous take." I pointed at her in her blue bustle. "But I didn't even know what movie that was from."

Hats Off came up. "And I'd never seen some of these."

"I didn't—" she said, looking at the screen.

"The Digimatte does a superimpose on the fibe-op image coming in and puts it on disk," I said, showing her. "That image goes back through the loop, too, and the fibe-op source randomly checks the pattern of pixels and automatically rejects any image that's been changed. Only you weren't trying to change the image. You were trying to duplicate it. And you succeeded. You matched the moves perfectly, so perfectly the Brownian check thought it was the same image, so perfectly it didn't reject it, and the image made it onto the fibe-op source." I waved my hand at the screen, where she was dancing to "42nd Street."

Behind us, the oldate said, "Who's in this *Magnificent Seven* scene?" but Alis didn't answer him. She was watching the shifting routines, her face intent. I couldn't read her expression.

"How many are there?" she said, still looking at the screen.

"I've found fourteen," I said. "You rehearsed more than that, right? The ones that got past the ID-locks are almost all dancers with the same shape of face and features you have. Did you do any Ann Millers?"

"*Kiss Me, Kate,*" she said.

"I thought you might have," I said. "Her face is too round. Your features wouldn't match closely enough to get past the ID-lock. It only works where there's already a resemblance." I pointed at the screen. "There are two others I found that aren't on the disk because they're in litigation. *White Christmas* and *Seven Brides for Seven Brothers.*"

She turned to look at me. "*Seven Brides*? Are you sure?"

"You're right there in the barnraising scene," I said. "Why?"

She had turned back to the screen, frowning at Shirley Temple, who was dancing with Alis and Jack Haley in military uniforms. "Maybe—" she said to herself.

"I told you dancing in the movies was impossible," I said. "I was wrong. There you are."

As I said it, the screen went blank, and the oldate said loudly, "How about that guy who says, 'Make my day!' Do you have him?"

I reached to start the disk again, but Alis had already turned away.

"I'm afraid we don't have Clint Eastwood either. The scene from *Magnificent Seven* has Steve McQueen and Yul Brynner," she said. "Would you like to see it?" and busied herself punching in the access.

"Does he have to shave his head?" his friend said.

"No," Alis said, reaching for a black shirt and pants, a black hat. "The Digimatte takes care of that." She started setting up the tape equipment, showing the oldate where to stand and what to do, oblivious of his friend, who was still talking about Charles Bronson, oblivious of me.

Well, what had I expected? That she'd be overjoyed to see herself up there, that she'd fling her arms around me like Natalie Wood in *The Searchers*? I hadn't done anything. Except tell her she'd accomplished something she hadn't been trying to do, something she'd turned down standing on this very boulevard.

"Yul *Brynner*," the oldate's friend said disgustedly, "and no Charles Bronson."

On the Town was on the screen again. Alis switched it off without a glance and called up *The Magnificent Seven*.

"You want Charles Bronson and they give you Steve McQueen," the oldate grumbled. "They always make you settle for second best."

That's what I love about the movies. There's always some minor character standing around to tell you the moral, just in case you're too dumb to figure it out for yourself.

"You never get what you want," the oldate said.

"Yeah," I said, "'there's no place like home,'" and headed for the skids.

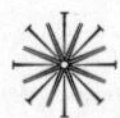

VERA MILES: *[Running out to corral, where RANDOLPH SCOTT is saddling horse]* You were going to leave, just like that? Without even saying good-bye?

RANDOLPH SCOTT: *[Cinching girth on horse]* I got a score to settle. And you got a young man to tend to. I got the bullet out of that arm of his, but it needs bandaging. *[RANDOLPH SCOTT steps in stirrup and swings up on horse]*

VERA MILES: Will I see you again? How will I know you're all right?

RANDOLPH SCOTT: I reckon I'll be all right. *[Tips hat]* You take care, ma'am. *[Wheels horse around and rides off into sunset]*

VERA MILES: *[Calling after him]* I'll never forget what you've done for me! Never!

I WENT HOME AND STARTED WORK. I DID THE ONES THAT MATtered first—restoring the double cigarette-lighting in *Now, Voyager,* putting the uranium back in the wine bottle in *Notorious,* reinebriating Lee Marvin's horse in *Cat Ballou*. And the ones I liked: *Ninotchka* and *Rio Bravo* and *Double Indemnity*. And *Seven Brides,* which came out of litigation the day after I saw Alis. It was beeping at me when I woke up. I put Howard Keel's drink and whiskey bottle back in the opening scene, and then ff'd to the barnraising and turned the pan of cornbread back into a jug before I watched Alis.

It was too bad I couldn't have shown it to her; she'd seemed so surprised the number had made it onto film. She must have had trouble with it, and no wonder. All those lifts and no partner—I wondered what equipment she'd had to lug down Hollywood Boulevard and onto the skids to make it look like she was in the air. It would have been nice if she could see how happy she looked doing those lifts.

I put the barnraising dance on the disk with the others, in case Russ Tamblyn's estate or Warner appealed, and then erased all my transaction records, in case Mayer yanked the Cray.

I figured I had two weeks, maybe three if the Columbia takeover really went through. Mayer'd be so busy trying to make up his mind which way to jump he wouldn't have time to worry about AS's, and neither would Arthurton. I thought about calling Heada—she'd know what was happening—and then decided that was probably a bad idea. Anyway, she was probably busy scrambling to keep her job.

A week anyway. Enough time to give Myrna Loy back her hangover and watch the rest of the musicals. I'd already found most of them, except for *Good News* and *The Birds and the Bees*. I put the *dulce de leche* back in *Guys and Dolls* while I was at it, and the brandy back in *My Fair Lady* and made Frank Morgan in *Summer Holiday* back into a drunk. It went slower than I wanted it to, and after a week and a half, I stopped and put everything Alis had done on disk *and* tape, expecting Mayer to knock on the door any minute, and started in on *Casablanca*.

There was a knock on the door. I ff'd to the end where Rick's bar was still full of lemonade, took the disk of Alis's dancing and stuck it down the side of my shoe, and opened the door.

It was Alis.

The hall behind her was dark, but her hair, pulled into a bun, caught the light from somewhere. She looked tired, like she had just come from practicing. She still had on her lab coat. I could see white stockings and Mary Janes below it, and an inch or so of pink ruffle. I wondered what she'd been doing—the "Abba-Dabba Honeymoon" number from *Two Weeks with Love*? Or something from *By the Light of the Silvery Moon*?

She reached into the pocket of the lab coat and held out the opdisk I'd given her. "I came to bring this back to you."

"Keep it," I said.

She looked at it a minute and then stuck it in her pocket. "Thanks," she said, and pulled it out again. "I'm surprised so many of the routines made it on. I wasn't very good when I started," she said, turning it over. "I'm still not very good."

"You're as good as Ruby Keeler," I said.

She grinned. "She was somebody's girlfriend."

"You're as good as Vera-Ellen. And Debbie Reynolds. And Virginia Gibson."

She frowned, and looked at the disk again and then at me, as if trying to decide whether to tell me something. "Heada told me about her job," she said, and that wasn't it. "Location assistant. That's great." She looked over at the array, where Bogart was toasting Ingrid. "She said you were putting the movies back the way they were."

"Not all the movies," I said, pointing at the disk in her hand. "Some remakes are better than the original."

"Won't you get fired?" she said. "Putting the AS's back in, I mean?"

"Almost certainly," I said. " 'But it is a fah, fah bettah thing I do than I have evah done before. It is a—' "

"*Tale of Two Cities,* Ronald Colman," she said, looking at the screens where Bogart was saying good-bye to Ingrid, at the disk, at the screens again, trying to work up to what she had to say.

I said it for her. "You're leaving."

She nodded, still not looking at me.

"Where are you going? Back to River City?"

"That's from *The Music Man,*" she said, but she didn't smile. "I can't go any further by myself. I need somebody to teach me the heel-and-toe work Eleanor Powell does. And I need a partner."

Just for a moment, no, not even a moment, the flicker of a frame, I thought about what might have been if I hadn't spent those long splatted semesters dismantling highballs, if I had spent them out in Burbank instead, practicing kick-turns.

"After what you said the other night, I thought I might be able to use a positioning armature and a data harness for the lifts, and I tried it. It worked, I guess. I mean, it—"

Her voice cut off awkwardly like she'd intended to say something more, and I wondered what it was, and what it was I'd said to her. That Fred might be coming out of litigation?

"But the balance isn't the same as a real person," she said. "And I need experience learning routines, not just copying them off the screen."

So she was going someplace where they were still doing liveactions. "Where?" I said. "Buenos Aires?"

"No," she said. "China."

China.

"They're doing ten liveactions a year," she said.

And twenty purges. Not to mention provincial uprisings. And antiforeigner riots.

"Their liveactions aren't very good. They're terrible, actually. Most of them are propaganda films and martial-arts things, but a couple of them last year were musicals." She smiled ruefully. "They like Gene Kelly."

Gene Kelly. But it would be real routines. And a man's arm around her waist instead of a data harness, a man's hands lifting her. The real thing.

"I leave tomorrow morning," she said. "I was packing, and I found the disk and thought maybe you wanted it back."

"No," I said, and then, so I wouldn't have to tell her good-bye, "Where are you flying out of?"

"San Francisco," she said. "I'm taking the skids up tonight. And I'm still not packed." She looked at me, waiting for me to say my line.

And I had plenty to choose from. If there's anything the movies are good at, it's good-byes. From "Be careful, honey!" to "Don't let's ask for the moon. We have the stars" to "Come back, Shane!" Even "Hasta la vista, baby."

But I didn't say them. I stood there and looked at her, with her beautiful, backlit hair and her unforgettable face. At what I wanted and couldn't have, not even for a few minutes.

And what if I said "Stay"? What if I promised to find her a teacher, get her a part, put on a show? Right. With a Cray that had maybe ten minutes of memory, a Cray I wouldn't have as soon as Mayer found out what I'd been doing?

Behind me, on the screen, Bogart was saying, "There's no place for you here," and looking at Ingrid, trying to make the moment last forever. In the background, the plane's propellers were starting to turn, and in a minute the Nazis would show up.

They stood there, looking at each other, and tears welled up in Ingrid's eyes, and Vincent could mess with his tears program forever and never get it right. Or maybe he would. They had made *Casablanca* out of dry ice and cardboard. And it was the real thing.

"I have to go," Alis said.

"I know," I said, and smiled at her. "'We'll always have Paris.'"

And according to the script, she was supposed to give me one last longing look and get on the plane with Paul Henreid, and why is it I still haven't learned that Heada is always right?

"Good-bye," Alis said, and then she was in my arms, and I was kissing her, kissing her, and she was unbuttoning the lab coat, taking down her hair, unbuttoning the pink gingham dress, and some part of me was thinking, *This is important,* but she had the dress off, and the pantaloons, and I had her on the bed, and she didn't fade, she didn't morph into Heada, I was on her and in her, and we were moving together, easily, effortlessly, our outstretched hands almost but not quite touching on the tangled sheets.

I kept my gaze on her hands, flexing and stretching in passion, knowing if I looked at her face it would be freeze-framed on my brain forever, klieg or no klieg, afraid if I did she might be looking at me kindly, or, worse, not be looking at me at all. Looking through me, past me, at two dancers on a starry floor.

"Tom!" she said, coming, and I looked down at her. Her hair was spread out on the pillow, backlit and beautiful, and her face was intent, the way it had been that night at the party, watching Fred and Ginge on the freescreen, rapt and beautiful and sad. And focused, finally, on me.

MOVIE CLICHE #1: The Happy Ending.
Self-explanatory.

SEE: *An Officer and a Gentleman, An Affair to Remember, Sleepless in Seattle, The Miracle of Morgan's Creek, Shall We Dance, Great Expectations.*

IT'S BEEN THREE YEARS, DURING WHICH TIME CHINA HAS GONE through four provincial uprisings and six student riots, and Mayer has gone through three takeovers and eight bosses, the next to last of whom moved him up to executive vice-president.

Mayer didn't tumble to my putting the AS's back in for nearly three months, by which time I'd finished the whole *Thin Man* series, *The Maltese Falcon,* and all the Westerns, and Arthurton was on his way out.

Heada, still costarring as Joan Blondell, talked Mayer out of killing me and into making a stirring speech about Censorship and Deep Love for the Movies and getting himself spectacularly fired just in time for the new boss to hire him back as "the only moral person in this whole poppated town."

Heada got promoted to set director and then (that next-to-last boss) to assistant producer in charge of new projects, and promptly hired me to direct a remake. Happy endings all around.

In the meantime, I programmed happy endings for Happily Ever After and graduated and looked for Alis. I found her in *Pen-*

nies from Heaven, and in *Into the Woods,* the last musical ever made, and in *Small Town Girl.* I thought I'd found them all. Until tonight.

I watched the scene in the Indy again, looking at the silver tap shoes and the platinum wig and thinking about musicals. *Indiana Jones and the Temple of Doom* isn't one. "Anything Goes" is the only number in it, and it's only there because one of the scenes takes place in a nightclub, and they're the floor show.

And maybe that's the way to go. The remake I'm working on isn't a musical either—it's a weeper about a couple of star-crossed lovers—but I could change the hotel dining room scene into a nightclub. And then, the boss after next, do a remake with a nightclub setting, and put Fred (who's bound to be out of litigation by then) in it, just in one featured number. That was all he was in *Flying Down to Rio,* a featured number, thirtyish, slightly balding, who could dance a little. And look what happened.

And before you know it, Mayer will be telling everybody the musical's coming back, and I'll get assigned the remake of *42nd Street* and find out where Alis is and book the skids and we'll put on a show. Anything's possible.

Even time travel.

I accessed Vincent the other day to borrow his edit program, and he told me time travel's a bust. "We were *this* close," he said, his thumb and forefinger almost touching. "Theoretically, the Casimir effect should work for time as well as space, but they've sent image after image into a negative-matter region, and nothing. No overlap at all. I guess maybe there are some things that just aren't possible."

He's wrong. The night Alis left, she said, "After what you said the other night, I thought maybe I could use a data harness for the lifts," and I had wondered what it was I'd said, and when I showed her the opdisk, she'd said, "*Seven Brides for Seven Brothers.* Are you sure?"

"It's not on the disk," I'd said, "it's in litigation," and it had stayed in litigation till the next day. And when I checked, it had been in litigation the whole time I looked for her.

And for eight months before that, in a National Treasure suit the Film Preservation Society had brought. The night I saw *Seven Brides,* it had been out of litigation exactly two hours. And had gone back in an hour later.

Alis had only been working at A Star Is Born for six months. *Brides* had been in litigation the whole time. Until after I found her. Until after I told her I'd seen her in it. And when I told her, she'd said, "*Seven Brides for Seven Brothers*? Are you sure?" and I'd thought she was surprised because the jumps and lifts were so hard, surprised because she hadn't been trying to superimpose her image on the screen.

Brides hadn't come out of litigation till the next day.

And a week and a half later, Alis came to me. She came straight from the skids, straight from practicing with the harness and the armature that she'd thought might work, "after what you said the other night." And it had worked. "—I guess," she'd said. "I mean—"

She'd come straight from practice, wearing Virginia Gibson's pink gingham dress, Virginia Gibson's pantaloons, wearing her costume for the barnraising dance she'd just done. The barnraising dance I'd seen her in six weeks before she ever did it. And my theory about her having somehow gone back in time was right after all, even if it was only her image, only pixels on a screen. She hadn't been trying to discover time travel either. She had only been trying to learn routines, but the screen she'd been rehearsing in front of wasn't a screen. It was a negative-matter region, full of randomized electrons and potential overlaps. Full of possibilities.

Nothing's impossible, Vincent, I think, watching Alis do kick-turns in her sequined leotard. *Not if you know what you want.*

Heada is accessing me. "I was wrong. The Ford Tri-Motor's at the beginning of the second one. *Indiana Jones and the Temple of Doom*. Beginning with frame—"

"I found it," I say, frowning at the screen where Alis, in her platinum wig, is doing a brush step.

"What's wrong?" Heada says. "Isn't it going to work?"

"I'm not sure," I say. "When's the Fred Astaire suit going to be settled?"

"A month," she says promptly. "But it's going right back in. Sofracima-Rizzoli's claiming copyright infringement."

"Who the hell is Sofracima-Rizzoli?"

"The studio that owns the rights to a movie Fred Astaire made in the seventies. *The Purple Taxi*. I figure they'll settle. Three months. Why?" she says suspiciously.

"The plane in *Flying Down to Rio*. I've decided that's what I want."

"A biplane? You don't have to wait for that. There are tons of other movies with biplanes in them. *The Blue Max, Wings, High Road to China*—" She stops, looking unhappy.

"Do they have skids in China?" I say.

"Are you kidding? They're lucky to have bicycles. And enough to eat. Why?" she says, suddenly interested. "Have you found out where Alis is?"

"No."

Heada hesitates, trying to decide whether to tell me something. "The assistant set director's back from China. He says the word is, it's Cultural Revolution 3. Book burnings, reeducation, they've shut at least one studio down and arrested the whole film crew."

I should be worried, but I'm not, and Heada, who knows everything, pounces immediately.

"Is she back?" she says. "Have you had word from her?"

"No," I say, because I have finally learned how to lie to Heada, and because it's true. I don't know where she is, and I haven't had word from her. But I've gotten a message.

Fred Astaire has been out of litigation twice since Alis left, once between copyright suits for exactly eight seconds, the other time last month when the AFI filed an injunction claiming he was a historic landmark.

That time I was ready. I had the Beguine number on opdisk, backup, and tape, and was ready to check it before the watch-and-warn had even stopped beeping.

It was the middle of the night, as usual, and at first I thought I was still asleep or having one last flash.

"Enhance upper left," I said, and watched it again. And again. And the next morning.

It looked the same every time, and the message was loud and clear: Alis is all right, in spite of uprisings and revolutions, and she's found a place to practice and somebody to teach her Eleanor Powell's heel-and-toe steps. And she's going to come back, because China doesn't have skids, and when she does, she's going to dance the Beguine with Fred Astaire.

Or maybe she already has. I saw her in the barnraising number in *Brides* six weeks before she did it, and it's been four since I saw her in *Melody*. Maybe she's already back. Maybe she's already done it.

I don't think so. I've promised the current A Star Is Born James Dean a lifetime supply of chooch to tell me if anybody touches the Digimatte, and Fred's still in litigation. And I don't know how far back in time the overlap goes. Six weeks before she did it was only when I *saw* her in *Seven Brides*. There's no telling how long before that her image was there. Under two years, because it wasn't in *42nd Street* when I watched it the first time, when I was first starting Mayer's list, and yeah, I know I was splatted and might have missed her. But I didn't. I would know her face anywhere.

So under two years. And Heada, who knows everything, says Fred will be out of litigation in three months.

In the meantime, I keep busy, doing remakes and trying to make them good, getting Mayer to talk ILMGM into copyrighting Ruby Keeler and Eleanor Powell, working for the Resistance. I have even come up with a happy ending for *Casablanca*.

It is after the war, and Rick has come back to Casablanca after fighting with the Resistance, after who knows what hardships. The Café Américain has burned down, and everybody's gone, even the parrot, even Sam, and Bogie stands and looks at the rubble for a long time, and then starts picking through the mess, trying to see what he can salvage.

He finds the piano, but when he tips it upright, half the keys fall out. He fishes an unbroken bottle of scotch out of the rubble and sets it on the piano and starts looking around for a glass. And there she is, standing in what's left of the doorway.

She looks different, her hair's pulled back, and she looks thinner, tired. You can see looking at her that Paul Henreid's dead and she's gone through a lot, but you'd know that face anywhere.

She stands there in the door, and Bogie, still trying to find a glass, looks up and sees her.

No dialogue. No music. No clinch, in spite of Heada's benighted ideas. Just the two of them, who never thought they'd see each other again, standing there looking at each other.

When I'm done with my remake, I'll put my *Casablanca* ending in Happily Ever After's comp for the tourates.

In the meantime, I have to separate my star-crossed lovers and send them off to suffer assorted hardships and pay for their sins. For which I need a plane.

I put the "Anything Goes" number on disk and backup, in case Kate Capshaw goes into litigation, and then ff to the Ford Tri-Motor and save that, too, in case the biplane doesn't work.

"*High Road to China,*" I say, and then cancel it before it has a chance to come up. "Simultaneous display. Screen one, *Temple of Doom*. Two, *Singin' in the Rain*. Three, *Good News* . . ."

I go through the litany, and Alis appears on the screens, one after the other, in tap pants and bustles and green weskits, ponytails and red curls and shingled bobs. Her face looks the same in all of them, intent, alert, concentrating on the steps and the music, unaware that she is conquering encryptions and Brownian checks and time.

"Screen eighteen," I say. "*Seven Brides for Seven Brothers,*" and she twirls across the floor and leaps into the arms of Russ Tamblyn. And he has conquered time, too. They all have, Gene and Ruby and Fred, in spite of the death of the musical, in spite of the studio execs and the hackates and the courts, conquering time in a turn, a smile, a lift, capturing for a permanent moment what we want and can't have.

I have been working on weepers too long. I need to get on with the business at hand, pick a plane, save the sentiment for my lovers' Big Farewell.

"Cancel, all screens," I say. "Center screen, *High Road to*—" and then stop and stare at the silver screen, like Ray Milland craving a drink in *The Lost Weekend*.

"Center screen," I say. "Frame 96-1100, no sound. *Broadway Melody of 1940,*" and sit down on the bed.

They are tapping side by side, dressed in white, lost in the music I cannot hear and the time steps that took them weeks to practice, dancing easily, without effort. Her light brown hair catches the light from somewhere.

Alis swings into a turn, her white skirt swirling out in the same clear arc as Eleanor's—check and Brownian check—and that must have taken weeks, too.

Next to her, casual, elegant, oblivious to copyrights and takeovers, Fred taps out a counterpoint ripple, and Alis answers it back and turns to smile over her shoulder.

"Freeze," I say, and she stops, still turning, her hand outstretched and almost touching mine.

I lean forward, looking at the face I have seen ever since that first night watching her from the door, that face I would know anywhere. We'll always have Paris.

"Forward three frames and hold," I say, and she flashes me a delighted, an infinitely promising, smile.

"Forward realtime," I say, and there is Alis, as she should be, dancing in the movies.

THE END

ROLL CREDITS

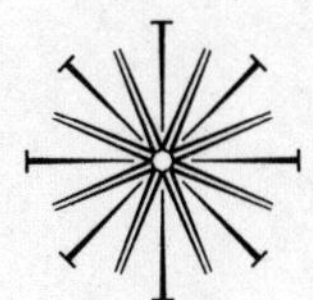

D.A.

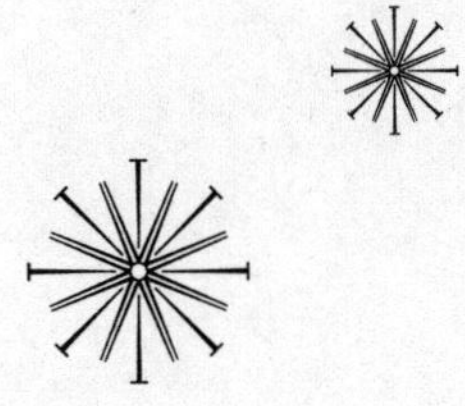

I WAS AT SCHOOL, STUDYING FOR MY UCLA ENTRANCE EXAM and talking to Kimkim, when my phone rang.

One of Ms. Sionov's many obnoxious rules is absolute silence in the media center. "Theodora," she said, glaring at me. "You know the rules. No phones. Hand it over."

"I turned my phone off and put it in my compack when I came in," I told Ms. Sionov as I looked in another compartment.

"Then why is it ringing? You had your phone on and were messaging Kimkim, weren't you?"

"No," I said, which was technically true. I wasn't messaging her, I was talking to her. And the phone I was talking to her on wasn't the phone that was ringing. It's ridiculous not to let us message each other in the media center, and Kimkim's a computer genius, so she rigged up a subliminal-sound flatphone that goes on my wrist so I can talk to her and have it look like all I'm doing is leaning on my hand, thinking about something. "Honestly, it isn't on," I said.

"I'll bet," Ms. Sionov said, holding out her hand for the phone. "Where *is* your partner in crime today?"

"Interview at CU," I said, still searching. "It must be a schoolwide override."

"Then why isn't everyone else's phone ringing?"

Which was a good point. I dug some more and finally found

the phone. "See," I said, showing her the dark screen. "I told you it was off." I hit "display," and the words "Assembly 1 P.M. Mandatory Attendance" came up.

"I told you it was an override," I said.

Ms. Sionov grabbed the phone away from me to look, and right then Fletcher Davis's phone began to ring and then Ahmed Fitzwilliam's. And Ms. Sionov's.

She handed me my phone and ran to turn hers off. While she was gone, I forwarded Kimkim the message. "What's up?" I added, gathering up my stuff and starting for the auditorium.

"No idea," she messaged back. "Mine just rang, too. Do you think the snowboard team finally won a match?"

"That wouldn't be Mandatory Attendance." Our principal, Mr. Fuyijama, *loves* calling assemblies, to announce fire drill evacuation routes or the revised lunch schedule or the junior varsity sudoku team's taking second place at State—but those are all Optional Attendance. Assemblies to announce university acceptances and scholarships are Mandatory Attendance, but it couldn't be that. We were still in the middle of entrance-exam-and-interview season. Which was why Kimkim wasn't here.

"Can you make it back by one?" I messaged her.

"Just barely," she answered. "Save me a seat."

I maneuvered my way down the crowded hall, where everybody was asking everybody else if they knew what the assembly was about. Nobody seemed to know. "I hope it isn't the 'responsible behavior' talk," I heard Sharlanne say.

"Oh, frick," I messaged Kimkim. "Please don't let it be one of Mr. Fuyijama's speeches."

"I'll find out if it is," Kimkim messaged back. As I said, Kimkim's a computer genius. She can hack into anything, including the Euro-American Union Department of Defense. And Mr. Fuyijama's daily planner.

"Thanks," I said, starting toward the girls' bathroom so I could hide out in one of the stalls if it turned out to be one of his *very long* speeches, but before I could cross the hall, Coriander Abrams came careening down the hall, clutching her phone and squealing, "Ohmigod! Ohmigod! A Mandatory Attendance Assembly! Theodora, do you know what that means?" She grabbed my arm and dragged me into the auditorium, squealing all the way. "This could be it! Do you think I have a chance? Tell me, honestly, do you? Isn't this absolutely *incred*?"

When she finally let go of me (her friend Chelsea had come up and was hugging her and shrieking, "I know it's you! Ohmigod, a cadet! You are *so* lucky!" and she had to let go of me so the two of them could dance around), I messaged Kimkim, "Never mind. I know what it is."

I should have guessed. I mean, the Academy's all anyone's talked about since the IASA recruiter was here last September to give her little pep talk. As if anybody at Winfrey High needed a pep talk. Three fourths of them had already applied, and the other fourth would have if they'd thought they could pass the entrance exams. I don't know why they even bother sending a recruiter.

It was one of the many annoying aspects of having to go to school. I had wanted to do remote learning like everybody else, but my mom was a nostalgia freak, and she had somehow talked my dad into it.

"I thought you said you wanted me to be independent and not go along with the crowd," I'd said to him.

"I do. And what better place to do that than *in* a crowd?" he'd said, and told me a long and pointless story about the time he'd set off a stink bomb in the lunchroom.

So for the last three years, I've had to put up with Ms. Sionov's ridiculous phone rules, locker combinations, school lunches, Mandatory Attendance assemblies, and everybody drooling to get into the Academy.

It's almost impossible to do—they only take three hundred candidates a year, and less than half of them are from the Euro-American Union, so there's fierce competition. Candidates have got to score astronomically high (how appropriate!) on the Academy's entrance exams, have to have taken tons of math and science classes, be in perfect physical condition, and pass four separate levels of psychological tests and interviews.

But even that's not enough. With over fifty thousand eager applicants to choose from, IASA uses all sorts of strange algorithms and extra criteria to make its picks, and nobody knows exactly what they are. The recruiter who'd come to our school had said meaningless things like "Cadets must demonstrate dedication, determination, and devotion" and "We're looking not for excellence, but for the exceptional," and when Coriander asked her, "What can I do to improve my chances of being chosen?" she'd replied, "The Academy wants not only the crème de la crème, but the cream of the crème de la crème."

"I'd suggest you learn to milk a cow," I'd told Coriander.

"Oh, shut up," she'd said. "You're just jealous because I've passed the first three levels of the application process."

Some years it seems the Academy selects mostly kids who've taken astrophysics and exobiology (even though we haven't found any life anywhere out there that's bigger than a virus), and other years ethics. Or Renaissance history. Five years ago, there'd been a study that seemed to indicate students in schools had a statistical edge over home- and remote-schooled kids, which meant everyone going to Winfrey High except me was there because they thought it would increase their chances of getting an appointment.

And, apparently, for one person, it had.

My bet was that it was Coriander. She'd taken Renaissance history *and* ethics *and* exobiology and everything else she could think of, had gone out for sports, forensics, and community service with a vengeance, and had so completely monopolized the questioning of the recruiter that I'd finally raised my hand just to shut her up for a minute.

"Yes, you have a question, Ms.—?" the recruiter asked me, smiling. She was one of those perky PR types IASA sends out.

"Baumgarten," I said. "Theodora Baumgarten. Can you explain to me why anybody in their right mind would want to go to the Academy? I mean, I know it's so you can become an astronaut and go into space, but why would anybody want to? There's no air, you're squashed into a ship the size of a juice can, and it takes years to get anywhere interesting. If you get there and aren't killed first by a meteor or a solar flare or a systems malfunction."

The entire student body had turned and was staring uncomprehendingly at me as if I was speaking ancient Sumerian or something. The recruiter gave me a cold, measuring glance, and then turned and said something to Mr. Fuyijama.

"You're gonna get detention," Fletcher said.

"Any other questions?" the recruiter said, pointedly avoiding looking in my direction.

"Yes," Coriander said. "How many space engineering classes do I need to take?"

"I hope you weren't planning to apply to the Academy," Kimkim said as we left the auditorium, "because I think you just blew whatever chance you had."

"Good," I said. "I have no desire to leave terra firma."

"Really? You have no desire to go to the Academy at all?"

"No," I said. "Do you?"

"Of course," Kimkim said. "I mean, Mars and the rings of Saturn and all that. And getting to be a cadet. I'd love to go, but I don't have the math grades."

At that point, Coriander had stormed up and snarled, "You'd better not have ruined my chances with that little stunt," and apparently I hadn't. As we went into the auditorium now, Mr. Fuyijama beamed at her proudly from the stage.

Whoever was announcing the appointment apparently wasn't there yet. I looked for a seat way in the back in case it was the recruiter, waiting to see where Coriander and her cadre of screeching friends sat before I sat down as far away from them as possible. I stuck my compack next to me to save the seat for Kimkim, who still wasn't here. She'd messaged confirmation that the assembly was indeed to announce the appointment of a cadet. "At least we won't have to listen to a speech," she said.

I wasn't so sure of that. Mr. Fuyijama was on the stage at the podium, messing with the holopoint controls and saying, "Is this on?" into the microphone. Chelsea Goodrum sat down one row in front of me, squealing into her phone.

"You know it's going to be you, Coriander! Where are you sitting?" she demanded. Apparently Coriander told her because she began to wave wildly. "Come over here!" she said. "No, there are plenty of seats!"

Oh, frick, I thought, and stood up, but the auditorium was almost full, I couldn't see two other seats together anywhere except next to Chelsea, and it was too late. Mr. Fuyijama was saying, "Take your seats, students!"

I sat down, hoping Coriander hadn't had time to move either, but no, here she came with four of her shrieking friends. "This is the most incred thing ever!" Chelsea screamed, hugging her. "You're going to be a *cadet*!"

"Take your seats," Mr. Fuyijama said again, "and please turn your phones off," a totally unnecessary order since all wireless bands were automatically jammed at the beginning of every assembly.

"It's starting," I messaged Kimkim. "Where are you?"

"Denver. I'll be there in ten minutes."

"Today we're here to celebrate a tremendous honor," Mr. Fuyijama said, "the appointment of a student to the International Space Academy. Winfrey High is extremely proud to have had one of its students chosen for this honor, one of many honors we have had over the years," and proceeded to name every single one of them. It should have sent everyone to sleep, but the whole auditorium listened intently, except for Coriander's friends, who were squeezing her arms and whispering excitedly.

"Did I miss anything?" Kimkim messaged me seven hundred and twenty-two honors later.

"No," I sent back. "Did you know Winfrey High has won the Regional Koi-Growing Contest six years running? Where are you?"

"Over by the west door. I can't get to you."

"It's just as well," I sent, and told her about Coriander, who was now emitting little whimpers. "At least if you're by the door, you might be able to escape."

Unlike the rest of us. Mr. Fuyijama droned on for several more geological ages and then said, "But none of those honors come close to the one we're here to bestow today. I'd like to welcome Admiral H. V. Washington, deputy chief of staff of the Space Administration."

There was thunderous applause. "Ohmigod, they sent an *admiral*!" Coriander squealed.

The admiral came over to the podium. "Every year IASA appoints candidates from all over the American-European Union to the Academy. These students have had to undergo a rigorous four-tiered application-and-interview process and have had to demonstrate the qualities of—"

Oh, no, not you, too, I thought. "Why don't they just give it to Coriander and put the rest of us out of our misery?" I messaged Kimkim. "Everyone knows it's her."

"Not everyone," she messaged back. "Nearly half the money's on Matt Sung."

"What do you mean, nearly half the money? Is there a pool?"

"'Betting pools are strictly forbidden at Winfrey High School,'" she quoted. "Of course there's a pool. Do you want to place a last-minute bet?"

"Yes," I said. "Who else is in the running besides Coriander and Matt? Tomas Rivera?"

"No, he didn't pass the second-level interview."

"You're kidding." I'd thought Tomas was a shoo-in. He had great grades, great SATs. He'd taken nationals in gymnastics.

"Our cadets, in other words," the admiral was saying, "are not just the best of the best, but the very best of the best of the best."

"Some of the sophomores are voting for Renny Nickson," Kimkim messaged.

"Renny? I thought he wanted a Rhodes."

"Not if he can get an Academy appointment instead. Nobody would turn down a chance to be a cadet. That's why the Academy announces its picks before the universities do."

"And today's appointment exemplifies that excellence," the admiral said.

It sounded like he was winding up. If I wanted in the pool, I'd better do it now. "Put me down for Matt," I said, and then glanced at Coriander. She was squeezing the hands of her friends on either side of her and biting her lip. And if sheer wanting to be a cadet was part of the criteria, she'd win it hands down. She'd been trying to get in ever since first grade. And hadn't that recruiter said something about determination and devotion? "Wait," I said. "Change my pick to Coriander."

"It gives me great pleasure to announce—"

Coriander's eyes were shut tight and she was murmuring, "Please, please, please . . ." and squeezing the color out of her friends' hands.

"—an appointment to the International Space Academy for—" He paused and looked straight at Coriander.

"I told you it was Coriander," I typed. "Actually, this is a good thing. It means we won't have to put up with her any—"

"Theodora Baumgarten," the admiral said.

There was stunned silence, during which I had time to think, *I must have heard that wrong,* and then, *Very funny,* and to look around to see who was behind this particular stink bomb.

Coriander shouted, "Theodora *Baum*garten?" and I knew he'd really said it.

"Wait," I said, and the auditorium erupted in excited applause.

Fletcher grabbed my hand and pumped it up and down. "Wow!" he shouted over the clapping. "Congratulations!"

"But—" I tried to look at my phone.

"Oh, creez! Congratulations!" Kimkim's message read. "Why didn't you tell me you'd applied?"

"I didn't," I murmured, and tried to pull my hand free so I could message her, but Chelsea grabbed it, squeezed it, and then pushed me to the end of the row. "Go on! Get down there! What are you waiting for?"

I looked down at the stage. The admiral was smiling up at me from the stage and applauding, and Mr. Fuyijama was beaming and beckoning to me.

"There's been some mistake," I said, but no one was listening. They were patting and hugging me and shoving me down the steps toward the stage. "Can I touch you?" Marla Chang said in an awestruck voice, and Ms. Sionov grabbed me and kissed me. "You've always been my favorite student!" she cried.

"No, Ms. Sionov, you don't understand," I said, and then I was on the stage and Mr. Fuyijama was pumping my hand.

"Mr. Fuyijama, there's been a mistake—"

"I can't tell you how proud Winfrey High is of you!" he beamed, and pushed me at the admiral, who saluted and handed me a certificate.

I read it, hoping he'd just read the name wrong, but there it was in official-looking print, "Theodora Jane Baumgarten." *This can't be happening to me,* I thought. "This isn't mine," I said and tried to hand the appointment back to him.

"You're supposed to salute back and say, 'Cadet Baumgarten reporting for duty,'" Mr. Fuyijama whispered.

"But I'm not—" I said. "Admiral, I didn't apply for the Academy—" and everybody must have thought I was saying, "Cadet Baumgarten reporting for duty," because they started to applaud again. The admiral shook my hand and gave me an envelope.

"There's been a mistake. This isn't my—" I said, but Mr. Fuyijama was shaking my hand again and a swarm of students took the opportunity to close in around the admiral and begin bombarding him with questions.

"Mr. Fuyijama, I have to talk to you," I said. "This is all a mistake—"

"It certainly is," Coriander said, storming up. "Theodora *can't* have gotten an appointment. She didn't even take deep-field astronomy."

Mr. Fuyijama was looking at her like she was a bug, which would have been enjoyable if I hadn't been in so much trouble. "The Academy chooses for all sorts of skills," he said.

"But she can't have gotten the appointment over me," Coriander said. "She's *not* cadet material."

Mr. Fuyijama ignored her. "I've messaged your parents," he said. "They should be here any minute."

"Help," I messaged Kimkim, who I still couldn't see anywhere, and tried again with Mr. Fuyijama. "My appointment is a mistake. They mixed up the names or something."

"Don't let Coriander upset you," he said. "She was a fine candidate, but so are you, so are all of Winfrey High's students. We have one of the most outstanding schools in the country, and—"

It was hopeless. I tuned him out and looked around for the admiral. I couldn't see him anywhere. "Where did the admiral go?"

"He had to leave," Mr. Fuyijama said. "He has several more appointments to announce this afternoon."

"But I have to talk to him—" Oh, thank goodness, here was Kimkim. "Where have you *been*?" I said, pulling her off to the side of the stage. "You have to help me. Nobody will listen when I tell them there's been a mixup."

"Mixup?" she said.

"Yes, of *course* it's a mixup. I can't have been chosen. I didn't even apply to the Academy."

"You didn't?" she said happily, and flung her arms around me. "Oh, I'm so glad! I thought you'd applied without telling *me*, your best friend, and I was so hurt—"

"Why would I apply? I've told you a hundred times I don't want to go into space. I want to go to UCLA."

She looked sheepish. "I know, but I thought you were just saying that because you were afraid you couldn't get in. But how could there be a mixup?"

"I don't know. Maybe there's somebody else with the same name."

"Two Theodora Baumgartens? Unlikely."

"Well, maybe there's a Theodore Baumgarten. Or a Theodora Bauman. Come on, maybe we can catch the admiral before he leaves," I said, and we headed backstage.

"Wait, Theodora!" Mr. Fuyijama said before we'd gone two steps. "Your mother's here."

"I'll go see if I can catch him," Kimkim said, and darted off as Mr. Fuyijama and my mom closed in on me. "I'm so *proud* of you!" she said. "I knew we made the right decision in sending you to school. You didn't want to come, remember? And now look at you, a cadet!" She and Mr. Fuyijama beamed at each other. "I still can't believe it!"

"Where's Dad?" I said. He knew I didn't want to be a cadet. He'd see this was all a ghastly mistake.

"Cheyenne," Mom said. "As soon as I heard, I left a message for him to come to the school. Why didn't you *tell* us you'd applied?"

"Because—"

Mr. Fuyijama patted me on the shoulder. "Shouldn't you be getting home, young lady, and getting ready to go?"

For your information, I am not going anywhere, I thought.

"What am I saying?" Mr. Fuyijama went on, smiling coyly. "You've probably had your kit all packed and ready to go for months."

"Mr. Fuyijama's right," my mom said. "We need to get you home. You only have a few hours."

"A few—?"

"I'll call your father," Mom said, steering me toward the door and away from Kimkim. "He can meet us there."

"Mom, what do you mean, a few hours?" I said, but she was talking to Dad.

"Bob? Where are you? Oh, dear. Well, turn around and go back home. We're on our way."

Kimkim appeared, shaking her head. "The admiral'd already left."

"What does my mom mean, I only have a few hours?" I asked her.

"Didn't you listen to anything the recruiter said when she was here? Cadets go straight to the Academy after they're appointed," Kimkim said, grabbing the letter the admiral had given me and opening it. "It says they'll pick you up in exactly—oh, gosh, two hours and forty minutes."

"Let me talk to Dad," I said to Mom, who was still on the phone. Dad knew I didn't want to go into space. We'd talked about it after the recruiter came. "Hand me the phone."

Mom shook her head. "I'm talking to Grandma. You can talk to your dad when we get home. Yes, isn't it marvelous?" she said, presumably to Grandma, and then, presumably to me, "Get in the car. Yes, of *course* she'll want you to come over and say good-bye. Come on, we need to go. Good-bye, Kimkim."

"Kimkim's coming with me," I said, grabbing her arm and pushing her into the car. "She's going to help me pack."

Mom nodded absently, still talking to Grandma. She switched on the car and pulled away from the school. "Would you call Bob's parents for me? And Theodora's piano teacher? I'm sure she'll want to see her before she leaves."

"You've got to find out the admiral's phone number for me," I messaged Kimkim so Mom couldn't hear what we were saying, "so I can call him and explain—"

"I'll try," she messaged back. "Academy numbers are all classified."

"Do you think I should phone Aunt Jen and Aunt Lucy?" my mom called back to me.

"No," I said, and Kimkim put in helpfully, "She doesn't have much time, and she's got to pack, Mrs. Baumgarten."

"I suppose you're right. You should have done that beforehand, like Coriander Abrams. Her mother said she packed her kit the same day she filled out her application. Oh, look," she said, pulling into the driveway, "Aunt Jen and Lucy are already here."

They were, along with Grandma, Grandpa, Grandma and Grandpa Baumgarten, and about a hundred neighbors, all holding up a big laserspark banner twinkling Congratulations, Cadet Baumgarten!

The online news crews were all there, too, holding mikes, and it took me half an hour to get into the house and another fifteen minutes to escape to my room, where Kimkim was working away at my computer. "Here," she said, handing me a printout.

"What is it?" I said eagerly. "The admiral's phone number?"

"No, it's the list of what you're allowed to take. Fifteen-pound weight limit. No pets, no plants, no weapons."

"Because they know at this point I'd like to shoot them. I don't need lists," I said, throwing it in the wastebasket and going over to stand beside her. "I *need* the admiral's phone number."

"I can't get to it," Kimkim said. "I've been trying to hack into the Academy officer roster for the last half hour. It's got firewalls, moats, ramparts, the works. I'm not surprised. With fifty thousand candidates, they'd be inundated with students trying to find out the officers' numbers so they could call them and beg them to be let in, but it means I can't get in either."

"Of course you can," I said. "The database you can't hack hasn't been invented. What about calling the airport? Mr. Fuyijama said the admiral had to go announce more appointments."

"I already did. IASA refused to authorize an in-flight emergency call, and the plane's onboard number is just as protected as the admiral's."

My mom poked her head in the door. "Theodora? You need to come cut your cake."

"I'm still packing," I said, grabbing my duffel bag off my closet shelf and throwing some underwear into it.

"It'll only take a minute," she said firmly. "The governor's here."

Oh, frick. "Have you heard from Dad?"

"No, but he should be here any minute. Come on. Everyone's waiting."

"I'll be right there," I said, and called up Dad, but there was no answer. "I'll only be a minute," I said to Kimkim. "There has to be some kind of emergency number where we can talk to somebody. Keep trying!" and went out to the dining room.

Everyone in town was there, gathered around a sheet cake with a spaceship and silver stars spelling out "Blast off!" Mom handed me a huge piece, and I gulped it down, nodding while two dozen people I'd never seen before told me how lucky I was, and finally escaped on the pretext of taking Kimkim some cake. She waved it away, intent on her hacking, so I ate it.

"It's no use," she said. "I can't get in anywhere. IASA, the Academy cadet roster, everything's blocked."

"But there has to be a number where the cadets can call them if they've got questions."

"There is," she said, her eyes on the screen. "It's automated. Press '1' for a list of forbidden kit items. Press '2' for the Academy course schedule. Sixteen menu choices, but none for 'If you wish to speak to an operator' or 'I think there's been a mistake.' You don't remember the name of that recruiter, do you?"

"No. Did you check the name thing?"

"Yes. There's no Theodore Baumgarten, or Ted, or Dora. Or Bauman or Bauer or Bommgren. The closest thing I found was a Theopholus Bami, and he lives in New Delhi. And is four years old."

"Oh. I know—look up the Academy rules. Those can't be encrypted, they're public record, and there's got to be something in there about turning down an appointment."

My mom poked her head in again. "Your dad's just pulled in," she said.

Dad. Thank goodness. I waded through the crowd in the dining room again, which now seemed to contain everyone in the state of Colorado, all eating cake, and outside. "Dad, I have to talk to you. I didn't apply to the Academy—"

"You didn't?"

"No. I—"

"That's wonderful! You did just what I always told you to do—follow your own path, be independent, don't do what everybody else is doing, and look what it got you! An Academy appointment!"

"No, Dad, you don't understand. I don't want this appointment. I don't want to go to the Academy!"

"That's what you said your first day of school, remember? And do you remember what I told you?"

"The stink bomb story?"

He laughed. "No, I told you to try it for a week and then see how you felt. You're just having cold feet. When does she leave?" he asked Mom, who'd come up carrying two pieces of cake.

She handed us each one. "In twenty minutes."

"Twenty *minutes*?!" I said, looking at my digital. According to it, I still had over an hour.

"IASA called. They said they knew how eager cadets always are to go, so they're sending the escort over early."

"I have to pack," I said, and shot back into my room. "You have to do something. *Now*," I told Kimkim.

"I'm trying," she said. "I looked up the Academy appointment regulations, but there's nothing in them about turning an appointment down, and I still can't get through to anybody. I'm afraid you're going to have to go to the Academy to get this straightened out. It's the only way you're going to be able to talk to someone in person."

"I am *not* going to the Academy," I said, tossing clothes and shoes into the duffel bag she'd gotten out. "I'll hide till the escort leaves. What about your basement?"

"That won't work," she said, coming over and taking out the clothes I was putting in. "They'll think you've been kidnapped or something. Remember that cadet in Barcelona whose girlfriend tied him up so she could take his place? They'll think Coriander killed you and send out an APB. Look," she said, picking up the list and handing it to me, "you go with them and talk to whoever's in charge of admissions. I'll keep working from this end, and as soon as I've got something, I'll message you. Do your mom and dad have a lawyer?"

Mom knocked. "Theodora, your escort's here," she said.

"Give me two minutes," I shouted, frantically trying to find "3 pr. tube socks, white."

"Here's your toothbrush and toothpaste," Kimkim said, "and your phone."

"Come on, Cadet Baumgarten," my dad said, opening the door. "You don't want to keep the Academy waiting."

"Dad, what's our lawyer's name?"

"Oh, for the admission papers and things, you mean? We'll take care of all that. You just go on and have a good time." He scooped up the half-packed duffel bag and led me out through the patting, handshaking crowd to the waiting hover. "It's a good thing you didn't do what I did in high school," he said, handing me into the hover. "If you'd set off a stink bomb, they'd never have let you in."

If only I'd known, I thought. The pilot leaned across me, shut the door, and took off. I took out my phone. "Help," I messaged Kimkim.

I decided there was no point in trying to explain things to the pilot, especially after he said, "Boy, are you lucky! I'd sell my soul to get into the Academy!" I would just have to explain things again to the person in charge once I got there, and besides, in spite of what Kimkim had said, I was seriously considering making a run for it when he let me out at the gates, but he landed me inside the high, razor-wire-tipped walls and walked me into the main building past two heavily armed sentries and handed me over to a man in an IASA uniform.

"I want to talk to the person in charge of admissions," I said to him.

"Name?"

"Theodora Baumgarten," I said, hoping against hope it wasn't on his list, but he found it immediately, handed me an ID badge, and weighed my bag.

"You're two pounds over," he said, opening it and taking out my phone. "You can get rid of this. It won't work in the Academy."

Oh, frick, I hadn't considered that possibility. I'd have to message Kimkim and tell her—

"I have a sentimental attachment to it," I said. "You can take my curling iron instead."

The door behind us opened and two girls came in.

"Oh, look at this! I can't believe we're here!" one of them said, clutching her chest just like Coriander, and the other one kept repeating, "Ohmigod, ohmigod, ohmigod!" till I thought she was going to hyperventilate.

"You're still overweight," the IASA guy said. "You sure you don't want to give up your phone?"

"I'm sure," I said, pulling out my iPod and some DVDs.

He shrugged. "Suit yourself," he said, handed me back the bag, and turned to the Hyperventilator. "Name?"

"Excuse me," I said, moving back in front of her. "I asked to see the person in charge of admissions."

"You'll have to talk to your sector officer," he said, looking at the list. "H-level. Second elevator on the right."

I took it down to H, messaging Kimkim the news about the phone on the way down. "Working on it," she answered immediately, so at least the phone worked in this part of the Academy. They must just jam the student areas, which meant till Kimkim found a way around it, I'd have to sneak off to an area where it did work.

If I was here that long. Which I might be, since the fourth-year cadet waiting for me on H-level looked at me totally blankly when I told him I wanted to see the admissions person.

"Never mind," I said. "Take me to the head of the Academy."

"You mean the Commander?"

"Yes," I said firmly.

"This way," he said, and led me down a long cement corridor, up an even longer ramp, and into another elevator. He pushed "3," and we went up for a very long way. It opened on an accordion-pleated tunnel, like a jetway, ending in a narrow, curved corridor lined with doors.

He stopped in front of one of them, opened it, and stepped aside so I could enter. "Is this the Commander's office?" I asked.

"No. Wait here," he said, and walked away, and before I could start after him, the Hyperventilator had swooped down on me.

"Isn't this exciting?" she squealed. "Come on!" She grabbed my arm and dragged me into the room, which was clearly not the Commander's office. It was a room the size of a closet with curved walls and two bunks. "I can't believe we're in the same cabin!"

Cabin—?

She'd plopped down on the lower bunk. "Come on, get strapped in! We launch in five minutes! Aren't we lucky?" she said, busily fastening straps. "All the other classes had to spend their first semester earthside before they got to go up."

The elevators, the jetway, the curving corridor—"We're in a *spaceship*?" I said, calculating whether I could make it down that jetway to the elevator in two minutes.

"I know, I can't believe it's happening either!"

An alarm began to sound. "All cadets to their acceleration couches."

I dived for the remaining bunk.

"You do the chest straps first," the Hyperventilator said. "Just think, in a few hours we'll be on the Ra!"

"The Ra?" I said, struggling with the straps. They were so in love with the Academy, they'd named it after a god?

"That's what cadets call the Academy space station, the *Rob-*

ert A. Heinlein. The *RAH,* get it? And now we're cadets! Can you *believe* this is actually happening?"

"No."

"Me neither!" she said. "Don't you think you'd better put your emesis bag on?"

I threw up all the way to the *RAH*.

"Gosh, I didn't think it was possible to throw up at four g's," the Hyperventilator said. "Maybe you'll feel better when we go into freefall."

I didn't. I went through my vomit bag and hers and threw up on the bunk, the walls, the Hyperventilator, and, once we were weightless, on the air in front of me, where it formed disgusting-looking yellowish-brown globules that floated around the cabin for the rest of the trip.

"What on earth did you eat?" the Hyperventilator asked.

"Cake," I said miserably, and vomited again.

"It can't last much longer," she said, ducking a large globule floating toward her. "You can't have anything left."

Also not true.

"You'll be okay once we get to the *RAH,*" she said.

"Rah, rah, rah," I said weakly, and proved her wrong by throwing up all over the cadet sent to unstrap us, the connecting deck, and the airlock.

At least this *will convince them there's been a mistake,* I thought as the cadet half carried me to my quarters, but he said cheerfully, "A touch of space sickness, huh?" He lowered me onto my bunk. "Happens to every cadet."

"I'm *not* a cadet," I said, and then, even though I wanted to lie there in my bunk and die, said, "I want to see the Commander."

"I know how you feel," he said. "My first day up here, I wanted to go home, too. You'll feel better after a shower and a nap."

"No, I won't. I demand to see the head. Now," I said, and got up to show him I was serious, but the minute I did, I felt wildly light-headed and on the verge of toppling, as if I were in a canoe about to tip over.

"Coriolis effect," he said, grabbing my arm and lowering me back onto the bunk. "It takes a couple of days to get used to."

"I won't live that long," I muttered, and he laughed again.

"I need to go get the other cadets settled in, and then I'll come back and see how you're doing," he said, covering me up with a Mylar blanket. "If you need me before that, just hit 'send.'" He handed me a communicator. "And don't worry. A little thing like space sickness won't get you thrown out of the Academy."

"But I *want* to be—" I began, but he was already gone, and the thought of getting up off the bunk to go after him, or even of pressing the button on the communicator, sent the room toppling over again.

I'll just lie here very, very quietly till he comes back, I thought, and then insist on seeing the Commander, but I must have been asleep when he came back, because when I opened my eyes, the Hyperventilator was unpacking her kit on the other bunk. "Oh, good, you're awake," she said. "We're going to be bunkmates! Isn't that incred! I'm Libby, I mean, Cadet Thornburg. Are you feeling better?"

"No," I said, though I was, a little. At least I was able to sit up. However, when I tried to stand, the room gave a sudden lurch, and I had to grab for the wall, and it, the other walls, and Libby seemed to be leaning ominously toward me. I reared back and nearly fell over.

"It's because of the Coriolis effect from the spin on the space station. It makes everything seem to tilt toward you. Isn't it incred?"

"Umm," I said. "How long does it take to get used to it?" It must not be that long. She was moving around without any trouble. Or maybe that was one of the things IASA tested for in its four-tiered screening process.

"I don't know. I wanted to get a head start," she said, stowing clothes in the locker above her bunk, "so I practiced in an artificial-gravity simulator before I came. Three weeks, maybe?"

I would never last three weeks. Which meant I had to get in to see the Commander now. I pressed the communicator button and then spent the time till the fourth-year got there working on standing up, walking over to the door, and fighting the urge to grab onto something, anything, at all times.

The fourth-year looked surprised to see me on my feet. I told him I wanted to see the Commander. "Don't you want to wait till you feel steadier?" he asked, looking at my vomit-spattered clothes. "And have a chance to clean up?"

"No."

"Okay," he said doubtfully. "What did you want to see the Commander about?"

If I told him, he'd stare blankly at me or say everyone with space sickness felt that way. "There's a problem with my application," I said.

"Oh, then, you want the registrar."

"No, I—" I began and then decided the registrar was exactly who I wanted to see. He'd have the applications on file, and when he saw I didn't have one, he could correct the mistake immediately. "Okay, take me to the registrar's office."

"That's not necessary," he said. "You can message him from here." He switched on the terminal above my bunk.

"No," I said. "I want to see him in person."

"Okay, wait here, and I'll see if he's available."

"No," I said, letting go of the wall with an effort. "I'm coming with you."

It was the longest walk of my life. I couldn't seem to overcome the feeling that everything, including the fourth-year, was about to pitch forward onto me and/or that I was about to float away, and I periodically had to latch onto handgrips and/or the fourth-year in spite of myself.

"It's because the gravity's only two-thirds that of earth," he said. "You'll get used to it. You're lucky it's not a full g. The more rotation, the more Coriolis effect. Any less, though, and there's bone loss. Two thirds is a happy medium."

"That's what you think," I muttered, showing no signs of getting used to it, even though he led me through what seemed like miles of tube-like corridors and locks and ladders, ending finally in an office not much bigger than my cabin. A guy who looked like my dad was seated at a console.

"What can I do for you, Cadet Baumgarten?" he asked kindly.

I poured out my whole story, hoping against hope he wouldn't give me another of those I-don't-understand-what-language-you're-speaking looks.

He didn't. He said, "Oh, dear, that's terrible. I can't imagine how that could have happened."

Relief flooded over me.

"I'll look into this immediately. Cadet Apley," he called into an inner office, "find me Cadet Baumgarten's file." He turned back to me. "Don't worry. We'll get this straightened out."

A young woman's voice called out to him, "The files for the new cadets haven't been transmitted yet, sir."

"Well, tell them I need it as soon as possible."

"Yes, sir," she said.

"Don't worry, Cadet Baumgarten," he said. "We'll get this straightened out. I intend to launch a full investigation." He stood up and extended his hand. "I'll notify you as soon as we've determined what happened."

I ignored his hand. "How long will that be?"

"Oh, it shouldn't take more than a week or two."

"A *week* or two?" I said. "But you've made a mistake. I'm not supposed to be here."

"If that is the case, you'll of course be sent home immediately," he said, showing me the door. "In the meantime, may I congratulate you on your rapid adaptation to artificial gravity. Very impressive."

If I could have thrown up on him, I would have, but there was no cake left. Instead, I planted myself in front of him as firmly as was possible in two-thirds g and said, "I want to make a phone call."

"Cadets aren't allowed phone calls for the first two weeks of term. After that, you can make one two-minute earthside call a month," he said.

"I know my rights," I said, trying not to sway backward. "Prisoners are allowed a phone call."

He looked amused. "The *RAH* is not a prison."

Wanna bet? "It's my legal right," I said stubbornly. "A *private* phone call."

He sighed. "Cadet Apley," he called into the inner office, "set up a Y49TDRS link for Cadet Baumgarten," and handed me a satellite phone. "Two minutes. There'll be a six-second lag. This will count as next month's call," he said, and went into the inner office and shut the door.

They were probably listening in, but I didn't care. I called Kimkim. "I'm so sorry," she said. "I didn't know they were taking cadets straight up to the *Heinlein*. Are you okay?"

"No," I said. "Did you find out my mom and dad's lawyer's name?"

Seconds passed, and then she said, "Yes, I talked to her."

"What did she say?"

More seconds. "That an Academy appointment was considered a legally binding contract."

Oh, frick.

"So I went online and found a lawyer who specializes in Academy law."

"And?" Creez, this lag was maddening.

"He said he only handled cases of cadets who'd been eliminated from the Academy and were trying to get reinstated. He said he couldn't find any record of a case where a cadet had wanted *out*."

"Did he say how these cases he handled *got* eliminated?" I asked, thinking maybe I could do whatever it was they did.

"Failing their courses, mostly," she said. "But, listen, don't do anything that might mess up your chances at UCLA. That's why these cadets file lawsuits, because flunking out of the Academy pretty much ruined their chances of getting into any other university."

Worse and worse. "Listen, you've got to figure out some way we can talk." I told her about the one call a month.

"I'll see what I can do. They didn't take your phone away from you, did they?"

"No," I said.

"Did they say anything about how this call worked?"

"They called it a Y49TDRS, whatever that is."

"It means it's relayed through tracking, data, and relay satellites," she said. "A Y49 shouldn't be too hard to patch into, but it may take—"

There was a buzz. "Call over," an automated voice said.

I spent the next day and a half checking my phone for messages and hoping Kimkim hadn't been about to say, "It may take months for me to come up with something," or, worse, "It may take extensive modifications to your phone's circuits," and worrying that if the registrar had been listening in, it didn't matter. They'd jam whatever Kimkim tried.

Then classes started, and I spent every waking moment trying to keep up with cadets who'd not only taken astrogation and exobotany, but knew how to dock a shuttle, read a star chart, and brush their teeth while weightless. First-year cadets had to spend half of each watch in the non-rotated sections of the *RAH,* learning to live and work in microgravity. Most of them (including, of course, Libby) had taken classes in weightlessness on Earth, and the rest had clearly been chosen for their ability to float from one end of the module to the other without crashing into something, a gene I obviously lacked. The second day, I sneezed, did a backward triple somersault, and crashed into a bank of equipment, an escapade that gave me the idea of pleading a bad cold and asking to see the doctor—a medical discharge surely couldn't hurt my chances at UCLA—but when I went to the infirmary, the medic said, "Stuffiness in the head is a normal side effect of weightlessness," and gave me a sinus prescription.

"What about chronic vertigo?" I asked. I was actually down to only a couple of episodes a day, but it had occurred to me that "inability to tolerate space environment" might be a way out.

"If it hasn't disappeared a month from now, come see me," he said, and sent me back to EVA training. Luckily, I didn't sneeze during my spacewalk and go shooting off into space, but being outside and linked to the *RAH* only by a thin tether reminded me just how dangerous space was.

Well, that, and the fact that those dangers were the second favorite topic of the cadets at mess and during rec periods. If they weren't talking about the difficulty of detecting fires in a weightless environment (there aren't any flames, just a hard-to-see reddish glow), they were recounting gruesome tales of jammed oxygen lines and carbon monoxide buildup and malfunctioning heating units which froze students into cadet-sicles. Or speculating on all the things that *might* happen, from unexpected massive solar flares to killer meteors to explosive decompression. All of which made it clear I needed to get off of here *soon*. I messaged the registrar during my study period, but he said he was still waiting for the cadet files.

There was still no word from Kimkim. I checked my phone every time I had the chance and tried to send her periodic Maydays, but each time the display said, "Number out of range," which was putting it mildly.

I messaged the registrar again. Still waiting.

You're *still waiting*? I thought. At least he had an office of his own. He didn't have to share with Miss Ohmigod, This Is So Incred! Libby adored everything about the Academy—the sardine-can cabins, the rehydrated food, the exhausting schedule of lectures and labs and exercise and freefall training. She even loved the falling-off-a-log vertigo. "Because then you know you're really in space!"

And she wasn't the worst one. Several of the cadets acted like they were in a cathedral, wandering the corridors with their mouths open and speaking in hushed, reverent tones. When I mentioned that the place smelled like a gym locker, they looked at me like I was committing heresy, and went back to the cadets' favorite topic of conversation, how *lucky* they were to be here. By the end of a week, I was ready to walk through an airlock without a spacesuit just to get away from them.

I was also worried about how I was going to talk to Kimkim, if and when she figured out a phone connection, and about finding a safe place to stash my phone so the registrar couldn't suddenly confiscate it. I checked the *RAH*'s schematics, but there was nowhere a person could go to be alone on the entire space station. Every classroom and lab was used every hour of every watch.

So were the mess, the gym, and the weightless modules, and when I'd gone to the infirmary, there hadn't been separate examining rooms, just a tier of cots.

There was temporary privacy in the shower (very temporary—water is even more limited than the phone call times) and there was supposed to be "private time" half an hour before lights-out, but it wasn't enforced, and Libby's half of the cabin was always crammed with cadets discussing how *exciting* it had been to learn to use the zero-g toilet. I began to actually miss Coriander.

I checked the schematics again, looking for anything at all that might work. The inner room of the registrar's office might in a pinch, though when I'd gone over to ask him what was taking the files so long, I'd been told the section was off-limits to first-years. So was the docking module, and all the outer sections were exposed to too much radiation to make them practical.

The only other possibility was the storage areas, which in the super-compact world of the *RAH* meant every space that wasn't being used for something else—floors, ceilings, walls, even the airlocks. The diagrams showed all those spaces as filled with supplies, but it occurred to me (during a private-time discussion about the joys of learning to sit down in two-thirds g) that once those supplies had been used, the place they'd been might be empty.

I noted some of the possible spots and for the next few days spent my rest period exploring, and finally came up with a space between the plastic drums of nutrients for the hydroponics farm. It wasn't very big, and it was above the ceiling, but luckily it was in the freefall area, and I'd finally figured out how to propel myself from one location to another in it without major damage. I half drifted, half rappelled my way up (over?) to the ceiling, squeezed into the space (which turned out to be a perfect size, big enough, but too small to drift around in), replaced the hatch, and spent a blissful fifteen minutes alone.

It would have been longer, but I remembered a class was scheduled to come in sometime soon, and I couldn't afford to get caught. When I got back to my cabin, I memorized the freefall-area-use schedule and checked for a message from the registrar.

There wasn't one, but on my schedule was "Conference Registrar's office. Tuesday. 1600 hours." Which meant I wouldn't need a hiding place after all.

"I've gone over your application," the registrar said, "and everything appears to be in order."

"In order?" I said blankly.

"Yes," he said, looking at the console. "Application, entrance exams, endurance test results, psychological battery scores. It's all here."

"Application?" I said, standing up too fast and nearly shooting over the desk at him. "I told you, I didn't apply!"

"I also sent for the interviewer assessments and the minutes of the selection committee. You did in fact apply—"

"I did *not*—"

"—and were duly appointed."

"I want to see that application. It must be a forgery—"

"Conflicted feelings among new cadets are not unusual. A strange new environment, separation from family, performance anxiety can all be factors. Did you perhaps have a friend who also wanted to get into the Academy?"

"Yes, but . . . I mean, *she* wanted in the Academy, I didn't. I didn't—"

He nodded sagely. "And now you feel by accepting your appointment you're betraying that friend—"

"*No,*" I said. "I did not write that application. Let me see it."

"Certainly," he said, hit several keys, and the image of the application came up on the screen.

"Theodora Jane Baumgarten," it read. *This is like a bad dream,* I thought. Birth date, address, school . . . Before I could read the rest of it, the registrar had hit the next screen and the next. "You see?" he said, blanking the last screen before I could get a good look at it. "And quite an impressive application, if I may say so. I think you'll make an excellent addition to the Academy."

"I want to see the Commander," I said.

"She'd only tell you the same thing." He hit several more keys, and the terminal spat out a slip of paper. "I've made an appointment for you with Dr. Tumali. He'll help you sort out any conflicting feelings you—"

"I don't *have* any conflicting feelings. I *hate* this place, and I want to go home," I screeched at him, and stormed out, slamming the door behind me. Well, sort of. Slams aren't terribly impressive at two-thirds g, and after I'd done it, I realize I should have demanded another phone call instead, this one to my mother. She'd said she'd secretly hoped I'd apply. Maybe she'd decided to do it for me. Or maybe Coriander had, as some kind of hideous joke. Or Mr. Fuyijama. The more cadets he had, the better Winfrey High looked.

But even if they'd filled out an application and forged my signature, they couldn't have faked the entrance exams or the interviews. It made no sense, and I had no time to think about it. I had an essay due on asteroid mining and a lunar geography exam to study for. "Help," I messaged Kimkim.

The display lit up. "Number out of range."

Three days later, when I had decided I was going to have to do something drastic to get myself expelled and forget UCLA, my phone rang in the middle of rest period. "What was that?" Libby said drowsily.

"A killer meteor," I said, switching the phone to "message."

"Are you there?" the display read.

"Yes," I messaged, "hang on," and took off at a run for the freefall area. And nearly got caught by a group of second-years playing weightless soccer. I had to wait till they'd finished and left to swing up to my hiding place, hoping Kimkim hadn't concluded she'd lost me in the meantime.

As soon as I was inside the space, I switched the phone to "voice" and said, "Kimkim, are you there?"

There was no answer. *Oh, frick,* I thought, and then remembered the lag.

"I'm here," she said. "Sorry I took so long. I had trouble setting up an encryption so the Academy can't eavesdrop on us."

"That's okay," I said. "I need you to get a look at my Academy application."

"I thought you said you didn't apply."

"I *didn't,* but the registrar showed me something that looked like one. I need you to find out what kind of signature verification it's got on it, an R-scan or a thumbprint, and what site notarized it."

"You think IASA faked it?"

"IASA or somebody else. You didn't submit an application in my name, did you?"

"I resent that," she said. "If I was going to fake one, I'd have faked my own."

She called back two days later in the middle of tensor calculus to tell me she couldn't get to my application. "I was finally able to hack into the Academy's database and the cadet applications files, but I can't get into yours."

"Because it doesn't exist," I said after I got to my hiding place.

"No, I mean, there's a file with your name on it, but I can't get access."

"What about having someone they won't connect with me make the request?"

"I already tried that. I used my sister's friend's friend in Jakarta. She couldn't get in either. Neither could any of the professional hackers I contacted. It's blocked. I can get into the other applications, but not yours."

"Well, keep trying," I said, and hung up. I stuck the phone down the front of my uniform, crawled over to the hatch, and began to slide it open.

And heard voices below me.

The soccer players weren't supposed to be in here till 1900 hours. I slid the hatch silently shut and flattened myself against it, listening. "It's my bunkmate," Libby was saying. "I've *tried* to be friends with her, but she acts like she doesn't want to be here."

You're right, I thought. *In more ways than one.*

"Libby's right. Her bunkmate's got a terrible attitude," one of her friends said. "I have no idea how she got appointed when there are thousands of candidates who'd *love* to be here."

"I know the Academy must have had a good reason for picking her," Libby said, "but . . ." and launched into a ten-minute list of my shortcomings, which I had no choice but to lie there and listen to. "That's why I asked you to meet me here," she said when she was finally finished. "I need your advice."

"Tell the dean you want a different bunkmate," another friend said.

"I can't," Libby said. "Inability to foster healthy personal relations is the number one reason for failing first-year."

"Cut her EVA tether next time she's outside," the first friend said, which didn't exactly sound like fostering healthy personal relations to me.

"Maybe you should introduce her to Cadet Griggs," another voice said. "It sounds like they'd be perfect for each other."

"Who's Cadet Griggs?" Libby asked.

"He's a third-year in my exochem class. Jeffrey Griggs. He doesn't like anything or anybody."

"I sat next to him in mess last week, and he was completely insufferable," the first one said. "And conceited. He claims he didn't even have to apply to get in. He—what was that?"

I must have kicked one of the nutrient drums in my surprise. I held my breath, praying they didn't investigate.

"He claims he was so brilliant they just appointed him without his taking any entrance exams or anything."

"You should definitely introduce them, Libby, and maybe they'll move in together, and your problem will be solved, and so will hers."

My problem is *solved*, I thought.

As soon as they left, I called Kimkim. "I need you to get into the cadet application files."

"I told you, I can't get anywhere near your application."

"Not mine," I said. "Cadet Jeffrey Griggs's. He's a third-year."

She said the name back to me. "What am I looking for?"

"The application," I said.

She called back the next day. "There's no application on file for Jeffrey Griggs."

"I knew it. Listen, I need you to go through all the cadet files for the last five years and see how many others are missing."

"I already did. I went back eight years and found four more: one last year, two four years ago, one seven."

"I need you to find out where they are now."

"I did, and you're not going to like the answer. All but one of them are still in the Academy or working for IASA."

"What about the one who isn't?"

"Medical discharge. 'Inability to tolerate space environment.' Her name's Palita Duvai. She's in graduate school at Harvard," Kimkim said. "Do you want their names?"

"Yes," I said, even though I knew the registrar would say five missing applications didn't prove anything. He'd claim they'd been accidentally erased, and if it wasn't an accident, then why hadn't they posted phony applications like the one they'd shown me?

I asked Kimkim that.

"I don't know," she said, "but it's definitely not an accident. When I looked up their IASA assignments, I found something else. Next to their ranks are the letters 'D.A.' It's part of Jeffrey's class rank, too—'Third-year Cadet, D.A.' "

D.A. District Attorney? Didn't Apply? Dragged Away Kicking and Screaming?

"I looked it up in the IASA lexicon, but it wasn't there," she said. "Do you want me to try to find out what it stands for?"

"I don't think that will be necessary," I said. I signed off, went back to my cabin and got the slip of paper the registrar had given me with the psychiatrist appointment on it, wrote, "D.A.," on the back, and took it up. I handed it, folded, to one of the guards, told him to slide it under the registrar's door, and went back to my cabin to wait.

I didn't even make it halfway. A fourth-year cadet was waiting for me before I even reached the dorm section. "Cadet Baumgarten?" she said. "The registrar wants to see you," and took me back up to his office.

"Come in, Ms. Baumgarten," the registrar said. "Sit down." I noted that the slip of paper was on his desk. And that he hadn't called me Cadet Baumgarten.

"The cadet said you wanted to—" I began, and then absorbed what he'd said. Ms. Baumgarten, not Cadet Baumgarten. I sat down.

"I'm sorry to have taken so long getting back to you," he said. "The first few weeks of term are always so hectic. However, I wanted to tell you that we've completed the check on your application, and you were correct. A mistake in our admissions software wrongly identified you as a candidate. The IASA sincerely regrets the error and any inconvenience it may have caused you."

"Inconvenience–!"

"You will be reimbursed for that inconvenience and your lost class time," he went on smoothly. "I understand you want to go to UCLA. We've already spoken to them and explained the situation, and they've agreed to reschedule your interview at your convenience. If you encounter any other problems, feel free to contact me." He handed me a folder. "Here are your discharge papers."

I opened the folder and read the papers. Next to "Reason for Discharge," it read, "Medical–Inability to Tolerate Space Environment."

"You're free to leave whenever you wish," the registrar said. "We've reserved a space for you on tomorrow's shuttle. It leaves at 0900 hours. Or, if you prefer, we'd be happy to arrange for a civilian shuttle, and if there's anything else we can do, please let us know."

He stood up and came around the desk. "I hope your time with us hasn't been too unpleasant," he said, and extended his hand.

And all I had to do was shake it, go pack my kit, and get on that shuttle, and I'd be back on blessed Earth and on my way to UCLA. It was extremely tempting.

"Sorry," I said, folding my arms across my chest. "Not good enough."

"Not–? If you're worried about questions from your friends and family regarding your leaving the Academy, I'll be happy to issue a statement explaining that inner-ear problems made it impossible for you to adjust to the Coriolis effect. Medical discharges carry no stigma–"

"I don't want a medical discharge. I want to know the truth. Why did you hijack me? And how many people have you done it to besides me? I know of at least ten," I lied. "What do you want with us? And don't tell me you don't have enough candidates."

"Actually, that's exactly why we hijacked you," he said, and called into the inner office. "Commander! I think you'd better take over!"

The Commander came in. At least, she was wearing a commander's uniform and insignia, but she couldn't be the Commander. She was the recruiter who'd come to Winfrey High. "Hello, Ms. Baumgarten," she said. "It's nice to see you again."

"You!" I said. "You kidnapped me because of that question I asked in assembly, to punish me."

"Yes and no," she said. "Punishment was the farthest thing from my mind. And I prefer the word 'shanghaied' to 'kidnapped.'"

"Shanghaied?"

"Yes. It comes from the practice in the port of Shanghai in the 1800s of ship captains' using unorthodox methods for obtaining crews for long, dangerous voyages. When they couldn't get the sailors they needed any other way, they drugged them, carried them aboard, and held them prisoner till they were out to sea. Not a nice technique, but sometimes necessary."

"I don't believe you," I said. "You have thousands and thousands of people who are dying to go to the Academy every year."

"You're right," she said. "Last year we had nine thousand students who successfully completed all four tiers of the screening policy. From those, we chose three hundred, which meant they were the most determined and dedicated of those nine thousand."

"And every one of them's *thrilled* to be here," I said.

"Exactly. They love the Academy, they love IASA, and that sort of intense devotion is absolutely necessary. Space exploration is an impossibly challenging and dangerous, often deadly, undertaking. Without complete belief in what they're doing, it couldn't be done. But that sort of devotion can also be a handicap. Explorers who are too in love with the jungle end up being bitten by snakes or eaten by tigers. To survive, IASA has to have people who are fully aware of the jungle's dangers and disadvantages and not the least enchanted by its beauties.

"Which means, along with astrogation and the ability to live in confined quarters, we also recruit for skepticism, independence, and questioning of authority—in short, for people who don't like the jungle. Unfortunately, those people generally do everything they can to avoid it, which is why we are forced to—"

"Shanghai people," I said. "Let me get this straight. The reason you wanted me to come to the Academy was because I didn't want to?"

"Yes."

"And what was I supposed to do here?"

"Precisely what you did. Refuse to be impressed, challenge authority, break the rules. Your determination to communicate with your friend was particularly educational. We obviously need to do a much better job of preventing hacking. Also, we've learned not to put D.A. even on interior records. And it's clear we need to reexamine the necessity of providing private space for our cadets. You've performed a valuable service," she said. "IASA thanks you." She extended her hand.

"I'm not done asking questions yet," I said. "Why do you have to shanghai people? Why didn't you just *ask* me?"

"Would you have come?"

I thought about that day she'd come to Winfrey High to recruit applicants. "No."

"Exactly," she said. "Besides, bringing D.A.s here involuntarily ensures the critical mindset we're looking for."

"It also ensures that when they find out, they'll be so furious they won't want to have anything to do with the Academy or IASA," I said.

"True," she said ruefully, "but they don't usually find out. You're only the second one."

"Was the first one Palita Duvai?" I asked.

"No," she said. "Unfortunately, Cadet Duvai's medical discharge was real. Inner-ear complications."

But if she wasn't the one, I thought, frowning, *then that meant uncovering the conspiracy didn't automatically mean a discharge, and that meant—*

"The other D.A.s concluded that either there'd been a bureaucratic foul-up or they'd been so outstanding they hadn't needed to apply."

Jeffrey Griggs, I thought.

"Or they eventually gave up trying to go home and decided that, in spite of the food and the solar flares, they liked the Academy." She shook her head. "I underestimated your dislike of space. And your friend's hacking and communication abilities. Tell me, is Kimkim interested in becoming a cadet?"

"That depends on what you're recruiting for," I said. "If you want a great hacker, yes. If you're looking for another D.A., then no, definitely not, she'd probably have to be dragged up here kicking and screaming. And the sooner the better."

The Commander grinned. "I really am sorry to lose you. I think you would have made an excellent D.A." She leaned back. "Have we answered all your questions?"

"No," I said. "I have two more."

"You want to know what D.A. stands for?"

"No, I already know that. Devil's advocate."

She looked at the registrar. "I told you she was good." She smiled back at me. "You want to know who the other cadet was who figured out what had happened."

"No, I know that, too. It was you."

She nodded.

"Did you decide you liked the Academy in spite of its shortcomings?" I asked.

"No," she said. "I thought it was a complete mess, and that if they didn't get some people in charge who knew what they were doing and change things, it was going to fall completely apart."

"I think you're right," I said. "You've got to get some private space on board before somebody kills somebody, and surely something can be done about the food. And you've got to get a lot more cadets with computer skills up here."

"We'll see what we can do," the Commander said, and extended her hand. "Welcome aboard."

I saluted her. "Cadet Baumgarten reporting for duty," I said.

"You said you had two questions," the registrar said. "What was the other one?"

"Which of you won the pool?"

"I did," the Commander said, and grinned at the registrar. "I *told* you she was good."

Yes, well, they don't know how good. Or how much trouble they're letting themselves in for. If it's independence, questioning authority, and bending the rules they want, Kimkim and I can come up with all kinds of stuff. I went straight to my hiding place and called her.

The display lit up. "Illegal transmission," it read. "Not allowed."

I waited, and in a couple of minutes Kimkim said, "Sorry. It took me a while to route around their jamming devices. I found out what 'D.A.' stands for."

"So did I," I said. "I definitely think you should reconsider applying for the Academy. And I think it would be a good idea to pack your kit now so you won't have to do it at the last minute."

"I already did," she said.

"Good," I said. "I've got a list of stuff I need you to bring when you come up. First, I want you to ask my dad for his stink bomb formula. . . ."

ACKNOWLEDGMENTS

Remake was written before the Internet Movie Database and all the other online movie information sites existed, so I owe a huge vote of thanks to all the people who helped me find movie references and movie quotations; come up with examples of chase scenes, tears, and happy endings; and figure out who played that one guy in that one movie, you know the one, I don't remember the title, but it was about a chorus girl. I couldn't have done it without them:

Scott and Sheryl Kippen
all the rest of the UNC Sigma Tau Deltans
my secretary Laura Norton Lewis
and my daughter Cordelia and her college statistics classes at Nebraska Wesleyan

"Here's lookin' at you, kids!"

PHOTO: © G. MARK LEWIS

CONNIE WILLIS has received seven Nebula Awards and eleven Hugo Awards for science fiction, and her novel *Passage* was nominated for both. Her other works include *Doomsday Book, Lincoln's Dreams, Bellwether, Impossible Things, Remake, Uncharted Territory, To Say Nothing of the Dog, Fire Watch, Blackout, All Clear, Crosstalk,* and *A Lot Like Christmas*. She is an SFWA Grand Master and has been named to the Science Fiction Hall of Fame. Connie Willis lives in Colorado with her family.

conniewillis.net